"The genius of Moyes...
[is that she] peers deftly
into class issues,
social mores, and
complicated relationships
that raise as many questions
as they answer. And yet
there is always resolution.
It's not always easy,
it's not always perfect,
it's sometimes messy and
not completely satisfying.
But sometimes it is."

—BOBBI DUMAS, NPR

EW YORK TIMES BESTSELLING AUTHOR

# Praise for **Still Me**

"Delightful."                                    **—People**

"Entertaining."                        —Associated Press

"**Still Me** offers a warm conclusion to the **Me Before You** trilogy . . . resulting in the best entry in the trilogy yet. . . . Moyes has crafted a clear-eyed tale of self-discovery and the sacrifice required to live a life honestly in pursuit of the things you love. [It will] keep you sighing with delight to the very last page."                    **—Entertainment Weekly**

"Jojo's work never fails to bring a smile to my face . . . a must read!"                          —Emilia Clark

"While the series may have started off as a romance, Jojo Moyes has turned Louisa Clark's story into one about learning to be, and to love, yourself."

**—Bustle**

"You sobbed through **Me Before You.** You sped through **After You.** And now, Lou is back in **Still Me.** . . . Don't miss this funny, romantic third installment."                        **—HelloGiggles**

# THE PEACOCK EMPORIUM

Jojo Moyes is the #1 **New York Times** bestselling author of **Still Me, After You, Me Before You, The Horse Dancer, Paris for One and Other Stories, One Plus One, The Girl You Left Behind, The Last Letter from Your Lover, Silver Bay,** and **The Ship of Brides.** She lives with her husband and three children in Essex, England.

Look for the Penguin Readers Guide in the back of this book. To access Penguin Readers Guides online, visit penguinrandomhouse.com.

Also by Jojo Moyes
Available from Random House Large Print

**Still Me**
**The Horse Dancer**
**Paris for One and Other Stories**

# The Peacock Emporium

## Jojo Moyes

RANDOM HOUSE
LARGE PRINT

Copyright © 2004 by Jojo's Mojo Limited

Published in the United States of America by Random House Large Print in association with Penguin Books, an imprint of Penguin Random House LLC, New York.

First published in Great Britain by Hodder & Stoughton, an imprint of Hachette UK, 2004
Published in Penguin Books 2019

Cover design: Roseanne Serra
Cover image: Karen Radkai / Condé Nast via Getty Images

The Library of Congress has established a Cataloging-in-Publication record for this title.

ISBN: 978-1-9848-8298-1

www.penguinrandomhouse.com/large-print-format-books

FIRST LARGE PRINT EDITION

Printed in the United States of America

10  9  8  7  6  5  4  3  2  1

This Large Print edition published in accord with the standards of the N.A.V.H.

To my mother and father,
Lizzie Sanders and Jim Moyes.
With love and thanks.

# The Peacock Emporium

# Part One

# 1

## Buenos Aires, 2001: The Day I Delivered My First Baby

It was the third time in a week that the air-conditioning had gone out at the Hospital de Clinicas, and the heat was so heavy that the nurses had taken to holding battery-operated plastic fans over the intensive-care patients in an effort to keep them cool. Three hundred had come in a box, a present from a grateful stroke survivor in the import-export business, one of the few users of the state hospital who still felt dollar-rich enough to give things away.

The blue plastic fans, however, had turned out to be almost as reliable as his promises of further drugs and medical equipment. All over the hospital, as the air dripped with the noisy heat of a Buenos Aires summer, you could hear the sudden "¡Hija di puta!" of the nurses—even the normally devout ones—as they had to beat them back into life.

I didn't notice the heat. I was trembling with my own cool fear, that of a newly qualified midwife who has just been told they will be delivering their first baby. Beatriz, the senior midwife who had overseen my training, announced this with a deceptively casual air and a hard slap on my shoulders as she went off to see whether she could steal any food from the geriatric ward to feed one of her new mothers. "They're in Two," she said, gesturing to the delivery room. "Multigravida, three children already, but this one doesn't want to come out. Can't say I blame it, can you?" She laughed humorlessly, and shoved me toward the door. "I'll be back in a few minutes." Then, as she saw me hovering by the door, hearing the muffled wails of pain inside, said, "Go on, Turco, there's only one end it can come out, you know."

I walked into the delivery room with the sound of the other midwives' laughter still in my ears.

I had planned to introduce myself with some authority, to reassure myself as well as my patient, but the woman was kneeling on the floor pushing at her husband's face with a white-knuckled hand, and mooing like a cow, so I thought a handshake inappropriate.

"She needs some drugs, please, Doctor," said the father, as best he could through the palm against his chin. His voice, I realized, held the deference with which I addressed my hospital superiors.

"Oh, sweet Jesus, why so long? Why so **long**?" She was crying to herself, rocking backward and forward on her haunches. Her T-shirt was drenched with sweat, and her hair, scraped back into a ponytail, was wet enough to reveal pale lines of scalp.

"Our last two came very quickly," he said, stroking her hair. "I don't understand why this one won't come."

I took the notes from the end of the bed. She had been in labor almost eighteen hours: a long time for a first baby, let alone a fourth. I fought the urge to shout for Beatriz. Instead I stared at the notes, attempting to look knowledgeable, and tried mentally to recite my way through medical checklists to the sound of the woman's keening. Downstairs, in the street, someone was playing loud music in their car: the insistent synthesized beat of **cumbia**. I thought about closing the windows, but the idea of that dark little room becoming even hotter was unbearable. "Can you help me get her on the bed?" I asked her husband when I could stare at the notes no longer.

When we had hoisted her up, I took her blood pressure and, as she grabbed at my hair, timed her contractions and felt her stomach. Her skin was feverish and slippery. The baby's head was fully engaged. I asked her husband about her previous history, and found no clues. I looked at the door and wished for Beatriz. "Nothing to worry about," I said, wiping my face, and hoped that there wasn't.

It was then that I saw the other couple, standing almost motionless in the corner of the room by the window. They did not look like the normal visitors to a state hospital: they would have been more suited, in their bright, expensive clothes, to the Swiss hospital on the other side of the plaza. The woman's hair, which was expensively colored, was pulled back into an elegant chignon, but her makeup had not survived the sweltering 104-degree heat, and had settled in lines and pools around her eyes, and was now sliding down her shining face. She held her husband's arm and stared intently at the scene in front of them. "Does she need drugs?" she said, turning to me. "Eric could get her drugs."

She looked too young to be the woman's mother, I thought absently. "We're too far along for drugs," I said, trying to sound confident.

They were all looking at me expectantly. There was no sign of Beatriz.

"I'll just give her a quick examination," I said. No one looked like they were going to stop me, so I was left with no option but to do one.

I placed the pregnant woman's heels against her buttocks and let her knees drop. Then I waited until her next contraction and, as gently as I could, felt around the rim of the cervix. This could be painful in advanced labor, but she was so tired by then that she barely moaned. I stood there for a minute, trying to make sense of it. She was fully dilated, yet I couldn't feel the baby's head. Suddenly I felt a little leap of excitement. I gave them all a reassuring smile and moved to the instrument cupboard, hoping that what I was seeking had not yet been looted by another department. But there it was—like a small, steel crochet hook: my magic wand. I held it in my palm, feeling a kind of euphoria at what was about to happen—about what I was about to make happen.

The air was rent by another wail from the woman on the bed. I was a little afraid to do this unsupervised, but I knew it was not fair to wait any longer. And now that the fetal heartbeat monitor no longer worked, I had no way of knowing if the baby was in distress.

"Keep her still, please," I said to the husband, and, timing carefully between contractions, reached in with the hook and nicked a tiny hole in the extra set of waters that I'd realized were blocking the baby's progress. Even above the woman's moans, and the traffic outside, I heard the beautiful tiny popping sound as the soft membrane conceded to me. Suddenly there was a gush of fluid and the woman was sitting up and saying, with some surprise and not a little urgency, "I need to push."

After that I don't remember much clearly. I remember seeing the soft, shocking thatch of dark hair, then grabbing the woman's hand and placing it there so that she could be encouraged by it too.

I remember instructing her to push, and that when the baby began to emerge I was shouting as loudly as I had when I went to football matches with my father, with relief and shock and joy. And I remember the sight of that beautiful girl as she slithered into my hands, the marbled blue of her skin turning a rapid pink, like a chameleon's, before she let out a welcome lusty cry of outrage at her delayed entry into the world.

And, to my shame, I remember that I had to turn my head because, as I clipped the cord and laid her on her mother's chest, I realized that I had begun to cry, and I did not want Beatriz to give the other midwives something else to laugh about.

Beatriz appeared at my shoulder, mopping at her brow, and gestured behind her. "When you're done," she said quietly, "I'm going to nip upstairs and see if I can find Dr. Cardenas. She has lost a lot of blood, and I don't want her to move until he's taken a look." I hardly heard her, and she knew it. She kicked my ankle. "Not bad, Ale," she said, grinning. It was the first time she had called me by my real name. "Next time you might even remember to weigh the baby."

I was about to respond in kind, but I became aware that the atmosphere in the room had changed. Beatriz did too, and halted in her tracks. Where normally there was the enraptured cooing of the new mother, the soft murmur of admiring relatives, there was only a quiet pleading: "Diego, no, no, Diego, please . . ."

The smartly dressed couple had moved beside the bed. The blond woman, I noticed, was trembling, a peculiar half-smile on her face, her hand reaching tentatively toward the baby.

The mother was clutching the child to her chest, her eyes closed, murmuring to her husband, "Diego, no, no, I cannot do this."

Her husband was stroking her face. "Luisa, we agreed. You know we agreed. We cannot afford to feed our children, let alone another."

She would not open her eyes, and her bony hands were wrapped around the overwashed hospital shawl. "Things will get better, Diego. You will get more work. Please, **amor**, please, no—"

Diego's face crumpled. He reached over and began, slowly, to pry his wife's fingers off the baby, one by one. She was wailing now: "No. No, Diego, **please!**"

The joy of the birth had evaporated, and I felt sick in the pit of my stomach as I realized what was happening. I made to intervene, but Beatriz, with an unusually grim expression on her face, stayed me with a tiny shake of her head. "Third one this year," she muttered.

Diego had managed to take the baby. He held her tight to his chest without looking at her, and then, his own eyes closed, held her away from him. The blond woman had stepped forward. "We will love her so much," she said, her reedy upper-class accent trembling with her own tears. "We have waited so long . . ."

The mother became wild now, tried to climb from the bed, and Beatriz leaped over and held her down. "She mustn't move," she said, her voice sharpened by her own unwilling complicity. "It's very important that you don't let her move until the consultant is here."

Diego wrapped his arms around his wife. It was hard to tell whether he was comforting her or imprisoning her. "They will give her everything, Luisa, and the money will help us feed our children. You have to think of Paola, of Salvador . . . Think of how things have been—"

"My **baby!**" screamed the mother, unhearing, clawing at her husband's face, impotent against Beatriz's apologetic bulk. "You cannot take her." Her fingernails left a bloodied welt, but I don't think he noticed. I stood by the sink as the couple backed toward the door, my ears filled with the raw sound of a pain I have never forgotten.

And to this day I cannot remember any beauty in the first baby I brought into this world. I remember only the cries of that mother, the expression of grief etched on her face, a grief I knew, even with my lack of experience, that would never be relieved. And I remember that blond woman, traumatized, yet determined as she crept away, saying quietly: "She will be loved."

A hundred times she must have said it, although no one was listening.

"She will be loved."

# 2

## Framlington Hall, Norfolk, 1963

The train had made six unscheduled stops between Norwich and Framlington, and the infinite glacial blue sky was darkening, although it wasn't even teatime. Several times Vivi had watched the guards jump down with their shovels to scrape another snowdrift from the tracks, and her impatience at the delay was now offset by a perverse satisfaction.

"I hope whoever's picking us up has snow chains on," she said, her breath clouding the carriage window so that she had to smear a viewing hole with her gloved finger. "I don't fancy pushing a car through that."

"You wouldn't have to push," said Douglas, from behind his newspaper. "The men'll push."

"It'd be terribly slippery."

"In boots like yours, yes."

Vivi looked down at her new Courrèges footwear, quietly pleased that he had noticed. Completely unsuitable for the weather, her mother had said, adding sadly to Vivi's father that there was "absolutely no telling her" at the moment. Vivi, usually compliant in all things, had been uncharacteristically determined in her refusal to wear Wellingtons. It was the first ball she had been to unchaperoned, and she was not going to arrive looking like a twelve-year-old. It had not been their only battle: her hair, an elaborate confection of bubble curls swept up on her crown, left no room for a good woolen hat, and her mother was in an agony of indecision as to whether her hard work in setting it had been worth the risk of her only daughter venturing into the worst winter weather on record with only a scarf tied around her head.

"I'll be fine," she lied. "Warm as toast." She offered up silent thanks that Douglas couldn't tell she was wearing long johns under her skirt.

They had been on the train almost two hours now, an hour of that without heating: the guard had told them that the heater in their carriage had given up the ghost even before the cold spell. They had planned to travel up with Frederica Marshall's mother in her car, but Frederica had come down with glandular fever (not for nothing, Vivi's mother observed dryly, was it called the "kissing disease") and so, reluctantly, their parents had let them travel up alone on the train instead, with many dire warnings about the importance of Douglas "looking after" her. Over the years, Douglas had been instructed many times to look after Vivi—but the prospect of Vivi alone at one of **the** social events of the year had apparently given this a weighty resonance.

"Did you mind me traveling with you, D?" she said, with an attempt at coquettishness.

"Don't be daft." Douglas had not yet forgiven his father for refusing to let him borrow his Vauxhall Victor.

"I simply don't know why my parents won't let me travel alone. They're so old-fashioned . . ."

She'd be all right with Douglas, her father had said, reassuringly. He's as good as an older brother. In her despairing heart, Vivi had known he was right.

She placed one booted foot on the seat next to Douglas. He was wearing a thick wool overcoat, and his shoes, like most men's, bore a pale tidemark of slush. "Everyone who's anyone is going tonight, apparently," she said. "Lots of people who wanted invites couldn't get them."

"They could have had mine."

"Apparently that girl Athene Forster's going to be there. The one who was rude to the Duke of Edinburgh. Have you seen her at any of the dances you've been to?"

"Nope."

"She sounds awful. Mummy saw her in the gossip columns and started on about how money doesn't buy breeding or some such." She paused, and rubbed her nose. "Frederica's mother thinks there's going to be no such thing as the Season soon. She says girls like Athene are killing it off, and that that's why they're calling her the Last Deb."

Douglas, snorting, didn't look up from his paper. "The Last Deb. What rot. The whole Season's a pretense. Has been since the Queen stopped receiving people at court."

"But it's still a nice way to meet people."

"A nice way to get nice boys and girls mixing with suitable marriage material." Douglas closed his paper and placed it on the seat beside him. He leaned back and linked his hands behind his head. "Things are changing, Vee. In ten years' time there won't be hunt balls like this. There won't be posh frocks and tails."

Vivi wasn't entirely sure but thought this might be linked to Douglas's obsession with what he called "social reform," which seemed to cover everything from George Cadbury's education of the working classes to communism in Russia. Via popular music. "So what will people do to meet?"

"Everyone will be free to see anyone they like, whatever their background. It'll be a classless society."

It was hard to tell from his tone of voice whether he thought this was a good thing or was issuing a warning. So Vivi, who rarely looked at newspapers and admitted to no real opinions of her own, made a noise of agreement, and looked out of the window again. She hoped, not for the first time, that her hair would last the evening. She should be fine for the quickstep and the Gay Gordons, her mother had said, but she might want to exercise a little caution in the Dashing White Sergeant. "Douglas, will you do me a favor?"

"What?"

"I know you didn't really want to come . . ."

"I don't mind."

"And I know you hate dancing, but if we get a few tunes in and no one's asked me, will you promise me a dance? I don't think I could bear to be left on the side all night." She pulled her hands briefly from the relative warmth of her pockets. Pearl Frost lay evenly over her nails. It glittered, opalescent. "I've practiced loads. I won't let you down."

He smiled now and, despite the cold of the carriage, Vivi felt herself grow warmer. "You won't be left on the side," he said, placing his own feet on the seat beside her. "But yes, silly. Course I will."

Framlington Hall was not one of the jewels of England's architectural heritage. Its initial air of antiquity was deceptive: anyone with only a basic knowledge of architecture could deduce swiftly that its Gothic turrets did not sit comfortably with its Palladian pillars, and that the unquiet red of its brick had not been weathered by more than a handful of seasons. It was a structural mongrel, a hybrid of all the worst nostalgic longings for a mythical time past.

Its gardens, when not buried under several feet of snow, were rigidly formal; the lawns carefully manicured and dense as the pile of an expensive carpet, the rose garden arranged not in a gently tangled wilderness but in rows of brutally pruned identical bushes in a blood-bright shade meticulously bred or grafted in laboratories in Holland or France. It was less a garden than, as one visitor had noted, a kind of horticultural concentration camp.

Not that these considerations bothered the steady stream of guests who, overnight bags in hand, had been disgorged onto the salted drive that curved round in front of the house. Some had been personally invited by the Bloombergs, who had themselves designed the hall, some had been invited through the Bloombergs' better-placed friends, with their express permission, to create the right atmosphere. And some had simply turned up, hoping, astutely, that in the general scale of things a few extras with the right sort of faces and accents were not going to bother anyone. The Bloombergs, with a freshly minted banking fortune and a determination to keep the debutante tradition alive for their twin daughters, were known as generous hosts. And things were more relaxed these days—no one was going to turf anyone out into the snow. Especially when there was a newly decorated interior to show off.

Vivi had thought about this at some length as she sat in her room (towels, toiletries, and a two-speed hairdryer provided), at least two corridors from Douglas's. She had been one of the lucky ones, thanks to Douglas's father's business relationship with David Bloomberg. Most of the girls were being put up in a hotel several miles away, but she was to stay in a room almost three times the size of her own at home, and twice as luxurious.

Lena Bloomberg, a tall, elegant woman who wore the jaded air of someone who had long known that her husband's only real attraction to her was financial, had raised her eyebrows at his more extravagant welcomes, and said there was tea and soup in the drawing room for those who needed to warm themselves, and that if Vivi needed **anything at all**, she should call—although not Mrs. Bloomberg, presumably. She had then instructed a manservant to show her to her room—the men were in a separate wing—and Vivi, having tested every jar of cream and sniffed every bottle of shampoo, had sat for some time before getting changed, reveling in her unheralded freedom, and wondering how it must be to live like this every day.

As she poured herself into her dress (tight bodice, long lilac skirt, made by her mother from a Butterick pattern) and swapped her boots for shoes, she could hear the distant hum of voices as people walked past her door, an air of anticipation seeping into the walls. She had been looking forward to the ball for weeks. Now that it was here, she was filled with the same sort of dull terror that she used to feel when going to the dentist. Not just because the only person she was likely to know was Douglas, or because, having felt terribly liberated and sophisticated on the train, she now felt very young, but because set against the girls, who had arrived, stick-limbed and glowing in their evening wear, she seemed suddenly lumpen and inadequate. Glamour didn't come easily to Veronica Newton. Despite the feminine props of hair rollers and foundation garments, she was forced to admit that she would only ever be pretty ordinary. She was curvy at a time when beauty was measured in skinniness. She was healthily ruddy when she should have been pale and wide-eyed. She was still in dirndl skirts and shirtwasters when fashion meant A-line and modern. Even her naturally blond hair was unruly, wavy, and strawlike, refusing to fall straight like that of the models in **Honey** or **Petticoat**, instead floating in wisps around her face. Today, welded into its artificial curls, it looked rigid and protesting, rather than the honeyed confection she had envisaged. Adding insult to injury, her parents, in some uncharacteristic burst of imagination, had nicknamed her Vivi, which meant people tended to look disappointed when they were introduced to her, as if the name suggested some exoticism she didn't possess. "Not everyone can be the belle of the ball," her mother said, reassuringly. "You'll make someone a lovely wife."

I don't want to be someone's lovely wife, thought Vivi, gazing at her reflection and feeling the familiar drag of dissatisfaction. I just want to be Douglas's passion. She allowed herself the briefest rerun of her fantasy, now as well-thumbed as the pages of a favorite book—the one in which Douglas, shaking his head at the unexpected beauty of her in her ball gown, whirled her on to the dance floor and waltzed her around until she was giddy, his strong hand placed firmly on the small of her back, his cheek pressed against hers . . . (It owed an awful lot, she had to admit, to Walt Disney's **Cinderella**. It had to, as things tended to get a bit blurry after the kissing.) Since arriving here, her daydream kept being interrupted by slim, enigmatic Jean Shrimpton lookalikes, who tempted him away with knowing smiles and Sobranie cigarettes. So she had started a new fantasy, in which, at the end of the evening, Douglas escorted her back to this huge bedroom, waited longingly at the open door, and then finally, tenderly, walked her over to the window, gazed at her moonlit face, and—

"Vee? Are you decent?" Vivi jumped guiltily as Douglas rapped sharply on the door. "Thought we might nip downstairs early. I bumped into an old schoolfriend and he's saving us a couple of glasses of champagne. Are you nearly done?"

"Two secs," she shouted, layering mascara on her eyelashes and praying that tonight would be the one in which he was forced to look at her differently. "I'll be right there."

He looked perfect in black tie, of course. He looked taller and straighter, his shoulders square in the crisp dark cloth of his jacket. When she'd told him he looked handsome, jokingly, to hide the intensity of longing his appearance had provoked in her, he'd laughed gruffly and said he felt like a trussed-up fool. Then, as if embarrassed to have forgotten, he had complimented her too. "You scrub up pretty well, old girl," he said, putting his arm round her and giving her a brotherly squeeze. It wasn't quite Prince Charming, but it felt radioactive on her bare skin.

"Did you know we're now officially snowed in?"

Alexander, Douglas's pale, freckled schoolfriend, had brought her another drink. It was her third glass of champagne, and the paralysis she had initially felt when confronted by the sea of glamorous faces before her had evaporated. "What?" she said.

He leaned in so that she could hear him over the noise of the band. "The snow. It's started again. Apparently no one's going to get past the end of the drive until they bring more grit tomorrow." He, like many of the men, was wearing a red coat ("Pink," he corrected her), and his aftershave was terribly strong, as if he hadn't been sure how much to use.

"Where will you stay?" Vivi had a sudden picture of a thousand bodies camped on the ballroom floor.

"Oh, I'm all right. I'm in the house, like you. Don't know what the rest will do, though. Keep going all night, probably. Some of these chaps would have done that anyway."

Unlike Vivi, most of the people she could see around her looked as if they stayed up until dawn as a matter of course. They all seemed so confident and assured, uncowed by their grand surroundings. Their poise and chatter suggested there was nothing particularly special about being in this stately home. The girls wore their dresses easily, with the insouciance of those for whom smart evening wear was as familiar as an overcoat.

And despite the incongruous elegance of the wedding-cake ballroom, it had not been long before the band had been persuaded to drop its playlist of traditional dances, and strike up something a little more modern. An instrumental version of "I Wanna Hold Your Hand" had sent girls squealing on to the dance floor, shaking their elaborately coiffed heads and shimmying their hips, leaving the matrons on the sidelines to shake their own heads in perplexed disapproval, and Vivi to conclude, sadly, that she was unlikely to get her waltz with Douglas.

Not that she was sure he'd remembered his promise. Since they had come into the ballroom, he had seemed distracted. In fact, Douglas hadn't seemed much like himself at all, smoking cigars with his friends, exchanging jokes she didn't get. She was pretty sure he wasn't talking about the imminent collapse of the class system—if anything, he looked disturbingly at home among the black ties and hunting coats. Several times she had tried to say something to reestablish their shared history, to recall a degree of intimacy. At one point she had boldly made a joke about his smoking a cigar, but he hadn't seemed particularly interested—he had listened with what her mother always called "half an ear." Then as politely as he could, he had rejoined the other conversation.

She had started to feel foolish, so she had been almost grateful when Alexander had paid her some attention. "Fancy a twist?" he had said, and she had to confess that she had only learned the classic dance steps. "Easy," he said, leading her on to the floor. "Stub a cigarette out with your toe, and rub a towel on your behind. Got it?" He had looked so comical that she had burst out laughing, then glanced behind her to see whether Douglas had noticed. But Douglas, not for the first time that evening, had disappeared.

At eight a master of ceremonies announced that there was a buffet, and Vivi, a little giddier than when she had arrived, joined a long line of people queuing for sole Veronique or boeuf bourguignon and wondered how to balance her extreme hunger with the knowledge that none of the girls around her were eating more than a few sticks of over-cooked carrots.

Almost accidentally, she had become embedded in a group of Alexander's friends. He had introduced her in a manner that was faintly proprietorial, and Vivi had found herself tugging at her bodice, conscious that she was revealing quite an expanse of flushed cleavage.

"Been to Ronnie Scott's?" said one, leaning over her so that she had to hold her plate away from her.

"Never met him. Sorry."

"It's a jazz club. Gerrard Street. You should get Xander to take you there. He knows Stan Tracey."

"I don't really know—" Vivi stepped back, and apologized when she jogged someone's drink.

"God, I'm starving. Went to the Atwoods' do last week and all they served was salmon mold and consommé. I had to pay the girls to give me theirs. Thought I'd bloody faint with hunger."

"Nothing as mean as a mean buffet."

Vivi found herself moving accommodatingly sideways as several conversations continued around her. She was starting to feel discomfited by the way Xander's hand had "accidentally" brushed her behind several times.

"Anyone seen Douglas?"

"Chatting to some blonde in the picture gallery. I gave him a wet willie as I went past."

"Another dance, Vivi?" Alexander held out a hand, and made to lead her back on to the dance floor.

"I—I think I'll wait this one out." She put a hand to her hair, and realized, with dismay, that her curls no longer felt smooth and round, but had collapsed in stiff fronds.

A queue was snaking out of the downstairs bathroom, and Vivi, standing alone as the chatter and noise ebbed and flowed around her, found that by the time she'd reached its head she genuinely needed to go. Suddenly, with "Vivi! Darling! It's Isabel. Izzy? From Mrs. De Montfort's? Don't you look fab!," the now limited space between her and the lavatory door was filled.

The girl, whom Vivi only vaguely remembered, wheeled in front of her, inelegantly hoicking up her long pink skirt with one hand, and planted a kiss just behind Vivi's ear. "Darling, I couldn't just nip in front of you, could I? I'm absolutely **dying**. Going to disgrace myself if I . . . **Marvelous**." The door swung open in front of them, Isabel vanished inside, and Vivi found herself crossing her legs, a vague need turning into an uncomfortably urgent one.

"Bloody cow," said a voice from behind her.

Vivi flushed guiltily, imagining this to be directed at her. "She and that Forster girl have been completely monopolizing Toby Duckworth and the Horseguards all night. Margaret B-W's terribly upset."

"Athene Forster doesn't even like Toby Duckworth. She just fools around because she knows he's going to pash on her."

"Him and half the bloody Kensington barracks."

"I don't know how they can't see through her."

"They certainly get to see enough **of** her." There was a ripple of laughter through the queue and Vivi plucked up the courage to glance behind her.

"Her parents hardly speak to her, I'm told."

"Are you surprised? She's getting quite a reputation."

"You know the rumor is that she . . ."

The voices behind her dropped to a murmur, and Vivi turned back to the door lest she was thought to be eavesdropping. She tried, unsuccessfully, not to think about her bladder. Then she tried, even less successfully, not to think about where Douglas might be. She had hardly seen him all night, and when she had, he had seemed like some unreachable stranger, not like **her** Douglas at all.

"Are you going in?" The girl behind her was gesturing at the open door. Isabel must have vacated it without a word to her. Feeling cross and stupid, Vivi stepped into the lavatory, then swore as the hem of her skirt flushed dark with the unidentified watery slick on the marble floor.

She peed, tugged, dissatisfied, at her hair, patted her face with her compact to dull the sweaty sheen, tried inexpertly to add solid mascara to her already spidery lashes. There was nothing fairy tale about her appearance now, she mused. Unless you brought the Ugly Sisters into the equation.

The impatient knocking on the door had become too insistent to ignore; she emerged into the hallway, primed to apologize, but no one was looking at her.

The row of girls was gazing away from her toward the gaming room, where there was an obvious commotion. Vivi, along with the rest, slowly followed the sound of clattering and sporadic exclamation, feeling the air grow suddenly chill. There was the sound of a strangulated horn, and Vivi observed that the hunting-horn-blowing competition, which Xander had told her about, must have started. But this horn was not being blown with any finesse; the air was expelled in gasps, as if someone was breathless, or laughing.

Vivi stopped in the entrance to the gaming room, behind a group of men, and gazed around her. On the opposite side of the huge room, someone had opened the French windows onto the front lawns so that stray snowflakes blew in at an acute angle. She wrapped her arms around herself, feeling her skin goose-pimple. She realized she had trodden on someone's foot, but the man did not notice. He was staring straight ahead, his mouth partially open as if, in his alcoholic daze, he couldn't believe what he was seeing.

For there, wheeling between the roulette and blackjack tables, was a huge gray horse, its nostrils flared and eyes rolling as it trod nervously back and forth, its hooves still covered in snow, surrounded by a sea of gleefully appalled faces. On its back was the palest girl Vivi had ever seen, her dress hoisted up to reveal long, alabaster legs, her feet still clad in sequined party slippers, long dark hair flowing behind her, one bare arm lifted as she steered the animal expertly in and out of the tables by its halter and reins, a brass horn raised to her lips with the other. Vivi noted absently that, unlike her own already mottled arms, the other girl's did not give the slightest suggestion of cold.

"View halloa!" One of the pink-coated young men in the corner was blowing a horn of his own. Two others had climbed onto the tables for a better view.

"I don't bloody believe this."

"Jump the roulette tables! We'll pull them all together!"

Vivi could see Alexander in the corner, laughing and raising a glass as if in mock salute. Beside him, several matronly chaperones were conferring anxiously, gesticulating toward the center of the room.

"Can I be the fox? I'll let you catch me . . ."

"Ugh. God, that girl would do **anything** for attention."

Athene Forster. Vivi recognized the dismissive tones of the girl in the queue for the lavatory. But, like the rest, she was captivated by the unlikely sight before them. Athene had pulled her horse to a halt and was bent low over his neck, entreating a group of young men in low, gravelly tones: "Anyone got a drink, loves?"

There was a kind of knowledge in her voice; a crack of grief that would be audible even at her happiest. A sea of glasses was proffered toward her, glinting under the thousand-watt brilliance of the crystal chandeliers. She dropped her horn, lifted a glass, and downed the contents in a single gulp to local applause. "Now, which of you darlings is going to light me a cigarette? I dropped mine jumping out of the rose garden."

"Athene, old girl, you don't fancy giving us a Lady Godiva, do you?"

There was a ripple of laughter. Which came to an abrupt stop. The band was silenced, and Vivi glanced behind her, following the sound of a whispered exclamation.

"What on **earth** do you think you're doing?" Lena Bloomberg had arrived in the center of the room and stood squarely facing the wheeling horse, her white-knuckled hands planted firmly on her hips. Her face was pink with suppressed fury, her eyes glittering as brightly as the rocks round her neck. Vivi's stomach clenched in anticipation.

"Did you hear me?"

Athene Forster didn't look remotely cowed. "It's a hunt ball. Old Forester here was feeling a bit left out."

Another ripple of laughter.

"You have **no right**—"

"As far as I can see, he's got more right than you to be here, Mrs. Bloomberg. Mr. B. told me you don't even hunt."

The man beside Vivi swore admiringly under his breath.

Mrs. Bloomberg opened her mouth as if to speak, but Athene waved a hand at her casually. "Me and Forester just thought we might make things a little more . . . **authentic**." Athene reached down for another glass of champagne, downed it, then added so quietly that only those closest to her could hear it, "Unlike this house."

"Get off—get off my husband's horse immediately! How **dare** you abuse our hospitality in this way." Lena Bloomberg would have been an imposing figure at the best of times; her height and the air of authority bestowed by huge wealth had evidently left her unused to being crossed. The suggestion of controlled fury had vacuumed any residual mirth from the room. People were looking anxiously at each other now, wondering which of the two participants would crack first.

There was a painful silence.

It appeared to be Athene. She gazed at Mrs. Bloomberg steadily for a short eternity, then shifted and began to turn the horse slowly back between the tables, pausing only to accept a cigarette.

The older woman's voice cut through the stilled room: "I had been warned not to invite you, but your parents assured me that you had grown up a little. They were patently wrong, and I can promise you that as soon as this is over I shall let them know so in no uncertain terms."

"Poor Forester," Athene crooned, lying along the horse's neck. "And he was so looking forward to a little poker."

"You should think yourself lucky that the weather does not permit me to have you thrown out of here on your ear, young lady." Mrs. Bloomberg's icy tones followed Athene as she walked the horse back toward the French windows.

"Oh, don't worry about me, Mrs. Bloomberg." The girl turned her head with a lazy, charming smile. "I've been turfed out of **far** classier establishments than this." Then, with a kick of her jeweled slippers, she and the horse leaped over the small stone steps and cantered, nearly silently, into the snowy dark.

There was a loaded silence, and then, on the instructions of the rigid hostess, the band struck up again. Groups of people exclaimed at each other, pointing at the snowy hoofmarks on the polished floor, as the ball sputtered slowly back to life. The master of ceremonies announced that the horn-blowing competition would take place in the Great Hall in five minutes, and that dinner was still being served in the dining room. Within minutes, all that was left of Athene's appearance was a ghostly imprint in the imaginations of those who had seen her—its edges already diminished by the prospect of the next piece of entertainment—and a few pools of melted snow on the floor.

Vivi glanced over at Douglas. Standing by the huge fireplace, his eyes had not left the now closed French windows, just as they had not left Athene Forster as she sat on her huge horse, a few feet from him. While those around him had been appalled, or shocked, giggling in nervous excitement, there had been something else in Douglas Fairley-Hulme's expression. Something still and rapt. Something that made Vivi fearful. "Douglas?" she asked, making her way over to him, trying not to slip on the wet floor.

He didn't appear to hear her.

"Douglas? You promised me a dance."

It took several seconds for him to notice her. "What? Oh, Vee. Yes. Right." His eyes were drawn back to the doors. "I—I've just got to get a drink first. I'll bring you a glass. Be right back."

———

That was the point, Vivi realized afterward, at which she had been forced to acknowledge that there was going to be no fairy-tale ending to her evening. Douglas hadn't returned with the drinks, and she had stood by the fireplace for almost forty minutes, a vague, glassy smile on her face, trying to look purposeful rather than like someone who had been left on the side like a spare part. When she realized that the group by the flower arrangement were remarking on her lonely sojourn, and the same waiter had been past three times, finally to ask if she was all right, she accepted Alexander's second offer to dance.

At midnight, there had been a toast, and some strange, unofficial game involving a young man with a fox's tail attached to his jacket who went hurtling through the house, hotly pursued by several of his pink-coated friends with hunting horns. One had slipped and fallen hard on the waxed floor, knocking himself unconscious by the main staircase. But another had poured the contents of a stirrup cup into his mouth, and he had come to, spluttering and gagging, got up, and carried on the chase as if nothing had happened. At one o'clock Vivi, who was wishing she could go back to her room, said she would accompany Alexander to the blackjack table, where, unexpectedly, he won seven pounds. In a fit of exuberance, he told her she should have the lot. The way he said that she was his "lucky charm" made her feel a bit nauseated—that, or the amount of champagne she had drunk. At half past one she saw Mrs. Bloomberg in animated discussion with her husband in what looked like his private office. Just visible was a pair of prostrate female legs, in shimmering oyster tights. Vivi recognized them as belonging to a red-haired girl she had seen earlier, being sick out of a window.

At two o'clock, some unseen church-tower timepiece acknowledged the hour and confirmed for Vivi that Douglas was not going to keep his promise, that she was not going to find herself held gently in his arms, that there was going to be no longed-for kiss at the end of the evening. Surrounded by the chaos around her, the girls shrieking, their faces now flushed and bleary, the boys sprawled drunkenly on sofas or brawling incompetently, all she wanted was to be alone and cry.

"Xander, I think I'm going to go to my room."

His arm was slung casually round her waist and he was talking to one of his friends. He turned toward her, surprised. "What?"

"I'm really tired. I hope you don't mind. I've had a perfectly lovely evening, thank you very much."

"You can't go to bed now." He reeled backward theatrically. "Party's only just starting."

His ears, she noted, were scarlet, and his eyelids

had slid halfway over his eyes. "I'm sorry. You've been awfully kind. If you bump into him, would you mind telling Douglas I've—I've retired for the evening?"

A voice behind Alexander barked, "Douglas? I don't think Douglas is going to be too bothered." Several of the men exchanged glances and let off a rapid volley of laughter.

She made her way out of the gaming room, her arms crossed miserably across her chest, no longer caring how she looked. The people around her were too drunk to pay any attention anyway. The band was taking a break, and Dusty Springfield sang a melancholy melody over loudspeakers that made Vivi set her face against tears.

"Vivi, you can't go up yet." Alexander was right behind her. He reached out and pulled her round by her shoulder. The angle of his head told her everything she needed to know about how much he'd had to drink.

"I'm really sorry, Alexander. Honestly, I've had a super time. But I'm tired."

"Come . . . come and have something to eat. They'll be doing kedgeree in the breakfast room soon." He was holding her arm, his grip a little tighter than was comfortable. "You know . . . you look very pretty in your . . . your dress." His eyes were now fixed on her **embonpoint**, and alcohol had removed any trace of reticence from his gaze. "Very nice," he said. And then, just in case she had missed the point, "Very, very nice."

Vivi stood in an agony of indecision. To turn away from him now would be the height of impoliteness to someone who had made such an effort to entertain her. And yet the way he was staring at her chest was making her uneasy. "Xander, perhaps we can meet for breakfast."

He didn't seem to have heard her. "The problem with skinny women," he was saying, directly at her chest, "and there're so many bloody skinny women these days . . ."

"Xander?"

". . . is that they have no breasts. No breasts to speak of." As he spoke, he tentatively lifted a hand toward her chest.

"Oh! You—" Vivi's upbringing had left her with no adequate response. She turned, and walked briskly from the room, one hand placed protectively over her bosom, ignoring the rather half-hearted entreaties behind her.

She had to find Douglas. She wouldn't be able to sleep until she did. She needed to reassure herself that, no matter how unreachable he had been this evening, once they had left this place he would be her Douglas again: kind, serious Douglas, who had mended punctures on her first bicycle, who, her dad said, was a "thoroughly decent young man," and who had taken her to see **Tom Jones** twice at the cinema. She wanted to tell him how awful Alexander had been (and harbored a newly flourishing secret hope that this dastardly behavior might spur him on to realize his true feelings).

It was easier to search now, as the crowds had thinned into small, sedentary gatherings. The older guests had departed for their rooms, some dragging protesting charges in their wake, and outside at least one tractor could be heard trying to clear a path away from the house. Douglas was not in the gaming room, or in the main ballroom, the adjoining corridor, underneath the grand staircase, or drinking with the pink coats in the Reynard bar. No one noticed her now, the late hour and alcohol consumption having rendered her invisible. But it seemed to have rendered him invisible too; she had wondered several times, in her exhausted state, whether, given his expressed dislike for such pompous, class-ridden occasions, he might have crept home after all. Vivi sniffed unhappily, realizing that she had been so wrapped up in her own private fantasy of having him escort her to her own room that she had never considered she might need to know where his room was. I'll find Mrs. Bloomberg and she'll tell me. Or I'll just knock on every door in the other wing until someone can find him for me.

She went past the main stairs, stepping over the seated couples propped against banisters. Weary now, she passed rows of ancestral portraits, their colors unmellowed by age, their gilt frames suspiciously bright. Under her feet the plush red carpet now bore carelessly stubbed cigarettes and the odd discarded napkin. Outside the kitchens, from which now emanated the smell of baking bread, she passed Isabel, laughing helplessly on the shoulder of an attentive young man. She didn't seem to recognize Vivi now.

Several feet beyond the corridor came to an end. Vivi glanced up at the heavy oak door, checked behind her to make sure that no one could see her, and let out a huge yawn. She bent down to remove her shoes, which had begun to pinch several hours earlier. She would put them back on when she found him.

It was as she raised her head that she heard it: a scuffling sound and the odd grunt, as if someone had fallen down drunk outside and was trying to raise themselves. She stared at the door from behind which the noise had come, and saw it was just ajar, a sliver of Arctic breeze slipping down the side of the corridor. Vivi, shoeless, crept closer, holding one arm across herself against the encroaching cold. She paused, then opened the door silently, and peered round at the side of the house.

She initially thought that the woman must have fallen down because he seemed to be supporting her, trying to prop her up against the wall. She wondered if she should offer to help. She then grasped, in swift, successive jolts, that the rhythmic sounds she had heard were emerging from these people. That the woman's long pale legs were not the limp limbs of a drunk, but wrapped tautly round him like some kind of serpent. As Vivi's eyes adjusted to the dark, she recognized, with a start, the woman's long, dark hair, falling chaotically over her face, and the lone sequined slipper, upon which stray flakes of snow were settling.

Vivi was simultaneously repulsed and transfixed, staring for several seconds before she grasped, with a flood of shame, what she had been witnessing. She stood, leaning against the half-opened door, that sound echoing grotesquely in her ears, jarring against the thumping of her heart.

She had meant to move, but the longer she stood there, the more paralyzed she became, even though her arms were mottling in the night air, and her teeth chattering. Instead of escaping, she leaned against the cool of the oak door and felt her legs disappear from under her: she had understood that while the tones were those she had never heard before, this man's voice was not. That the back of the man's head, his pink-tinged ears, the sharp edge where his hair met his collar, were familiar to her: as familiar as they had been twelve years ago, when she had first fallen in love with him.

# 3

She might not have made Deb of the Year (and now that she was "respectable" no one discussed why), but there were few observers of society who doubted that the nuptials of Athene Forster, described as the so-called Last Deb, It Girl, or, among some of the less forgiving society matrons, something far less complimentary, and Douglas Fairley-Hulme, son of the Suffolk farming Fairley-Hulmes, could be hailed as the Wedding of the Year.

The guest list sported enough old money and double-barreled names to grant it a prominent position in all the society pages, along with some rather grainy black-and-white pictures. The reception was held at one of the better gentlemen's clubs in Piccadilly, its customary air of tobacco-scented pomp and bluster temporarily smothered by spring blooms and swathed drapes of white silk.

There was the groom, universally decreed to be "a catch," whose serious manner, clean-cut good looks, and family fortune had left heartbroken potential mothers-in-law across several counties. Even as he stood, formal and stiff in his morning suit, the occasion weighty upon his broad shoulders, his obvious happiness kept breaking through, evident in the way he kept glancing across the room to locate his bride, his eyes softening as he saw her. It was also patently obvious that, despite the presence of his family, his best friends and a hundred others, all of whom wanted to pass on their warmest wishes and congratulations, he would rather they had been alone.

And then there was the bride. Her dewy eyes and bias-cut silk dress, which skimmed a figure that might easily have seemed too thin, had led even her more fervent detractors to note that whatever else she was (and there was no shortage of opinions in that department), she was certainly a great beauty. Her hair, more usually seen cascading wildly down her back, had been glossed and tamed to sit regally on the crown of her head, held in place by a tiara of real diamonds. Other girls' skin might have been grayed by the white of the silk, but hers reflected its marble smoothness. Her eyes, a pale aquamarine, had been professionally outlined, and shimmered under a layer of silver. Her mouth formed a small, secretive smile that revealed none of her teeth, except when she turned to her husband and broke into a wide, uninhibited grin, or when she occasionally locked lips with him in a suggestion of some private, desperate passion, that made those around them laugh nervously and look away.

Justine Forster now sat smiling out gamely from the top table. Having tried to ignore that her already habitually choleric husband was still cross that the date of the wedding had interrupted his annual veteran-soldiers' trip to Ypres and had mentioned it on no fewer than three occasions already (once during the speech!), she was now trying to ignore her daughter, who, two seats away, appeared to be giving her own husband a verbatim account of the "girl-to-girl" chat she had unwisely embarked upon the previous evening.

"She thinks the Pill is immoral, darling," Athene was whispering, snorting with laughter. "Says that if we head off to old Dr. Harcourt to get a prescription, there'll be a shrieking hot line to the new pope before we know it, and we'll be cast into flaming damnation."

Douglas, who was still unused to such frank discussion of bedroom matters, was doing his best to appear composed while fighting off a now familiar wave of longing for the woman beside him.

"I told her I thought the pope might be a bit busy to worry about little old me swallowing birth-control bonbons, but, apparently, no. Like God, Paul VI—or VIII or whatever he is—knows **everything**: if we're thinking impure thoughts, if we're considering copulation purely for pleasure, if we're not putting enough in the collection plate." She leaned toward her husband and said, in a whisper just loud enough for her mother to hear: "Douglas, darling, he probably even knows where you've got your hand right now."

There was a sudden spluttering from Douglas's left, and he tried, but failed, to silence his wife, then with both hands clearly visible, asked his new mother-in-law whether he might get her some water.

Douglas's embarrassment did not last long. He had swiftly decided that he loved Athene's irrepressibility, her lack of concern for the social mores and confines that had dictated their lives so far. Athene shared his embryonic views that society was increasingly unimportant, that they could be pioneers, expressing themselves as they liked, doing what they liked, heedless of convention. He had to fit it all round his job on his father's estate, but Athene was happy doing her own thing. She wasn't terribly interested in doing up their new house—"The mothers are so good at that kind of thing"—but she liked riding out on her new horse (his pre-wedding present to her), lying in front of the fire reading, and, when he wasn't working, going up to London for dances, to the cinema, and, most of all, spending as much time as they could in bed.

Douglas had not known it was possible to feel like this. He spent his days in a state of distracted tumescence, for the first time in his life unable to focus on work, the duties of family and career inheritance. Instead his antennae were tuned to a frequency of soft curves, flimsy fabrics, and salty smells. Try as he might, he couldn't seem to get inflamed by the things that had inspired him or fed his growing preoccupation with the wrongs of the ruling classes, and the vexed question of whether wealth redistribution meant that he should give up some of his land. Nothing was as relevant, as **interesting** as it had been. Not when compared to the carnal delights of his bride. Douglas had once confessed to his friends that he had never become more involved with a woman than he would with a new car (both, he had said, with the shallow confidence of youth, were best replaced within a year by a new model). The young man who had always maintained a skeptical distance from the messy doings of the full-blown love affair now found himself dragged into a vacuum of—well, what was it? Lust? Obsession? The words seemed somehow inadequate for the blind unthinkingness of it, the skin-upon-skin neediness of it, the gloriously greedy voluptuousness of it. The hard, thrusting—

"Going to give the old girl a quickie?"

"What?" Douglas, flushing, stared at his father, who had appeared unannounced at his shoulder. His small, wiry frame stood characteristically straight in his morning suit, his weather-beaten, normally watchful face softened by alcohol and pride.

"Your mother. You promised her a dance. She fancies a quick whirl if I can get them to strike up a quickstep. Got to meet your obligations, my boy. Your car will be here soon, after all."

"Oh. Right. Of course." Douglas stood, struggling to regroup his thoughts. "Athene, darling, will you excuse me?"

"Only if your gorgeous father promises to give this old girl a quickie too." Her smile, flickering behind innocently wide eyes, made Douglas wince.

"Delighted, my dear. Just don't mind me if I wheel you past old Dickie Bentall a few times. I like to show him that there's life in the old dog yet."

"I'm heading off, Mummy."

Serena Newton turned away from her wiener schnitzel (beautifully done, but she wasn't sure about the creamed mushrooms) and looked with surprise at her daughter. "But you can't leave until they've gone, darling. They've not even brought their car around yet."

"I promised Mrs. Thesiger I'd babysit for her tonight. I want to go home first and get changed."

"But you never said. I thought you were coming home with Daddy and me."

"Not this weekend, Mummy. I promise I'll be back in a week or two. It was lovely to see you."

Behind her there was a round of applause as the young groom took his bride onto the dance floor.

Vivi, glancing away from her mother's enquiring gaze, didn't flinch. She had got rather good at hiding her feelings these last months.

Her mother reached out a hand. "You've hardly been home in ages. I can't believe you're rushing off like this."

"Hardly rushing off. I told you, Mummy. I've got to babysit tonight." She smiled, a broad, reassuring smile.

Mrs. Newton leaned forward, placed a hand on Vivi's knee, and dropped her voice: "I know this has been terribly hard for you, darling."

"What?" Vivi couldn't hide her sudden color.

"I was young once, you know."

"I'm sure you were, Mummy. But I really have to go. I'll say goodbye to Daddy on my way out." With a promise to call, and a twinge of guilt at her mother's hurt expression, Vivi turned and made her way across the room, managing to keep her face toward the doors. She understood her mother's concern: she looked older now. Loss had etched new shadowy echoes of knowledge on her face, grief sharpening its once puddingy outline into planes. It was ironic, really, she mused, that she should start acquiring the characteristics she had so desired— slimness, a kind of jaded sophistication—through losing the very thing she had wanted them for.

And, despite being naturally home-loving, Vivi

had done her best to return to her family as little as possible over the last few months. She had kept her telephone conversations brief, avoiding all references to anyone outside the family, had preferred to stay in touch with her parents through short, cheerful dispatches on jokey postcards, had insisted time after time that she couldn't possibly come back for Daddy's birthday, the village fete, the Fairley-Hulmes' annual tennis party, pleading work commitments, tiredness, or an illusory round of social invitations. Instead, having found work in the offices of a fabric company a little way from Regent's Park, she had thrown herself into her new career with a missionary zeal that left her employers astonished daily at her capacity for hard work, her babysitting families grateful for her perpetual availability, and Vivi frequently too exhausted, when she returned to her shared flat, to think. And this suited her just fine.

After the hunt ball, Vivi had realized that whenever she mentioned Douglas's name with anything but sisterly interest her parents had gently steered her away from him, perhaps knowing even then that he had longings she could not fulfill. He had never given her any indication, after all, that his affection for her held anything more than the most innocent brotherly interest.

Now, having seen him look another way entirely,

she had resigned herself to her fate. Not that she was going to have to find someone else, as her mother had repeatedly suggested. No, Vivi Newton now knew herself to be one of an unlucky minority: a girl who had lost the only man she would ever love, and who, having considered the alternatives carefully, had decided she would rather not settle for anyone else.

It was pointless telling her parents, who would fuss, protest, and assure her that she was far too young to make such a decision, but she knew she would never marry. It was not that she was so hurt she could never love again (although hurt she had been—she still found it difficult to sleep without her "little helpers," prescription benzodiazepine) or, indeed, that she had some idea of herself as a doomed romantic heroine. Vivi had just concluded, in the fairly straightforward manner that she concluded most things, that she would rather live alone with her loss than spend a lifetime trying to make someone else match up.

She had dreaded this trip, had considered a thousand times what legitimate excuse she could find for not coming. She had spoken to Douglas only once, when he had arranged to meet her in London, and found his patent happiness and what she could only imagine to be his new air of sexual confidence almost unbearable. Heedless of her discomfort, he had held her hands and made her promise that she would come: "You're my oldest friend, Vee. I really want you there on the day. You've got to be there. Come on, be a sport."

So she had gone home, cried for several days, and then been a sport. She had smiled when she had wanted to wail and beat her breasts like women in Greek tragedies, and pull the brocade drapes and wedding banners from their hangings, and scratch that awful, awful girl's face and take swings at her head, her hands, her heart to destroy whatever it was about her that Douglas loved most. And then, shocked that she was capable of thinking such dark thoughts about any human being (she had once cried for an entire afternoon after accidentally killing a rabbit), she had smiled again. She was hoping against hope that if she presented a peaceable front for long enough, if she kept persuading herself to keep living a seemingly normal life, one day at a time, some of her apparent equilibrium might become real.

Athene's mother had caught her daughter smoking on the stairs. Dressed in her bridal gown, legs splayed, puffing away like a charlady on a cigarette she had solicited from one of the bar staff. She informed her husband of this discovery in quietly outraged tones. "Well, she's not my responsibility now, Justine." Colonel Forster leaned back on his gilt chair, and tamped tobacco into his pipe, refusing to look his wife in the face, as if she too was complicit in this indiscretion. "We've done our duty by the girl."

His wife stared at him for a moment, then turned to Douglas, who had been swilling a brandy in his hand. "You do understand what you've taken on?" Her tone suggested that her daughter had not been forgiven for her earlier indiscretion.

"The finest girl in all England, as far as I'm concerned." Douglas, full of alcohol, bonhomie, and sexual anticipation, felt magnanimous, even to his sour-faced in-laws. He had been remembering the night he had asked her to marry him, a day that separated the two lives of Douglas into a kind of Before and After Athene. It was less the marking of some rite of passage than a fundamental shift in who he was. To him, now, a married man, that day seemed to signify a crossing-over: a vast leap across a divide that had seen him on one side as someone searching, tentatively trying out new attitudes and opinions, new ways to be, and on the other marked simply as a Man. Athene had bestowed that upon him. He felt like a rock to her shifting, mercurial self, her separateness bestowing on him a sense of solidity, of surety. She crept up him like ivy, clinging and beautiful, a welcome, parasitic sprite. He had known from the night he first saw her that she was meant for him: she had prompted an ache, an unexpected sense that something was lacking, that some fundamental part of him was, without him having previously known it, **unfulfilled**. She made him think like that, lyrically, fatalistically. He had not known such words were even in his vocabulary. Previously when he had considered marriage it had been with a kind of moribund expectation: it was the thing that one did when one found a suitable girl. It would be expected of him and, as usual, Douglas would fulfill those expectations. But she had stood in the elevator of the London restaurant where they had just eaten, and, heedless of the people queuing behind them, she had wedged her childlike feet in the lift doors and, laughing breathlessly—as if, when the words had bubbled unexpectedly out of his trembling mouth, he had suggested something extraordinarily amusing— had said yes. Why not? What fun. They had kissed then, joyfully, greedily, as the lift doors trundled back and forth in a frenzy of thwarted purpose, and the queue of people behind them had grown, muttered crossly, and eventually taken the stairs. And he had realized that his life was no longer on some predestined course, but had been diverted by fantastic possibility.

"You need to knock some sense into her," said Colonel Forster.

Douglas's head jolted backward.

"**Anthony**." Justine Forster pursed her lips. She opened her compact and examined her eye makeup. "She . . . It's just that she can be a bit of a handful."

"I like her like that." Douglas's tone was one of contented belligerence.

She had dragged him to dance halls run by black people in some of the less savory parts of London, chiding him if he expressed anxieties, exhorting him instead to dance with her, to join her in drinking, laughing, **living**. And because she seemed perfectly at ease in those places, his worst fears rarely materialized, and he was forced to confront his own conceptions of poor people, or black people, or, at any rate, people unlike himself. Along with his fears, he had made himself shed a few inhibitions, smoked and drunk dark rum, and when they were alone allowed himself to approach Athene sexually in a way that he had been brought up to think of as not just daring but probably illegal.

Because she didn't mind. She didn't care about shopping, or fashion, or furnishings, or the things that had bored him about so many of the girls he knew. If anything she was careless with her possessions—at the end of a dance she would remove her shoes, complaining that they were a bore, then fail to bring them home. There would always be another pair of shoes, she would say, laughing. Worrying about things was such a **bore**.

"Yes. Well, dear, don't say we didn't warn you." Justine Forster was eyeing a piece of wedding cake as if it might spring up and bite her.

"Very silly girl," said Colonel Forster, lighting his pipe.

"What?"

"Our daughter. No point beating around the bush. She's jolly lucky to have married at all."

"**Anthony.**" Mrs. Forster glanced at Douglas fearfully, as if this damning commentary might prompt her new son-in-law to announce a change of heart.

"Oh, come on, Justine. She's surrounded by feckless young people, and it's made her feckless. Ungrateful and feckless and silly."

"I don't think she's feckless." Douglas, who would have been appalled to think his own parents might discuss him in this way, felt the need to defend his bride. "I think she's brave, and original, and beautiful."

Athene's father regarded him as if he'd just admitted to being a pinko. "Yes. Well, you don't want to go admitting all that to her. Don't know where it might lead. Just see if you can settle her down a bit. Otherwise she'll end up as no use to anyone."

"He doesn't mean it, Douglas, dear. He just means that we—we've probably been a little lax with her at times."

"Lax with who?" Athene appeared at Douglas's shoulder. He smelled Joy and cigarette smoke, and his innards clenched. "Are you talking about me?"

"We were just saying that we're very glad you're

settling down." With a wave of her hand, Justine Forster suggested she would like the conversation closed.

"Douglas and I have no intention of settling down, do we, darling?" Douglas felt her cool hand on the back of his neck. "Not if it means ending up like **you**."

"I'm not going to talk to you, Athene, if you're going to be deliberately rude."

"Very silly girl," muttered her father.

Douglas was feeling extremely uncomfortable. "I think you're being rather unfair on Athene," he ventured.

"Douglas, dear, well-meaning as you are, you have no conception of what Athene has put us through."

Athene leaned down and picked up Douglas's brandy, as if to examine its contents, then swallowed the amber liquid in one gulp. "Oh, Douglas, don't listen to them," she said, replacing the glass and pulling at his arm. "They're such bores. This is our day, after all."

Within minutes of their being on the dance floor he had almost forgotten the exchange, lost in his own private appreciation of her silk-clad curves, the scent of her hair, the light feel of her hands on his back. When she looked up at him, her eyes were glittering with tears.

"We don't have to see them now that we're

married." It wasn't a question, but she appeared to demand some kind of reassurance. "We don't have to spend half our time as stuffed shirts, sitting in horrid old family gatherings."

"We can do whatever we want, my darling," he whispered into her neck. "It's just us now. We can do whatever we want." He enjoyed the sound of his own voice, the authority and comfort it promised.

She held him tighter in a surprisingly strong grasp, her face buried in his shoulder. Over the sound of the music, he had been unable to make out her reply.

"Won't be a minute," said the girl in the cloakroom. "Some of the tickets have got separated from the coats."

"Fine," said Vivi, her foot tapping with impatience to be gone. The sounds of the reception were dulled now, muffled by the expanse of carpet that lined the hallways and stairs. Past her, elderly dowagers were helped to powder rooms, and small, shoeless children skidded up and down under the quietly outraged gaze of rigid, uniformed staff. She wouldn't return home until Christmas. It was likely that Douglas and that woman—she still could not bring herself to say her name, worse still to describe her as "his wife"—would be away for Christmas. His family had always been big on skiing, after all.

It might be easier, now that it was clear her mother

understood. And if her longing for her parents became too much, she could always invite them up to London, persuade her father to make a weekend of it. She could show them the antiques market behind Lisson Grove, take them to the zoo, hail a taxi to the Viennese tea rooms in St John's Wood and feed them frothy coffee and spiced pastries. By then she might not think about Douglas at all.

Her coat was taking an age. Beside her, she noticed, two men were smoking, deep in conversation, their own tickets held loosely in their hands.

"Still, you've got to admit, he's done all right for himself. I mean, if you're going to get marched down the aisle by anyone . . ."

She didn't even flinch now. Vivi pretended to be absorbed by a carved engraving on the wall, wondering again how much longer it would be before this outward stillness was echoed internally.

Almost twenty minutes later, while Vivi was still waiting for her coat, her mother stood in front of her, in her good wool boucle suit, her clutch bag held in front of her like a shield. "I know it hasn't been easy," she was saying, "but I just don't think you should run away today. Come home with me and Daddy."

"I have told you—"

"Don't let them keep you away from your home.

The car's gone. And they'll be away for at least two weeks."

"It's really not that, Mummy."

"I'm saying no more, Vivi. I just couldn't let you leave without talking to you properly. Just don't keep staying away. I don't like to think of you alone in London. You're still so young. And, besides, we miss you, Daddy and I."

Vivi was staring, unseeing, at her empty hand in front of her.

Her mother continued.

"Daddy really wants to see you. He wants you to help us choose a dog. He's finally agreed to having one, you see, but he thinks it would be nice for the two of you to do it together." Her mother's expression was hopeful, as if childish pleasures could still cancel out adult pain. "A spaniel, perhaps? I know you've always liked spaniels."

"Is it green?"

"Sorry?"

The attendant tried to hide her exasperation under a smile. "Is your coat the green one? Big buttons?"

She was pointing to a row behind her. Vivi glimpsed the familiar bottle color. "Yes," she whispered.

Mrs. Newton's eyes were dark with sympathy. She smelled of Vivi's childhood, and Vivi fought an urge to hurl herself into her mother's arms and allow herself to be comforted.

"I know how much you felt for Douglas. But Douglas . . . well, he's found his—his path in life, and you just have to get on with things. Put it behind you."

Vivi's voice was unnaturally stiff. "I have put it behind me, Mother."

"I hate to see you like this. So sad . . . and . . . well, I just want you to know . . . even if you don't want to talk to me . . . and I know girls don't always want to confide in their mothers . . . that I do understand." She reached out and stroked Vivi's hair, smoothing it away from her face, an unthinking maternal gesture.

No, Mummy, you don't understand, Vivi thought, her hands still trembling, her face still whitened by what she had heard. Because this pain did not stem from the origins her mother assumed. That pain had been almost easy. For some kind of equanimity had been possible while she could at least comfort herself with the thought that he'd be happy. Because that was it, loving someone, wasn't it? The knowledge that, if nothing else, you wanted them to be happy.

While her mother might have had some comprehension of her pain, her longing, her sense of grief at losing him, she would not have understood the conversation Vivi had just been forced to overhear.

Or why Vivi knew already, with a pain that was searing her core, that she would never repeat it to anyone.

"Still, you've got to admit, he's done all right for himself," the man had said. "I mean, if you're going to get marched down the aisle by anyone . . ."

"True. But . . ."

"But what?"

"Let's face it, he's going to need to keep an eye out, isn't he?"

"What?"

"**Come on** . . . Girl's a little tart."

Vivi had stood very still. The man's voice had lowered to a murmur, as if he had turned away to speak. "Tony Warrington saw her on Tuesday. A drink for 'old times,' she told him. They used to walk out together, back when he lived in Windsor. Except her idea of **old times** was a bit too closely related to **good times**, if you know what I mean."

"You're kidding me."

"Not a week before the wedding. Tony said he hadn't even wanted to. Bad form and all that. But she was all over him like a rash."

Vivi's ears had started to ring. She put out a hand to steady herself.

"Bloody hell."

"Exactly. But keep it to yourself, old boy. No point ruining the day. Still . . . you've got to feel rather sorry for poor old Fairley-Hulme."

# 4

Douglas leaned back in his chair, sucked ruminatively at the end of his ballpoint pen, and gazed at the densely covered pages of plans in front of him. It had taken him several weeks, working long into the evening, but he was pretty sure he'd got them right.

He had based his ideas partially on a mix of the ideals of the great social reformers, a kind of utilitarian blueprint for living, and something in America he'd read about—a more communal way of doing things. It was pretty radical, admittedly, but he thought it might work out rather well. No, he corrected himself, he **knew** it would work out well. And it would change fundamentally the face of the estate.

Instead of the huge herd of Friesians—the rules and regulations about which, since the introduction of the Common Agricultural Policy, his father had repeatedly complained could turn a sane man into a raving imbecile—a hundred acres would be turned over to a self-supporting community. The participants could live in the derelict tied cottages, doing them up themselves with timber from the Mistley wood. There was a water source near there, along with old barns that could be used for small numbers of livestock. If they got in craftsmen and artisans, they could even start a studio down there, sell their pottery or whatever, perhaps giving back a small percentage of the profits in return.

Meanwhile the four fields on Page Hill, the ones currently turned over to sugar beet, could be divided into small holdings to allow local people to grow their own vegetables. There was a growing market for home-produced food, an increasing number of people who wanted to "get back to nature." The Fairley-Hulmes would charge a minimal rent, and take food as partial payment. It would be like a return to the tenanted farm, a return to the ancestral ways of the family but without the feudal attitude. And the scheme would be self-supporting. Perhaps even profitable. If it worked really well, the surplus money could be plowed into some other project, perhaps an educational program. Like one that taught the delinquents in town something productive, perhaps about land management.

The estate was too big for one man to manage. He had heard his father say so a million times, as if Douglas himself were not quite man enough to be included in this. There was the estate manager, of course, the head herdsman and the farmhands, the gamekeeper and the odd-job man, but ultimate responsibility for what went on belonged with Cyril Fairley-Hulme, a responsibility he had held now for almost forty years.

The brief period of self-examination that had followed his meeting Athene had made Douglas realize he had never felt truly comfortable with the idea of inheriting the Dereward estate. It didn't feel earned somehow: in an age when nepotism and feudalism were dying a slow death, it didn't seem right that he should take on this self-aggrandizing mantle, that he, not yet out of his twenties, should assume a right to the estate and responsibility for the lives of all who depended on it.

The first time he had broached this with his father, the older man had looked at him as if he were a Commie. He might even have used the word. And Douglas, who was astute enough to understand that his father was not likely to take a plan that was only half thought-out seriously, had swallowed his words and gone off to oversee the disinfecting of the milking parlor.

But now he had a concrete set of proposals, which even his father would have to admit was likely to take the estate forward into the future. He could follow in the tradition of those great reformers: Rowntree and Cadbury, those who had thought that making money was an insufficient aim unless it led to social and environmental betterment. He conjured up images of contented workers eating home-produced food and studying to better themselves instead of liquefying their weekly wages down at the White Hart. It was 1965. Things were changing fast, even if the inhabitants of Dere Hampton were unwilling to acknowledge it.

He placed the pages neatly together, laid them reverently in a card wallet, and tucked it under his arm. He did his best to ignore the pile of letters to which he had yet to reply. He had spent much of the last month fending off complaints from ramblers and dog-walkers over the fact that he had erected a post-and-rail fence along the middle of the thirty-acre fields that led down to the wood to let the two sides for sheep grazing. (He had always fancied sheep. He still remembered fondly a youthful stay with a Cumbrian sheep farmer who counted his animals using an ancient and incomprehensible dialect: **Yan, tan, tethera, pethera, pimp, sethera, lethera, hovera, covera, dik** . . .) That the villagers could still walk down the field had not pacified them: they didn't like, they said, being "penned in." Douglas had been tempted to retort that they were lucky to have access to it at all, and that if the estate wasn't made financially secure by such measures it would be sold off in parcels for development, like the once-grand Rampton estate four miles away. And see how they would like that.

But conscious that, as a Fairley-Hulme, he had at

least to pay lip service to villagers' opinions, he had suggested they write their complaints in letter form and he would do his best to address them.

He glanced at his watch, then tapped his fingers on the side of the desk, a mixture of nervousness and excitement. His mother should be preparing lunch. When his father retreated into his office for his usual half-hour of "paperwork" (often involving the brief closure of his eyes—just for resting purposes, you understand), he would present his ideas. And perhaps make his own, more contemporary mark on the Dereward estate.

Douglas Fairley-Hulme's mother had not got off to a good start with Athene. She failed to see how anyone could. The girl was a wearisome sort, always making impossible demands of Douglas but rarely wanting to do anything wifely and supportive in return. But Cyril had told her she should try a little harder to make friends. "Have a coffee morning or something. Douglas says she gets bored. Easier for him if you two are friends."

She had never particularly enjoyed the company of other women. Too much gossiping and worrying over things that didn't matter. One of the disadvantages of being the matriarch of the estate was that people expected her to have conversations all the time, that she should chat about fripperies at charity mornings and fetes, when all she really wanted was to be at home with her garden. But it was rare that Cyril made a specific request of her, so she had set off dutifully on the two-mile cross-country walk that led to Philmore House, the large, Queen Anne–style residence that, on his marriage two years ago, Cyril had given to his only son.

Athene had been wearing her nightclothes, even though it was well past eleven, and she had not seemed remotely concerned at having been caught in them. "I'm awfully sorry," she had said, not looking sorry at all. She had appeared momentarily surprised, and then flashed a bland, charming smile. "I'm not receiving people today." She had reached up to stifle a yawn, her seersucker robe revealing the flimsiest of nightdresses and, worse, a good length of pale **décolletage** underneath, even though any of the estate men might have been passing.

Douglas's mother had felt quite unbalanced by this extraordinary breach of decorum. "I had thought we might have a cup of coffee together," she said, forcing a smile. "We've hardly seen you up at the house lately."

Athene had glanced behind her, an air of distracted irritation hovering around her, as if her mother-in-law might have been followed by a phalanx of visitors, all demanding tea and conversation.

"Cyril was—we were both wondering how you were."

"You're terribly kind. I've just had rather a lot on." Athene's smile wavered a bit when her mother-in-law did not budge. "And today I'm feeling rather tired. Which is why I'm not really receiving anyone."

"I thought we might have a little chat. About things—"

"Oh, I don't think so. But it's very kind of you to think of me."

"There are a couple of things we'd like you to—"

"Lovely to see you. I'm sure we'll see you again soon."

And, after that brief exchange, the least demonstrative goodbye and not even a hint of an apology, Athene had closed the front door. And her mother-in-law had been almost too stupefied to be offended.

In fact, despite being a woman of some certainty, she wasn't even quite sure how to describe this turn of events to her husband. What could she say in condemnation? That the girl had received her in her nightdress? Cyril might find that charming— worse, he could start imagining things, and she knew where **that** might end. That Athene had declined to offer her coffee? Cyril would say simply that she should have telephoned before she went on the walk. Her husband's determination always to be **fair** was one of the things that irritated her most. She decided to say nothing, but when Douglas arrived she took him to one side and told him straight: if his wife didn't want to dress herself with a little dignity, then she shouldn't answer the door. There was a family name to uphold. When he had looked at her with incomprehension, she had felt a sudden fearful protectiveness, combined with a distant annoyance that the boy was so like his father. You spent their entire youth warning them, but it made no difference when it came to girls like that.

Cyril Fairley-Hulme put down his napkin and glanced at the clock, as he did every day during the short minutes between finishing his lunch and heading into his study.

"Very nice," Cyril said quietly. Then, as if making some long-pondered observation, "You can't beat a good game pie."

"Delicious. Thank you, Mother." Douglas crumpled his napkin into a ball on the table.

"It's one of Bessie's. I'll tell her you liked it. Do you have time for some coffee?" The dining table had been laid, as it always was, with a neat formality and good china despite the mundanity of the occasion. She lifted the plates, and walked, straight-backed, from the room.

Douglas watched her go, feeling the words leaden in his mouth, at odds with the racing feeling in his chest.

His father took some minutes meditatively tamping his pipe, then lighting it, his thin, tanned face creased into well-worn lines of concentration.

Then he glanced at his son, as if surprised that he hadn't left. "Dennis is sowing the tubers this afternoon."

"Yes," said Douglas. "I'm going to head up there when I leave."

His father looked down at his pipe. "Waiting for harvest?" he said lightly.

"What? Oh—" It was often difficult to recognize when his father was joking. "Oh, no. Actually, Father, I wanted to talk to you about something."

His father leaned back, and exhaled a thin plume of smoke, his face briefly relaxing. "Fire away," he said genially.

Douglas looked at him, and then down, trying to remember where he'd put his folder. He stood, fetched it from the dresser, then began to pull out pages, laying them carefully on the table in front of his father.

"What's this?"

"What I wanted to talk to you about. Some ideas I've had. For the estate."

Douglas stood back, watching as his father leaned forward to take a closer look.

"Ideas for the estate?"

"I've been thinking for ages. I mean, since the stuff with the CAP, and you talking about giving up on the dairy side of things. We might look at doing things a bit differently."

Cyril watched his son's stammering explanation

impassively. Then he lowered his head toward the page. "Pass me my glasses."

Douglas held out the spectacles. He could hear his mother in the kitchen placing crockery on the tray. He could hear the blood in his ears. He stuffed his hands into his pockets, then took them out again, fighting the urge to leap forward and point to separate paragraphs on the pages.

"There's a map under there," he said, unable to contain himself any longer. "I've color-coded the fields according to usage."

Time seemed to drag, then stall. Outside, the dogs barked manically at some offender. Douglas, staring at his father's face, saw not even a flicker of emotion as he methodically scanned the pages.

His father removed his glasses, and sat back slowly in his chair. His pipe had gone out and, after examining it, he laid it on the table beside him. "This what they taught you at agricultural college, was it?"

"No," said Douglas. "Actually they're pretty well all my own ideas. I mean, I've been reading up and everything, about kibbutzes—and you know all about Rowntree, of course, but—"

"Because, if so, we wasted every bloody penny sending you there."

It came out with force, as if the words had been shot from a gun, and Douglas jumped, as if they had physically hit him.

His father's face, as ever, revealed almost nothing. But there was a brightness behind his eyes that suggested intense hidden anger.

They sat in silence, eyes locked.

"I thought you had sense. I thought we'd raised you with some notion of what was right and—"

"This is right." Douglas heard his own voice rise in protest. "It is right to give something back to people. It is right that everyone gets a share in the land."

"Give it all away, shall I? Dish it out in parcels to anyone who wants it? Ask them to form a queue?"

"It would still be our land, Dad. It would just enable other people to work it. We don't even use it all properly."

"You think people round here want to work the land? Have you actually **asked** any of them? The young people don't want to be plowing and drilling. They don't want to be out in all weathers pulling weeds and spreading muck. They want to be in the cities, listening to popular music and all sorts. Do you know how long it took me to find enough hands just to get the hay in last year?"

"We'd find people. There are always people who need jobs."

His father jabbed at the papers with disgust. "This is not some social experiment. This is our blood, our sweat in this soil. I can't believe I've taught my son everything I know about this estate, only to have him want to give it away. Not even sell it, mind. Give it away. You—you're worse than a **girl**."

He spat the words at his son, as if he were bilious. Douglas had rarely heard his father's voice raised against him, and discovered he was shaking. He tried to collect his thoughts against his father's concentrated anger and saw his mother, standing stationary in the doorway, tray in hand.

Without a word, his father stood up and stomped past her, ramming his hat onto his head as he went.

Douglas's mother placed the coffee on the table, and stared at her son. He wore the same look of contained shock and misery as when he was eight and his father had beaten him for letting one of the dogs get into the calving shed. She fought the urge to comfort him, and instead asked cautiously what had happened.

For several minutes Douglas didn't answer, and she wondered whether he was trying to hold back tears. He gestured toward some papers on the table. "I had some ideas for the estate." He paused, then spoke in a strangled voice: "Father didn't like them."

"Shall I look?"

"Feel free."

She sat down carefully in her husband's chair and scanned the pages. It took her several minutes to grasp what he was proposing, and she stared at the colored map, slowly building a picture of her son's vision.

Her initial sympathy for her son was replaced by her own swiftly increasing anger. Young people could be so thoughtless. They never considered what previous generations had had to go through.

"I suggest you throw these on the fire," she said, sweeping them into a pile.

"What?"

"Get rid of them. If you're lucky, your father will forget this conversation ever happened."

Her son's face was a mask of frustration and incredulity. "You're not even going to consider them?"

"I have considered them, Douglas, and they are . . . inappropriate."

"I'm twenty-seven years old, Mother. I deserve to have a say in the running of the estate."

"You **deserve**?" Her chest was tight, and her voice came in short bursts: "That's all your generation cares about—what you supposedly deserve. Your ideas are an insult to your father, and until you can comprehend that I suggest you and I end this conversation here."

Douglas had both hands on the table now, was leaning down on straightened arms, as if he had been almost felled by her response. "I can't believe you're both reacting like this."

The last ounce of maternal sympathy she had felt for him evaporated. "Douglas, sit down," she commanded, and placed herself opposite him. She took a deep breath, trying to make her words measured. "I'm going to tell you something about your father, young man. You have no idea what he has been through, keeping this estate together. You have no idea. When he inherited it, it was almost bankrupt. Wheat prices were the lowest in memory, the farm workers were heading off to the city because we couldn't afford to pay them, and we couldn't give the wretched milk away. He had to sell nearly all his family furniture, all the paintings except for the portraits, his own mother's family jewelry, the only reminder he had of her, I might add, just to keep it alive."

She stared at her son, determined that he should understand the gravity of what she was telling him. "And you'd be too young to remember this properly, but in the war the estate was requisitioned—we even had German POWs here. Did you know that? Your own father's brother killed in the air, and we had to take Germans"—she spat the word—"just to keep the thing going. Dirty thieves they were, stealing food and all sorts. Even bits off the farm machinery."

"They didn't steal anything. It was the Miller boys."

She shook her head. "Douglas, he has worked those fields day in and day out, rain, snow, sleet, and hail, for his whole adult life. I have had him come home with hands raw from pulling weeds, and his back burned blood red from working twelve hours in the sun. I remember nights when he's eaten and fallen asleep at the table. When I've woken him, he's gone off to fix the tenants' roofs, or sort out their drainage. This is the first time we've had enough money for him to relax a bit. The first time he's allowed himself to let other people help him. And now you, his hope, his pride, his heir, you tell him you want to give it away to a bunch of beatniks, or whatever they are."

"It's not like that." Douglas was blushing.

His mother had said her piece. She stood, poured the coffee, added the milk, and then pushed a cup to her son. "I'd like this to be the last time we discuss this," she said, the heat gone from her voice. "You're a young man with big ideas. But this estate is bigger than your ideas. And we haven't held it together for so long to let you unravel everything we've done. Because, Douglas, it's not even yours to give away. You are a trustee, a custodian."

"But you said—"

"We said the estate would be yours. What we did not say, at any time, is that it should be diverted from its natural purpose. Which, first, is farming and, second, to provide a home and a living for successive generations of Fairley-Hulmes."

There was a long silence. Her tone, when she

spoke, was conciliatory: "When you have children, you'll understand a little better."

Douglas, his head lowered, sat and stared into his cup.

When he arrived home the house was empty. It was possessed of the cold stillness that spoke of many hours of inoccupancy.

He hung his coat in the echoing hall and made his way to the kitchen, his feet absorbing the chill of the cold linoleum. For the first year of his marriage he had frequently found that his supper consisted of breakfast cereal or bread and cheese. Athene was not a natural homemaker and, after a few early charred efforts, had lost interest in even pretending to be one. More recently, without telling his mother, he had employed Bessie, one of the longest-standing estate wives, to keep their kitchen stocked and put the odd pie or casserole into the refrigerator. He knew she thought Athene scandalous. In a vague attempt to protect his wife's domestic reputation he had explained that flour made her skin break out in hives.

A cheese pie was sitting on the shelf. Douglas placed it in the range, closed the door, and scanned the kitchen table for an explanatory note. Often they told him little: "Darling Douglas, back soon—A." Or "Nipped out for breath of fresh air," or "Gone for a spin." Increasingly she didn't leave a note at all. Tonight he didn't mind. He didn't know if he wanted to talk to anyone at the moment, even his wife.

He pulled a plate from the cupboard, glancing at the framed snapshot of Athene he had taken in Florence. That first year had been wonderful. They had spent three months traveling around Italy, driving Douglas's red MGB Roadster, staying at tiny **pensiones**, and frequently offending the **padronas** with their uninhibited expressions of love. Athene had made him feel like a king, screaming delightedly at his driving on the winding mountain roads, draping herself over him as they sipped coffee in pavement cafés, wrapping herself round him needily in the dark. On their return, despite the newly decorated house, her horse, his gift of driving lessons, and her own car—she was a hopeless driver, and he had long since ceased becoming exasperated by the dents in the bumper—she had gradually become a little less adoring, a little less easy to please. She was not interested in his plans for wealth redistribution. He had hoped she'd be inspired. The idea for it had come from her, after all. "Let's give it all away," she had said, one summer afternoon as they picnicked alone by the trout river. "Let's decide who's most deserving in the village, and then give it away in parcels." She was joking, of course. Like when she announced she had a terrible need to sing jazz and he had booked lessons for her as a surprise.

In fact, over the past few weeks, not that he liked to dwell on it, Athene had been rather demanding. He never knew where he stood—one minute she was flirtatious, clingy, trying to charm him into some outlandish plan, the next she was cold and distant, as if he had fallen foul of some unspoken rule. If he dared ask what he had done, she would explode with exasperation, and ask why he couldn't just let her alone. He had not dared approach her in the dark. He was still smarting from the time two weeks earlier when she had physically shoved him off her, accusing him of being like "some slobbering animal."

He glanced up at the picture of the smiling, uncomplicated wife. It was a fortnight until their second wedding anniversary. Perhaps they might return to Italy for a week or two to give them both a change of scene. He needed to spend some time away from the estate, give himself time to bite down on his disappointment. Perhaps a holiday would make her less irritable, less mercurial.

She arrived shortly before eight, raising her eyebrows in surprise when she saw the scoured dinner plate in front of him. She was wearing an ice-blue dress and a new white high-collared coat. "I didn't realize you would be home so early."

"Thought you might want company."

"Oh, darling, I'm sorry. If you'd said I'd have made sure I was here. I took myself off to Ipswich for the afternoon, to go to the pictures." She was plainly in a good mood. She swept down to kiss his forehead, leaving an echo of her scent in the air before him.

"Mother said she stopped by earlier."

Athene was removing her coat, her back to him. "I suppose she still wants me to present a trophy at the village fete. I have told her it isn't my scene."

Douglas stood up and walked to the liquor cabinet, where he poured himself two fingers of whiskey. "You could try, Athene. She's not so bad. You could try, for me."

"Oh, let's not have words. You know I'm no good with families, Douglas."

It was a pointless conversation, one which had been repeated too many times already.

"I saw the most fabulous film. French. You must see it too. I was so carried away by it I nearly didn't come home at all." Her laughter, perhaps deliberate, took any threat from her words.

Douglas watched her as she moved lightly around the room: the focus of it, yet not belonging to it. Perhaps she would always look like this to him: something otherworldly, floating, refusing to be tied down by the ropes of domesticity. He wished, briefly, that he could tell her about his exchange with his father. That he could express his humiliation, his disappointment at the reaction of the man whose good opinion he valued more than anything in the world. Perhaps lay his head against her and be comforted. But he had learned that Athene would alight on any potential fault line in his relationship with his parents and do her best to widen it. She didn't want him so closely linked to his family: she wanted to cast them adrift.

He took a long drink of his whiskey. "I thought we might go away."

She turned, something unreadable on her face. "What?"

"To Italy."

It was as if he had proposed satiating some hidden hunger. She moved toward him, her eyes not leaving his. "Back to Florence?"

"If you like."

She gave a little gasp, then threw her arms round him with a kind of childish abandon. "Oh, yes. Yes, let's go back to Italy. Oh, Douglas, what a wonderful idea."

He put down his glass and stroked her hair, stunned that it had been so easy to make things right between them. He could feel her limbs, sinuous against his, and felt the battened-down stirrings of desire. She lifted her face to his, and he kissed her.

"When shall we go? Soon? It will take us hardly any time to pack up." Her voice was greedy, urgent.

"I thought we could go for our anniversary."

Her eyes were on some distant horizon now, her thoughts already overseas. It was like her face had changed shape, softened and blurred at the edges, as if she were seen through a Vaselined lens.

"We could even stay at the Via Condolisa."

"But where shall we live?"

"Live?"

"In Italy."

He drew in his chin and frowned. "Not to live, Athene. I thought we could have a trip for our anniversary."

"But I thought—" Her face closed off as she grasped the ramifications of what he was saying. "You don't want to move there?"

"You know I can't move there."

There was a sudden desperation in her. "But let's move away from here, darling. Away from your family. And mine. They're always dragging us down with their obligations and expectations. Let's go. Not even to Italy. We've been there. To Morocco. It's meant to be fabulous in Morocco." Her arms were tight round his waist, her eyes burning intently into his.

Douglas felt suddenly very tired. "You know I can't go to Morocco."

"I don't see why not." Her smile was bruised, wavering.

"Athene, I have responsibilities."

She moved away from him then. Stepped back and shot him a hard look. "God, you sound exactly like your father. Worse. You sound like **my** father."

"Athene, I—"

"I need a drink." She turned her back on him, and poured herself a large measure of whiskey. He noticed, as she poured, that for a new bottle the level had dropped rapidly. She stayed turned away from him for some minutes. Normally Douglas might have approached her, placed a comforting hand on her shoulder, offered some murmured words of affection. Tonight, however, he was just too exhausted to play games with his impossible, flighty wife.

She turned to him. "Douglas. Darling. I never ask you for anything. Do I? Really?"

There was little point in contradicting her. Douglas stared at her pale, unreadable face, at the sadness suddenly visible in it. He hated the thought that it might be his failure as a husband that was responsible for it.

"Let's go. Let's leave here. Say yes to me, Douglas. **Please.**"

He had a brief insane impulse to throw their possessions into a single suitcase and roar up the drive in the MG, Athene delighted and wrapped round him, then disappear into a Technicolor future in some exotic foreign land.

Athene's gaze hadn't wavered.

"I need a bath," he said. And, wearily, turned toward the stairs.

# 5

## The Day I Broke Somebody's Heart

Oh, I know I don't look the type. You're probably thinking I've never inspired passion in anyone. But I did, a long time ago, before middle age and gray hair covered up what few attributes I ever had. His name was Tom, and he was a dear, sweet lad. Not the best-looking chap, but an absolute brick. He was solid as a rock. Good family. And he adored me.

He wasn't the type to talk much. Men didn't in those days. Not in my experience, anyway. But I knew he adored me from the way he used to wait on the corner every evening to walk me home from the office, to the beautiful pieces of ribbon and lace he would save me from the remnants pile at his father's factory. His family was in haberdashery, and he was learning the business from his father. That's how we met. He was a big chap, with a broad chest and strong arms. Used to carry bolts of fabric for me, piled three or four on his huge shoulders as easily as if he were tipping his jacket behind him.

He used to come in with trays of buttons and bits of trimming, lovely Victorian lace that he'd rescued from boxes just starting to go damp. He left them for me wordlessly, laid out, as if he were a dog presenting me with a bone. I used to make my own clothes then, and when I was dressed up he could always point out one of his buttons, or a piece of his velvet trim. I think it made him rather proud.

And he never pushed me. He never made any great declarations, or announced his intentions. I had told him that I'd never marry. I was very certain of that, and I thought it only fair to tell him from the beginning. But he just nodded, as if that was a fair decision, and decided to adore me anyway. And, gradually, I found I worried less and less about whether I was leading him on, or being unfair, and I just enjoyed his company.

The sixties were a pretty tricky time to be a single girl. Oh, I know you think it was all Mary Quant and free love and nightclubs and the like, but there were very few of us really living that kind of life. For girls like me, from respectable families, who didn't have a "fast streak," the times were pretty confusing. There were girls who did, and girls who didn't, and I was never sure which of those I should be. (Although I nearly did, with Tom. Several times. He was very good about it, all things considered, even when I told him I'd decided to be a virgin for life.) And there was this pressure for one to be **à la**

**mode**, to wear the latest fashions, whether they be Biba or the King's Road, or, like mine, made from Butterick and Vogue patterns. But our parents were all rather scandalized, so one was under this huge pressure to wear a miniskirt or whatever and yet felt rather embarrassed to be doing so.

Perhaps I just wasn't liberated enough. There were plenty who were. But Tom seemed to understand and like me, whatever I was, or however I tried to be, and we had a rather lovely time for a couple of years.

So it was a bit of a shame that he had to suffer so on the first occasion that he was introduced to my parents.

I had invited them to London to see a show. My mother was excited about it, and Daddy was rather sweet too, although he wouldn't have said as much, as I had hardly been home in a year. I had booked us tickets for **Hello, Dolly!** at the Theatre Royal and a light supper afterward at one of the new Golden Egg restaurants, and I was going to treat everybody because Mr. Holstein had just given me a pay raise and a promotion from secretary to office manager, which was terrifically exciting. I had mulled things over for ages and ages, and in the end I thought I would probably invite Tom too, because he was such a sweetheart, and I knew it would mean a lot to him if he was to meet my parents, and I knew they'd like him. They had to. There was nothing to dislike about him. The show was marvelous. Mary Martin was Dolly Levi—I'll never forget how gorgeous she looked, even though we had all secretly wished to see Eve Arden. And Mummy was so pleased to see me that she kept sneaking her hand into mine and squeezing it, and making meaningful little glances at Tom. I know she was rather relieved to see a man on the scene after such a long time, and he had brought her a box of New Berry Fruits. So it was rather a lovely evening until the dinner. Mummy said, gazing around her, that the Golden Egg was "certainly very . . . 'colorful' ": the food was fine, and I splashed out on a bottle of wine, even though Daddy said he would not let me spend my new salary on entertaining my "old folks." And Tom just sat and beamed quietly in that way of his, and talked to Mummy for ages about ribbons and things from before the war and how his father had once met the prime minister's wife when she ordered some fine Belgian lace.

And then she said it.

"I meant to tell you, darling. Things are not good in the Fairley-Hulme household."

I stared at my fish for a moment, then looked up, my expression carefully blank. "Oh?"

Daddy snorted. "She's bolted."

"Who's bolted?"

"Oh, Henry. That's such an outdated term. Athene Forster. Sorry, Fairley-Hulme. She's run off with some salesman from up north, of all things. Made the most awful mess of everything. The families are desperate to keep it out of the papers."

It was as if she thought her words would no longer have an effect on me.

"I don't read the papers." My fish had turned to powder in my mouth. I forced myself to swallow, and took a sip of water. Tom, poor thing, was plowing through his food, oblivious. "How—how is Douglas?"

"Hoping she'll come back, poor boy. He's absolutely devastated."

"Always looked like trouble, that one," my father added.

Their voices had receded, and I wondered, briefly, if I might faint. Then I looked at Tom and, for the first time, noticed with mild revulsion that he kept his mouth open while he ate.

"Of course, her parents are absolutely furious. They've actually disinherited her. They're telling everyone she's gone abroad for a bit. I mean, it's not as if she hadn't pushed her luck before she married Douglas. She didn't have any real friends, did she? Or much of a reputation, come to that."

My mother shook her head pensively and swept nonexistent crumbs from the tablecloth. "Douglas's parents have taken it very badly. It reflects awfully on everyone. The chap sold vacuum cleaners, door to door, would you believe? **Vacuum cleaners.**

Poor Justine. I saw her at the Trevelyans' bridge evening two weeks ago and it's turned her quite gray."

It was then that she must have seen my expression. She gave me a concerned stare, which turned into rather a hard one, and then she glanced at Tom. "Still, you don't want us wittering on about people you don't know, do you, Tom? Frightfully rude of me."

"Don't mind me," said Tom. His mouth was still open.

"Yes. Well. Let's think about pudding. Who's for pudding? Anyone?" Her voice had risen almost an octave. She gave me another hard look, the kind that can only travel from mother to daughter.

I don't think I heard another thing she said.

I didn't go back home. Not then. But it wasn't fair on Tom to continue seeing him. Not under the circumstances.

# Part Two

# 6

2001

They always argued on the way to parties. Suzanna was never sure why, although she could always ascribe it to something: their lateness, his habit of waiting until the last minute to check that the back door was locked, her perpetual inability to find anything decent to wear. Perhaps it was anticipating the strain of being nice to each other for a whole evening. Or perhaps, she sometimes felt, it was just her way of ensuring that there would be no intimacy between them later, when they arrived home. Tonight, though, they had not argued. It was no great victory given they had traveled to the Brookes's house separately. Neil arrived late from work via train and taxi, and when Suzanne had greeted him at the dinner table, her smile calcified on her face, and her jocular "We thought you weren't coming" squeezed through gritted teeth.

"Ah. Have you met the other half of the Peacocks? Neil, isn't it?" Their hostess, in her pearls, expensive but dated silk blouse, and Jaeger-style skirt, had shepherded him gently into his seat. Her clothes had told Suzanna everything she had needed to know about the night ahead. That she was about to be patronized, rather than admired, for her urban ways. That they had probably only been invited because of her parents.

"Got held up at a meeting," Neil had said apologetically. "Why make an issue of it?" he whispered later, when she scolded him in the corridor. "No one else seems to think it matters."

"It matters to me," she had said, then forced a smile as her hostess stepped out of the living room and, tactfully avoiding looking too closely at them, asked whether anyone would like a top-up.

It had been a long evening, Neil covering his awkwardness with mildly inappropriate jocularity. Everyone else there had apparently known each other for some time, and slipped frequently into conversation about people she didn't know, making repeated references to events from years past: the rained-off summer fete of two years ago, the primary-school teacher who ran off to Worcester with poor old Patricia Ainsley's husband. Someone had heard she'd had a baby. Someone else had heard that Patricia Ainsley was now a Mormon. The room was overheated, so even before the main course was served Suzanna's face had become flushed, and occasional beads of sweat ran down her spine, hidden by her overly fashionable shirt.

They all knew, she was sure of it. She felt that despite her smiles, her assurances that, yes, she was happy to be living in Dere Hampton again, that it was lovely having a bit more time on her hands, that it was good to be closer to one's family, they must be able to tell she was lying. Her husband's studied unhappiness—gamely making conversation with the opinionated vet—must radiate like a glowing neon sign floating above them. We're Unhappy. And It's My Fault.

Over the past year, she had become an expert at gauging the state of people's marriages, and she recognized the women's tense smiles, the barbed comments, the men's blank expressions of withdrawal. Sometimes it made her feel better to see a couple who were obviously so much unhappier than they were, sometimes it made her feel sad, as if it proved that the simmering anger and disappointment were inevitable in everyone.

The worst, however, were the couples who were clearly still in love and whose length of tenure together seemed to have deepened something, to have wound them more tightly around each other. She knew all the signs: the conversational "we," the frequent touches to small of back, to hand or even cheek, the quiet smiles of attentive satisfaction when the other spoke. Sometimes even the combative argument punctuated by laughter, as if they could still flirt with each other. Then Suzanna would find herself staring, wondering what glue she and Neil were lacking; whether it was something she could still find to hold them together.

"I thought that went quite well," said Neil, bravely, as he started the car. They had been the second to leave, perfectly acceptable. He had offered to drive so that she could drink; a conciliatory gesture, she knew, but somehow she didn't feel generous enough to acknowledge it.

"They were okay."

"But it's good—I mean, getting to know our neighbors. And no one sacrificed a pig. Or threw their car keys into the middle of the room. I had been warned about these rural dinner parties." She knew he was forcing himself to sound lighthearted.

Suzanna tried to quell the familiar irritation. "They're hardly our neighbors. They're almost twenty minutes away."

"From our house, everyone's twenty minutes away." He paused. "It's just good to see you making friends in the area."

"You make it sound like my first day at school."

He glanced at her, apparently assessing just how mulish she was determined to be. "I only meant that it's good you're . . . putting down a few roots."

"I've got the roots, Neil. I've always had the bloody roots, as well you know. It's just that I didn't want to be planted here in the first place."

Neil sighed. Rubbed his hand through his hair. "Let's not do this tonight, Suzanna. Please?"

She was being horrible, she knew it, and it made her feel even more cross, as if it was his fault for making her behave in this way. She stared out of the window: hedge, hedge, tree, hedge. The never-ending punctuation of the countryside. The debt counselor had suggested couples therapy. Neil had looked receptive, as if he would go. "We don't need that," she had said bravely. "We've been together ten years." As if that made them unbreakable.

"The kids were sweet, weren't they?"

Oh, God, he was so predictable.

"I thought that little girl handing round the crisps was delightful. She was telling me all about her school play and how unfair it was that she got to be a sheep instead of a bluebell. I told her someone was obviously pulling the wool over—"

"I thought you said you didn't want to start all this tonight?"

There was a short silence. Neil's hands tightened on the steering-wheel. "I only said I thought the children were nice." He glanced sideways at her. "It was a perfectly innocent remark. I was just trying to make conversation."

"No, Neil, there's no such thing as an innocent remark when it comes to you and kids."

"That's a bit unfair."

"I know you. You're completely transparent."

"Oh, so what if I am? Is it really such a sin, Suzanna? It's not like we've been married five minutes."

"Why does that have to come into it? Since when was there a time limit on having kids? There's no rule book that says, 'You've been married for blah years, better get procreating.'"

"You know as well as I do that things get harder once you hit thirty-five."

"Oh, don't start on that again. And I'm not thirty-five."

"Thirty-four. You're thirty-four."

"I know how bloody old I am."

There was a kind of adrenaline rush within the car, as if being alone had liberated them from the constraints of having to appear happy.

"Is it because you're frightened?"

"No! And don't you **dare** bring my mother into this."

"If you don't want them, why can't you just say so? At least then we'll know where we stand—I'll know where **I** stand."

"I'm not saying I don't want them."

"Well, I've got no idea what you **are** saying. For the past five years every time I've brought the subject up you've jumped down my throat as if I'm suggesting some great horror. It's only a baby."

"For you. It would be my life. I've seen how it takes over people's lives."

"In a good way."

"If you're a man." She took a deep breath. "Look, I'm not ready yet, okay? I haven't **done anything** with my life, Neil. I can't just go straight to having kids without having achieved anything. I'm not that kind of woman." She crossed her legs. "To be honest, I find the whole prospect depressing."

Neil shook his head. "I give up, Suzanna. I don't know what I have to do to make you happy. I'm sorry we had to move back here, okay? I'm sorry we had to leave London, and I'm sorry you don't like where we're living, and you're bored, and you don't like the people. I'm sorry about tonight. I'm sorry that I've been such a bloody disappointment to you. But I don't know what to say anymore that isn't bloody **wrong**."

There was a prolonged silence. He didn't usually give up this easily, and it made Suzanna uneasy.

Neil turned off the main road on to an unlit lane, his lights flicking on to full beam, sending rabbits fleeing into the hedgerows.

"Let me take on the shop." She said it without looking at him, facing straight ahead, so that she didn't have to see his reaction.

She heard his deep sigh. "We haven't got the money. You know we haven't."

"I'm sure I can make a go of it." She added, hope-fully, "I've been thinking. We can sell my painting to make the deposit."

"Suze, we've just got out of debt. We can't afford to go dropping ourselves back in it."

She faced him. "I know you're not keen, but I need this, Neil. I need something to occupy me. Something of my own. Something that isn't bloody coffee mornings and village gossip and my bloody family."

He said nothing.

"It will really help me." Her voice had become pleading, conciliatory. Its fervency surprised even her. "It will help **us**."

Perhaps it was something in her tone. He pulled over and gazed at her. Outside, a mist was descending.

"Give me a year," she said, and took one of his hands. "Give me a year, and if it's not working, I'll have a baby."

He looked stunned. "But if it is working—"

"I'll still have a baby. But at least then I'll have something else. I won't turn into one of **them**." She gestured behind her, referring to the other women at dinner, who had spent a good part of the evening comparing grisly tales of birth and breastfeeding, or talking about the awfulness of other people's children with veiled contempt.

"Ah. The neo-natal Nazis."

"Neil—"

"You really mean it?"

"Yes. Please, I just think it will make me a bit happier. You want that, don't you?"

"You know I do. I've only ever wanted you to be happy."

When he looked at her like that, she could still occasionally garner a fleeting glimpse of how she used to feel about him: allied to someone for whom you felt not irritation or dull resentment, but gratitude and anticipation, and a lingering sexual hunger. He was still handsome. She could look at him and see that he was the type who would age well.

In moments like this, she could just remember what it had felt like for them to be close.

"You don't have to sell your painting. It's too personal. And it would be better to hold on to it, keep it as an investment."

"I don't think I could cope with you working longer hours than you do already." It was not living without him that frightened her, but how good she was getting at it.

"I didn't mean that." He cocked his head to one side, blue eyes softened and considerate. "You could always ask your father for money. For the deposit. He always said he'd put some by for you."

He had broken the spell. Suzanna removed her hand from his, and shifted so that, once again, she faced away from him. "I'm not going through all that again. We've had to take enough from him already. And I don't want his money."

At first they hadn't thought of it as debt: they were simply living as everyone did, a short distance beyond their means. Double income, no kids. They adopted a lifestyle they believed they deserved. They bought huge matching suede sofas, spent weekends with like-minded friends at noisy West End restaurants, felt entitled to "treat themselves" for the most minor disappointment. Suzanna, cushioned by Neil's income, and the fact that both of them secretly liked her spending more time at home, took a succession of part-time jobs: working in a women's clothes shop, driving for a friend who opened a florist, selling specialized wooden toys. None captured her imagination enough to make her want to stay, to deprive herself of morning coffee with girlfriends at pavement cafés, time spent browsing, or the pleasure of cooking elaborate meals. Then, seemingly overnight, everything had changed. Neil had lost his job at the bank, replaced by someone he described afterward as the Ball-Breaking He-Woman from Hell. His sense of humor had vanished, along with their cash flow.

And Suzanna had started shopping.

At first she had done it just to get out of the flat. Alternating between petulant outrage and miserable self-loathing, he became the worst of himself.

So she had left him to it, and cheered herself up with expensive soaps, ready meals, the odd bunch of flowers. She told herself she deserved it, her sense of entitlement sharpened by Neil's filthy temper.

She persuaded herself that there were things they needed, such as new bed linens, matching curtains, antique glass.

It was only a short stop from there to her own personal makeover. She couldn't possibly get a new job with her existing wardrobe; her hair needed cutting and highlighting; the stress of Neil's job had left her skin in desperate need of specialist facials.

It had made her feel better at first, gave her purpose, and filled a need. But even as she spent, she knew she had been infected by a kind of madness, that the brightly lit interiors and rows of cashmere sweaters, the fawning shop assistants and beautifully packaged boxes, were increasingly less effective at diverting her attention from the looming reality at home. She gleaned little satisfaction from her acquisitions: the initial rush of the purchase would wear off faster and faster so that she would sit at home, surrounded by crisp shopping bags, blinking in bemusement or, occasionally, weeping after she had felt brave enough to calculate what she had spent. She became an early riser, always up in time for the postman.

There was no point in worrying Neil.

It had taken him almost six months to make the

discovery. It had not been the high point of their marriage, to say the least. Pushed beyond his own depression, Neil had questioned her sanity and announced that it was she, and not his redundancy, who was making him impotent. Finally allowing herself to unleash the anger she had bottled up for so long, she had told him in return that not only was he cruel, but unfair and unreasonable. Why should his problems have to affect her life so much? She still considered it a matter of quiet pride that she had not said what she really thought. That she had not used the **failure** word, even if, when she looked at him, she felt it.

Then her father had mentioned the house, and although she was still furious with him about the will, Neil had persuaded her that they had no choice—unless they wanted to be declared bankrupt. The horror of that word still had the capacity to chill her.

And so, almost nine months ago, Suzanna and Neil had sold their London flat, which paid off the debts on Suzanna's credit cards and the lesser debt Neil had run up before he managed to get a new job, and bought a small, unshowy car. Lured by the prospect of a three-bedroom flint-fronted estate house, almost rent-free and renovated by her father, they had moved back to Dere Hampton, where Suzanna had grown up, and which she had spent the last fifteen years doing her best to avoid.

When they came in, the little house was cold: Suzanna had forgotten to set the timer on the heating again. Neil whistled and blew on his hands. He was still enthusiastic about all aspects of country living, persuading himself that their move was about quality of life rather than downsizing, choosing only to see the advantages of chocolate-box cottages and rolling green acres, rather than the reality his wife experienced: people who knew, or thought they knew, everything about you, the claustrophobia of years of shared history, the subtle policing of women with too much money and too little time.

The answering machine was flashing, and Suzanna fought a guilty thrill of hope that it might be one of her London friends. They were ringing less often now, her lack of availability for coffee or early evening drinks in wine bars slowly fraying what she now knew must have been pretty tenuous threads of friendship. It didn't stop her missing them. She was tired of having to think about what she said before she said it; frequently she found it easier, as she had this evening, to say almost nothing at all.

"Hello, darlings. I hope you're both out having fun somewhere. I just wondered whether you'd had a think about Lucy's birthday lunch on the sixteenth. Daddy and I would so love it if you could make it, although we quite understand if you've got something else on. Let me know."

Always so careful not to suggest any obligation or imposition with that cheerful yet slightly apologetic tone. The subtlest hint of "We know you're having problems, and we're keeping our fingers crossed for you." Suzanna sighed, knowing that, having missed several Christmases and numerous other family gatherings, there were few excuses to avoid her family now that they were, geographically at least, so close.

"We should go." Neil had taken off his coat and was pouring himself a drink.

"I know we should."

"Your dad will probably find some reason to go out anyway. You two are pretty good at avoiding each other."

"I know."

Neil liked being part of her family. He had little of his own, with one seldom-visited and barely missed mother now several hundred miles away. It was one of the reasons he took such a conciliatory approach with hers.

Neil put down his glass and walked over to her. He put his arms around her and pulled her to him gently. She felt herself concede, unable to shake off her natural rigidity entirely. "It would mean so much to your mum."

"I know, I know." She placed her hands on his waist, unsure whether she was holding him or just holding him away. "And I know it's childish. It's just the thought of everyone wittering on about how fantastic Lucy is, and what a marvelous job she's got and look how beautiful and blah blah, and everyone making out that we're this superhappy family."

"Listen, it's not exactly easy for me to listen to that stuff either. Doesn't make me feel like the superstar son-in-law."

"I'm sorry. Maybe we just shouldn't go."

Suzanna was the decorative one of the family. Its genetic mythology had ascribed to her beauty and financial haplessness, to her younger brother, Ben, a countryman's wisdom beyond his years, while Lucy had been the brainy one, able at the age of three to recite great swathes of poetry, or ask in all serious-ness why such and such a book was not as good as the author's last? Then, slowly, some kind of meta-morphosis had taken place. While Ben became, as everyone had expected, a kind of younger, merrier echo of their straightforward, stoic, occasionally pompous father, Lucy, far from becoming the pre-dicted bespectacled recluse, had blossomed, become frighteningly assertive, and now, in her late twen-ties, headed up the digital division of some foreign media conglomerate.

Suzanna, meanwhile, had gradually realized that decorativeness was no longer enough when one reached one's thirties, that her lifestyle, and lack of financial acumen, had ceased to be endearing and now seemed simply self-indulgent. She didn't want to think about her family.

"We could go and look at shops tomorrow," she said. "I've seen a place in town that's up for rent. Used to be a bookshop."

"You don't waste any time."

"There's no point in hanging around. Not if I've only got a year."

He was evidently relishing this unusual intimacy, enjoying holding her close. She would have liked to sit down, but he seemed unwilling to let her go.

"It's in one of those little lanes, the cobbled ones off the square. And it's got a Georgian window at the front. Like the Olde Curiosity Shoppe."

"You don't want something like that. If you're going to do it, do it properly, with a great big plate-glass window. Something people can see your stock through."

"But it's not going to be that sort of shop. I told you before. Look, come and see it before you say anything. I've got the estate agents' number in my bag."

"Now, there's a surprise."

"I might ring them now. Leave a message. Just to let them know I'm interested." She could hear the excitement in her voice. It sounded strange to her, as if it came from somewhere else.

"Ring in the morning. It's not going to go at eleven thirty at night."

"I just want to get on with it."

He squeezed her. He smelled of soap powder, and the slightly stale yet inoffensive human scent of the end of the day. "You know, Suze, we should go to this lunch. We're fine. We're earning again. You can tell them about your shop."

"But not the baby stuff."

"Not the baby stuff."

"I don't want to tell any of them about it. They'll start going on about it, and Mum will get all excited and try to hide it, and then, if nothing happens, they'll all be walking on eggshells, wondering whether they can say anything. So, no baby stuff."

He spoke into her hair. "I bet Lucy hasn't got baby stuff."

"Neil, no."

"Look, ring them in the morning. We'll go, and we'll be bloody cheerful and have a nice day."

"We'll pretend to have a nice day."

"You might surprise yourself."

She snorted. "I'd certainly do that."

Surprisingly, considering it had been nearly eight months, that night they made love. Afterward Neil had become almost tearful and told her how much he really loved her, that he knew this meant everything was going to be all right.

Suzanna, lying in the dark, just able to make out the beamed ceiling she hated, had felt none of his sense of emotional release but rather a mild relief that they had done it. And a sneaking hope, which she was reluctant to admit even to herself, that she had earned herself a couple of months' grace before she had to do it again.

# 7

Dere Hampton was usually described in tourist brochures as "Suffolk's most beautiful market town," with the Norman church and antique shops providing a lure for ambling tourists throughout the summer months, and the occasional stoic walkers in winter. Its older inhabitants referred to it simply as "Dere," and its younger folk, who could usually be found on Friday nights drinking cheap cider and catcalling to each other in its market square, as "an effing dump, with nothing to do." They were not being unreasonable. It was fair to say it was a town more in love with its history than its future, and even more so since it had filled with commuter families pushed out from London. Its tall, elegant, pastel-colored Georgian buildings stood dovetailed by Tudor houses, with tiny windows and beams, that lurched over the pavement like ships in high seas, all arranged in a haphazard network of narrow cobbled lanes and small courtyards that branched out from the square. It held at least two of nearly all the shops one might need—butcher, baker, newsstand, hardware store, and an increasing proliferation of those that one might not.

It had been almost two months before Suzanna realized what bothered her about the town most: that during working hours it was almost exclusively female. There were headscarved matrons in green waistcoats picking up roasts from butchers with whom they were on first-name terms, young mothers pushing prams, carefully coiffed women of a certain age seemingly doing nothing much more than killing time. But apart from those who worked in the shops, or tradesmen, or schoolboys, there were almost no men. They were presumably off on the predawn trains to the City, returning to cooked meals and long-lit houses after dark. It was, she muttered crossly to herself, as if she'd been transported back to the 1950s. She had lost count of the number of times she had been asked what her husband did and, almost a year on, was still waiting for that question to be directed to herself.

Although she would have protested initially that she had nothing in common with those women, she could see herself in the way they shopped, wandering around the town's only department store with the measured gait of someone who had both money and time.

Suzanna was not sure what category her shop would fall into. As she sat, surrounded by boxes of stock, conscious that not only was her cash register still not working but that the electrician had failed to tell her which lightbulbs she needed for the spotlights, she was not sure that it was going to be a shop at all. Neil had rung twice to check whether she was certain she needed to buy quite so much stock in advance, while the water company had sent several letters demanding money even before she had opened.

For someone so recently haunted by debt, Suzanna was unworried by any of this. For the weeks that she had held the keys, she had just enjoyed being there, slowly turning the image she had held for the past months into a reality. She had loved traveling around to investigate possible suppliers, at trade exhibitions or tiny backrooms behind London's Oxford Street, meeting young designers eager to showcase their works, or more established ones who could talk her through years of trade. She loved having a purpose, being able to talk about "my shop," to make decisions based upon her own taste, choosing only what she thought beautiful and unusual.

And then there was the shop itself. The exterior had been given a fresh lick of white paint and the interior was slowly taking shape, nudged along by visits from local plumbers, carpenters, and her own amateur ability with a paintbrush. She knew they thought her picky and overdeliberate, but the decisions as to where things should go were complicated because it was not going to be a conventional shop. It was, instead, a mixture of things: a coffee room, for which the back wall held an old church pew, several tables and chairs, and a reconditioned Italian coffee machine. It was a secondhand shop, offering a few disparate items simply because she liked the look of them. It had some clothes, some jewelry, some pictures, some ornaments. It had some modern things. And that was about as specific as it got.

She had begun to place a variety of objects in the window. Initially, to make it look inhabited, she had put some of the more beautiful things she had bought during her "shopping" phase and never been able to use: brightly beaded bags, oversized glass rings, an antique picture frame with a modern abstract print. When the stock came, she had felt unwilling to alter her arrangement, so she had simply added to it: beautiful concentric circles of Indian bangles, old dresser drawers full of glowing metallic pens, spice bottles with silver lids in a variety of colors.

"It's like a sort of doll's house. Maybe an Aladdin's cave," Neil had said, when he had dropped by at the weekend. "It looks very—erm—pretty. But are you sure people are going to understand what it is you're about?"

"What does it have to be about?"

"Well, what kind of shop is it going to be?"

"My kind of shop," she said, and enjoyed his look of confusion.

Suzanna was creating something that was entirely her vision, diluted by no husband or partner. Free to do whatever she wanted, she found herself stringing bargain fairy-lights around the shelves, putting up little painted signs in her own intricate handwriting, coloring the floorboards a pale violet because the shade had taken her fancy. She arranged the tables and chairs, bought cheap from a house-clearance shop and painted with tester pots, into the kind of arrangements she would have liked when she got coffee with her girlfriends. She was, she realized, looking at the chairs, making herself a little corner of something magical, perhaps a little cosmopolitan, a place where she could once again feel at home, separate from the provincial eyes and attitudes that now surrounded her.

"So, what kind of shop are you?" one of the antique dealers had said, after eyeing the frame in her window. His voice had held just the faintest note of derision.

"I'm . . . an emporium," she had said, and ignored his raised eyebrows as he left to return to his own shop. And that's what she had called it, the Peacock Emporium, the sign painted in chalk blue and white, a stenciled drawing of a peacock feather beside it. Neil had looked at it with a mixture of pride and fearfulness; he confessed later that he had wondered whether, with his name on the door, he might face bankruptcy again if it folded.

"It's not going to fold," said Suzanna firmly. "Don't be so negative."

"You're going to have to work bloody hard," he said.

Even Neil's anxieties didn't bother her. She found it harder to argue with him at the moment. She was sleeping well.

Apart from the stock, she had bought nothing for weeks.

"Are you open?"

Suzanna glanced up from her spot on the floor. The religious-icon candles had seemed like a good idea at the London wholesaler's, but now, as she watched green padded waistcoat after green padded waistcoat pass the window, either oblivious or squinting through the glass in a vaguely disparaging manner, she wondered whether she had been too cosmopolitan in her tastes. They looked beautiful next to the beaded bags but, as Neil kept saying, there was no point in her buying beautiful things if no one around here would be prepared to buy them.

"Not quite. Probably on Monday."

The woman walked in anyway, closed the door behind her, and gazed around with a rapt expression. She wasn't wearing a green waistcoat but a maroon anorak, and a hand-knitted multicolored woolen hat from which her gray hair stuck out at right angles. At first glance Suzanna might have written her off as a trainee bag lady, but on looking closer, she noted that her shoes were expensive, as was her purse.

"Doesn't it look **lovely** in here? Very different from how it was before."

Suzanna struggled to her feet.

"This shop was a grocer's, you know, when I was a girl. There was your fruit over this side . . ." She gestured to where Suzanna's tables and chairs now stood. ". . . And on this side the vegetables. Oh, and they used to do fresh eggs. They kept their own chickens out the back, you know. I don't suppose you'll be doing that." She laughed, as if she had said something amusing.

"Right. Well, I'd better be—"

"What are the tables for? Are you going to serve food?"

"No."

"People like a bit of food."

"You need a license for that. I'm going to serve coffee. Like espresso."

"Espresso?"

It was moments like this that made Suzanna's renewed optimism falter. How could she sell coffee in a town whose inhabitants didn't even know what espresso was? "It's a type of coffee. Quite strong. Served in small cups."

"Well, I suppose that's a good way to keep your profits up. The tea house on Long Lane serves their tea in very small cups. I suppose it keeps their profits up too."

"It's meant to be in small cups."

"I'm sure they'd say the same, dear." She moved over to the window, muttering to herself as she fingered the objects on display. "What's this meant to be, then?" She held up the abstract painting.

"I don't believe it's meant to **be** anything." There was a hint of steel in Suzanna's voice.

The woman peered closely at it. "Is it **modern art**?" She said the words as if she was speaking a foreign language.

"Yes." Please don't let her say, "A child could do that," Suzanna thought.

"I could do that. If I did one like it, would you sell it for me?"

"I'm not really a gallery. You need to talk to a gallery."

"But you're selling that one."

"It's a one-off."

"But if you sell it, there's no reason why you shouldn't be able to sell another. I mean, it proves there's a demand."

Suzanna could feel herself losing patience. She had a short fuse at the best of times, and these were not the best of times.

"It's been lovely talking to you, but I'm afraid I really must get on." Suzanna held out an arm, as if to steer the woman toward the door.

But the woman had rooted herself to the center of the floor. "Grew up in this town, I did. I'm a seamstress by trade, but I moved away when I married. Lots of us did, then."

Oh, God. She was going to want to talk **history**. Suzanna looked around desperately for an excuse to get rid of her.

"My husband died three years after we married. Tuberculosis. Spent almost six months in a Swiss clinic, and then he died anyway."

"I'm sorry."

"I'm not. He was rather a stupid man. I only realized it after I'd married him. We didn't have children, you know. He preferred his mouth-organ."

Suzanna let out a snort. "What?"

The woman brushed vaguely at her hair. "He didn't know what to do, dear. I did, because my mother had told me. I told him on our wedding night, and he was so horrified that he said no, thank you, he'd rather play his mouth-organ. So that's what we did every night, for two years. I read my book in bed, and he played his mouth-organ."

Suzanna found herself laughing despite herself. "I'm sorry. Did you—did you find anyone else?"

"Oh, no. No one I wanted to marry. I had rather a lot of affairs, which were nice, but I didn't want someone in my bed every night. They might have wanted to play some musical instrument too. Goodness knows what I might have ended up with."

The woman, apparently haunted by visions of bass drums and tubas, gave a tiny shake of her head. "Yes, it's all changed. I've only been back here six months, and it's all changed . . . Are you local?"

"I was born here, but we lived in London until last year." She wasn't sure why she had told the truth: she had a feeling that the less she told this woman, the better.

"So you're a returnee too! How exciting. Well, we've each found a kindred spirit. I'm Johanna Creek. You can call me Mrs. Creek. What's your name?"

"Peacock. Suzanna Peacock."

"We had peacocks in the house where I grew up. It's just outside the town, on the Ipswich road. Dreadful birds they are, make the most hideous noise. They used to do their business all over our windowsills."

She turned and put a hand up to her hat, as if to check it was still there. "Well, Suzanna Peacock, I can't stand around here chatting all day. I'm afraid I'll have to get on. I've got to get a shepherd's pie from the Women's Institute market. I'll come back when you open and have one of your small cups of coffee."

"Oh, good," said Suzanna, dryly.

Before she left, Mrs. Creek stared again at the abstract painting, as if memorizing it in preparation for her own version.

Suzanna arrived home at almost half past nine. Neil was sitting with his feet on the coffee table, an empty bowl and a plate littered with a few crumbs next to them. "I was about to send out a search party," he said, turning his head away from the television.

"What's for dinner?"

He looked mildly surprised. "I haven't made anything. I thought you might be back in time to cook."

She removed her coat, feeling suddenly cross and tired. "I'm opening in three days' time, Neil. I'm run off my feet. I thought just this once you might cook for me."

"You might have eaten already. Besides, I didn't know what time you'd be back."

"You could have rung."

"You could have rung me."

Suzanna stomped into the little kitchen. The sink was still full of the morning's breakfast things. "Well, as long as you're all right, Neil, don't worry about me, will you?"

His voice lifted in protest: "I only had bloody bread and cheese. I've hardly been cooking myself up a banquet."

She began slamming cupboard doors, searching for something easy to prepare. She hadn't had time to go to the supermarket for a couple of weeks, and the shelves contained little more than the odd split lentil or opened stock cube. "You could have washed up."

"Oh, for crying out loud! I leave the house at a quarter to six in the morning. Do you want me to wait here until you've had your breakfast?"

"Just forget it, Neil. You look after yourself, and I'll look after myself, and then at least we both know where we stand."

There was a brief silence, and he appeared in the kitchen doorway. There wasn't enough space for them both, and he moved as if to steer her out into the living room. "Don't be so melodramatic, Suze. Look, you sit down and I'll cook you something."

"You haven't left me any bread." She peered into the plastic packet.

"There were only two slices."

"Oh, just go away, Neil. Go and lie on the sofa."

He threw up his arms in exasperation. It was only then that she noticed how tired he looked, that his face was shadowed with gray. "Don't be such a bloody martyr. If this shop is going to make you so bloody grumpy I'm already wishing you hadn't taken it on."

He launched himself back onto the sofa, which was too big for the room, picked up the remote, and began to flick through the channels.

She stood in the kitchen for a few minutes, then came and sat on the chair opposite him, clutching a bowl of cereal, not looking at him. It was the least arduous way of showing him how fed up she was.

Abruptly, Neil turned off the television. "I'm sorry," he said, into the silence. "I should have thought about the bread. It's just that by the time I get off the train in the evening, all I can think about is getting home."

He had disarmed her. "No, I'm the one who should be sorry. I'm just tired. It'll be better when the shop opens."

"I am pleased you've got the shop. I shouldn't have said that. It's been nice seeing you so . . . so—"

"Busy?"

"Animated. I like seeing you animated. You seem less bothered by . . . stuff than you have been."

Even the cereal felt like an effort. She put it on the table in front of her. "Less time to think, I suppose."

"Yup. Too much time to think—always a recipe for disaster. Try not to do it myself." He smiled wanly. "Want me to see if I can get the day off for your opening?"

She sighed, acknowledging his smile. "No . . . don't worry. I don't think I'll do a grand opening. I don't even know if it's going to be Monday, the way things are going. And you'd better not upset the boss. Not this soon into the job."

"If you're sure." He gave her another tentative smile, then settled back into the sofa, picked up his newspaper, and flicked through the pages.

Suzanna sat wondering why she had instinctively not wanted him there. She knew it sounded daft, ungenerous, even. But she just wanted something that was hers, pure and pleasurable, untainted by her and Neil's history. Uncomplicated by **people**.

# 8

The old lady stood in the doorway wearing her good tweed coat, a straw hat with cherries set on her head at a rakish angle, and her patent-leather handbag in front of her. "I would like," she announced, "to go into Dere."

Vivi turned, the roasting dish spitting lethally in her gloved hands, and searched frantically for a spare section of the stove on which to rest it. She took in the hat and bag, and her heart sank. "What?"

"Don't say 'what.' It's rude. I am ready to go to town. If you wouldn't mind fetching the car."

"We can't go to town, Rosemary. The children are coming for lunch."

A flicker of confusion passed across Rosemary's features. "Which children?"

"All of them. They're all coming for Lucy's birthday lunch, you remember?"

Rosemary's cat, which was so bony and decrepit that, when lying outside, it had several times been mistaken for roadkill, scrambled its way onto the kitchen work surface and shakily toward the roast beef. Vivi removed an oven glove and gently placed the mutely protesting animal back on the floor, then promptly burned herself on the roasting pan.

"In that case I'll just get a quick trip in before they come."

Vivi sighed inwardly. She fixed a smile on her face and turned back to her mother-in-law. "I'm awfully sorry, Rosemary, but I've got to get lunch ready and lay the table. And I haven't dusted the front room. Perhaps you could ask—"

"Oh, he's far too busy to be running me around. You don't want to go bothering him." The old lady lifted her head imperiously, and glanced at the window. "Just run me to the Tall Trees then. I'll walk the rest of the way." She waited, then added, pointedly, "With my stick."

Vivi checked the beef, and slid the roasting tray back into the lower oven. She walked over to the sink and ran cold water over her throbbing fingers. "Is it urgent?" she asked, her voice carefully light. "Could it wait until after tea, perhaps?"

Her mother-in-law stiffened. "Oh, don't mind me. My trips are never urgent, are they, dear? No, I'm far too ancient to have anything important to do." She peered dismissively at the other tray on the worktop. "Nothing as important as the needs of a few **potatoes**."

"Now, come on, Rosemary, you know I—"

But with a loud emphatic slam of the door, which

belied her apparent frailty, Rosemary had vanished back into the granny annex.

Vivi closed her eyes and took a deep breath. She would pay for that later. But, then, most days she ended up paying for something.

Normally she would have dropped whatever she was doing to do the old lady's bidding, just to avoid any unpleasantness. But today was different. She had not had the three children together in the house for several years and, having got this far, she was not going to jeopardize Lucy's birthday lunch by running Rosemary around when she should be ladling beef fat over the potatoes. Because with her mother-in-law it was never just a matter of taking her into town—Rosemary would suggest a diversion, or that Vivi accompany her to pick up some dry cleaning (and Vivi could carry it). Or announce that what she really needed, after all, was to get her hair done, and would Vivi mind waiting? She had become particularly demanding since they had persuaded her she was no longer capable of driving herself. They were still wrestling with the insurance over the ruined fence at Paget's farm.

"Any chance of a cup of tea? Cooking the books always makes me thirsty."

Vivi was sitting at the kitchen table. Having found the collection of tired pencils and compacts that passed for her makeup bag, she was trying to brighten herself up a bit, to blot down the high color and slight sheen she always got from cooking. "I'll bring one through," she said, after a defeated glance in the little mirror. "Does Daddy want one?"

"Dunno. I expect so." Her son, all six foot four of him, ducked with practiced ease under the lintel as he left the kitchen and walked back down the corridor. "Oh, I didn't tell you?" he called over his shoulder. "We forgot to pick up the flowers. Sorry."

Vivi stilled, put her compact on the table, then walked briskly after him. "What?"

"Don't say 'what.' It's rude." Her son grinned, mimicking his grandmother. "Dad and I forgot to pick up those flowers this morning. Got a bit tied up at the feed shop. Sorry."

"Oh, **Ben**." She stood in the doorway of the study, her hands dropped in exasperation.

"Sorry."

"One thing. The one thing I asked you two to do for me, and you leave it till five minutes before they all arrive to tell me you've forgotten."

"What did we forget?" Her husband lifted his head from the books. "Cup of tea?" he said hopefully.

"The table arrangements. You didn't pick them up like I asked you."

"Oh."

"I'll pick you some, if you want." Ben glanced out of the window. He had spent more than an hour in the study and was restless to get outside again.

"There are no flowers, Ben. It's February, for goodness' sake. Oh, I am disappointed."

An unaccustomed note of crossness had crept into her voice. "I wanted everything to be perfect today. It's a special day."

"Lucy's not going to care if there are no table arrangements." Her husband shrugged, and ruled a line underneath some numbers.

"Well, I care. And it's a terrific waste of money, spending on flowers that we can't even be bothered to pick up." She would get nowhere with them. Vivi gazed up at the clock, wondering vainly whether she could whiz into town and pick them up herself. With luck, and a decent parking space, she could be in and out in twenty minutes.

Then she remembered Rosemary, who would either want to come too or treat Vivi's brief visit as further evidence that her needs were not just considered unimportant but could be trampled over in a barbarous manner. "Well, you can jolly well pay for them," she said, wiping her hands on her apron, and reaching behind her to untie the strings, "and explain to Mr. Bridgman why we're ordering flowers that we apparently don't want."

The two men looked at each other, exchanging the blankest of glances.

"Tell you what," said Ben. "I'll go. If you'll let me take the Range Rover."

"You'll take your mother's car," came her husband's voice. "Pick us up a bottle of sherry for your grandmother while you're at it . . . You won't forget that cup of tea, darling, will you?"

Vivi had been married for precisely nine years when her mother-in-law came to live with them, and fifteen when her husband capitulated and agreed to build her an annex so that they could watch the odd American cop show without having to pause every five minutes to explain the plot, be able to cook food containing garlic or spices, and, just occasionally, read the newspapers in bed on a Sunday morning without an imperious knock at the door and a demand to know why the orange juice wasn't on its normal shelf in the fridge.

There had been no question of her going into a home. The house had been hers. She might not have been born there, she was fond of saying, but she could see no reason why she shouldn't die there. Even though the land was now farmed by tenants, and there was no longer much in the way of livestock, she liked to look out of her window and remember the past. It was a great **consolation** to her. Besides, Vivi occasionally mused, in a rare mutinous thought, why would she want to move anywhere else when she had a built-in cook-cleaner-chauffeur permanently at her disposal? Not even a five-star hotel would provide that.

The children, having grown up with Granny down the corridor and who, like their father, largely left their mother to deal with her, treated the old lady with a mixture of benevolence and irreverent humor, most of which, thankfully, she could not hear. Vivi scolded them for mocking her favorite phrases, or for their veiled references to the fact that she smelled not of Parma violets but of something rather more pungent and organic, but she had loved them too, for putting the old lady in perspective on the dispiriting days when Rosemary's demands made her seem impossible.

Even her carefree, even-tempered son had to admit that Rosemary was not the easiest old lady. Irascible and opinionated, with a firm belief in tradition and an oft-spoken disappointment in her family's failure to live up to it, she still apparently considered Vivi to be a kind of working guest in the house, even after some thirty years of marriage.

And, frail and forgetful as she was, she had not gone quietly down that good corridor. Rosemary's already heightened emotions at the building of the annex had subsequently wavered between a stubborn resentfulness that she was being "pushed out" to a secret pride in her renewed independence. Vivi had carefully decorated the new rooms in a combination of French cherry stripes and **toile de Jouy** (the one thing Vivi had always been good at, Rosemary had been forced to acknowledge, was fabrics), and they were untainted by young people's incomprehensible music, and endless streams of their monosyllabic friends, dogs, racket, and muddy boots.

This didn't stop her making surreptitious and repeated references that she had been "cast out" or "shoved off," occasionally in front of her remaining friends. Her own grandmother, she said pointedly, at least once a week, had taken over the good parlor as her living quarters, and children were **allowed** to go and pay court to her and occasionally read to her.

"I've got **The Clubber's Guide to Ibiza** here," said Ben, cheerfully. "That and **Basic Tractor Maintenance.**"

"We could dig out **The Joy of Sex.**" Lucy giggled. "Remember Mum and Dad used to hide that in their wardrobe?"

"Who's hiding in the wardrobe?" said Rosemary crossly.

"Lucy!" exclaimed Vivi, blushing. She had bought it on her thirtieth birthday, in a last-ditch attempt to be something of a siren, back when they had been "trying" for Ben. Her husband had been rather shocked, then put off by the illustrations. "No wonder he's grown all that facial hair," he'd said dismissively. "I'd want to disguise myself after that little lot."

Vivi did her best not to mind. She reminded

herself constantly of all the good things she had: a beautiful home, wonderful children, a loving husband, so she endured Rosemary's barbs and capricious demands, and left him in the dark as to their true extent. He didn't like family discord: it made him retreat into his shell like a snail, where he would lurk, slightly crossly, until everyone else had "sorted themselves out." It was why he didn't like this business with Suzanna and the others. "Well, I think you should sit down and explain it to her," Vivi had ventured, on more than one occasion.

"I've told you, I don't want all that business stirred up again," he would respond abruptly. "I don't have to explain myself to anyone. Especially not to someone who's just been given a bloody house to live in. She's just going to have to learn to live with it."

Suzanna stood on the front step of her parent's home, as Neil took the bottle of wine and the flowers from the back of the car.

"You got carnations," she said, grimacing.

"And?"

"They're awful. Such mean-looking flowers."

"In case it had escaped your notice, Suze, we're not exactly in a position to be buying rare orchids. Your mum'll be happy with whatever we give her."

Suzanna knew it was true, but it didn't stop her feeling ill-tempered. She had felt like this ever since they had pulled into the drive and she had seen the mustard-colored sprawling farmhouse, the huge oak door of her childhood. She could hardly remember a time when this house had been a comfort to her. She knew it must have, sometime before the differences between her and her siblings had become pronounced, before she could see them reflected in her father's complicated gaze, and her mother's overblown efforts to pretend they were invisible. Before they had been written, legally, into her family's future. Her stomach lurched, and she glanced at the car. "Let's go home," she whispered, as Neil stepped up beside her.

"What?"

From inside came the distant sound of manic yapping.

"Let's go—let's just go now."

Neil raised his eyes to heaven, his arms dropping exasperatedly by his sides. "Oh, for God's s—"

"It'll be awful, Neil. I just can't cope with them en masse. I'm not ready."

But it was too late. There was the sound of a footfall, then of someone wrestling with the catch, and the door swung open, allowing out an overexcited Jack Russell and the smell of roast meat. Vivi shooed the yapping dog back inside, then straightened herself and beamed. She brushed her hands on her apron, then held them wide open before her. "Hello, my darlings. **Oh**, it's **good** to see you. Welcome home."

"Don't give me anything with shellfish. Those shrimps made my lips blow up. I nearly ended up going to the doctor. I couldn't go out for two days."

"You were very poorly." Vivi was dishing out potatoes. She noted with satisfaction that the beef fat had made them lacy and golden.

"Some women pay good money for that now, Gran," said Ben. "Can I have a couple more spuds? That one there, Mum. The burned one."

"Implants," said Lucy.

"What?"

"Women. Put them in their lips to make them look fuller. Perhaps they should have just eaten some of Mum's potted shrimp. No meat for me, Mum. I'm off red meat at the moment. Didn't you have those once, Suze?"

"I never had implants."

"Not implants. Injections. In your lips. During your self-improvement phase."

"Thanks a lot, Lucy."

"You had injections in your lips?"

"They were only temporary." Suzanna looked down at her plate. "It's just collagen. It's meant to give you more of a pout."

Vivi, appalled, turned to her son-in-law, her serving spoon raised in her hand. "And you let her do this?"

"You think I had any say in the matter? You

remember what she was like then. It was all hair extensions, false nails—I never knew whether I was coming home to Cher."

"Oh, don't exaggerate, Neil. They were only temporary. I didn't like them anyway." Suzanna, cross, pushed her vegetables around her plate.

"I saw you with them. I thought it looked like someone had stuck two inner tubes to your face. Very spooky."

"Inner tubes?" said Rosemary. "On her face? What's she want to do that for?"

Suzanna glanced at her father who, head down, was pretending not to have heard the exchange. He had spent most of his time talking to Neil who, as usual, he treated with ridiculous courtesy, as if he were still grateful to the younger man for the huge favor he had done in taking Suzanna off his hands. Neil always told her she was being ridiculous when she said this out loud, but she couldn't see why her parents always made such a fuss about him being prepared to do things like iron his own shirts, put the rubbish out, or take her to dinner. Like she was somehow genetically predisposed to do all the housework.

"Well, I think Suzanna is quite pretty enough without any . . . enhancements." Vivi, seated, handed around the gravy. "I don't think she needs any help at all."

"Hair's looking good, Suze," said Lucy. "I like it

when it's its proper color." Lucy's own hair, a much lighter shade than Suzanna's, woven through with highlights, was cut into a businesslike bob.

"Like Morticia Addams," said Ben.

"Who?" Rosemary leaned forward over her plate. "Is someone going to help me to potatoes? I don't seem to have any potatoes."

"They're coming around, Gran," said Lucy.

"Morticia Addams. Out of **The Addams Family.**"

"The Stoke-by-Clare Adamses?"

"No, Grandma. Someone on telly. Did you see Radiohead in concert, Luce?"

"He was a fascist, you know. In the war. Dreadful family."

"Yup. They were excellent. I've got a copy if you want."

"Used to serve cold cuts every evening for supper. Never a decent meal there. And they kept pigs."

Vivi turned to Suzanna. "And you must tell us all about your shop, darling. I'm dying to hear. Have you got an opening date yet?"

Suzanna stared at her plate, took a deep breath, and glanced at Neil, who was still talking to her father. "Actually, it's open."

There was a brief silence.

"Open?" said Vivi, uncomprehending. "But I thought you were going to have an opening party."

Suzanna looked uncomfortably at Neil, who gazed at his plate with a don't-bring-me-into-this expression. She swallowed. "It was only a small thing."

Vivi stared at her daughter and blushed, so delicately that only those watching carefully—like her son, son-in-law, and other daughter—would have noticed. "Oh," she said, methodically spooning gravy onto her plate. "Well. You didn't want us lot clogging the place up, I'm sure. You want proper customers, don't you? Was it . . . Did it go well?"

Suzanna sighed, cowed by guilt and simultaneously resentful that, within minutes of lunch beginning, she had been made to feel this way. It had all seemed perfectly rational when she had justified her decision to herself. It was bad enough that she had been forced to move back into the shadow of her family, surely it wasn't too much to ask that she carve herself a bit of space away from them? It wouldn't be her shop, otherwise, just another extension of her family's interests. Yet now, listening to Vivi trying to cover the hurt in her voice with a series of mindless observations, aware of the weight of her siblings' accusatory stares, it seemed somewhat less easy to explain.

"Where is it, Suze?" She could hear icy politeness in Ben's voice.

"Just off Water Lane. Two down from the takeout."

"Nice for you," he said coolly.

"You'll have to drop in some time," she said, smiling gamely.

"We're a bit busy at the moment." He looked at his father. "Got some projects going on in the barns, haven't we, Dad?"

"I'm sure we'll all find time to pop in soon." Her father's tone was neutral.

Suzanna's eyes filled inexplicably with tears.

Vivi had left the table to fulfill some unspecified task in the kitchen. They could hear her down the corridor, muttering something to the dog.

"Well, that was nice of you, Suze." Lucy's voice cut across the table.

"Lucy . . ." Her father's voice held a warning.

"Well, how much would it have hurt her to invite Mum? Even if none of the rest of us came, she could have invited Mum. She was really proud, you know? She told everyone about your bloody shop."

"Lucy."

"You'll have made her look a right idiot in front of her friends."

"I didn't mean to hurt her."

"No, you never do."

"It wasn't even a proper opening. I didn't serve drinks or anything."

"All the more reason why it wouldn't have hurt to invite her. God, after all Mum and Dad have done for you—"

"Lucy—"

"Look, let's not—" Neil interrupted, gesturing toward the doorway, from which Vivi was emerging again. "Not now . . ."

"I almost forgot to put the pudding on. Wasn't that silly of me?" Vivi said, seating herself again, and looking around the table with the vaguely assessing eye of the practiced hostess. "Has everyone got everything? Is it all right?"

"Delicious," said Neil. "You've excelled yourself, Vivi."

"I haven't got any mustard," said Rosemary, accusingly.

"Yes, you have, Gran," said Lucy. "It's on the side of your plate."

"What did you say?"

Ben leaned across the table, pointing with his knife. "There," he said, revealing it to her. "Mustard."

Vivi had been on the verge of crying—Suzanna could see the telltale reddening round her eyes. She glanced at Neil across the table and knew that he had seen it too. She found she had lost her appetite.

"We've got some news," said Neil.

Vivi smiled at him. "Oh, yes?" she said. "What is it?"

"Suzanna's decided to think of someone other than herself," said Lucy. "That would be news."

"Oh, for God's sake, Lucy." Her father's cutlery crashed down on the tabletop.

"We're going to have a baby. Not yet," Neil added hurriedly. "Next year. But we've decided it would be the right time."

"Oh, darlings, that's wonderful." Vivi, face brightening, had leaped from her place at the table and reached round to hug Suzanna.

Suzanna, stiff as a board, sat staring at her husband in silent fury. He refused to meet her eyes.

"Oh, I'm so pleased for you. How lovely!"

Lucy and Ben exchanged glances.

"What's going on? I wish you would all speak up."

"Suzanna's going to have a baby," said Vivi loudly.

"Not yet." Suzanna found her voice. "I'm not going to have one yet. Not till next year. In fact, it was meant to be a—a surprise."

**I'm going to kill you**, Suzanna mouthed at Neil.

"Isn't that wonderful, darling?" Vivi placed her hand on her husband's arm.

"Not really, no," he said.

The room fell silent—apart from at Rosemary's end of the table, where some kind of internal gastric explosion had sent Ben and Lucy into barely stifled giggles.

Their father placed his knife and fork on his plate. "They're still virtually bankrupt. They're living in rented accommodation. Suzanna has just set up a business, even though she has absolutely no experience in running anything, let alone a household budget, successfully. I think the last thing they should be doing is bringing children into the equation."

"**Darling**," Vivi remonstrated.

"What? Can't we tell the truth now? In case she decides to absent herself from the family again? I'm sorry, Neil. In other circumstances it would be wonderful news. But until Suzanna has grown up a bit and learned to accept her responsibilities I think it's a bloody awful idea."

Lucy had stopped giggling. She looked at Suzanna, and then at Neil, who had flushed a deep red. "That's a bit harsh, Dad."

"Just because something's not easy to hear, Lucy, doesn't mean it's harsh." Her father, having apparently exceeded his daily quota of spoken words, resumed eating.

Vivi reached for the Yorkshire puddings, her face taut with anxiety. "Let's not talk about this today. It's so seldom we have everyone together. Let's just try to have a nice lunch, shall we?" She held aloft her glass. "Shall we make a toast to Lucy, perhaps? Twenty-eight. A wonderful age."

Only Ben joined her.

Suzanna lifted her head. "I thought you'd be pleased I set up a business, Dad," she said slowly. "That I was trying to do something for myself."

"We are pleased, darling," said Vivi. "Aren't we?" She placed her hand on her husband's arm.

"Oh, stop trying to pretend, Mum. He never thinks anything I do is good enough."

"You're twisting my words, Suzanna." He kept eating in small, regular mouthfuls. His voice stayed steady.

"But not your meaning. Why can't you ever just give me a break?"

It was like speaking into a vacuum. Suzanna stood up abruptly. "I **knew** this would happen," she said, burst into tears, and fled from the table.

They listened to her footsteps fading down the corridor, and the sound of a distant door slamming.

"Happy birthday, Luce," said Ben, raising a glass ironically.

Neil pushed back his chair, and wiped his mouth with his napkin. "Sorry, Vivi," he said. "It was delicious. Really delicious."

His father-in-law did not raise his head. "Sit down, Neil. You'll help no one by galloping after her."

"What's the matter with her?" said Rosemary, turning stiffly toward the door. "Morning sickness, is it?"

"Rosemary . . ." Vivi pushed a strand of hair off her forehead.

"You stay," Lucy said, placing her hand on Neil's shoulder. "I'll go."

"Are you sure?" Neil eyed his food, unable to hide his relief that he might be allowed to finish his lunch in peace.

"Trust her to hijack Lucy's birthday celebration."

"Don't be unkind, Ben," said Vivi. She glanced wistfully at Lucy's departing back.

Rosemary reached over to help herself to another potato. "I suppose it's all for the best." She jabbed one with a shaking fork. "Just as long as she doesn't turn out like her mother."

The barns had all changed. Where, at the rear of the farm, there had been three semi-derelict timber shelters for hay, straw, and pieces of rusting farm equipment, there were now two double-glazed barn conversions, fronted by gravel parking areas, advertised as "all-inclusive offices."

"You all right?"

Lucy appeared at Suzanna's left, and sat beside her. Suzanna noted that her sister had the even, glowing complexion that spoke of winter sun and expensive skiing holidays, then, with a jolt, that Lucy had joined the ever-increasing list of people she envied. "So, when did all this happen?" She cleared her throat, and gestured toward the barns.

"Started a couple of years ago. Now that Dad's letting the land, he and Ben are working on ways to make the rest of the estate earn more money."

There was something about "he and Ben" that made Suzanna's eyes fill again with tears.

"They're holding shoots on the other side of the wood too. Breeding pheasants."

"Never thought of Dad as a shooter."

"Oh, he doesn't do it himself. He gets Dave Moon to do it. He's got dogs and everything.

"They charge a fortune," Lucy added approvingly. "Last season paid for Dad's new car." She picked at a piece of lichen near her shoe, then lifted her head and smiled. "You'll never guess—when Dad was younger he became briefly obsessed with the idea of giving it all away. All the land. Gran told me. Can you imagine Dad, the great stickler for tradition, as a kind of communist Robin Hood?"

"No."

"Nor me. I thought she had a touch of Alzheimer's to begin with, but she swears it's true. She and Grandpa talked him out of it." She hugged her knees. "Boy, I'd have loved to have been a fly on the wall for that conversation."

In the distance, dotted along the narrow field by the river, there were twenty or so black and white sheep, seemingly stationary. Her father had never been particularly successful with his sheep. Too prone to disgusting diseases, he would say.

"I hardly recognize it around here." Suzanna's voice was small.

Lucy's was brisk in response. "You should come home more often. It's not as if you live miles away."

"I wish I bloody did." Suzanna buried her face in her arms again. She cried for a few more minutes, and then, sniffing, looked sideways at her younger sister. "He's so bloody horrible to me, Luce."

"He's just pissed off that you hurt Mum's feelings."

Suzanna wiped her nose. "I know I should have invited her. I just—I just get sick of living in their shadow. I know they've helped out since we lost the money and everything, but nothing's the same, now that . . ."

Lucy turned to her, then shook her head. "It's the will, isn't it? You're still going on about the will."

"I'm not going on about it."

"You'll have to let this go, you know. You don't want to run the estate. You never have. You told me it would drive you mad."

"That's not the point."

"You're letting it poison everything. And it's making Mum and Dad really unhappy."

"But they're making **me** unhappy."

"I can't believe you're obsessing over what happens to Dad's money after he dies. I can't believe you're prepared to split this family apart over something that isn't yours in the first place. He's not going to leave either of us short, you know."

"It's not **about** Dad's money. It's about the fact that he believes in some outdated system where boys matter more than girls."

"Primogeniture."

"Whatever. It's just wrong, Lucy. I'm **older** than

Ben. It's wrong, and it's divisive, and it shouldn't happen in this day and age."

Lucy's voice rose in exasperation. "But you've never wanted to run the estate."

"It's not the bloody point."

"So you'd rather it be broken up and sold off, just so you can have an equal share?"

"No, Lucy. I just want an acknowledgment that I—that we—are as important as Ben."

Lucy made as if to stand. "It's your problem, Suze. I feel just as important as Ben.

"Look, no one else is going to say this to you, but you need to get this into perspective, Suzanna. This all bears no indication of what Dad thinks of you. If anything, you got more attention than either me or Ben when we were young." She held up a hand, silencing Suzanna's protest. "And that's fine. You probably needed it more. But you can't blame him for everything that's happened since. He's given you a house, for God's sake."

"He hasn't given it to us. We're paying rent."

"A peppercorn rent. You know as well as I do that you've got it for good if you want it."

Suzanna fought a childish urge to say she didn't want it and she hated that little house with its tiny rooms and its cottagey beams. "It's because he feels guilty. He's overcompensating."

"God, you sound spoiled. I can't believe you're thirty-five."

"Thirty-four."

"Whatever."

Perhaps conscious that her tone had been a little hard, she nudged Suzanna with her elbow, a conciliatory gesture. Suzanna, who had started to feel chilly, wrapped her arms around her knees and wondered how her sister, at twenty-eight, had achieved this level of certainty, this self-possession.

"Look. It's Dad's right to divide things up as he chooses. And things might change, you know. You just need a bit more going on in your own life and then it won't matter."

Suzanna swallowed the bitter retort. There was something particularly galling about being patronized by one's baby sister, hearing an echo of family discussions that had taken place without her. Especially if you knew she was right.

"Make a go of this shop and Dad will have to look at you differently."

"If I make a go of this shop Dad will die of shock."

She was shivering now. Lucy was getting to her feet with the balanced ease of someone for whom exercise was a daily ritual. Suzanna, standing, thought she heard her own knees creak. "Sorry," she said. And then, after a pause, "Happy birthday."

Lucy held out her arm. "Come on, let's go inside. I'll show you the tin of biscuits Gran gave me for my birthday. It's the exact one Mrs. Popplewell gave her for Christmas two years ago. Besides, if we stay out much longer she'll convince herself that you're giving birth already."

Vivi sat down heavily on the stool, and began to wipe the day from her face. She was not a vain woman—there were only two pots on her dressing table, one for cleansing and one a supermarket moisturizer—but tonight she looked at the reflection before her and felt immensely tired, as if someone had placed an intolerable weight on her shoulders. I might as well be invisible, she thought, for all the influence I have in this family. As a younger woman, she had shepherded her three children around the county, had supervised their reading, eating, and brushing of teeth, had refereed their squabbles and dictated what they should wear. She had fulfilled her maternal tasks with certainty, rebuffing their protests, setting their boundaries, confident in her own abilities.

Now she was incapable of intervening in their fights, of helping to lighten their unhappinesses. She tried not to think about the opening of Suzanna's shop: that discovery had made her feel like such an irrelevance she had been almost winded.

"That dog of yours has been at my slippers."

Vivi turned. Her husband was examining the heel of his leather slip-ons, which had been visibly gnawed.

"I don't think you should let it upstairs. I don't know why we don't put it in a kennel."

"It's too cold outside. The poor thing would freeze." She turned back to her reflection. "I'll nip into town tomorrow and get you another pair."

They completed their ablutions in silence. Vivi, slipping into her nightdress, wished she hadn't recently finished a book. Tonight she could have done with a little escape.

"Oh. Mother wants to know if you can dig her out a baking tray. She wants to make scones tomorrow and she doesn't know where hers has gone."

"She left it in the walled garden. She used it to feed the birds."

"Well, perhaps you could bring it in for her."

"Darling, I think you might have been a little hard on Suzanna today." She kept her tone light, tried to avoid any hint of reproach.

Her husband made a dismissive sound, but his lack of a response gave her courage. "You know, having a child might be the making of her. She and Neil have had such problems. It would give them a new focus." Her husband was staring at his bare feet. "Douglas? She's trying so hard."

It was as if he hadn't heard.

"Douglas?"

"And what if my mother's right? What if she does end up like Athene?"

# 9

The Dereward estate was one of the largest in that part of Suffolk. Backing on to what later became known as Constable country, it dated back to the 1600s, was unusual in that it had housed an almost unbroken ancestral line, and its land, which was notably hilly for the region, was well placed for a variety of uses, from arable farming to game fishing, and contained an exceptional—some said uneconomic—number of tied cottages. Most estate houses that oversaw some 450 acres were rather grander, perhaps with a portrait gallery or ballroom to indicate the gravitas of the incumbent family. The Dereward estate took some pride in its history—its family portraits were renowned for not just showing every heir in the past four hundred years but for detailing, in rather bald language, the manner of their death. From the turn of the twentieth century, various attempts had been made to portray some female members of the family, just as there had been increasing protests about the possibility of the house falling to the female line of the family. But the wives and daughters tended to look a bit half-hearted, as if they were not convinced of their right to pictorial immortality. The Fairley-Hulmes, as Rosemary was fond of saying, had not survived four hundred years by swaying to fashion and political correctness. For traditions to last, they had to be strong, shored up with rules and certainty. For one so strident on the matter, she spoke little about her own family's history—with good reason: Ben had looked her up on an Internet genealogy database and discovered that Rosemary's family hailed from a slaughterhouse in Blackburn.

The last portrait would have been Suzanna's mother's. A young artist had been commissioned on Athene's eighteenth birthday to paint it and, several decades on, it had become Important. But it was now Suzanna's, and lived with them in the cottage, although Vivi had repeatedly assured her that she would be more than happy for Athene to take her rightful place on the wall. "She's very beautiful, darling, and if it would be meaningful for you to have her up, then that's where she should be. We can get that frame restored, and it will look lovely." Vivi was always bending over backward, always so anxious to spare everybody's feelings. As if she had none of her own.

Suzanna had told her that the reason she liked to have the portrait in her own house was simply that it was beautiful. It was not as if she remembered

Athene; Vivi had been the only mother she had known. She couldn't articulate the real reason. It was to do with guilt, resentment, and that, for as long as her father found it nearly impossible to talk about his first wife, she felt it difficult to confront him with the evidence that he had had one. It was since she had let her hair grow dark again, since she had acquired, as Neil called it, something of her mother's fierce beauty, that her father had found it so difficult even to look at her at all. "Athene Forster," it read, the writing just visible against the crumbling gilt of the frame. Perhaps in deference to Suzanna's feelings, it had never explained the manner of her death.

"You going to put that up? Is it for sale?"

Suzanna eyed the young woman who stood, head cocked, in the doorway.

"She's like you," the girl said cheerfully.

"It's my mother," Suzanna said reluctantly.

The picture hadn't looked right in the cottage: it was too grand. Athene, with her glittering eyes and her pale, angular face, had filled the sitting room and left little space for anything else. Now, staring at it in the shop, Suzanna realized it didn't belong here either. The mere fact that this stranger was inspecting it made her feel uncomfortable, exposed. She turned it to the wall. "I was just taking it home," she said, and tried to suggest, through her tone, that the conversation was closed.

The girl's blue-black hair was pulled into two plaits, like a schoolgirl's, although she was clearly older. "I nearly lost my virginity on your stairs. Drunk as a skunk, I was. Can I have an espresso?"

Suzanna, moving toward the espresso machine, didn't bother to turn around. "You must be mistaken. This used to be a bookshop."

"Ten years ago it was a wine bar. The Red Horse. For a couple of years, anyway. When I was sixteen we all used to get hammered on Diamond White in the market square on Saturday nights, then come in here to cop off with each other. It's where I met my bloke. Snogging away on those stairs. Mind you, if I'd known then . . ." She trailed off, laughing. Suzanna wrestled with levers and coffee measurements, grateful that the din of the machine temporarily drowned the need to talk. She had envisaged that people would come in here, sit down, and talk to each other while she would preside over it all from the safety of the counter. But in the two months that she had been open, she had found that, more often than not, they wanted to talk to her, whether she felt sociable or not.

"They closed the bar down in the end. Not surprising, really, with all the underage drinking that went on."

Suzanna placed the filled cup on a saucer with two sugar lumps, and carried it carefully to the table.

"That smells gorgeous. I've been walking past for weeks, and I kept meaning to come in. I love what you've done with it."

"Thank you," said Suzanna.

"Have you met Arturro, in the deli? Big man. Hides behind his salamis when women go in the shop. He gave up doing coffee about eighteen months ago because his machine kept breaking down."

"I know who you mean."

"Liliane? From the Unique Boutique? The clothes shop on the corner."

"Not yet."

"They're both single. Both middle-aged. I think they've been hankering after each other for years."

Suzanna, mindful that she didn't want herself discussed in this manner, said nothing. The girl sipped her coffee. Then she leaned back in her chair, and noticed the small pile of glossy magazines in the corner. Suzanna had bought them a week ago, hoping it would deter customers from always wanting to talk to her. The girl smiled easily, and began flicking through **Vogue** with the kind of relish that suggested she didn't get to read too many magazines.

She sat there for almost twenty minutes, during which the two men who ran the motorbike spares shop dropped in to down quick, silent fixes of strong coffee, and Mrs. Creek made her twice-weekly foray around the shelves. She never bought anything, but she had given Suzanna several years' worth of her

life story, including her career as a dressmaker in
Colchester, the Unfortunate Incident on the Train,
and tales of her various allergies, which included
dogs, beeswax, certain synthetic fibers, and soft
cheese. "You don't have any beeswax here, do you?"
she said, sniffing.

"Or soft cheese," said Suzanna evenly. Mrs. Creek
had bought one coffee, and complained, grimacing,
that it was "a little bitter for my taste." "The Three-
Legged Stool, up the road, they put Coffee-mate
in theirs, if you ask. And they give you a free bis-
cuit," she said hopefully. Then, as Suzanna ignored
her, she added, "You don't need a food license for
biscuits." She had left shortly before twelve, having made, as she told the girl, "a promise to play a
little gin rummy with one of the elderly ladies up at
the center. She's a bit of a bore," she confided, in a
stage whisper, "but I think she's a bit lonely."

"I'm sure she'll be glad to see you," said the girl.
"There are a lot of lonely people in this town."

"There are, dear, aren't there?" Mrs. Creek had
adjusted her hat, looked meaningfully at Suzanna,
and tottered briskly out into the watery spring
sunshine.

"Can I have another coffee?" The girl stood up,
and walked with her cup to the counter.

Suzanna refilled the machine. As she was about
to start it up, she felt the girl's eyes on her. She saw
that she was being quietly assessed.

"It's an odd choice, running a coffee shop," the girl said. "I mean, for someone who doesn't like people."

Suzanna stood quite still. "It's not really a coffee shop," she said tartly. She glanced down at her hands, which were holding the cup. Then she added, "I'm just not big on small talk."

"You'd better learn, then," the girl said. "You won't stay afloat long otherwise, no matter how beautiful your shop is. I bet you've come up from London. London people never talk in shops." She glanced around. "You need some music. Always cheers things up, music."

"Oh?" Suzanna was fighting irritation. This girl appeared to be some ten years younger than her, and was presuming to tell her how to run her business.

"Am I being a bit blunt? Sorry. Jason always tells me I'm too blunt with people. It's just it's a really nice shop, really magical, and I think it will do really well as long as you don't keep treating every customer like you wish they weren't there. Can I have sugar with that?"

Suzanna pushed the bowl toward her. "Is that how I come across?"

"You're hardly welcoming." Seeing Suzanna's dismayed expression, she corrected herself: "I mean, I don't care, because I'll talk to anyone. But there's a lot of others around here who'd be put off. Is it London you're from?"

"Yes," said Suzanna. It was easier than explaining.

"I grew up on the estate near the hospital. Meadville, you know it? But it's a funny old town. Very green Wellies. Very up itself. You know what I'm saying? To be honest, there's a lot around here who aren't going to give you a second glance because everything in your window will just look weird to them. But there are some people who feel they don't fit in. People who don't want to sit with their Lapsang souchong and some headscarfed old blue rinse braying at the next table. I reckon if you were a bit friendlier you'd get a lot of trade from them."

Despite herself, Suzanna found the corners of her mouth lifting in recognition of the girl's description. "You think I should become a kind of social service."

"If it brings the punters in." The girl popped a sugar cube into her mouth. "You need to make money, don't you?" She gave Suzanna a sly look. "Or is this shop your **little hobby**?"

"What?"

"I didn't know whether you were one of those— you know, 'Hubby works in the City. She needs a little hobby.'"

"I'm not one of those."

"Once your customers knew they were welcome, you could put a notice up saying, 'Don't talk to me.' If you get the right sort of regulars they'll understand . . . I mean, if talking to people is really that painful . . ."

Their eyes locked and they grinned. Two grown women, recognizing something in each other, yet too old to acknowledge that they were making friends.

"Jessie."

"Suzanna. I'm not sure I can do that chatty stuff."

"Are you getting enough customers not to?"

Suzanna thought of Neil's knitted brow when he went over the figures. "Not really."

"You pay me in coffee, I'll come and help for a couple of hours tomorrow. Mum's picking up my Emma for a couple of hours before night school, and I'd rather do this than the Hoovering. It's nice to do something different."

Suzanna stiffened, unbalanced by the idea that she was being maneuvered. "I don't think there's enough work for two."

"Oh, there will be. I know everyone, you see. Look, I've got to go. Think about it, and I'll turn up tomorrow. If you don't want me, I'll have a coffee and go. Yeah?"

Suzanna shrugged. "If you're sure."

"Oh, hell. I'm late. His nibs'll be doing his conkers. See you." Jessie tossed some money onto the counter—the right amount, it turned out—threw her coat over her shoulder, and flew out into the lane. She was tiny. Watching her go, Suzanna thought she looked like a child. How can someone like that have a child herself, she thought, while I still feel unready?

She was unwilling to admit it, even to herself, but Suzanna was cultivating a new crush. She knew this because every day, in the few minutes before she closed the shop to buy her daily sandwich from the deli, she found herself checking her appearance, and reapplying her lipstick. It was not her first: during her marriage to Neil she thought she'd probably averaged one a year. They ranged from her tennis coach, who had the most compellingly muscular forearms she'd ever seen, to her friend Dinah's brother.

Nothing ever **happened**, as such. She either adored them from afar, building up a kind of parallel life and personality for them in her imagination— that was often far more desirable than theirs actually was, or allowed herself a swiftly intimate friendship, in which questions hung in the air unspoken, and tended to evaporate when the man surmised that she was prepared to take it no further. She was not being unfaithful, she would tell herself, just enjoying a little window-shopping, nurturing the kind of frisson that tended to disappear with security and domesticity.

Except that in this case she wasn't sure who her crush was focused **on**. Arturro's delicatessen

employed three of the most handsome young men
Suzanna had ever seen. They were lithe, dark, and
filled with the cheerful exuberance of those who not
only know they are beautiful but are made more
so in a town without competition. They shouted
cheerful insults to each other, hurling cheeses and
jars of olives with what Suzanna saw as a sublime
grace, while Arturro hovered benignly behind the
counter.

For a town that appeared to view anything more
foreign than the tired offerings of the local Chinese
takeout as too challenging, and still had reservations about the tandoori restaurant, Arturro's deli
was always well populated. The townswomen, in to
purchase their weekly cheese platter or posh coffee-
morning biscuits, would stand in their orderly
queue, breathing in the dense aromas of peppered
salami, Stilton, and coffee, eyeing the young men
with polite amusement (while occasionally reaching
up to smooth the odd stray hair). The younger girls
would stand in the queue and giggle, whispering to
each other, then remembering only when they got
to the counter that they didn't have any money.

The men's eyes held the knowing glint that spoke
of summer evenings full of laughter, squealing rides
on stylish scooters, nights of guilty promise. I'm
too old for any of them, Suzanna told herself, in
a determinedly maternal manner, while wondering if increased levels of poise and sophistication

outweighed the definite lines on her face and the increasingly square outline of her behind.

"Can I have a mortadella, tomato, and olive sandwich on brown? No butter, please."

Arturro blushed as he acknowledged her order.

"Busy today," Suzanna said, as one of the young men leaped up a stepladder to reach a brightly wrapped **panettone**.

"And you?" He spoke quietly and Suzanna had to lean forward to hear him.

"Not very. But it's early days." She painted on a bright smile.

Arturro handed her a paper bag. "I am coming in tomorrow to see. Little Jessie came in this morning and invited us. Is this okay?"

"What? Oh, yes. Yes, of course," she said. "Jessie's helping me out."

He nodded approvingly. "Nice girl. I know her a long time."

As Suzanna wondered which of the three young men might constitute Arturro's "us," he walked heavily to the end of the counter, and pulled an ornate tin of amaretti biscuits from a high shelf. He walked back and handed it to her. "For your coffee," he said.

Suzanna looked down at it. "I can't take this," she said.

"It's for good luck. For your business." He smiled shyly, revealing two tiny rows of teeth.

"Uh-oh, Arturro's on the pull." There was a cat-call behind her. Two of the young men were gazing at him, their arms crossed across their white aprons, mock disapproval on their faces. "You got to watch out, ladies. Next stop Arturro will be offering you a free taste of his salami . . ."

There was stifled laughter in the queue. Suzanna found herself blushing.

"And you know what they say about Italian salami, eh, Arturro?"

The big man turned toward the till, lifted an arm the width of a ham, and let off a volley of what Suzanna assumed was Italian abuse.

"**Ciao**, signora."

Suzanna left the deli blushing, trying not to smile too hard in case it made her look like the kind of woman who becomes overexcited when given a bit of attention.

When she got back to the shop she discovered she had forgotten to pick up her sandwich.

Jessie Carter had been born in the Dere maternity hospital, the only daughter of Cath, who worked in the bakery, and Ed Carter, who had been one of the town's postmen until his death from a heart attack two years ago. It was fair to say her life had not been exotic. She had grown up with her friends on the Meadville estate, attended Dere Primary, then gone on to Hampton High School, which she had left at

sixteen with two GCSEs in art and home econom-
ics, and a boyfriend, Jason, who became the father
of her daughter, Emma, two years later. Emma
hadn't been planned, but was much wanted and
Jessie had never regretted her arrival—especially as
Cath Carter was the most devoted of grandmothers,
which meant Jessie had never been tied down in the
way that some girls complained of.

No, it was not Emma who caused any constraints
on her life. If she was honest, it was Jason. He was
completely possessive, which was stupid, really, as
she'd only ever been with him and had no intention
of going elsewhere. But he was a great laugh, when
he wasn't being an arse, and a great dad, and there
was a lot to be said for a bloke who really loved you.
Passion, that was the key. Yes, they fought, but they
did loads of making up too. Sometimes she thought
they probably fought just to get to the making-up
bit. (Well, there had to be **some** reason for it.) And
now that the council had given them a house, not
that far from her mum's, and he had got used to the
idea of her doing night school, and was earning a
bit himself by driving the delivery van for the local
electrical store, things were getting better for them.

Suzanna discovered all of this within the first
forty minutes or so of Jessie's tenure at the shop.
Initially, she didn't mind the chatter. Jessie had
cleaned the entire shop almost effortlessly as she
spoke, properly lifting and sweeping under all the

chairs, had reorganized two shelves and washed up all the coffee cups from the morning. It had made the shop feel warmer, somehow. And she had helped give the Peacock Emporium its most profitable afternoon ever, drawing a seemingly endless trail of locals through the doors with magnetic efficiency. There had been Arturro, who had come alone, had drunk his coffee with the considered attention of the connoisseur, and answered Jessie's relentless questions with shy pleasure. After he left, Jessie had pointed out that he had spent much of the time gazing through the window at the Unique Boutique, as if hopeful that Liliane might emerge from its smoked-glass door and join him.

There had been the ladies from the department store, where Jessie's aunt worked, who had oohed and aahed over the wall hangings and ducked under the glittery mobiles and fussed over the glass mosaics and eventually bought one each, exclaiming at their extravagance. There had been Trevor and Martina from the hairdresser's behind the post office who had known Jessie since school, and had bought one of the raven-black feather dusters, because it would look good in the salon. There had been several young people Jessie knew by their first names, probably from the estate, and there had been Jessie's mother and daughter, who had come in and sat for a good three-quarters of an hour, admiring almost everything they could see. Emma was a carbon copy of her mother, a self-possessed seven-year-old in myriad shades of pink who pronounced the amaretti biscuits "weird, but nice, especially the sugar," and said that when she was grown-up she was going to have a shop "exactly the same. Except in my shop I'm going to give people bits of paper and they can do drawings to put on the walls."

"That's a good idea, petal. You could put your favorite customers' drawings in the best spot." Jessie seemed to treat all her daughter's pronouncements seriously.

"And put frames on them. People like to see their pictures in frames."

"There you go," said Jessie, giving a final polish to the coffee machine. "Retail psychology. How to make your customers feel valued."

Suzanna, while acknowledging the benefit of extra customers, was feeling a little overwhelmed by Jessie and her extended family. She felt uneasy at the sight of someone else behind the counter, and the reorganization of her shelves (even though they undoubtedly looked better). The shop hadn't felt hers in the same way since Jessie had been in it.

In fact, after the peaceful previous weeks, so many people had come in that afternoon that Suzanna had had to fight a sneaking sense of inadequacy and a faint jealousy that this girl could have succeeded so apparently effortlessly where she had failed.

This is stupid, she told herself, heading into the

cellar to fetch up some more bags. It's a shop. You can't afford to keep it all to yourself. She sat down heavily on the stairs—now polluted by the ghosts of snogging teenagers—and surveyed the downstairs shelves, which had apparently once held illegal game that you could order with your vegetables. Perhaps it wasn't that Jessie was better at it, perhaps it was that she didn't like the feeling of belonging, of obligation and expectation that a close relationship with your customers seemed to engender. It was all veering a bit too close to the idea of **family**.

I'm not sure I'm cut out for this, she thought. Perhaps I only liked the decorating, creating something beautiful. Perhaps I should do something where I hardly have to deal with people at all.

She flinched as Jessie's head appeared at the top of the stairs. "You okay down there?"

"Fine."

"Mum brought us in some nice orange juice. Figured you'd probably had enough of coffee."

Suzanna forced a smile. "Thanks. I'll be right up."

"You want any help?"

"No, thank you." Suzanna tried to convey in her tone that she would rather have five minutes on her own.

Jessie glanced to her left. "There's someone else in you've got to meet. Liliane from across the road—I used to do cleaning for her. She's just bought that pair of earrings, the ones in the case."

They had been the most expensive item in the shop. Briefly forgetting her previous reservations, Suzanna half ran up the stairs.

Liliane MacArthur's face was as closed as Jessie's was open. A tall, slim woman with the kind of mutely reddened hair beloved by Dere Hampton's female population, she eyed Suzanna with the practiced once-over of someone who had learned the hard way that women, especially those a good twenty years younger than herself, were generally not to be trusted.

"Hi," said Suzanna, immediately awkward. "Glad you spotted the earrings."

"Yes. I like topaz. Always have."

"They're Victorian, but you can probably see that from the box."

Jessie was wrapping it in an intricate arrangement of raffia and tissue paper. "They for you, Liliane?"

The older woman nodded.

"They'll go lovely with that blue coat of yours. The one with the high collar."

Liliane's expression softened slightly. "Yes, I thought that."

"How's your mum, Liliane?" Jessie's mother leaned over, so that she had an uninterrupted view past the till.

"Oh, much the same . . . She's had some problems holding her cup lately."

"Poor thing. I saw on the telly you can get all

sorts with special handles and things now to make it easier. Specially for people with arthritis. Ask Father Lenny, he can usually get stuff like that," Jessie said.

"He's our priest," explained Cath, "but he's like a Mr. Fixit. He'll get hold of anything for you. If he doesn't know someone, he'll track it down on the Internet."

"I'll see how we go."

"It's a very cruel thing, the arthritis." Cath shook her head.

"Yes," said Liliane, her head down. "Yes, it is. Well, I'd better get back to the shop. I'm glad to meet you, Mrs. Peacock."

"Suzanna, please. You too." Suzanna, her hands twitching uselessly at her sides, tried to loosen her smile as Liliane closed the door quietly behind her. She felt, even if she didn't hear, the "poor thing" lingering in the air as the older woman left.

"First husband died," murmured Jessie. "He was the love of her life."

"No. Roger was."

"Roger?" Suzanna said.

"Second husband," said Cath. "He told her he didn't want children, and she loved him so much she agreed. Two days before her forty-sixth birthday he ran off with a twenty-five-year-old. She was pregnant. God, there's no justice. Eighteen years Liliane gave to that man. She's never been the same."

"Lives with her mum now."

"She had no choice, not with things being the way they are . . ."

As Liliane crossed the road, the lumbering figure of Arturro could be seen heading toward her. On seeing her, he picked up speed, his arms swinging as if he was unused to traveling at such a pace. With a nod of recognition and only a faint pause, she disappeared into her shop.

Arturro stopped inelegantly, like a large vehicle needing more space to apply the brakes, his face still set toward the door of the Unique Boutique. Then he glanced toward the Peacock Emporium, his expression almost guilty, and entered.

Jessie, who had seen the whole thing, switched on the coffee machine, calling innocently, "Come for a top-up, Arturro?"

"If you don' mind," he said quietly, and sat heavily on the stool.

"I knew you'd be back for a second cup. Italians love their coffee, don't they?"

Suzanna felt her earlier misgivings melt away. Through the window, she could just make out the older woman, safely back in her own domain, mistress of the buttoned-up and held-in, surrounded by her expensive fabric armory. There was something in Liliane's brittle exterior, her discomfort with casual conversation, the pain only hinted at in her demeanor that made her fearful, as if she were witnessing the Ghost of Christmas Future.

"Do you want to come again?" she asked Jessie later, after Arturro, and Cath with Emma in hand, had gone. They had placed the chairs upside-down on the tables and Jessie was sweeping the floor, while Suzanna counted her takings. "I'd really like it if you did," she added, trying to feed some conviction into her voice.

Jessie had smiled, her wide, unguarded smile. "I can do till school pick-up, if that's any good to you."

"After today I don't see how I can manage without you."

"Oh, you'd be all right. You just need to get to know everyone. Get them coming through the door every day."

Suzanna peeled off several notes and held them out. "I can't pay much to begin with, but if you increase takings like that again, I'd make it worth your while."

After a moment's hesitation, Jessie took them and thrust them into her pocket. "I wasn't expecting anything for today, but thanks. You sure you won't get bored of me prattling on all the time? I drive Jason mad. He says I'm like a stuck record."

"I like it." Suzanna thought she might eventually believe that. "And if not, I'll put up one of those notices you mentioned—'Don't talk to me.'"

Suzanna locked the till, noting, as she began her nightly routine for closing, that it was the first evening in which there had been a hint of peach-colored daylight remaining. Gradually it built in strength, illuminating the interior of the shop, transforming the blues into a rich neutral glow, crisscrossing them with the shadows of the window frames. Outside, the narrow lane was already nearly empty of people: things closed down early in the town, and only the shopkeepers remained to say goodnight to each other as night fell. She loved this part: loved the silence, loved the feeling that she'd spent a day working for herself, loved the knowledge that the imprints she left on the shop would remain until she opened it again the next morning. She moved around almost silently, breathing in the myriad fragrances that lingered in the air from wax-papered soap and Byzantine bottles of scent, hearing in the silence the laughter and chatter of the day's customers, as if each had left some spectral echo behind them. The Peacock Emporium had been a pleasurable dream, but today it had felt magical somehow, as if the best of both the shop and its customers had rubbed off on each other. She rested against a stool, seeing something ahead of her other than the disappointments and restrictions she had been picturing as her future, seeing instead a place of possibilities where she could be herself, her better self.

She found herself smiling. On nights like tonight, she didn't want to leave: she harbored a secret desire to swap the pew for an old sofa, and bed down for the night. The shop felt so much more hers than the cottage.

As she was dragging in the pavement sign, Arturro walked by, took it wordlessly from her, and placed it carefully inside. "Beautiful evening," he said, his head tucked inside a soft red scarf.

"Gorgeous," she said. "A Marsala sunset."

He laughed, and lifted a heavy hand as he made to leave.

It was time to go. Neil was coming home early, especially, he said, to cook her a meal, although she knew it was because of the big match, which began before he normally reached the cottage. But that was okay. She fancied a long bath anyway.

She walked around the shop, straightening things, giving the surfaces a wipe, then placed the cloth in the sink. She checked that the till was turned off and, as she stood at the counter, noticed that the painting was still turned toward the wall. On a whim, she reversed it, so that Athene, revealed, became instantly burnished, incandescent. The evening sun, burning with the urgent intensity that told of its imminent disappearance, reflected off the canvas, gleamed in points off the old gilded frame.

Suzanna stared at her. "Night, Mother," she said.

Then she glanced around the shop, flicked off the lights, and headed for the door.

# 10

The underpants were in the middle of the dining-room table. Still wrapped in cellophane, stacked like breakfast pancakes, still advertising their "discreet, comfortable security." They were as untouched as when Mrs. Abrahams had left them outside Rosemary's door that morning, their current placement under the Venetian chandelier a mute, furious protest.

Vivi and Rosemary had had some spats over the years, but Vivi could not remember one as bad as that which had resulted from the visit of the Incontinence Lady. She couldn't remember having been shouted at so long and hard, could not remember seeing that level of puce, stammering fury on Rosemary's face, the threats, the insults, the slamming of doors.

Vivi removed the underwear from the table, walked along the corridor, and stuffed them under the old pew as she passed it. She reached the end and knocked tentatively. "Rosemary, will you want lunch today?" She stood for some minutes, her ear pressed to the wood. "Rosemary? Would you like some stew?"

There was a momentary pause, then the television volume increased, so that Vivi withdrew, eyeing the door nervously.

It had seemed a sensible idea. She hadn't felt strong enough to broach it with Rosemary herself, but as the person who did the household laundry she had become aware that her mother-in-law's **control**, for want of a better word, was not what it had been. Thanking Mr. Hoover for the automatic washing machine, she had found herself, several times this month, loading Rosemary's bed linens sporting rubber gloves and a pained expression. And it wasn't just the bed linens: over a period of months, Vivi had become aware that Rosemary's undergarments had significantly lessened in number. She had waited until she was out, then searched the annex. Initially, she had discovered the offending items soaking in Rosemary's bathroom sink. More recently, Rosemary had taken to hiding them. In the past weeks Vivi had discovered them beneath Rosemary's sofa, in the cupboard under the sink, and even stuffed into an empty chopped-tomatoes can, high on a bathroom shelf.

When she had tried to discuss it with Douglas, he had looked at her with an expression of such unalloyed horror that she had backtracked, promising to sort it out herself. Several times she had sat with Rosemary at lunch, trying to muster the courage to ask whether she was having a bit of trouble with her "waterworks." But something in her mother-in-law's trenchant demeanor, the aggressive way she now shouted, "**What?**" whenever Vivi tried to broach some innocent topic, that prevented her. And then her GP, a matter-of-fact young Scottish woman, had presented her with a range of state-subsidized services that had meant Vivi could perhaps remedy this without having to talk directly about it to her mother-in-law.

Mrs. Abrahams—a plump, capable sort with a comforting manner that suggested not only that she had seen it all but had a plastic-backed non-sweat-inducing, discreetly wrapped solution for it—had arrived shortly before eleven. Vivi had explained the delicacy of the situation.

"Much easier if it comes from outside the family," Mrs. Abrahams said.

"It's not that I mind the washing, as such . . ." Vivi had trailed off, already feeling guilty of betrayal.

"But there are health and hygiene considerations as well."

"Yes . . ."

"And you don't want the old lady to lose her dignity."

"No."

"You leave it to me, Mrs. Fairley-Hulme. I tend to find that once they've got over the initial hurdle, most ladies are rather relieved of the help."

"Oh . . . good." Vivi had knocked on Rosemary's door, and placed her ear to the wood to see if the old lady had heard.

The door had opened, leaving Vivi crouched awkwardly.

"What are you doing?" Rosemary had stared crossly at her daughter-in-law.

Vivi righted herself. "Mrs. Abrahams to see you, Rosemary."

"What?"

"I'll make some coffee and leave you to it." She had scuttled into the kitchen, flushed, aware that her palms were sweating.

There had been peace for almost three minutes. Then the earth had cracked open, volcanic fire spewed forth, and, moments later, against the back-drop of some of the worst language Vivi had ever heard uttered in a cut-glass accent, she had witnessed Mrs. Abrahams walking briskly across the gravel to her neat little hatchback, her handbag clutched to her chest, glancing back at the house as various plastic-wrapped items were hurled after her.

"Douglas, darling, I need to talk to you about your mother." Ben had gone out for lunch. Rosemary was still locked in her annex. Vivi didn't think she could keep this to herself until bedtime.

"Mm?" He was reading the newspaper, thrusting forkfuls of food into his mouth, as if he was in a hurry to get out again. It was the drilling season, time to get the arable fields sown—he rarely hung around for long.

"I had a woman here, for Rosemary. To talk about . . . that thing we discussed."

He looked up, raised an eyebrow.

"Rosemary took it rather badly. I don't think she wants any help."

Douglas's head dropped, and his hand waved dismissively above it. "Send it all to the laundry, then. We'll pay. Best thing all around."

"I don't know if the laundry will take things that are . . . soiled."

"Well, what's the bloody point of it being a laundry, then? You're hardly going to send things that are clean."

Vivi didn't think she could bear the thought of the staff remarking upon the state of the Fairley-Hulmes' bedding. "I don't . . . I just don't think it's a good idea."

"Well, I've told you what I think, Vivi. If you don't want to send it away and you don't want to do it yourself, then I don't know what you want me to suggest."

Vivi wasn't sure either. If she said she just wanted a bit of sympathy, understanding, the faintest idea that she wasn't in this on her own, she knew Douglas would look at her blankly. "I'll sort something out," she said glumly.

Suzanna and Neil had not argued in almost five weeks. There wasn't a cross word, a mean-minded snipe, or a careless spat. Nothing. When she realized this, Suzanna had wondered whether things were changing, whether her marriage had begun to reflect the satisfaction that she was gleaning from her shop. Now on waking she felt, perhaps for the first time in her working life, something approaching anticipation when she thought about her day and the people who now populated it. From the moment she put her key in the door, her spirits lifted at the sight of the cheerful, stuffed interior, the brightly colored ornaments, the gorgeous scents of honey and freesia. And despite her reservations, Jessie's presence had not just worked for the shop economically: something of her Pollyanna-ish nature seemed to have rubbed off on herself too. Several times, Suzanna had caught herself whistling.

When she allowed herself time to think about it she realized it wasn't that she felt any closer to her husband, it was simply that, with both of them working long hours, they had neither the time nor the energy to fight. On three nights this week Neil had not been home before ten. Several times she had left the house before seven, only dimly aware that they had spent any time in the same bed. Perhaps this is how marriages like Dad and Mum's survive, she mused. They just make sure they're too busy to think about them.

Neil ruined it, of course, by bringing up the subject of their apparently imminent children. "I've been finding out about childcare," he said. "There's a nursery attached to the hospital that doesn't just take staff children. If we put our name on the list now, we might have a good chance of getting a place. Then you can keep working, like you wanted."

"I'm not even pregnant."

"It doesn't hurt to plan ahead, Suze. I was thinking, I could even take the baby there on my way to work in the morning so you wouldn't have to cut into your day too much. It makes sense, now that your shop's doing okay."

He couldn't keep the excitement from his voice. She knew that now he overlooked lots of things about her that had previously irritated him—her preoccupation with the shop, her persistent lack of courtesy toward Vivi, the fact that her exhaustion made her bad-tempered and killed her libido—all because of the greater favor she was about to pay him when the year was up.

Despite her promise, Suzanna did not feel the same sense of excitement, despite Jessie's breathless reassurances that it was the best thing that had ever happened to her, that having children made you laugh, feel, and love more than you ever dreamed possible. It wasn't just the sex thing that bothered her—in order to get pregnant they were going to have to embark on a fairly regular bout of sexual activity—it was the feeling that her promise had hemmed her in, that she was now bound by obligation to produce this thing, to harbor it in a body that had always been, quite comfortably, entirely hers. She tried not to think too hard about her mother. Which made her feel something else.

In one of his more irritating moments, Neil had put his arms around her and said she could always get some "counseling," and she had had to restrain herself physically from hitting him. "It would be perfectly understandable. I mean, it's no wonder you have reservations," he went on.

She had wriggled free of his grasp. "The only reservations I have, Neil, are because you keep harping on about it all the time."

"I don't mind paying for you to see someone. We're doing okay at the moment."

"Oh, just drop it, will you?"

His expression was sympathetic, and it somehow made her even more irritated. "You know," he said, "you're more like your dad than you think. You both just sit on your feelings the whole time."

"No, Neil. I just want to get on with my life and not obsess about some nonexistent baby."

"Baby Peacock," he mused. "Neil Peacock Junior."

"Don't even think about it," said Suzanna.

All of the schools in Dere Hampton broke for lunch between twelve thirty and one forty-five, and this stretch of the day was marked, outside the windows of the Peacock Emporium, by passing bunches of leggy schoolgirls in inappropriately customized uniforms, exasperated mothers dragging their younger charges away from the sweet shop, and the arrival of unhappily self-employed regulars, looking for what might just be coffee but was more usually a bit of human contact to break up their day. In honor of this being the first really hot day of the year, the door of the shop had been propped open and a solitary table and chairs left outside on the pavement.

It felt, Suzanna told herself, almost continental. She had not yet tired of staring out, through her meticulous arrangements, of the prismed-lit window, and still enjoyed standing behind her register, her clean white apron starched to old-fashioned stiffness. Sometimes she wondered if she hated Dere Hampton less than she had previously thought. Having created her own space, and imprinted her own character on it, she had felt, at times, almost proprietorial—and not just about the shop.

Jessie had soon learned to play to their respective strengths and today, dressed in a flower-printed dress and heavy boots, she was serving at the counter, often nipping out to make conversation with the cement-booted builders and the old ladies, while Suzanna walked around the shop with her jotter, totting up the remaining stock, noting with a vague disappointment how little she had sold in the past few weeks. It was not what you would call a roaring success but, as she frequently reassured herself, at least the shop was on its way to paying for itself. If it would only pick up a bit, Neil said, they could start repaying some of the capital outlay. Neil liked saying such phrases. She thought finance was one of the few areas left in which he had unchallengeable authority in their relationship.

Arturro had come in, drunk two espressos in quick succession, then left. Father Lenny had poked his head around the door, supposedly to ask Jessie if Emma was coming back to Sunday school, but also to introduce himself to Suzanna and remark that if she wanted any more fairy-lights he knew someone near Bury St. Edmunds who did them wholesale.

Mrs. Creek had come in, ordered a milky coffee, and sat outside for half an hour, removing her hat so that her wispy hair was exposed to the sun, looking as fragile as frostbitten grass. She told Jessie that this weather reminded her of the first time she had gone abroad, to Geneva, where her husband had been in the hospital. The airplane had been a terrific adventure and her arrival in a foreign country so exciting that she had almost forgotten the reason she was there, and managed to miss visiting time on the first day. Suzanna, occasionally venturing outside to pick up coffee cups, or just to feel the first rays of sun on her face, had heard her reminiscing with Jessie, who, chin in hand, was soaking up every last detail along with the sun. Her husband had been ever so cross, and refused to talk to her for two days. Afterward it had occurred to her that she could have fibbed, could have told him her airplane had been delayed. But she was never one to lie. You always ended up in a muddle trying to remember what you'd said to whom.

"Jason thinks I lie even when I don't," said Jessie cheerily. "We had a massive fight once because I didn't vacuum when I was ill. He likes to see those little lines in the carpet, you see, just to prove I've done it. But I had this food poisoning, chicken I think it was, so I just lay in bed.

"When he got home I was feeling a bit better and he accused me of sitting around on my arse all day, even though I'd managed to make his tea. And I was so cross I just hit him with the pan. You don't know how much I'd wanted to puke just peeling his spuds." She laughed guiltily.

"That's men, dear," said Mrs. Creek, vaguely, as if they were some kind of affliction.

"What did he do?" said Suzanna, struck by this casual depiction of violence, and unsure whether to take what Jessie had just said at face value.

"He hit me back. So I hit him with the pan again, and knocked out half his tooth." She gestured toward the back of her mouth, showing where the damage had been done.

Mrs. Creek had stared across the road, as if she hadn't heard. After a moment's stillness, Suzanna had smiled vaguely, as if she had forgotten to pick something up, then turned and walked back into the shop.

"Are you scared of him?" she asked, sometime later, when Mrs. Creek had gone. She had been trying to imagine Neil filled with enough violence to hit her.

"Who?"

"Your . . . Jason."

"Frightened of him? Nah." Jessie had shaken her head, her expression one of fond indulgence. She glanced at Suzanna and evidently decided the concern in her expression made some sort of explanation necessary. "Look, his problem is I'm better with words than he is. So I know how to really wind him up. And if he starts getting at me I just twist his words back, tie him in knots, which makes him feel stupid. I know I shouldn't, but . . . you know how they get on your nerves sometimes?"

Suzanna nodded.

"And sometimes I just get a bit carried away. And I don't leave him"—her smile faded—"I guess I don't really leave him anywhere to go."

There was a brief silence.

Outside, two schoolboys were kicking someone's bookbag back and forth across the road.

"I love this shop," said Jessie. "I don't know what it is about it, because it wasn't like this when it was the Red Horse, but it's like it's got a really good vibe to it. Do you know what I mean?"

"Yes. I thought when I came in first that it was just the smell of the coffee and stuff. Or perhaps all the pretty things. It's a bit of an Aladdin's cave, isn't it? But I think there's something about the shop itself. It always makes me"—she paused—"feel better."

The two boys had stopped, were examining something that one had pulled from his pocket, muttering in low voices.

The women watched them from the window.

"It's not what you're thinking," said Jessie, eventually.

"No," said Suzanna, who felt suddenly middle class and naïve. "Of course not."

Jessie had left at a quarter past two to pick up her daughter from school early and, with the head teacher's permission, take her for a birthday treat. If Emma fancied it, she said, they might buy ice-cream bars, and sit at the table outside the shop to eat them. "They go on a school trip to France next year," she said as she left. "I told her that was how the French eat and now all she wants to do is drag our chairs outside."

Suzanna was halfway down the cellar steps when she heard the door open. She shouted that she would be there in a second. She tripped up the last step, and swore softly as she nearly dropped her armful of suede-bound notebooks. Things invariably seemed easier when Jessie was there.

Her father stood in the middle of the shop, his arms crossed awkwardly as if he was unwilling to be seen standing too close to anything. He was staring down behind the counter. When Suzanna came in, he jumped.

"Dad," she said, blushing.

"Suzanna." He nodded.

There was a silence. She wondered, fantastically, whether he was going to apologize for his previous comments to her. But she was old enough to understand that his arrival in her shop was as conciliatory a gesture as he was likely to make. "You nearly missed me," she babbled, raising a smile. "I was out till about half an hour ago. You would have got Jessie . . . my assistant."

He had removed his hat and held it in his hands, a curiously courteous gesture. "I was just passing. Had to come in to meet my accountant, so I thought I'd . . . take a look at your shop."

Suzanna stood, clutching her notebooks. "Well, here it is."

"Indeed."

She made as if to peer behind him. "No Mum?"

"She's at home."

She put the notebooks on a table, and glanced at the objects around them, trying to see them through her father's eyes. "Fripperies and nonsense," she could imagine him saying. Who was going to want to spend good money on a mosaic candleholder, or a pile of secondhand embroidered napkins?

"Did Neil tell you? We're doing really well." It felt easier to pretend that this was Neil's venture too. She knew her father thought him a more sensible fellow.

"He didn't, but that's good."

"Turnover's up by—erm—around thirty percent on the first quarter. And I—I've just done my first inventory." The words sounded solid, reassuring, not the kind of words uttered by a feckless, irresponsible flibbertigibbet.

He nodded.

"I might have to take some tips from you soon about VAT. It looks impenetrable to me."

"It's just practice." He had been staring at the portrait of her mother. Suzanna glanced behind the counter, and saw it resting against the wall, facing outward. Her mother's enigmatic smile, which had never appeared maternal, now seemed inappropriately intimate in the public space. Jessie had loved it, saying she was the most glamorous woman she'd ever seen, and urged her to put it on the wall. Now it made Suzanna feel guilty, although she couldn't be sure why.

"What's that doing here?" He cleared his throat as he spoke.

"I'm not selling it, if that's what you're worried about."

"I was—"

"We're not **that** badly off for money."

Her father paused, as if he were weighing up his possible responses. He let out a little breath. "I was just curious, Suzanna, about what it was doing in a shop."

"Not 'a shop,' Dad. You make it sound like I was trying to offload it. **My** shop . . . I was going to put it on the wall." Defensiveness had made her snappy.

"What would you want to put it in here for?"

"I just thought it would be a good place for it to go. It doesn't—it doesn't really fit at home. The house is too small for it." She couldn't help herself.

Her father eyed it sideways, through narrowed eyes, as if he found it difficult to look directly at the image. "I don't think it should be left down there."

"Well, I don't know where else to put it."

"We can take it back to the bank if you want. They'll store it for you." He looked sideways at her. "It's probably worth a bit of money, and I doubt you've got it insured."

He never expressed any emotion when he talked

of Athene. Sometimes, Suzanna thought, it was as if when she had died he had decided she would be of no more lasting emotional importance to him than some distant relative who lined the upstairs corridors. The limited family history that had been made public to her and her siblings showed he had moved pretty swiftly on to Vivi after all. At other times she wondered if he had battened down his emotions because he found the memory of Athene just too painful, and she felt the familiar flush of her own implicit guilt. There were no boxes of clothes, no well-thumbed photographs. Only Vivi had saved any remnants of her: a yellowed newspaper cutting about the wedding of "the Last Deb," and a couple of photographs of her on a horse. Even those were only brought out when Douglas was elsewhere.

Her dad's presence in her shop, so apparently devoid of any emotional reaction, had the reverse effect on her. Is it so impossible for you to express anything about my mother? Suzanna suddenly wanted to shout. Even if it is supposedly for my sake, do you have to pretend she never existed? Do I have to pretend she never existed?

"You could hang it in the picture gallery." The words hung, too loud, in the air, Suzanna's voice holding a faint tremor of challenge. "Vivi wouldn't mind."

Her father had turned away from her, was bending to examine a piece of Chinese silk.

"I said Vivi wouldn't mind. In fact, she suggested getting the frame mended, and putting it up. Quite recently."

He picked up one of the miniature silk purses, examined the price, then placed it gently back on its pile. The timing of those actions, and the faint criticism she felt they implied, caused something to swell inside her, unbidden and unstoppable. "Did you hear what I said, Dad?"

"Quite well, thank you." He still wouldn't look at her. There was an excruciating delay. "I just . . . I just don't think it's appropriate."

"No. But, then, I suppose even if they're just on canvas you don't really want **women** cluttering up the ancestral line, do you?"

She wasn't sure where it had come from. Her father turned very slowly, and straightened up before her, his expression unreadable. She had the sudden sensation of being a small child found guilty of some misdemeanor and waiting, in silent terror, to discover her punishment.

But he simply replaced his hat on his head, a measured gesture, and turned to the door. "I think my parking meter's probably running out. I just wanted to tell you that your shop looks very nice." He lifted a hand, his head inclined toward her.

Her eyes had filled with tears. "Is that it? Is that all you're going to say?" She heard the shrill tones of a teenager in her voice, and knew, with fury, that he had heard them too.

"It's your painting, Suzanna," he said as he left. "You do with it what you want."

There was almost no sign of blotchiness left on Suzanna's face when Jessie returned, entering the shop apparently in midconversational flow, although she was plainly by herself.

"You can't believe the ice cream they sell now. When I was her age you were lucky to get a Strawberry Mivvi, or a Rocket. Do you remember those? With the different-colored stripes? Now it's all Mars bar lollies, Bounty this and Cornetta that. Unbelievable. And more than a quid each. Still, they're so enormous you wouldn't need lunch as well."

She moved to the till, almost unconsciously sweeping crumbs from the tabletop as she moved to collect stray receipts. "We got you a Crunchie ice cream. Did you know they did Crunchie ones? That's what me and Emma decided you'd like best."

"Thanks," said Suzanna, her face buried in her folder of invoices. "Can you stick it in the fridge?" She had been staring at them for almost twenty minutes now, unsure why she had got them out in the first place. Her father's visit had unbalanced her, sucked out her drive and enthusiasm.

"Don't leave it for long. It'll melt in there." Jessie

moved toward the tables scanning them for empty cups. "Anyone been in?"

"No one special."

That was the maddening thing about crying. You could do it only for a few minutes, and your skin, your nose would still display the telltale signs half an hour later.

Jessie's glance settled on her a fraction of a second longer than it would otherwise have done. "I had an idea while I was out. About Arturro," she said.

"Oh?"

"I'm going to get him together with Liliane."

"What?"

"I've had this idea, see. Tell me what you think . . ."

Suzanna could hear the sound of a cloth being run under a tap, as Jessie chattered on.

She spoke into her folder. "You know what I think, Jess? It's that people should just be left alone."

"Yes, but I think Arturro and Liliane have spent too long by themselves. It's become such a habit with them that they're both too frightened to break it."

"Perhaps they're happier like that."

"You don't really think so."

Oh, go away, thought Suzanna, exhausted. Stop trying to turn everyone into shinier, happier versions of themselves, and convince me I'm someone I'm not. Not everyone sees things like you do. But she said nothing.

Jessie stared at her for a minute. "Why don't you take a break? Go and have a walk. It's such a beautiful day outside."

"I'm **fine**, Jessie. Just give me a break, will you?" It came out more sharply than she'd intended. She caught the hurt in Jessie's expression, which was immediately disguised under an understanding smile.

"Oh, okay, you're right. I'll go," Suzanna said, grabbing her wallet, feeling perversely resentful that she was being made to feel guilty yet again. "Look, I'm sorry—take no notice of me. It's just hormones or something." And then hated herself for using that as an excuse.

She walked around the square for almost twenty-five minutes. It was market day, and she found herself meandering between the tightly packed stalls, savoring the brief period of invisibility, eyeing the cheap imported confectionery, the wholefood stall, the timeless arrangements of the greengrocers, while simultaneously fighting the inner voice reminding her that London markets had been so much more interesting, so much more vibrant and excitingly stocked.

Suzanna wondered, as she occasionally did, whether she would have felt the same way if her mother had lived. Sometimes she wondered if she felt this way precisely because her mother hadn't.

"Do you want something, love?"

"Oh. No. Thank you."

She shoved her hands into her pockets and moved on, the internal lightness she had felt at the start of the day having turned into something dull, leaden. Perhaps Neil was right. Perhaps she should just give in and have a baby. At least she would be doing the one thing everyone expected of her. She would probably love it when it came. Most people did, didn't they? It wasn't as if anything else had made her happy.

If it's my destiny, my biology, she asked herself, walking slowly back toward her shop, why does every bone in my body scream against it?

"You know what you should do?"

Suzanna closed her eyes, and opened them slowly. She had told herself firmly that, with only two hours before closing time, she wasn't going to take out any more of her bad mood on Jessie. Even a Jessie sporting a pair of child's angel wings and balancing a pair of frankly ridiculous pink sunglasses on her head. "What?" she said evenly.

"I was thinking about something Emma said. About drawings."

"You think I should get people to do drawings?" Suzanna, refilling sugar bowls, struggled to keep the sarcasm from her voice.

"No. But I was thinking about what we said

earlier, about getting people involved with the shop, building up regulars. Because that's what you're going to need around here. You could have a sort of Regular of the Week."

"You're joking?"

"No, I'm not. Look at what you've put on the walls—the old sheet music and the wills you pasted up. Every time someone's come in this afternoon they've stopped to read the wills, right?"

It had been one of her better ideas. The bundle of yellowed, calligraphied wills had been on a skip in London; she had kept them in a folder for years waiting for a chance to use them as wallpaper.

"And once they've spent that long in the shop, they've ended up buying something, right?"

"And?"

"So you do something similar in the window. But you do it about someone who comes in the shop. People are nosy around here, they like to talk, they like to know about each other's lives. So you do a little display on, say, Arturro. I don't know, a little written thing about his life in Italy, how he came to have the deli. Or perhaps just take one thing from his life—the best or worst day he can remember— and do a display around it. People would stop to read it and if they're vain, like most of them are, they might even want one of their own."

Suzanna fought the urge to tell Jessie that, the way she felt right now, the shop might not be around for long. "I don't think people will want to put their life in a window."

"You might not. But you're not like most people."

Suzanna looked up sharply. Jessie's face was guileless.

"It'll bring more people in. It'll get them interested in the shop. I bet I could get people to do it—just let me try it."

"Everyone in this town seems to know all there is to know about each other anyway."

"I'll do it myself. And if you don't think it's working, I'll stop. It's not going to cost you anything."

Jessie moved in front of her, her smile broad and sympathetic. Her wire wings bounced jauntily behind her. "I'll show you how it can work. Look, the next person who walks in here, I'll persuade them to let me do it to them. I promise. You'll find out all sorts of things you didn't know."

"You reckon?"

"Go on, it'll be fun."

"Oh, God, if it's Mrs. Creek, we'll have no room left in the window."

As Suzanna reached for the empty milk carton, the door swung open. The two women looked almost guiltily at each other. Jessie hesitated, then smiled, a broad, complicit smile.

The man glanced at them, as if unsure whether to enter.

"Would you like a coffee? We're still serving."

He was olive-skinned, tall, and he wore the uncomfortable expression of someone who considered that a warm day in England qualified as cold weather. He was dressed in the blue scrubs of the local hospital beneath an old leather jacket and looked exhausted.

Suzanna realized she was staring and looked abruptly at her feet.

"You do espresso?" His accent was foreign, but not one she could easily place. He glanced up at the board, then back at the two women, trying to gauge the reasons for the smaller one's barely suppressed merriment.

"Oh, yes," said Jessie, beaming at Suzanna and then at him. She grabbed a cup and placed it, with something of a flourish, under the spout of the espresso machine, motioning to him to sit down. "In fact, if you're prepared to spare me a few minutes, I reckon you can have this one on me."

# 11

The peacock bass is an aggressive, belligerent fish. Despite its deceptive iridescent beauty, it is mean enough to straighten a hook and bend a fishing rod almost double. Even a four- or five-pounder can wear a man out in under an hour. It evolved in the same waters as the piranha, the alligator, the armor-scaled pirarucus—creatures as big as cars, and routinely fights rivals even bigger or more dangerous than itself. In the flowing waters of the Amazon, its natural habitat, it can grow to thirty pounds, providing a sparring partner worthy of Moby Dick himself.

It is, in short, a mean fish, and when it shoots from the water, several feet up, it is easy to detect in that prehistoric eye a hunger for the fight. You can see its attraction to a young man keen to prove himself in the eyes of others. Or even an older one keen to retain his son's respect.

Perhaps this was why Jorge and Alejandro de Marenas liked to fish. They would pack up the fishing rods, take Jorge's big four-wheel drive to the airport, and catch a flight to Brazil to spend two, maybe three days flexing their muscles against this cichlid, then go home with satisfactorily broken tackle and bloodied hands, having satisfied some elemental sense of man's eternal struggle against nature. It was a biannual pilgrimage for them, and was the one place, Alejandro often thought, where they felt truly at ease with each other.

Jorge de Marenas was a plastic surgeon in Buenos Aires, and one of the best. His client list contained more than three thousand names, including many prominent politicians, singers, and television personalities. The women came to him increasingly young, for higher bosoms, slimmer thighs, noses like this television presenter, or bee-stung lips like that starlet. With a manner as smooth as the skin he re-created, he satisfied them all, injecting, hauling up, filling, and smoothing, often shaping and reshaping the same people over the years until they resembled more startled versions of themselves ten years previously. Except Alejandro's mother. He would not touch his wife. Not her plump, fifty-year-old thighs, her tired, furious eyes camouflaged by expensive makeup and the religious application of expensive creams. He didn't even like her dyeing her hair. She told her friends proudly that it was because he thought her perfect as she was. Though she believed, she told her son, that, as with builders and plumbers, the job waiting at home was always the last to be considered. Alejandro himself could not say which version was correct: his father seemed to treat his mother with the same detached respect that he treated everybody else.

For while his mother was almost stereotypically **Latina**—operatic, passionate, prone to dizzying highs and lows—he and his father were an emotional disappointment, both unusually even-tempered and, especially in the case of Alejandro, possessing what was often described as an almost off-putting reserve. His father defended him against this (frequently made) charge, saying the Marenas men had never felt the need to communicate as they did in soap operas, with angry, posturing confrontations or extravagant declarations of love. Possibly this was because Alejandro had been sent to boarding school from the age of seven, or possibly it was because Jorge possessed the air of calm that made him such a good surgeon. That biannual fight with the gamefish was the one occasion on which both father and son would let loose, their emotions briefly unbuttoned in the swirling waters, and their laughter, frustration, joy, desperation all expressed from the safety net of waders and a waistcoat full of hooks.

Usually, anyway. This time, for Alejandro at least, the uncomplicated physical pleasures of the trip had been muted by the conversation that was yet to come, the knowledge that although his chosen career had been considered by his family the worst hurt he could inflict on them, he was about to do worse.

The trip had been complicated from the start: Jorge was unsure whether he should be seen to go, conscious that many of his friends were not just missing their own fishing trips and a retreat to the family **estancia** but, faced with devalued fortunes and inaccessible savings, were now considering ways to leave the country altogether. He was doing okay, he said, but he didn't want to put his friends' noses out of joint. It didn't do to gloat about one's good fortune when so many were suffering.

Alejandro had meant to tell his father on the walk from the lodge, but Jorge had been preoccupied by a bite that had made his foot swell, so Alejandro carried his things and said nothing. His hat was tipped low against the sun, his mind whirring with projected arguments, anticipated confrontation. He had meant to tell Jorge when his father had tied on his plug, a gaudy thing the size of a horseshoe, with Indian festival decorations, the kind of lure that made European anglers shake their heads in disbelief—until they hooked their own bass, of course.

He had meant to tell him when they hit the water, but the sound of the rushing creek and his father's intense concentration had distracted him, forcing him to wait until the moment was lost.

Then, on their favored quiet stretch between the derelict shack and the standing timber pile, just as Alejandro found himself choking on the words that were fully formed in his mouth, his father had hooked a great brute of a thing, whose eyes, briefly visible even from thirty feet, caught theirs with the same mute fury as Alejandro's mother when Jorge announced he would be late home again. (It didn't do to get too angry, she said, after she had replaced the receiver. Not with things the way they were, and he the only man they knew still making money. Not with all those **putas** floating around him with their plastic grapefruit tits and adolescent arses.)

This **tucunaré**, as the Brazilians called it, was big even by Alejandro's father's standards. He announced its arrival with the excited yelp of a surprised child, as the plug was assaulted in the water with a sound like an explosion, and he motioned his son over with a frantic head gesture—he had needed both hands on his rod just to keep it in his grasp. Whatever conversation had been planned was swiftly forgotten.

Alejandro dropped his own rod and sprinted for his father, his eyes fixed on the furious commotion just under the water. The bass leaped from the water and both men let out a gasp at its size. Then in the split second in which they were stunned into immobility by what they had seen, it bolted for the maze of rotting tree trunks, sending the drag into the high-pitched screech of an aircraft plummeting toward earth.

"¡Mas rapido! ¡Mas rapido!" Alejandro yelled at his father as the older man strained against his line, everything but that combative fish forgotten. Shaking its head, the bass dislodged at least one of the hooks from the bait, its bright orange and emerald green scales shimmering as it fought the line, the gold-rimmed black eye of its caudal fin taunting them as it flashed above the water, as aggressive and alluring as the peacock's tail after which it was named. Alejandro felt his father falter a little, his mind spun by the sheer ferocity of their battle, and clapped him on the shoulder, glad for once that it was his father who had lured the magnificent fish, glad that it was he who had a chance to display his superiority in the water.

"Mierde, Ale, have you got your camera?" Finally, spent, they half sat, half lay together on the riverbank, the fish like a sleeping baby between proud new parents. Jorge caught his breath, then struggled to his feet. As he held it, still blank-eyed and furious in death, his middle-aged, tanned face was illuminated with hard-won triumph, a rare unguarded joy, his arms sore and flexed under each end as he held it up to the gods. It was the best day he had had in years, he said. A day to remember. Wait till he told them at the club. Was Ale sure he had the pictures?

Alejandro asked himself several times, afterward: How could I have told him then?

Jorge de Marenas decided to pop into his office before going home. The traffic headed out to the Zona Norte was always terrible at this time, and since the trouble had started, even a man like Jorge didn't feel safe sitting in a jam.

"Luis Casiro got his new Mercedes stolen, did I tell you? Didn't even have time to get his gun from his jacket before they had pulled him out. Hit him so hard he needed fourteen stitches." Jorge shook his head, gazing out at the traffic around him. "Fernando de la Rua has a lot to answer for."

To the right, Alejandro could see the Mothers of the Plaza de Mayo through the smoked-glass window, their headscarves white against the greenery around them, embroidered with the names of the Disappeared. Their apparently peaceful demeanor was deceptive, belying the thousands of photographs that had decorated the park for over twenty years: sons, daughters, whose murderers, each knew, might have passed them in the street. The economic downturn had not deterred them, but it had given the rest of the city's inhabitants a new focus, and they looked tired and ignored, upholders of yesterday's news.

Alejandro thought briefly of the baby girl he had delivered almost three months ago, those he had seen handed over subsequently, their births christened with tears, then pushed the thought from his mind. "Pa?"

"Don't tell your mother how much we had to drink last night. My head is sore enough as it is." His father's voice still carried the satisfaction of the catch. Beside them, a **colectivo**, visibly belching diesel fumes, slowed down enough for its departing passengers to hit the pavement running, while those waiting launched themselves on board.

"I think she is going through **the change**," his father said meditatively. "Women often become irrational then."

"I need to talk to you."

"She's got so paranoid about security she will hardly leave the house. She won't own up to this, of course. Not even if you ask her. She will make excuses, say the ladies are coming around for her charity works, or it's too hot to go out today, but she's no longer leaving the house." He paused, still cheerful. "And she's driving me mad." The size of the fish had made him garrulous. "Because she's not going out, she's dwelling on things, you know? Not just the economic or security situation, which I grant you is bad. You know you're more likely to be mugged in the Zona Norte now than in the slums? The bastards know where the money is, they're not stupid." Jorge exhaled, his eyes still fixed on the road ahead. "She's become obsessed about where

I am. Why am I ten minutes late back from the office? Didn't I know that she thought I'd had an accident?"

He glanced in the mirror, unconsciously checking that the coolbox containing the fish had not tipped over. "I think she thinks I'm having an affair. Whenever she asks me why I'm late, she immediately asks about Agostina. Agostina! Like she's going to give a second glance to an old man like me!" He said it with the confidence of someone who didn't truly believe his own comments.

Alejandro's heart was heavy. "Pa, I'm going abroad."

"Everything is magnified, you know? Because she has too much time to sit and think."

"To England. I'm going to England. To work in a hospital."

Jorge had definitely heard him now. There was a lengthy silence, not sufficiently interrupted by the traffic reports on the radio. Alejandro sat in the leather seat, his breath held against the coming storm. Eventually, when he could bear it no longer, he spoke quietly: "It's not something I planned . . ." He had suspected it would be like this, but still felt unprepared for the weight of guilt that had settled upon him, and for the explanations, apologies, that were already begging to be spoken. He stared at his hands, blistered and crisscrossed in an angry red from the nylon lines.

His father waited until the traffic report was finished. "Well . . . I think it's a good thing."

"What?"

"There is nothing for you here, Ale. Nothing. It is better you go and enjoy life somewhere else." His head sank into his shoulders, and he exhaled in a long, weary sigh.

"You don't mind?"

"It's not a question—you're a young man. It is right that you travel. It is right that you have some opportunities, meet some people. God knows, there's nothing in Argentina." He glanced sideways, and the look was not lost on his son. "You need to live a little."

The words that sprang to Alejandro's mind seemed inadequate so he closed his mouth on them.

"When are you going to talk to your mother?"

"Today. I got the papers through last week. I want to go as soon as possible."

"It's just . . . it's just the economic situation, right? There's nothing . . . nothing else that makes you want to leave?"

Alejandro knew that another conversation was hovering between them. "Pa, the state hospitals are on their knees. There are rumors that they don't have enough money to pay us by the end of the year."

His father seemed relieved. "I won't go to

the office. You need to talk to your mother. I'll drive you."

"She's going to be bad, huh?"

"We'll deal with it," his father said simply.

They traversed the three sides of the square and sat in traffic before the government buildings. His father placed a hand paternally on his leg. "So, who is going to help me hunt peacock bass, eh?" The unforced animation of before was gone. His father's professional mask was back in place, benign, reassuring.

"Come to England, Pa. We'll hunt salmon."

"A child's fish." It was said without resentment.

The Mothers of the Disappeared were ending their weekly march. As the car began to head back, Alejandro watched them as they folded their laminated posters carefully into handbags, adjusted embroidered headscarves, exchanged greetings, and held each other with the loose affection of long-standing allies before they headed for the gates and their lonely journeys home. The Marenas house, like many in the Zona Norte, looked neither like the flat-fronted, Spanish-influenced shuttered manses of central BA, nor a modern glass-and-concrete structure. It was a curious, ornate building set back from the street and, in architectural style, most closely resembled a Swiss cuckoo clock.

Around it, carefully sculpted hedges disguised the electric gate, the newly installed bars on the windows, and hid the security booth and guard at the end of the road. Inside, the wooden floors had long given way to shining expanses of cool marble, upon which sat expensive French rococo-style furniture, polished and gilded to within an inch of its life. It was not a comfortable-looking house, but while the front rooms spoke of a cool social superiority, inviting guests to admire rather than relax, the kitchen, where the family spent most of their private time, still housed a battered old table and several shabbily comfortable chairs. Their disappearance, Milagros, the maid, had sworn, would mean the immediate end of her twenty-seven-year tenure with the family. If they thought that after a hard day's cleaning she was going to squeeze her backside into one of those modern plasticky things, they had another think coming. As it was widely agreed that Milagros was often the only thing standing between Alejandro's mother and the sanatorium, the chairs stayed, to the unspoken satisfaction of all parties. And the kitchen remained the most used room in the seven-bedroom house.

It was here that Ale chose to speak to his mother, while his father supposedly busied himself in his study, and Milagros shuffled backward and forward across the marble floors with a mop to eavesdrop on the conversation. His mother sat upright at the table. With her helmet of blond hair, she was unrecognizable as the dark-haired beauty of the wedding photographs in gilt frames that littered the house.

"You are going where?" she said, for the second time.

"England."

"To train? You have changed your mind? You're going to be a doctor?"

"No, Mother, I'm still going to be a midwife."

"You're going to work in a private hospital? To advance your career?"

"No. Another state hospital."

Milagros had stopped all pretense of cleaning, and stood still in the center of the room to listen.

"You are going to the other side of the world to do the same job that you do here?"

He nodded.

"But why there? Why so far?"

His answers had been rehearsed so many times in his head. "There are no opportunities here. They are offering good jobs in England, proper wages. I can work in some of the best hospitals."

"But you can work here!" There was a rising note in his mother's voice that spoke of panic or hysteria. "Is it not enough that I lose one child? Must I lose two?"

He had known it was coming, but that did not make the blow any lighter. He felt the vaguely malevolent presence that he always did when Estela was discussed. "You're not losing me, Mother." His voice was that of a doctor speaking to his patient.

"You're moving ten thousand miles away! How is that not losing you? Why are you leaving me?" She appealed to Milagros, who shook her head in sorrowful agreement.

"I'm not moving **from** you."

"But why not America? Why not Paraguay? Brazil? Why not Argentina, for heaven's sake?"

He tried to explain how English hospitals were short of midwives, how those from other countries were being offered substantial financial rewards to fill the gaps. He tried to tell her that it would be good for his career, that he might end up working for one of the famous teaching hospitals, how the neonatal care was among the best in the world. She was always going on about their European ancestors—it would be good for him to experience Europe.

He considered telling her of the three babies he had watched handed over at birth because Argentina's economic collapse meant their parents were too poor to keep them, of the anguished cries of the still-bloodied mothers, the painfully set jaws of the fathers. He said nothing of the fact that while he had chosen to work with the city's dirt poor, nothing had prepared him for the lingering sorrow, or the sense of unwilling complicity he felt at the handing over of those children.

But he and his father did not talk to her of babies. They never had.

He knelt and took her hand. "What is there left for me here, Mama? The hospitals are dying. I could not afford to live in a slum on my salary. You want me to live with you until I am an old man?" He regretted the words as soon as he had spoken them, knowing she would be perfectly happy with such an arrangement.

"I knew you doing this—this **thing** would bring us no good."

When he had initially gone into medicine, his mother had been proud. What professions were of a higher status in Buenos Aires, after all? Only plastic surgeons and psychoanalysts, and there were one of each in the family already. Then, two years in, he had returned home to announce a change in career: he was not at home among the doctors, he had realized. His future lay elsewhere. He was going, he said, to work in obstetric care.

"You're going to be an obstetrician?" his mother had said, faint concern creasing her brow.

"No, I'm going to be a midwife."

It was only the second time Milagros had seen her mistress faint—the first was when they told her Estela had died. It was not a suitable profession for the son of Buenos Aires' most prominent cosmetic surgeon, and no profession for a red-blooded man, no matter what was said about equality and sexual liberation these days. To her friends, her son was only ever described as being "in medicine." It wasn't **seemly**. More importantly, she believed it might be, she confided to Milagros, the real reason why her beautiful son never brought girls home, why he didn't seem to display the arrogant machismo that should have been shot through the firstborn son of such a family. Then, even worse, he had chosen to work in the state hospital.

"So, when are you thinking of going?"

"Next week. Tuesday."

"Next **week**? Next week coming? Why so much hurry?"

"They need staff immediately, Mama. One has to take opportunities when they come."

Shock had made her rigid. She held a hand to her face, then crumpled. "If it had been your sister who wanted this profession, who wanted to move continents . . . that I could have coped with. But **you** . . . It's not **right**, Ale."

So what is right? he wanted to ask. But as always, he said nothing. Alejandro closed his eyes, and braced himself against his mother's hurt. "I'll be able to come back, two, maybe three times a year."

"My only son will be a visitor to my house. This is supposed to make me happy?" She didn't look at Alejandro but appealed to Milagros, who sucked her teeth. There was a lengthy silence. Then, as he had expected, his mother broke into a noisy burst of sobbing. She reached a hand across to him, her fingers waving vainly in the air. "Don't go, Ale. I promise I won't mind where you work. You can stay at the Hospital de Clinicas. I won't say a thing."

"Mama—"

"Please!"

She heard the certainty in his silence, and when she next spoke her voice held an edge of bitterness. She blinked against the tears. "All I wanted was to watch you succeed, get married, look after your children. And now you don't just deny me this, you would deny me yourself!"

Their impending separation made him generous. He knelt and held her hand, her jeweled rings cold against his skin. "I will come back. I thought you might see this as an opportunity for me."

She frowned at him, pushed his hair back from his eyes. "You are so cold, Ale. So unfeeling. Can't you see that you're breaking my heart?"

Alejandro was unable, as ever, to answer his mother's forceful logic. "Be glad for me, Mama."

"How can I be glad for you when I am grieving for myself?"

And that is why I am escaping from you, he said silently. Because all I have ever known from you is grieving. Because my head is full of it, always has been. And this way, finally, I might get a little peace. "We'll talk later. I have to go out now." He smiled, the patient, detached smile he reserved for his mother, and left her, with a kiss to her brow, sobbing quietly in the arms of her maid.

Considering that their sole purpose was to facilitate sexual excess and impropriety, the Venus Love Hotel, like other such establishments, was excessively bound up in rules and regulations. While any number of sexual aids might be ordered along with the room-service menu, and any kind of debauched proclivity catered for on the many adult videos available for private hire, the hotel was curiously prudish when it came to maintaining its code of conduct, its air of respectability. The building had the sober façade of a private house. Neither man nor woman was allowed to wait in a room alone, despite the inconvenience caused to illicit couples forced to rendezvous in nearby cafés, not so safe from prying eyes. A smoked-glass screen at reception meant that neither receptionist nor visitor could accurately gauge the identity of the other.

Except that one particular customer was known to the man behind the screen and had paid him generously on more than one occasion to ensure discretion. This customer had appeared in the gossip magazines enough times to be recognizable even from behind the twin barriers of smoked glass and sunglasses.

This meant that, with only a nod to the silhouette

before him, Alejandro was able to skip up the stairs two or three at a time and, at the appointed hour, knock on the discreetly numbered door that had been a private haven two or three times a week for almost eighteen months.

"Ale?" Never anything romantic. Never anything like **amor**. He preferred it like that.

"It's me."

Eduardo Guichane was one of Argentina's highest paid television hosts. On his chat show, which aired several times a week, he was flanked by several near-naked South American girls who made frequent, badly scripted references to his legendary sexual appetite. He was tall, immaculately dressed, and prided himself on a physique seemingly unchanged since his years of playing professional football. Argentina's favorite gossip magazine—**Gente**—repeatedly featured "stolen" pictures of him squiring some young woman who was not Sofia Guichane, or speculating as to whether, as was the case with his previous wives, he was being unfaithful to the former Miss Venezuela finalist. All planted by his publicist. "All lies," Sofia would mutter bitterly, lighting one of her omnipresent cigarettes. Eduardo had the libido of an armchair. Although his most frequent excuse had been exhaustion, she was wondering if his interests didn't lie in other directions.

"Boys?" said Alejandro cautiously.

"No! Boys I could cope with." Sofia blew smoke

at the ceiling. "I am afraid he is more interested in golf."

They had met at his father's surgery on a day after rioting when Alejandro had come, at his mother's request, to check that his father had made it to work safely. Sofia was on one of several visits. Having been celibate for four of the six years of her marriage, she had labored under the belief that a smaller, higher backside and several inches off her thighs might reignite her husband's passion. ("What a waste of American dollars that was," she said afterward.) Alejandro, struck by her beauty and by the shining dissatisfaction in her face, had found himself staring, and then, upon leaving, thought no more of her. But she had bumped into him in the foyer downstairs where, staring at him with the same curious hunger, she announced that she never normally did this sort of thing, then scribbled her number on a card and thrust it at him.

Three days later they met at the Fenix, a spectacularly lascivious love hotel, where intricate prints of the **Kama Sutra** decorated the walls, and beds vibrated at will. Her mention of their meeting-place had left him in no doubt as to her intention, and they had come together almost wordlessly, in a frenzied coupling that had left Alejandro dazed for almost a week afterward.

Their meetings had gradually achieved a pattern. She would swear that they could not meet again, that

Eduardo suspected something, had been quizzing her, that she had only got away with it by the skin of her teeth. Then, as he sat beside her, comforted her, told her he understood, she would weep, ask why she, as a young woman, should have to endure a sexless marriage, a life free of passion, when she was not even thirty. (Both were aware that this was not strictly true—the age at least—but Alejandro knew better than to interrupt.) And then, as he comforted her again, agreed that it was unfair, that she was too beautiful, too passionate to grow stale and dry like an old fig, she would hold his face and announce that he was so handsome, so kind, the only man who had ever understood her. And then they would make love (although that always sounded too gentle for what it really was). Afterward, smoking furiously, she would pull away and tell him that this really was it. The risks were too high. Alejandro would have to understand.

Several days, or occasionally a week, later she would call again.

His own feelings about the arrangement had often verged on the ambivalent. Alejandro had always been discreetly selective when it came to sexual partners, uncomfortable with the idea of falling in love. While he felt a sympathy for her predicament, he knew he didn't love Sofia; he wasn't even sure he always liked her. What they shared, and what neither had ever been quite brave enough to acknowledge, was a fierce sexual chemistry that ratified Sofia's enduring belief in her own desirability, and lifted Alejandro out of his habitual reticence, even if his exterior did little to suggest it.

"Why do you never look at me when you come?"

Alejandro closed the door quietly behind him, and stood over the prostrate figure of Sofia on the bed. He was used now to these abrupt opening gambits: it was as if the abbreviated nature of their meetings left no room for any kind of nicety. "I do look at you." He considered removing his jacket, then changed his mind.

Sofia rolled over on to her stomach so that she could reach the ashtray. The action caused her skirt to ride up her legs. A pornographic film was playing on the television; he glanced at it, wondered if she had been watching it while she waited for him.

"No, you don't. Not when you come," she said. "I watch you."

He knew she was right. He had never opened his eyes to any woman at that moment; no doubt his uncle, the psychoanalyst, would have said it betrayed something ungenerous about him, some determination not to reveal himself. "I don't know," he said. "I hadn't thought about it."

Sofia pushed herself upright, lifting one knee so that a long expanse of thigh was clearly visible. Normally this would have been enough to elicit powerful waves of desire in him; today he felt curiously detached, as if he were already thousands of miles from here.

"Eduardo thinks we should have a baby."

Next door someone opened a window. Through the wall, Alejandro could just make out the dull murmur of voices. "A baby," he repeated.

"You're not going to ask me how?"

"I think I understand the biology of it by now."

She wasn't smiling. "He wants to do it at a clinic. He says it will be the best way to make sure it happens quickly. I think it is just because he doesn't want to make love to me."

Alejandro sat on the corner of the bed. The couple on the television were now engaged in an orgiastic frenzy; he wondered whether Sofia would mind if he turned it off. He had told her several times that such films did nothing for him, but she would just smile as if she knew better, as if repeated exposure to them would change his mind. "I don't think making babies is something you can do by yourself."

She had kicked off her shoes in separate corners of the room—Eduardo liked things to be neat, orderly, she had told him before. When she was with Alejandro, she liked to scatter her clothes about, a kind of secret rebellion.

"I don't think he really wants a kid. All those diapers—plastic toys everywhere, baby puke on his shoulders. He just wants to look virile. You know he's losing his hair? I told him it would be cheaper for both of us if he got hair plugs. But he says he wants a baby."

"And what do you want?"

She looked at him sharply, smirked at his psychoanalytic tone. "What do I want?" She pulled a face, stubbed out her cigarette. "I don't know. Some other life, probably." She pushed herself off the bed and walked up to him, close enough for him to smell her perfume, and placed a cool hand against his cheek, letting it slide slowly over his skin. Her hair, which was loose around her shoulders, was slightly matted, as if she had spent some time lying on the bed before he arrived. "I've been thinking about you," she said. She leaned forward and kissed him, leaving the taste of lipstick and cigarettes on his lips. Then she cocked her head to one side. "What's up?"

She surprised him like this every now and then. He had believed her to be spoiled and self-absorbed, and yet occasionally she would pick up on some subtle change in atmosphere, like a dog.

He wondered whether there was any way to soften it. "I'm going away."

Her eyes widened. The woman on the screen had contorted herself into a position that made Alejandro uncomfortable for her. He was longing to turn off the television.

"For long?"

"A year . . . I don't know."

He had been primed for an explosion. But she merely stood very still, then sighed and sat down on the bed, reaching for her cigarettes.

"It's work. I've got a job in a hospital in England."

"England."

"I leave next week."

"Oh."

He moved closer to her, put a hand on her arm. "I shall miss you."

They sat like that for some minutes, vaguely conscious of the sound of muffled lovemaking next door. There had been a time when he would have found it embarrassing.

"Why?" She turned to him. "Why are you going?"

"Buenos Aires . . . is too full of ghosts."

"It has always been full of ghosts. Always will be." She shrugged. "You just have to choose not to see them."

He swallowed. "I can't." He reached for Sofia then, perhaps because she had not reacted as he had expected, suddenly desiring her, desperate to lose himself inside her. But she extricated herself from his grasp, twisting nimbly, and stood up. She lifted one hand to her hair, smoothed it, walked to the television, and flicked it off.

When she spoke, her eyes were filled with neither tears nor infantile fury, but a kind of resigned wisdom he hadn't seen before. "I should be mad at you for leaving me like this," she said, lighting another cigarette. "But I'm glad, Ale." She nodded, as if confirming it to herself. "It's the first time I've ever seen you do something, make a real decision. You've always been so . . . passive."

He felt a brief discomfort, not knowing if she was disparaging his sexual technique. But having lit her cigarette she took his hand, lifted and kissed it, a curious gesture. "Are you running to something? Or just running away?" Her hand held his firmly.

It was impossible to answer honestly, so he said nothing.

"Go, Turco."

"Just like that?"

"Go now. I don't want us to start making stupid promises about meeting again."

"I'll write if you want."

"Come on . . ."

He looked at her beautiful, disappointed face, feeling an affection that surprised him. The words he had prepared seemed trite.

She understood. She squeezed his hand, then gestured toward the door. "Go on. You know I was going to finish things anyway. You're not my type, after all."

He heard her tone harden determinedly, and walked toward the door.

"Just my luck, eh?" she said, laughing humor-lessly. "A husband who is dead to the touch, and a lover too haunted by ghosts to live."

Heathrow and its outskirts was the ugliest place Alejandro had ever seen. Dere Maternity Hospital was prettier, but even less friendly—especially, he realized, to those with darker skin. For weeks many of the midwives had refused to speak to him, apparently resentful of this male usurper in their female domain. Two weeks after he arrived, he had slept with a young nurse out of loneliness, and when he had apologized afterward had been told, bitterly, "God, you men are all the same." He was permanently cold. His mother, when she had called, had asked if he had a girlfriend yet: "A young man, your age," she said sadly, "you should be shopping around."

He had seen the sign outside the Peacock Emporium and, overcome by a wave of homesick-ness almost as strong as his exhaustion after a fourteen-hour shift (other midwives told him he was mad not to end a shift during a labor, but he did not consider it fair to leave a woman at her most vulnerable), he had pushed open the door and entered. He was not a superstitious man, but some-times you had to follow signs. Trying to shut them out didn't seem to have served him well this far.

He didn't tell the two women this, of course. Or
the bit about Sofia. Or Estela, come to that. If it
hadn't been for the blonde with the smiling face,
the first person who had appeared to want to hear
what he had to say, he might not have said anything
at all.

# 12

The problem with getting older was not so much that one got stuck in the past, Vivi often thought, but that there was so much more of the past to get lost in. She had been sorting through the old bureau in the sitting room, determined to put all those sepia-tinted photographs into an album, hopefully before the men came in, but suddenly it was going on half past five. She had found herself inanimate on the small sofa, absorbed in images of her earlier self, pictures she had not lingered over for years: clinging to Douglas's arm at various social functions, posing self-consciously in frocks, proudly holding newborn babies, and then, as they got older, looking increasingly less confident, her smile perhaps a little more painted on with each year. Perhaps she was being too hard on herself. Or perhaps she was being sentimental, projecting emotions on to herself that she felt overwhelmed by.

Suzanna had been an easy child. When Vivi considered the upheaval of her daughter's early years, and her own lack of experience as a mother, it amazed her that they had muddled through as well as they had. Suzanna's childhood had never been the problem: it was puberty, when those gawky, elongated limbs achieved a certain sylph-like elegance, and when those near-Slavic cheekbones had started highlighting the previously hidden planes of her face. The distant echo had patently disturbed Douglas's peace of mind. And Suzanna, perhaps reacting to some unseen vibration in the air, had gone off the rails.

Rationally, Vivi knew this was not her fault. No one could have offered Suzanna more unconditional love, or have better understood her complicated nature. But motherhood was never rational: even now, with Suzanna as settled as she ever had been—and Neil such a wonderful husband—Vivi still found herself suffused with guilt that somehow she had failed to raise this daughter to be happy. "No reason for her to be unhappy," Douglas would say. "She's had every advantage."

"Yes, well, sometimes it's not quite as simple as that." Vivi rarely ventured further into family psychology, as Douglas did not hold much truck with such discussions, and, besides, he was right in his way. Suzanna **had** had everything. They all had. The fact that Douglas and her two children were so contented had not alleviated her sense of responsibility—if anything, it had heightened it. Vivi had spent years wondering privately if she had

treated the children differently in some way, if sub-
consciously she had instilled in Suzanna a sense that
she was second best.

She knew how seductive that feeling could be.

Douglas said it was rubbish. His view of relationships was simple: you treated people fairly,
and expected the same in return. You loved your
children, they loved you back. You supported them
as much as you could, and in return they attempted
to do you proud.

Or, in Suzanna's case, you loved them and they
did their best to make themselves unhappy.

I don't think I can bear this any longer, she
thought, her eyes welling with tears as she looked at
a photo of eleven-year-old Suzanna, clinging fiercely
to Vivi's prematurely thickened waist. Somebody
has to do something. And I shall hate myself if I
don't at least try.

What would Athene have done? Vivi had long
since stopped asking herself that question: Athene
had been such an unknowable quantity it had been
impossible to predict her actions even when she had
been alive. Now, thirty-odd years later, she seemed
so insubstantial, her memory both so fierce and
simultaneously ephemeral, that it was hard to imagine her as a mother at all. Would she have understood
her daughter's complicated nature, which echoed her
own? Or would she have done even more damage,
dipping in and out of her daughter's life, her failure

to stick at motherhood another painful example of her irredeemably mercurial temperament?

You're lucky, Vivi told the invisible mother in the photograph, feeling suddenly envious, thinking of how Douglas had waved her away when she had attempted once again to bring up the subject of Rosemary and her laundry. It's easier to be a ghost. You can be romanticized, adored, can grow in the memory instead of diminish in reality. Then, pushing herself out of the chair, and noting the time, she scolded herself for the fanciful indulgence of envying the dead.

Alejandro arrived at the Peacock Emporium at a quarter past nine. He came in most days now but always at different times, according to the apparently random timetable of his shifts. He didn't speak much. He didn't even look at a newspaper. He just sat in the corner and sipped his coffee, occasionally smiling in response to Jessie's cheerful chatter.

Jessie, never slow in striking up a conversation, had made it her mission to find out all about the man she termed "the Gaucho Gyno," asking him questions in a manner that occasionally made Suzanna wince. Had he always wanted to be a midwife? Only since he realized he was not going to make the national football team. Did he like delivering babies? Yes. Did the women mind having a male midwife? Mostly no. He backed out gracefully when they did. He had found, he said, that if he wore a white coat no one batted an eyelid. Did he have a girlfriend? No. Suzanna had looked away when he answered that one, furious with herself for her faint but definite blush.

He didn't seem to mind Jessie's questions, although he often managed not to answer them directly. He sat close enough to the counter, Suzanna had noted, to express some degree of comfort with them. Suzanna herself made sure she was rarely close to him. He already felt, somehow, as if he were Jessie's. As if Suzanna attempting to be equally friendly with him would make everyone uncomfortable.

"How many babies did you deliver today?"

"Only one."

"Any complications?"

"Just a fainting father."

"Fantastic. What did you do?"

Alejandro had glanced down at his hands. "It was not very good timing. We only had time to move him out of the way."

"What—drag him?"

Alejandro had seemed faintly embarrassed. "We needed our hands. We had to push him with our feet."

Jessie loved to hear these stories. Suzanna, more squeamish, often had to turn up the volume of the music or invent some task in the cellar. It was all a little too close to home. But she frequently found herself staring at him, albeit surreptitiously. While his appearance would have failed to hook her attention in London, in the environs of the frighteningly Caucasian Suffolk town, and in the close confines of her little shop, he was a welcome breath of exoticism, a reminder of a wider world outside.

"Did he miss the birth?"

"Not quite. But I think he was a bit confused." He smiled to himself. "He tried to punch me when he came round, and then he called me 'Mother.'"

Jessie had wanted to do a display on him with a story about some miracle of birth ("It kind of fits, being a newish shop and all"), but Alejandro had been reluctant to agree. He didn't think, he said, in his quiet, courteous voice, that he could yet lay claim to being one of the shop's regulars. There was something decisive enough in his tone for Jessie to back off. And despite her compelling charm—Suzanna thought she could probably have flirted with a brick—Alejandro had failed to fulfill any of their expectations about Latin men. He neither swaggered, nor eyed them with a swarthy intent. He didn't even seem to have inbuilt rhythm.

"Probably gay," said Jessie as, with a polite goodbye, he left for work.

"No," said Suzanna, who wasn't sure whether wishful thinking had made her say it.

"You hurt yourself?" Jessie had injured her hand. Suzanna hadn't noticed it until Arturro asked when he came in for his morning espresso. He had lifted her hand from the counter with the tenderness of one used to treating food with reverence, and turned it to the light to reveal a large purplish-brown bruise across three fingers.

"Car door shut on me," said Jessie, and pulled it back with a smile. "Daft, aren't I?"

There was an unexpected embarrassed silence in the shop. The bruise was awful, a livid reminder of some extreme pain. Suzanna had glanced at Arturro's face, noted that Jessie refused to look directly at either of them, and was ashamed that she had not noticed it. She thought, perhaps, that if the subject were pursued tactfully, Jessie might confide in her, but as she ran through the possible questions she could ask, she became aware that every possible variation sounded not only intrusive but crass, and possibly patronizing too. "Arnica cream," Suzanna said eventually. "Seems to bring out the bruising quicker."

"Oh, don't worry. I've done that. We've got loads of it at home."

"Are you sure your fingers aren't broken?" Arturro was still eyeing Jessie's hand. "They look a bit swollen to me."

"No, I can move them. Look." She gave a gay

wave of her fingers, then turned back toward the wall. "Who shall we put in the first display, then? I really wanted to do Alejandro, but I think that story about the baby who got given up would make everyone cry."

"It was him, wasn't it?" said Suzanna, much later, when they were alone.

"Who?" Jessie was working on her display after all: she had targeted Father Lenny, who had conceded with some amusement, but only if she would mention that currently he had almost two hundred battery-operated back massagers for sale. ("They don't look much like back massagers to me," Jessie had said, dubiously holding one up. "I'm a priest," Father Lenny had exclaimed. "What else would they be?")

"Your boyfriend. Hurt your hand." She had felt it between them all afternoon—and she couldn't ignore it, even if it meant Jessie would take it badly.

"I shut them in the car door," said Jessie.

There was a short delay before Suzanna spoke: "You mean he did."

Jessie had been in the window. She got up off her knees, and backed out of the space, careful not to dislodge any of the items on display. She lifted her hand and examined it, as if for the first time. "It's really difficult to explain," she said.

"Try me."

"He liked it when I was just at home with Emma.

This all started when I did my night school. He just loses his temper because he gets insecure."

"Why don't you leave?"

"Leave?" She looked genuinely surprised, even, perhaps, offended. "He's not some wife-beater, Suzanna."

Suzanna raised her eyebrows.

"Look, I know him, and this isn't really him. He just feels threatened because I'm getting an education and he thinks that means I'm going to bugger off. And now there's this place, and that's something new as well. I probably don't help matters—you know I'm a terrible one for talking to everybody. Sometimes I probably don't consider how it looks to him . . ." She gazed meditatively at her half-finished window display. "Look, once he sees nothing's going to change, he'll go back to how he was. Don't forget, Suzanna, I know him. We've been together ten years. This is not the Jason I know."

"I just don't see that there's ever an excuse for it."

"I'm not making excuses. I'm explaining. There's a difference. Look, he knows he's done wrong. I'm not some cowering little victim. We just fight, and when we fight sometimes we fight nasty. I give as good as I get, you know."

In the long silence, the atmosphere in the shop seemed to contract. Suzanna said nothing, fearful of how it might sound, conscious that even her silence was suggesting some kind of judgment.

Jessie leaned back against one of the tables, and looked squarely at her. "Okay, what is it that really bothers you about this?"

Suzanna's voice was small. "The effect it might have on Emma? What it's teaching her?"

"You think I'd let anyone lay a hand on Emma? You think I'd stay in the house if I thought Jason might lay a hand on her?"

"I'm not saying that."

"So what are you saying?"

"That . . . I don't know . . . I'm just uncomfortable with any kind of violence," said Suzanna.

"Violence? Or passion?"

"What?"

It was the first time Jessie's face had darkened. "You don't like passion, Suzanna. You like things neatly packaged. You like to keep things buttoned up. And that's fine. That's your choice. But me and Jason, we're just honest about what we feel—when we love, we really love. But when we fight, we really fight. There aren't any half-measures. And do you know what? I'm more comfortable with that— even with the odd busted hand"—she held up her wrist—"than the opposite, which is feeling so not bothered by someone that you lead this cool, polite, parallel life with each other. Have sex once a week. Hell, once a month. Fight quietly so you don't wake the kids. What's that teaching anyone about life?"

"The two things don't necessarily . . ." Suzanna

trailed off, midsentence. Intellectually, she knew she could have disputed the sense in what Jessie had said, however forcefully it had been put, but even though it had not been meant maliciously, there was something so profoundly discomfiting about it that Suzanna could hardly speak.

It had been almost a relief when Vivi appeared that afternoon. Suzanna and Jessie, while outwardly polite, had lost a certain spontaneity in their dealings with each other, as if the conversation had been too premature for their infant friendship to survive its honesty. Arturro had drunk his coffee unusually quickly and, with a nervous thank-you, had left. Two other customers had talked loudly in the corner, oblivious, temporarily masking the long silences. But now that they were gone it had become painfully apparent that Jessie's normal chattiness had been deadened. Suzanna, making an uncharacteristic effort to talk to her customers as an attempt to bypass the strained atmosphere, found herself greeting her mother with an unusual warmth, which Vivi, flushed with pleasure at being hugged, had eagerly returned.

"So, this is it!" she exclaimed, several times, in the doorway. "Aren't you clever?"

"Hardly," said Suzanna. "It's only a few chairs and tables."

"But look at your lovely colors! All these pretty

things!" She bent and examined the shelves. "They're all exquisite. And so nicely arranged. I did want to come by—but I know you don't like to feel we're all breathing down your neck. And the couple of times I did come past you looked like you were busy . . . anyway. The Peacock Emporium," she said, slowly reading a label. "Oh, Suzanna, I'm so proud of you. It really is like nothing else around."

Suzanna's burst of warmth evaporated. It was as if, she thought, Vivi could never gauge the correct level of emotion: her overenthusiasm left the recipient unable to accept it gracefully. "Do you want a coffee?" She motioned to the blackboard listing, in an attempt to disguise her feelings.

"I'd love one. Do you make them all yourself?"

Suzanna fought the urge to raise her eyebrows. "Well. Yes."

Vivi sat carefully on one of the blue chairs and gazed over at the cushions on the pew. "You've used that fabric I gave you from the attic."

"Oh, that. Yes."

"It looks much better here. It could be almost contemporary, couldn't it, that print? You'd never think it was over thirty years old. An old boyfriend gave it to me. Am I all right here? Not in anyone's way?" She was holding her handbag in front of her with both hands, in the manner of a nervous elderly lady.

"It's a shop, Mum. You're allowed to sit anywhere. Oh, Jessie, this is my mum, Vivi. Mum, Jessie."

"Nice to meet you. I'll do your coffee," said Jessie, who was behind the machine. "What would you like?"

"What would you recommend?"

Oh, for God's sake, thought Suzanna.

"The latte is nice, if you don't like it too strong. Or we do a mocha, with chocolate in it."

"A mocha, I think. I'll treat myself."

"We'll need to top up on the chocolate flakes, Suzanna. Would you like me to get some more?"

"It's okay," she said, acutely conscious of Jessie's new formality. "I'll get some."

"No problem. I can go now."

"No, really. I'll get them." Her own voice sounded wrong, too insistent—like someone's boss.

"It really is stunning. You've completely changed the look of it. And you've got such an individual eye!" Vivi was gazing around her. "I love the smells, the coffee, and the—what is it? Oh, soap. And perfume. Aren't they beautiful? I shall tell all my friends to get their soaps here."

Normally, Suzanna noted, Jessie would already have seated herself beside Vivi, bombarding her with questions. She was instead focused on the coffee machine, her bruised hand now hidden under an overlong sleeve.

Vivi's hand reached to take Suzanna's. "I can't tell you how wonderful I think it is. Well done, darling. I think it's just marvelous that you made it happen all by yourself."

"It's early days yet. We're not in profit or anything."

"Oh, you will be. I'm sure you will. It's all so . . . original."

Jessie handed over the coffee with a muted smile, then begged to be excused so that she could unpack some jewelry that had just come in. "If that's okay with you, Suzanna?"

"Of course it is."

"This is delicious. Thank you, Jessie. Definitely the best coffee in Dere."

"That wouldn't be hard." Suzanna attempted a joke, hoping Jessie would smile. She didn't think she could bear any more of this.

Suzanna turned to Vivi, her face animated. "Guess what, Mum. We're going to play Cupid. Jessie's idea. We're going to get two local lonely hearts together without them knowing it."

Vivi sipped carefully at her coffee. "Sounds exciting, darling."

"I meant to tell you, Jess. I bought these. I thought you could use them—you know, like you said." She reached behind the counter and pulled out a small gold-wrapped box of chocolates. Jessie looked at it. "It was a really clever idea. I think you should do it. Pop them over there, you know, just before she leaves this evening. Or maybe first thing tomorrow."

Jessie's eyes held just a hint of a question, and some mute understanding passed between them.

"What do you think?"

"These are perfect," Jessie said, with her old, unguarded smile. "Liliane will love them."

Suzanna felt something in her relax; the shop itself seemed to breathe out, and brighten a little. "Let's all have a coffee," she said. "I'll make them, Jess. Some of Arturro's biscuits. Cappuccino for you?"

"No, I'm fine." She placed the chocolates back under the counter. "Better hide these in case he comes back in. There, you're in on a secret here, Mrs. Peacock. You're not to say a word."

"Oh, I'm not Mrs. Peacock," Vivi said benignly. "That's Suzanna's married name."

"Oh? So what's your last name?"

Suzanna cringed.

"Fairley-Hulme."

Jessie turned to Suzanna. "You're a Fairley-Hulme?"

Vivi nodded. "Yes, she is. One of three."

"Off the Dereward estate? You never said."

Suzanna felt oddly caught out. "Why would I?" she said, a little sharply. "I don't live on the estate. Strictly speaking, I'm a Peacock."

"Yes, but—"

"It's only a name." Suzanna's relief—that the

tension between her and Jessie had cleared—dissipated. She felt as if her family had physically intruded.

Jessie's gaze flickered between the two women, and settled back on the counter in front of her. "Still. It's all making sense now. I love the picture," she said to Vivi.

"Picture?"

"The portrait. Suzanna was going to put it up in here but she thinks it doesn't look right. I've heard about your family's portraits. Do you still let people in to see them in the summer?"

Jessie turned toward the painting, still sitting behind the legs of the counter. Vivi saw it, and flushed. "Oh, no, dear. That's not me. It—that's Athene—"

"Vivi's not my real mum," interjected Suzanna. "My real mum died when I was born."

Jessie did not speak, as if she was waiting for something to be added. But Vivi was now staring at the portrait, and Suzanna appeared to be thinking about something else. "No, now I see. Different hair. And everything . . ." Jessie trailed off, conscious that no one was listening.

Eventually Vivi broke the silence, tearing her gaze from the painting and rising to her feet. She placed her empty coffee cup carefully on the counter in front of Jessie. "Yes. Well. I'd better be off. I promised I'd drive Rosemary to see one of her old friends in Clare. She'll be wondering where I am." She pulled her silk scarf more tightly round her neck. "I just wanted to stop by and say hello."

"Nice to meet you, Mrs. Fairley-Hulme. Pop by again soon. You can try one of our flavored coffees."

Vivi made as if to pay at the till, but Jessie waved her away. "Don't be silly," she said. "You're family."

"You—you're very kind." Vivi picked up her handbag and moved toward the door. Then she turned back to Suzanna. "Listen, darling. I was wondering. Why don't you and Neil come to supper one night this week? Not a huge affair, like last time. Just a simple supper. It would be so lovely to see you."

Suzanna was tidying the magazines in the rack. "Neil doesn't get back till late."

"Come by yourself, then. We'd so love to have you. Rosemary's had . . . a difficult time, lately. And I know you'd cheer her up."

"Sorry, Mum. I'm really busy."

"Just you and me, then?"

Suzanna hadn't meant to be snappy, but something about the business with the surnames, or perhaps it was the portrait, had made her irritable. "Look, Mum, I told you. I have to do bookkeeping and all sorts of things after work now. I don't really get evenings to myself. Some other time, yes?"

Vivi buried her discomfort under a wavering smile. She placed a hand on the door handle and knocked a swinging mobile as she stepped backward, so that she had to brush it away from her head. "Right. Of course. Lovely to meet you, Jessie. Good luck with the shop."

Suzanna buried herself back in her magazines, refusing to meet Jessie's eyes. As Vivi exited, they could hear her muttering, as if to herself, even when she was out of the door. "Yes, it's really looking marvelous . . ."

"Jess," said Suzanna, several minutes later. "Do me a favor." She glanced up. Jessie was still looking at her steadily from over the counter. "Don't talk about it. To customers, I mean. Me being a Fairley-Hulme." She rubbed at her nose. "I just don't want it . . . becoming an issue."

Jessie's expression was blank. "You're the boss," she said.

"You'll never guess where I'm going."

Neil had burst in on her, and Suzanna, although largely concealed by bubbles, felt curiously exposed. One of the worst things about leaving their London flat had been having to share a bathroom. She fought the urge to ask him if he'd mind stepping outside. "Where?"

"Shooting. With your brother." He lifted his arms, cocking an imaginary rifle.

"It's the wrong time of year."

"Not now. On the first one of the next season. He

rang me up this morning, said they've got a spare place. He's going to lend me a gun and all the gear."

"But you don't shoot."

"He's well aware that I'm a beginner, Suze."

Suzanna frowned at her feet, which were just visible at the other end of the bath. "Just doesn't seem like your thing."

Neil loosened his tie, made a face at himself in the mirror as he examined some ancient shaving cut. "To tell you the truth, I'm looking forward to it. I've missed getting out and about since we lost the gym memberships. It'll be good to do something a bit active."

"Shooting's hardly running the four-minute mile."

"It's still outdoors. There'll be a fair bit of walking."

"And a huge lunch. Full of fat bankers stuffing their faces. You're hardly going to get in shape that way."

Neil folded his tie round his hand and sat down on the lavatory seat next to the bath. "What's the problem? It's not as if you're ever around at weekends. You're always in the shop."

"I told you it was going to be hard work."

"I'm not complaining, just saying I might as well do something with my weekends if you're going to be working."

"Fine."

"So what's the problem?"

Suzanna shrugged. "There's no problem. Like I said, I just didn't think it was your kind of thing."

"And it wasn't. But we live in the country now."

"It doesn't mean you have to start wearing tweeds and wittering on about guns and braces of pheasant. Honestly, Neil, there's nothing worse than a townie trying to pretend they're to the manner born."

"But if someone's offering me the chance to try something new, for free, I'd be a fool to turn it down. Come on, Suze, it's not as if we've had much fun recently." His head dropped to one side. "I tell you what, why don't you get someone to mind the shop and come too? You've got loads of time to organize it. You could be a beater or whatever they're called." He stood, and made a swishing motion with his hand. "You never know, the sight of you with a long stick," he grinned, suggestively, "might do wonders for us . . ."

"Ugh. My idea of hell. Thanks, but I think I can think of other ways to spend my weekends than killing small feathered creatures."

"Pardon me, Linda McCartney. I'll turn the roast chicken loose, shall I?"

Suzanna motioned for a towel and got out of the bath, revealing barely an inch of flesh before she had covered herself.

"Look, you're the one who keeps accusing me of

being boring and predictable. Why are you attacking me for trying something new?"

"I just hate people trying to be what they're not. It's phony."

Neil stood before her, stooping to avoid bumping his head on the beams. "Suze, I'm getting tired of having to apologize for myself. For being me. For every bloody decision I make. Because at some point you're just going to have to accept that we live here now. This is our home. And if your brother invites me shooting or walking or bloody sheep shearing, it doesn't mean that I'm phony. It just means I'm trying to accept opportunities as they come. That I, at least, am trying to enjoy myself occasionally. Even if you're still determined to see the worst in bloody everything."

"Well, hooray for you, Farmer Giles." She couldn't think of a more intelligent way to respond.

There was a long silence.

"You know what?" said Neil, eventually. "If I'm really, really honest, I've been thinking that you having this shop is not doing us any good at all. I'm glad it's making you happy, and I didn't want to say anything because I know it means a lot to you, but for quite a while I've been thinking that it's not helping us."

He rubbed his hand through his hair, then looked her straight in the eyes. "And the funny thing is, I'm wondering all of a sudden whether it has anything to do with the shop at all."

Suzanna held his gaze for what seemed like an eternity. Then she brushed past him, and hurried down the narrow corridor into their bedroom, where she noisily began drying her hair, her eyes shut tightly against the tears.

Douglas found Vivi in the kitchen. She had forgotten that she had promised a couple of cakes for the Women's Institute sale on Saturday, and had roused herself reluctantly from the soporific comfort of television and sofa. "You're all floury," he said, glancing at her sweater.

He had been for a drink with one of the local grain wholesalers: she smelled beer and pipe smoke on him as he bent to kiss her on the cheek.

"Yes. I think it knows I hate baking." Vivi used the flat side of a knife to even out the mixture in the tin.

"Don't know why you don't buy the things from the supermarket. Much less fuss."

"The older ladies expect home-made. There would be all sorts of talk if I gave them shop-bought . . ." She gesticulated toward the range. "Your supper's in the bottom oven. I wasn't sure what time you'd be back."

"Sorry. Meant to phone. Not that hungry, to be honest. Filled up on crisps and peanuts and rubbish."

He opened the top cupboard, looking for a glass, then sat down heavily and poured himself some whiskey. "I daresay Ben will take a second helping."

Along the corridor, there was the sound of hissing as Rosemary's elderly cat was apparently ambushed by the terrier. They could hear his claws scrabbling along the flagstones, and skidding into another room. The kitchen was silent again, interrupted only by the steady tick of the Viennese wall clock her parents had given them at their wedding, one of their few presents: it hadn't been that kind of a wedding. "I saw Suzanna today," Vivi said, still smoothing the cake mixture. "She's rather frosty. But the shop was beautiful."

"I know."

"What?" Vivi's head shot up.

Douglas took a long drink of his whiskey. "I meant to tell you. I went to see her last week."

Vivi had been about to place the cake tin in the oven. She stopped. "She never said."

"Yes, Tuesday, I think it was . . . I thought this silly row had gone on too long." Douglas was holding his glass in both hands. They were wind-chapped and red-knuckled, even though high summer was fast approaching.

Vivi turned back to the oven, placed the tin inside, and closed the door carefully. "And did you sort things out?" She struggled to keep the dismay from her voice, to smother the ferocity of her feelings of exclusion. She knew she was being childish, but she didn't know what was hurting her most: that after all her attempts at bridge building, neither father nor daughter had thought to mention it to her; or, if she dared admit it to herself, the fact that it hadn't been just Douglas who had been in that shop before her. "Douglas?"

He paused, and she wondered, with a brief madness, how long he had gazed upon that image. "No," he said, eventually. "Not really."

He sighed, an unusually mournful sound, and glanced up at her, his expression fatigued and vulnerable. She knew he was half expecting her to put her arms around him, to say something soothing, assure him that he had done the right thing and his daughter would come around. But, just this once, Vivi didn't feel like it.

# 13

## The Day I Realized I Did Not Have to Be My Father

My whole life I do not think I ever saw my father without oiled hair. I never knew what its real color was: it was a kind of perpetual slick dark shell, separated into tiny furrows by the tortoiseshell comb that protruded from his back pocket. He was from Florence, my grandmother would say, as if that explained his vanity. Then again, my mother did not look like an Italian mama, not the way you English think of one. She was very slim, very beautiful, even into her later years. You can see them in this photograph. They look like something from a movie, too glamorous for a little village like ours. I do not think my mother ever cooked a meal in her life.

I was six when they first left me with my grandmother. They used to work in the City, which I was told repeatedly was a place not fit for a child. They took a variety of jobs, often linked to the lower end of the entertainment business, but never seemed to

make much money—or, at least, any more than
they needed to maintain their own beauty. They
sent back envelopes of **lire** for my upkeep—not
enough to keep the hens in corn, my grandfather
said dismissively. He grew or raised almost all our
food—the only way, he would say, slapping my back,
that he was going to grow himself a fine young man.

They would come back every six months or so
to see me. At first I would hide behind my grandmother's skirts, hardly knowing them, and my father
would tut and then pull faces at me behind her back.
My mother would croon to me, smoothing my hair
and scolding my grandmother for dressing me like
a peasant, while I lay against her chest, breathing in
her perfume, and wondering how two such exotic
creatures could have created a lumpen animal like
myself. That was how my father used to describe
me, pinching at my stomach, exclaiming at my
chins, and my mother would scold him, smiling,
but not at me. Some years I didn't know whether I
loved or hated them. I knew only that I could never
live up to what they had wanted of a son, that even
I was possibly the reason they kept going away.

"You mustn't mind them," my grandmother
would say. "The City has made them sharp as
knives."

Then, the year I turned fourteen, they returned
with nothing for my grandmother, nothing for my
upkeep. It was apparently the fifth time in a row.

I was not meant to know this, and was sent to my room, where I peered through the door, straining to hear the rapidly raised voices. My grandfather, losing his temper, accused my father of being a wastrel, my mother a prostitute. "You still have enough money to put this shit on your faces, the shine on your new shoes. Yet you are good for nothing," he said.

"I don't have to listen to this," said my father, lighting a cigarette.

"Yes, you do. Call yourself a father? You could not even kill a chicken to feed your own son."

"You think I could not kill a chicken?" said my father, and I could imagine him pulling himself up to his full height in his pin-striped suit.

The parlor door slammed. As I ran to the window, I could see my father striding out into the yard. After several attempts, and much squawking, he managed to grab Carmela, one of the older hens, who had long since stopped laying. Facing my grandfather, he snapped her neck, and casually threw her body across the yard toward him.

A silence descended, and suddenly I felt my father's gesture had been almost a threat. I saw in him something I hadn't seen before, something mean and impulsive. My grandmother had seen it too: she wrung her hands, imploring everyone to come inside, to drink some **grappa**.

My mother glanced nervously from her father to her husband, unsure who to try to placate first.

The air seemed to grow still.

Then with a strangulated squawking sound, Carmela appeared at my father's foot, her head a little tilted, her expression malevolent. She hesitated, wobbled, and then made her way unsteadily past him, across the yard and into the chicken house. No one said anything.

Then my grandmother pointed. "She crapped on your suit," she said.

My father looked down and found his sharply pressed trousers polluted by Carmela's last protest.

My mother, her hand pressed to her lips, began to giggle.

My grandfather, his head raised high, turned on his heel and walked back into the house, his dismissive "Huh!" hanging in the still air behind him. "Even your son can wring the neck of a chicken," he muttered.

After that my father returned very seldom. I didn't care. My grandfather taught me about meat, about the differences between **pancetta** and **prosciutto**, between **dolce latte** and **panna cotta**, how to make pâté studded with figs and sealed in goose fat. He never once mentioned my appearance. Ten years later I opened my first shop, and from that day it was my turn to feed him, which I did, with pleasure, until he died.

Carmela was the one chicken we never ate.

# 14

Liliane stuck the key in the door of the Unique Boutique at twenty minutes to ten. She glanced down and, having wedged open the door with her foot, bent and picked up the small box of gold-wrapped chocolates on the step. She looked closely at them, turned them over twice in her hands, then looked left and right down the lane, her long coat billowing in the brisk breeze. She could just make out the frontage of Arturro's deli. She waited a moment more, and then, holding the chocolates along with her handbag, close to her chest, she pushed her way into her shop.

Across the road, from their vantage point behind Arturro's display, Suzanna and Jessie looked at each other. Then they burst into a fit of childish giggles.

The box of gold chocolates was the fourth gift they had left on the steps of the Unique Boutique: once a week was what they had decided. Any more would look obvious, any less and it might appear accidental. Suzanna and Jessie had developed all sorts of ploys to draw Liliane and Arturro into each other's company. When Liliane's handbag shelf fell down, they persuaded Arturro to pop over to mend it, telling him that she had so admired the work he had done in his own store. They had dropped hints about oil being good for arthritis, so that Liliane popped into the deli to pick up a bottle for her mother. They manufactured reasons—suddenly scrubbing tables, or whipping away chairs to be "fixed," why the two should be seated together when they came in for coffee. And occasionally they were rewarded: they would catch them glancing at each other with a kind of shy pleasure, or being startled if they dropped in at the Peacock Emporium and found the other already present. It was working, they told each other in gleeful whispers.

At Dere House, Vivi was preoccupied with culinary matters of her own: she had become haunted by Rosemary's fridge. Over recent weeks, she had discovered, among the liquefying vegetables and old medicine bottles, several discarded yogurts beside open packs of bacon, and raw chicken on plates, dripping blood into the open milk carton below. The words "listeria" and "salmonella" took on a horrible resonance, and Vivi found herself jumping anxiously when Rosemary talked of making herself "a little sandwich" or having a snack.

She had wanted to talk to Douglas about it, but

he had been rather dour and uncommunicative since the thing with Suzanna, and with the hay making he was out often till nine in the evening. She had considered whether any of her friends from the village might help, but she wasn't close enough to anyone for that level of confidence: she had never been one of those women who surrounded themselves with a "circle," and with the Fairley-Hulme name being what it was around here, any admission of difficulties at home seemed a kind of disloyalty. Vivi would watch the morning talk shows, with young people who thought nothing of revealing the most intimate details of their sex lives, or their problems with drugs or alcohol, and marvel. How, in the space of a generation, could we have been transported from an age in which everything had to stay within one's four walls to a point at which that attitude is now considered unhealthy? In the end, she called her daughter Lucy, who listened with the analytical detachment that had made her such a success in her job, then told her that Rosemary was getting to the age when she needed to go into a home.

"I wouldn't even suggest that to your father," said Vivi, in hushed tones, as if from the distance of the forty-acre field Douglas could somehow hear her treachery.

"You're going to have to do something," said Lucy. "Salmonella's a killer. A home help?"

Vivi didn't like to confess the little matter of the Incontinence Lady. "It's just that she's so stubborn. She doesn't even like it when I go into her kitchen. I have to make up all sorts of excuses for why I've replaced her food."

"She should be grateful."

"Well, yes, darling, but you know that word's not in Rosemary's vocabulary."

"It's a tough one. Can you not just put cling film over everything?"

"I tried that, but she decided to reuse it. She put the stuff from the chicken round a big lump of cheddar and I had to throw the whole thing out."

"Just tell her she's causing a health hazard."

"I did try, darling. Really. But she gets so cross, and won't listen. She just waves her hand at me and storms off."

"She probably knows," said Lucy, ruminatively. "That she's losing her marbles, I mean."

Vivi sighed. "Yes. Yes, I suppose she does."

"It would make me angry. And Granny's never been exactly a . . . benign character."

"No."

"D'you want me to have a word?"

"With whom?"

"I don't know. Granny? Dad? It sometimes comes easier when there's a gap between generations."

"You could try, dear, but I don't know what good

it will do. Your father's a bit . . . well, I think he's had enough of dealing with family problems at the moment."

"What do you mean?"

Vivi paused, feeling disloyal again. "Oh. You know. This silly thing with Suzanna."

"You're joking. They're not still harping on about that?"

"She's really rather hurt. And I'm afraid they've got to that awful stage where they can't say anything without making it worse."

"Oh, for God's sake, I can't believe they haven't sorted things out. Hold on a minute." Vivi heard the sound of muffled conversation, and a rapid agreement. Then her daughter's voice was back on the line. "Come on, Mum. You've got to put an end to this. They're behaving like a pair of idiots. They're as stubborn as each other."

"But what can I do?"

"I don't know. Bang their heads together. You can't let this drag on. You're going to have to make the first move. Look, Mum, I've got to go. I'm due in a meeting. Ring me tonight, okay? Let me know what you decide about Granny."

She was gone before Vivi had a chance to whisper her love. She sat, staring at the distantly humming receiver, and felt the familiar swell of inadequacy. So, why is this my responsibility? Vivi thought crossly. Why do I have to sort everybody out, or suffer the consequences? What is it exactly that I ever did?

Nadine and Alistair Palmer were splitting up. As the evenings grew lighter, Suzanna's quiet hours between closing the shop and before Neil came home—the time when she habitually pored over receipts at the kitchen table, sipping a glass of wine—had been increasingly interrupted by Nadine's telephone calls: "If he thinks I'm letting the children go for a whole weekend he's gone quite mad . . . You know, the lawyer thinks I should go for the holiday home too . . . I did decorate it, even if it is shared with his brother . . ."

At first she had been flattered to hear from her—for some time she had thought that Nadine, who still lived in London, had forgotten her. Several weeks later, she was exhausted by the calls, by the never-ending tales of postmarital injustice, and the myriad examples of pettiness to which once-loving couples could sink in their desire to punish each other.

"I can't tell you how lonely it is at night . . . I hear all sorts of noises . . . My mother thinks I should get a dog, but who's going to walk it now that I have to go to work?"

Nadine and Alistair had been the first among their circle to marry, only six weeks before Suzanna and Neil. They had honeymooned in the same part of France. Recently Nadine had asked three times whether she and Neil were okay, as if desperate for reassurance that she wasn't alone in her misery. Suzanna never said much more than "Fine." At first she had been rather shaken, but Nadine and Alistair were now the fourth couple among their old friends to have divorced, and she was less disturbed—perhaps less surprised—each time.

"He says he doesn't fancy me anymore. Not since the children. I told him, frankly, I haven't fancied him for years, but that's not what marriage is all about, is it?"

Of course, on her better days Suzanna knew this wasn't the case for everybody, that there were marriages where children cemented things and were a source of joy. In fact, she was never sure whether her friends had emphasized to her all the bad things about motherhood—the sleepless nights, the ruined bodies, the plastic toys and puke—out of a kind of misplaced sympathy that she hadn't yet embarked upon it. But, perversely, listening to Nadine weep about the prospect of her two young children spending time with Daddy's girlfriend, at the silence of a house on waking up without them, made her keenly aware that among the domestic trivia, mundanity, and pettiness, there was a deep and jealous passion. And something about that passion—even in the depths of Nadine's grief—set against her own carefully constructed lukewarm life, had begun to appeal.

The first time Neil met Suzanna, she had served him sushi. She had been working in a restaurant in Soho, and, having discovered that the mixture of raw fish and rice was almost fat free, was subsisting on it and Marlboro Lights in an attempt to drop down a dress size. (These days, she wondered why she hadn't spent her twenties wandering around in a bikini instead of fretting about nonexistent cellulite.) Neil had come in with clients. Having grown up in Cheam, with the uncomplicated rugby-club diet of the public-school boy, he had gamely tried everything she suggested, and only confessed to Suzanna afterward that if anyone else had tried to make him eat raw sea urchin he would have put them in a headlock.

He was tall, broad, and handsome, just a few years older than her, and bore the kind of sheen on his skin that spoke of a City salary and frequent trips abroad. He had tipped her almost thirty percent, and she had acknowledged that this gesture was not for the benefit of his companions. She had observed him across the table, listened to his whispered confession, conscious that a willingness to experiment in matters of appetite might suggest an openmindedness in other areas.

Neil, she discovered, over successive months, was

focused, uncomplicated, and, unlike her previous, only occasionally faithful boyfriends, utterly reliable. He bought her the things a boyfriend theoretically should—regular flowers, perfume after trips abroad, occasional weekends away, and, at appropriate intervals, impressively sized engagement, wedding, and eternity rings. Her parents loved him. Her friends eyed him speculatively, several with a sly persistence that told her he would never be alone for long. His flat had French windows that over-looked Barnes Bridge. He slotted into her life with an ease that convinced her they were meant to be together.

They had married young. Too young, her parents had worried, knowing nothing of her busy romantic history. She had batted away their concerns with the certainty of someone who knew themselves to be adored, who knew of no gaps for doubt to nestle in. She looked stunning in her cream silk dress.

If, later, she wondered whether she would ever again feel that first flush of excitement, that tingling anticipation for the sexual attention of another, she could usually rationalize it away. It was in-evitable that one would wish occasionally for a taste of the exotic. With a man who now frequently felt more like an irritating older brother than a lover, it was obvious that she would cast the odd covet-ous glance elsewhere. She, of all people, knew that shopping around could be addictive.

Ever since the row about the shooting, Neil had been withdrawn. Nothing was obviously wrong, just a cooling in their domestic climate. In some ways, Suzanna realized, it was the best thing he could have done. She was always better when she had to work for his attention. So, although Neil might initially have thought otherwise, things for them had been improving, even if only in increments.

Perhaps Neil knew it too, and perhaps that was why, for her birthday, he had brought her to London for sushi.

"I'll eat anything you throw at me," Neil had said, "as long as you don't make me eat one of those puddings."

"The pink testicles?"

"That's the one." Neil wiped his mouth with a napkin. "D'you remember when you made me eat one in Chinatown, and I had to spit it out in my gym bag?"

She smiled, pleased that the memory didn't carry with it any revulsion or irritation.

"It's the texture. I fail to understand how anyone can eat something the consistency of a pillow."

"But you eat marshmallows."

"Different. Somehow nothing testicular about them."

It had been the first evening she could remember when they had talked freely, without a second, silent conversation full of recrimination running under the surface. She had wondered, privately, whether it was just the pleasure of being in Central London, before deciding that most of her troubles were to do with analyzing things too much. A short memory and a sense of humor, that was what her grandmother had said were necessary for a successful marriage. Even if she herself had never displayed the evidence of either.

"You look nice," he had said, watching her over the green tea. And she had been able to forgive him the use of such a vapid word.

At ten fifteen, as they walked through a balmy, bustling Leicester Square, he had told her that they were not returning to Dere Hampton that night. "Why?" she had said, shouting over the Hare Krishnas and their tambourines. "Where are we going?"

"A surprise," he said. "Because we're doing better financially. Because you work so hard. And because my wife deserves a treat." And he had walked her to a discreetly luxurious hotel in Covent Garden, where the very window boxes spoke of good taste and the kind of attention that would guarantee a good night's stay, even if Suzanna had not already been brimming with pleasure at the way her evening was turning out. And in their room was an overnight bag that he had apparently packed that morning and spirited away. He had only forgotten her moisturizer.

Passion, in marriage, ebbed and flowed. Everyone said it. If, for a change, she gave him her full attention, if she tried to push aside all the things that annoyed her, that persisted in creeping in and polluting her finer feelings; if she tried to focus on the things that were good, then it wasn't impossible that they could recover it. "I love you," she had said, and felt a huge relief that, even after everything, she still meant it.

He had held her tightly then and, unusually for him, stayed silent.

At eleven fifteen, as they sipped room-service champagne, he had turned to face her, the coverlet slipping down his bare skin. She noted how pale he was. Their first year without a foreign holiday. In fifteen months he was going to be forty, he said.

And?

He had always wanted to be a dad before he was forty.

She said nothing.

And, he was thinking, if it took an average eighteen months to get pregnant, shouldn't they start trying now? He just wanted to be a dad, he said quietly. To have a family of his own. He had put down his glass and held her face between two warm hands. He looked a little apprehensive, as if he were aware that broaching this subject might breach the terms of their deal, that he might fracture the fragile peace that had made the evening magical.

But then, he hadn't known he was asking her something she had already decided. She had said nothing, but lay back, placing her own glass on the opposite table.

"You don't have to be afraid," he said softly.

In the blur of the champagne, she felt a little like a fish on dry land. Breathing, gasping, but somehow, finally, accepting of her fate.

Vivi walked up the hallway, puffing under the combined weight of her shopping bags, musing that her son was never in when she needed him. Reaching the kitchen, she allowed them to drop and held up her hands in the fading light to examine the red welts the handles had carved into her fleshy palms.

Douglas and Ben had failed to move their empty tea mugs from the table to the sink, so Vivi, who no longer sighed in resignation at the sight of their mess, did it for them. She swept up the crumby souvenirs of their lunch, stuck the plates in the dishwasher, and tidied scattered papers into piles. When she was unpacking the groceries on the kitchen table, she made out Rosemary's imperious tones in the drawing room, where she was in muffled conversation with Douglas. She considered popping her head around the door to say hello, but realized, guiltily, that she would rather have the extra five minutes by herself. She glanced up at the clock and noted, with a small stab of pleasure, that she could still catch the last few minutes of **The Archers.** "We'll just enjoy a bit of peace, won't we, Mungo?"

The terrier, hearing its name, trembled in stillness as it gazed intently at her, waiting in a state of permanent anticipation for some culinary scrap to fall.

"No luck, darling boy," said Vivi, placing the various meat products in the freezer. "I happen to know you've had yours."

When **The Archers** finished, Vivi stood for a moment, gazing out of the window as she had while she listened. The kitchen garden was at its best at this time of year, the herbs sending dusty waves of fragrance into the house, the lavender, campanula, and lobelia bulging from the old raised-brick beds, the creepers and climbers, dead brown skeletons in winter, now a riot of vigorous green. Rosemary had built this garden when she was first married: it was one of the few things for which Vivi felt uncomplicatedly grateful to her. For a while, she had thought Suzanna would take an interest in it: she had the same eye as Rosemary, a skill for arranging things so they were at their most beautiful.

She was inhaling the scent of the evening primrose and listening to the lazy drone of the bees when she detected that, over the gentle sounds of approaching evening, Rosemary's voice had taken on an unusually combative note. Douglas's was softer, as if he was reasoning with her. Vivi wondered, in vague discomfort, whether they were discussing her. Perhaps Rosemary had still not been forgiven for the aborted visit of the Incontinence Lady.

She turned from the window and placed the chops on the stovetop. She rubbed her hands on her apron and, with a heavy heart, walked toward the door.

"I can't believe you're even considering it."

Rosemary was seated on the nursing chair, even though she often had trouble getting out of it. Her hands were folded stiffly in her lap, and her face, set in anger, was turned away from her son as if she was refusing physically to acknowledge what he had to say. As she closed the door behind her, Vivi noted that her mother-in-law had buttoned her blouse lopsidedly, and was grieved that she could not mention it to her.

Douglas was standing by the piano, a tumbler of whiskey in his hand. To the left of him, the grandfather clock that had been in the family since Cyril Fairley-Hulme's birth offered up a discreetly regular quarter-chime. "I have given this plenty of thought, Mother."

"That may well be, Douglas, but I've said this to you before, you do not necessarily know what's best for this estate."

A faint smile played about his lips. "The last time

we had this conversation, Mother, I was twenty-seven years old."

"I'm well aware of that. And you had a head full of foolish ideas then too."

"I just don't think it makes financial sense for Ben to inherit the entire estate. It's not just about tradition, it's about finance."

"Would somebody like to fill me in as to what's going on?" Vivi's gaze flicked from her husband to her mother-in-law, who was still gazing mulishly toward the French windows. She tried to smile, but stopped when she realized no one else was.

"I had a few ideas I thought I should discuss with Mother—"

"And while I'm alive, Douglas, and I have a say in the running of this estate, then things will stay exactly as they are."

"I'm only suggesting that some—"

"I know very well what you're suggesting. You've said it enough times. And I'm telling you the answer is no."

"The answer to what?" Vivi moved closer to her husband.

"I refuse even to discuss this further, Douglas. You know very well your father had firm views on these things."

"And I'm sure Father would not have wanted to see anyone in this family made unhappy by—"

"No. No, I will not have it." Rosemary placed her

hands on her knees. "Now, Vivi, when is supper? I thought we were eating at seven thirty, and I'm sure it's past that already."

"Will one of you please tell me what you are discussing?"

Douglas placed his glass on the top of the piano. "I had some thoughts. About changing my will. About perhaps setting up some sort of trust that gives the children equal say in the running of the estate. Perhaps even before my death. But . . ."—his voice lowered—". . . Mother is unhappy about the idea of it."

"Equal say? For all three?" Vivi stared at her husband.

Douglas shrugged, his weathered face offering Vivi a complicit exasperation. "I tried. I can't say I've felt entirely happy about how things are."

"You tried?"

Rosemary struggled to lift herself from the chair, her weight resting on bony arms. Then she fell back and let out a grunt of irritation. "Do you have to ignore me? Douglas? I need your arm. Your **arm**."

"Does that mean you're just going to give in?"

"It's not giving in, old thing. I just don't want to make things worse than they already are." Douglas moved toward his mother and placed his arm under hers to elevate her.

"How can they be worse than they already are?"

"It's Mother's decision too, Vee. We all live here."

Rosemary, on her feet, tried, with some effort, to straighten herself. "Your dog," she announced, looking directly at Vivi, "has been on my bed. I've found hairs."

"You have to remember to keep your door shut, Rosemary," she said quietly, still staring at Douglas. "But that would solve everything, darling. Suzanna would be so much happier. All she needs is to feel equal. She doesn't actually want to run the thing. And the others wouldn't mind—I don't think they've ever been comfortable with the plans."

"I know, but—"

"Enough," said Rosemary, making her way toward the door. "Enough. I would like my supper now. I do not want to discuss this matter any further."

Douglas reached out a hand to Vivi's arm. His touch felt light, insubstantial. "Sorry, old thing. I tried."

As Rosemary passed her, Vivi found her breath had become tight in her chest. She watched Douglas turn to open the door for his mother and recognized that, as far as they were both concerned, the conversation was already over, the issue closed. Suddenly she heard her voice, loud enough to make Rosemary turn in her tracks, and uncharacteristically angry. "Well, I hope you'll both be terribly pleased with yourselves," she said, "when you've alienated the poor girl completely."

It was several seconds before her words registered with them.

"What?" said Rosemary, who was clutching Douglas's arm.

"Well, we've never told her the truth, have we? Don't look at me like that. No one's told her the truth about her mother. And then we wonder why she's grown up confused and resentful." Finally she had their full attention. "I've had just about enough—of all of it. Douglas, either you make her your heir or introduce some kind of equal trust, or you tell her the truth about her mother." She was breathing hard.

A brief silence followed. Then Rosemary lifted her head and began to speak, as if to someone mentally impaired: "Vivi," she said, deliberately, "this is not what this family does—"

"Rosemary," Vivi interrupted, "in case it has escaped your notice, I **am** this family. I am the person who makes the meals, who irons the clothes, who keeps the house clean, and who has done so for the last thirty years. I **am** the bloody family."

Douglas's mouth had opened fractionally. But she didn't care. It was as if a kind of madness had infected her. "That's right. I am the person who washes your dirty smalls, who is the butt of everyone else's bad moods, who cleans up after everyone else's pets, the person who does their best to try to hold the whole bloody thing together. I am this family.

I may have been Douglas's second choice, but that doesn't mean I'm second best—"

"No one ever said you—"

"And I deserve an opinion. **I—too—deserve—an—opinion.**" Her breath came in gasps, tears pricking her eyes. "Now, Suzanna is my daughter, as much as she is anybody's, and I am sick, **sick**, I tell you, of having **my** family divided over something as trivial as a house and a few acres of bloody land. It's unimportant. Yes, Rosemary, compared to my children's happiness, to my happiness, it really is unimportant. So there, Douglas, I've said it. You make Suzanna an equal heir, or you tell her the bloody truth." She reached behind her to untie her apron strings, wrenched it over her head, and tossed it onto the arm of the sofa.

"And don't call me 'old thing,'" she said, to her husband. "I really, really don't like it." Then, under the stunned gaze of her husband and mother-in-law, Vivi Fairley-Hulme walked past the kitchen, where Rosemary's elderly cat was making a youthful stab at the lamb chops, and out into the evening sun.

# 15

In Suzanna's teenage years, on days like these, Vivi would have described her as having woken up feeling "a bit complicated." It was nothing one could put one's finger on, the result of no tangible misfortune, but she had started her day with an invisible cloud hanging over her, a sense that her universe was askew and that she was only a hair's breadth from bursting into tears. On such days one could usually guarantee that inanimate objects would rise to the occasion: a piece of bread had got wedged in the toaster, and she had shocked herself trying to get it out with a fork; Neil had failed to put the rubbish out, as he'd promised. Today she had bumped into Liliane in the delicatessen when she'd nipped in to buy a box of sugared almonds, as suggested by Jessie for the next "love token," and been forced to whip them into her bag like a shoplifter. She, theoretically, became one when she left the shop having forgotten to pay for them. And when she finally arrived at the Emporium she had been ambushed by Mrs. Creek, who asked if Suzanna could donate some of her "bric-a-brac" for one of the pensioners' jumble sales.

"I don't have any bric-a-brac," she had said pointedly.

"You can't tell me all of this stuff is for sale," said Mrs. Creek, staring at the display on the back wall.

Mrs. Creek had then segued effortlessly into a story about dinner dances in Ipswich and how, as a teenage girl, she had supplemented her parents' income by sewing dresses for her friends. "You know, when the fashion first came out, people here were scandalized. We'd spent years scrimping on fabric during the war, you see. There was nothing. Lots of us went out dancing in dresses we'd made from our own curtains."

"Really," said Suzanna, flicking on switches and wondering why Jessie was late.

"The first one I ever made was in emerald silk. Gorgeous color, ever so rich. It looked like one of Yul Brynner's outfits in **The King and I**."

"Are you having coffee?"

"That's very kind of you, dear. I don't mind keeping you company." She sat on the seat near the magazines, looking inside her bag. "I've got photographs somewhere, of me and my sister. We used to share dresses then. Waists that you could stick your hands around." She breathed out. "Men's hands, that is. Of course, you had to nearly suffocate yourself with corsetry to get the look, but girls will always suffer to be beautiful, won't they?"

"Mm," said Suzanna, remembering to take the sugared almonds from her bag, and place them under the counter. Jessie could take them over later. If she ever decided to turn up.

"She's got a colostomy now, poor thing."

"What?"

"My sister. Crohn's disease. Causes her terrible trouble, it does. You have to make sure you don't bump into anyone, you know what I'm saying?"

"I think so," said Suzanna, trying to concentrate on measuring coffee.

"Sorry I'm late," said Jessie. She was dressed in cut-off jeans, with lavender-colored sunglasses on her head, looking summery and almost unbearably pretty. She was followed closely behind by Alejandro, who stooped as he entered. "His fault," she explained cheerfully. "He needed directing to the good butcher's. He's been a bit shocked by the state of the supermarket meat."

"It is shocking, that supermarket," said Mrs. Creek. "Do you know how much I paid the other day for a bit of pork belly?"

"I'm sorry," said Alejandro, who had registered Suzanna's set mouth. "It's hard for me to discover these things on my own. My shift hours never match anyone else's." His eyes held a mute appeal that made Suzanna feel both appeased and irritated.

"I'll make up the extra minutes," said Jessie, shedding her bag under the counter. "I've been hearing all about Argentinian steak. Tougher, apparently, but tastier."

"It's fine," Suzanna said. "Doesn't matter." She wished she hadn't seen the look that had passed between them.

"Double espresso?" said Jessie, moving behind the coffee machine. Alejandro nodded, seating himself at the small table beside the counter. Suzanna wished she hadn't worn these trousers. They picked up lint and fluff, and the cut, she saw, made them look cheap.

"We don't really eat meat," Jessie was saying. "Not during the week, anyway. Apart from chicken it's too expensive. But I do love roast beef. For Sunday lunch."

"One day I will find you some good Argentinian beef," Alejandro said. "We let our animals get older. You will know the difference."

"I thought old steers were meant to get stringy," said Suzanna, and immediately regretted it.

"But you tenderize your meat, dear," said Mrs. Creek. "You beat it with a wooden thing."

"If the meat is good," said Alejandro, "it should not need beating."

"You'd think the cow had been through enough."

"Beef dripping," said Mrs. Creek. "Now there's something you never see in the shops anymore."

"Can we talk about something else?" Suzanna was starting to feel queasy. "Jessie, have you finished that coffee?"

"You never told us"—Jessie turned to Alejandro, leaning over the counter—"about your life before you came here."

"Not much to tell," said Alejandro.

"Like why you wanted to be a midwife. I mean, no offense, but it's not a normal profession for a bloke, is it?"

"What is normal?"

"But you'd have to be pretty comfortable with your feminine side in a macho country like Argentina to do what you do. So why do you do it?"

Alejandro took his cup of coffee, and dropped two sugar cubes into the thick black liquid. "You are wasted in a shop, Jessie. You should be a psychotherapist. In my home it's the most prestigious job you can have. Next to a plastic surgeon, of course . . ."

Which was, Suzanna thought, as she began to unpack a new box of bags, a pretty neat way of not answering the question.

"I was just telling Suzanna I used to make dresses. Have I shown you these ones?" Mrs. Creek held out a fan of battered photographs.

"They're beautiful," said Jessie, obligingly. "Aren't you clever?"

"And what did you do, Suzanna, before you opened this shop?" His voice, with its strong accent, was low and comforting. She could imagine how it would be consoling to hear in childbirth. "Who were you in your past life?"

"The same person I am now," she said, aware that she didn't believe what she was saying. "I've got to nip out and pick up some more milk."

"No one is the same person forever," insisted Jessie.

"I was the same . . . but with less strong views on people minding their own business," she said, and slammed the till drawer.

"I come here for the atmosphere, you know," Mrs. Creek confided to Alejandro.

"Are you all right, Suzanna?" Jessie leaned over to get a better view of her expression.

"Fine. Just busy, okay? There's a lot to do today."

Jessie caught the implicit criticism and winced. "That fish," she said to Alejandro, as Suzanna shoved the mugs on the shelf around unnecessarily, "the one you used to catch with your dad, the peacock something."

"Peacock bass?"

"It's known for being really grumpy, right?"

Mrs. Creek coughed quietly into her coffee.

There was a short pause.

"I think maybe it has to be grumpy, as you call it, to survive in its environment," said Alejandro, innocently.

Suzanna threw a flashing glance their way, and closed the shop door hard behind her. They watched her striding up the lane, head down, as if walking into a fierce wind.

Father Lenny walked down Water Lane, turned left, and nodded through the window at the occupants of the Peacock Emporium and, on seeing Jessie's cheerful face, waved vigorously. He thought back to the conversation he had had earlier that morning.

It was Cath Carter who had initially sought his advice. Cath now had, on several occasions, invited him over supposedly to offer him tea and have a "catch-up," but really to solicit his opinion on her daughter's ever-burgeoning collection of bruises and "accidental" knocks. It wasn't like she hadn't a temper herself, she said, and she'd be a liar if she said she and Ed had never come to blows in all their years together, but this was different. And whenever she had tried to broach the subject with Jessie, she snapped at her to mind her own business, or words to that effect. There wasn't much he could offer. Cath believed Jessie would be offended if she thought they were discussing her, so he wasn't allowed to approach her. It wasn't serious enough, she said, to call the police. In the old days, when

Lenny was growing up, a couple of the older men would go around and rough the boy up a little, just to let him know they were on to him. Most of the time it worked. But there was no Ed Carter around anymore, and there was no way Cath or Jessie would want social services involved. So his hands were tied.

Until he turned up on his doorstep. The boy— for he was still a boy, no matter what maturity he thought paternity had conferred—had come to deliver a storage heater to the presbytery. Because no one had said anything, after all, about the two of **them** having a discreet word.

"You enjoying your new job, eh?"

"It's not bad, Father. Regular hours . . . Pay could be better."

"Ah, now, there's a universal truth."

The boy had looked at him, as if struggling to gauge his meaning, then lifted the heater with formidable ease, and carried it, as directed, into the front room, where he ignored the boxes of discount crockery and alarm clocks stacked high against the walls, partially obscuring two Virgin Marys and a St. Sebastian. "You want me to put it together for you? It'll take me five minutes."

"That would be grand. I have no gift with a screwdriver. Shall I go and find one?"

"Got me own." The boy had held it up, and Lenny had been suddenly uncomfortably aware of the strength in those shoulders, the potential force behind these currently contained movements.

The irony was that he was not a bad lad: generally well thought of, polite, brought up on the good part of the estate. And while not churchgoers, his parents were decent people. And the boy had never been in any trouble, had not been one of those he would occasionally scoop up from the market square in the early hours of Sunday, semiconscious from cheap cider and God only knew what else.

But that didn't mean he was **good**.

He stood, watching, as the metal legs were forcefully tightened to the body of the thing, the screws and nuts tightened with a spare efficiency. Then, as the boy prepared to right it, Lenny spoke: "So, how's your woman enjoying her new job?"

The boy did not raise his face from his work. "She says she likes it."

"It's a nice shop. Good to see something different in the town."

The boy grunted.

"And good for her to be earning some money, no doubt. Every little helps, these days."

"We did all right before she started there." The boy placed the heater upright on the rug.

"I'm sure you did."

Outside, two cars had come to an impasse in the road behind the churchyard. "Must be hard work for her."

The boy looked up, uncomprehending.

"It's obviously a more physical job than it looks." Lenny kept the boy's eyes, trying to look more at ease than he felt. He chose his words carefully, and delivered them slowly. "Must be, anyway, considering the number of injuries I hear she's been getting." He let the aftershock kick like a mule.

The boy started, glanced away from the priest and back again, his eyes flickering with discomfort. Then he bent and picked up his screwdriver, placing it in his top pocket. Although his face betrayed little emotion, the tips of his ears had flushed a deep red. "I'd best be off," he muttered. "Got other deliveries."

"I'm very grateful to you."

He walked down the narrow corridor after him. "You go easy on her now," Father Lenny continued, seeing the boy out. "She's a good girl. I know that with the support of a man like yourself she can find a way to hurt herself a little less often."

Jason turned to face Father Lenny. His expression was both hurt and furious, his shoulders hunched forward. "It's not what you—"

"Of course."

"I love Jess—"

"I know you do. And there are always ways to avoid these things, aren't there?"

The boy said nothing. He breathed out, as if he had considered, then decided against speaking. His walk, when he headed out to his van, contained a defiant hint of swagger.

"Because we wouldn't want the whole town concerned about her, after all?" the priest called, waving as the van door slammed and the vehicle skidded out of the driveway.

There were occasions on which he felt a longing for a larger life, broader horizons, as he turned back toward his neglected, long-undecorated house. But sometimes, Lenny thought, with some satisfaction, there were indeed benefits to living in a very small town.

Liliane MacArthur waited until the young men had disappeared across the square, their bags slung carelessly over their shoulders. Then, peering into the shop to ensure that she would be alone, she pushed open the door tentatively and walked in.

Arturro was busy at the back. At the sound of the bell he called that he would only be a minute, and she stood awkwardly in the center of the shop, sandwiched between the preserves and the dried pasta, smoothing her hair.

When he emerged, drying his hands on his large white apron, his face broke into a broad smile. "Liliane!" The way he said her name made it sound like someone announcing a toast.

She nearly smiled back, until she remembered why she was there. She reached into her bag and pulled out the box of sugared almonds. "I—I just wanted to say thank you . . . for the chocolates and everything. But it's starting to feel like too much."

Arturro looked blank. He gazed at the box in her hand, which she proffered to him, his own hand rising obediently to take it from her.

She pointed up at the chocolates on the shelf, keeping her voice low as if she were shielding it from other customers. "You're a very kind man, Arturro. And . . . it's been . . . well, I don't get many surprises. And it's been very kind of you. But I—I'd like it to stop now."

She held her handbag tight against her side, as if it was supporting her. "You see, I'm not sure what you . . . what you're expecting from me. I have to look after my mother, you see. I can't—there are no circumstances in which I'd be able to leave her alone."

Arturro moved a step closer to her. He ran a hand through his hair.

"I thought it only fair to let you know. I've been very touched, though. I wanted you to know that."

His voice, when it came, was thick, unwieldy. "I'm sorry, Liliane . . ."

She raised a fluttering hand, her expression anguished. "Oh, no. I don't want you to be sorry—I just . . ."

". . . but I don't understand."

There was a lengthy silence.

"The chocolates? All the gifts?"

He kept looking at her expectantly.

She studied his face now. "You left me chocolates? Outside my door?" Her voice was insistent.

He stared at the box in his hand. "They are from here . . . yes."

Liliane flushed. She glanced down at the box, then back at him. "It wasn't you? You didn't send any of these?"

He shook his head slowly.

Liliane's hand had lifted unconsciously to her mouth. She gazed around the shop, then wheeled toward the door. "Oh! Forgive me. I'm . . . Just a misunderstanding. Do—please, please forget what I said—" And then, her bag still clutched to her like a life raft, she ran from the delicatessen, her heels clattering on the wooden floor.

For some minutes Arturro stood in the middle of the empty shop, staring at the box of sugared almonds, the faintest remnant of her scent hanging in the air. He glanced at the nearly empty market square as the last of the delivery vans prepared to leave.

Then he looked up at the three white aprons recently abandoned on the hook by the door, and his face darkened.

A few hundred yards away, Suzanna was preparing to close the Peacock Emporium. Jessie had left almost half an hour previously, and she had been a little disconcerted to note that Alejandro had not gone with her. He was still there, having written a series of postcards and now reading a newspaper. He occasionally gazed out into the lane, his thoughts apparently far away.

For some reason, his presence had made Suzanna accident-prone. She had dropped a colored-glass vase just as she was about to hand it over to a customer and been forced to replace it, free of charge, with another. She had tripped up the last two steps into the cellar and half twisted her ankle. She had scalded herself twice on the coffee machine. If he had noticed any of this, he had said nothing. He just sipped at his coffee slowly.

"Don't you have anywhere to go to?" she asked, when there was nobody else left in the shop.

"You would like me to leave?"

Suzanna corrected herself, blushing at her transparency: "No—I'm sorry. I just wondered what was home for you."

He frowned at the window. "No place I want to spend much time in."

He had a woman's eyelashes: dark, curly, and silky. She hadn't noticed until now. "Does the hospital provide accommodation?"

"Not at first."

She waited.

"Then they discovered that many of the landlords around here do not want 'foreigners' as tenants." He smiled, raised an eyebrow at her concern, as if waiting for her to stumble over a long-held truth. "You, Suzanna, are one of the few people I have met here who is neither blond nor blue-eyed."

The way he looked at her made her flush. She pushed herself back from the counter and began to align the jars that held colored buttons, magnets, and boxes of pins, into rigid lines.

"It's fine. I got accommodation at the hospital."

Outside, the town had settled into a late-afternoon torpor. Its mothers had shepherded small charges home, and were now bracing themselves for the evening onslaught of tea, bath, and bed. Pensioners were transporting string bags or shopping trolleys with vegetables in paper bags from the market, single portions of brisket or meat pie.

Suzanna gazed around the interior of her shop, and felt weighed down by its carefully contrived perfection, its stasis. "How can you stand it here?" she asked.

"How can I stand what?" He had looked at her then, his head tilted to one side.

"After Buenos Aires. The small-townism. Like you say, landlords afraid of you because you're **different**."

He frowned, trying to understand.

"The way everyone has an opinion on everything and feels entitled to know your business. Don't you miss the city? Don't you miss the freedom of it?"

Alejandro put down his empty coffee cup. "I think perhaps you and I have different ideas about freedom."

She felt suddenly self-conscious and naïve. She knew nothing about Argentina, except the vague snippets she remembered from the television news: some riots, some financial crisis. Madonna as Eva Perón. God, she thought. And I accuse everyone else of being insular.

Alejandro stooped to pick up his backpack from under his table. He glanced out of the window, which was still glowing with refracted evening sun.

Something welled inside Suzanna. "She lives with someone, you know."

"Who?" He was still stooped over his bag.

"Jessie."

He hardly missed a beat. "I know."

She turned and started scrubbing the sink, furious and ashamed.

"I am no threat to Jessie."

It was a strange thing to say, made more so by the emphatic way in which he said it, as if he was trying to convince himself.

"I didn't mean . . . I'm sorry." Her head dipped toward the sink. She fought the urge then to tell him about Jason, to explain, to try to redress the childish jealousy she'd shown. She didn't want him to see her as everyone else seemed to. But to explain Jessie's relationship would put her among the very people she'd been criticizing—those who traded each other's domestic secrets as a kind of social currency.

"I hated living here, until I got this shop," she said. "I was a city girl. I like noise, bustle, anonymity. It's too hard to live in the place where you grew up—a small town like this. Everyone knows everything about you—your parents, where you went to school, where you've worked, who you've been out with. How you fell off the piano stool in your school recital."

She could feel him watching her, and the words tumbled out, unstoppable, while in some distant, sane part of her mind she wondered why she felt this desperate need to fill the silence.

"And, you see, because they know the things that have happened to you—some of them, at least—it means that people think they know you. There's no room for you to be someone else. Around here, I'm the same person I was at twelve, thirteen, sixteen. Set in aspic. And the funny thing is, I know I'm someone else entirely."

She stopped, her hands resting on the sides of the sink, and shook her head slightly. She had sounded ridiculous, even to herself.

"Anyway. The shop has changed all that," she

said. "Because even if I can't be someone else, the shop can. It can be anything I want it to be. Nobody has any expectations of it. I know it's not everyone's idea of a commercial venture. I know a lot of people around here think it's daft. But it's got a—" She wasn't sure what she was trying to say.

A car reversed slowly up the lane.

"I have seen her at the hospital," said Alejandro, standing still, his bag raised over his shoulder. "Sometimes I go down and pick the mothers up from outside A and E in a wheelchair. The ones who can no longer walk. I have seen her . . . waiting."

In the stainless steel of the taps Suzanna could make out her reflection—twisted, inverted. "You know . . . that she loves Jason, then." She spoke into her chest. Then, when there was no reply, she faced him . . .

"I only know what I see." He shrugged. "It is not my kind of love."

"No," said Suzanna.

They stood finally facing each other. His hands rested on the back of the chair. His face was in shadow so she could barely make out his expression.

A van's rear doors banged outside, breaking the frail threads of connection in the air. Alejandro looked out of the window, then his eyes locked onto hers for several seconds before he turned back toward the door. "Thank you for your hospitality, Suzanna Peacock," he said.

# 16

Douglas closed the door behind him, and stared at his wife's dog in frustration. He had been looking for Vivi, and walked the animal around the formal gardens in the hope of finding her. He had continued around to the new offices, down to the dairy yard, and even through the woodland at the back of the grain sheds. The dog had failed to pick up a bloody thing.

I need a sniffer dog to locate my wife, he thought, and let out a sigh at the irony. She had been so busy lately, had left his meals with polite notes, retired late to bed having discovered a multitude of urgent tasks in underused parts of the house. He was never sure where she would be anymore. Or what mood she would be in when he found her. He felt unbalanced by the wrongness of it all.

The dog got under his feet and yelped as he tripped over it. Douglas's mother, from behind the annex door, called out twice to see if it was him. Feeling mean, he pretended he hadn't heard: he didn't want to be sent on some other errand. He was weary from having to drive Rosemary into town twice this morning—the third time he had had to do so in a week. His mother, still smarting from Vivi's outburst a week earlier, no longer asked where she was, as if her daughter-in-law's verbal insurrection had breached some unspoken rule. If he wasn't feeling so sorry for himself it might have made him laugh. This, he understood, uncomfortably, was what his wife had been complaining of these last months. That, and the faint, but distinctively unpleasant aroma that now lingered in the passenger seat of the Range Rover.

Douglas picked up the note on the kitchen table. It had not been there when he left the house this morning, or an hour earlier when he had returned to deliver Rosemary home, and the sight of it made him both annoyed and sad, as if his marriage had been requisitioned by two childish strangers.

Vivi, the note informed him in neat handwriting, would be out for a while. His and Ben's lunches were in the oven, and needed only twenty minutes' reheating. She could not, apparently, guarantee the same punctuality for herself.

He reread the note, then screwed it up in his broad hand and hurled it across the kitchen, so that the dog went scurrying after it across the flagstones.

Then, noting that her car keys were on the peg, he glanced out of the window, rammed his cap on his head, and left the house via the kitchen door, ignoring the imperious muffled voice calling his name behind him.

Alejandro pulled the airmail letter from his pigeon-hole, registered the familiar stamp, and stuffed it into his pocket as he walked wearily across the hospital grounds to his bed, some twenty-two hours since he had last seen it. He might still be relegated to the graveyard shifts, but while the hospital was assiduous in noting, at every opportunity, that it was an equal-opprtunity organization, he had, by virtue of his sex, struck lucky in his accommodation. It had been agreed that the nurses and midwives would not feel comfortable sharing their quarters with a man, no matter how polite. When it became apparent that finding him local lodgings was going to be a problem, someone had hit upon the solution of giving him what would have been the caretaker's flat, had the hospital still employed one for the nurses' block. He might have to unblock the odd sink, or change the odd fuse, joked the accommodation manager, but Alejandro had just shrugged. He hadn't been able to afford his own flat at home. Two bedrooms and a kitchen big enough to house a table seemed fair exchange for a few odd jobs.

And yet, several months into his tenancy, Alejandro found the place depressed him, even on a day like today when it was flooded in sunlight. He had never understood the ability, so often seen among women, to imprint their own character on a space and, in a living situation that might be temporary, he lacked the will to try. Its bland beige decor and hard-wearing furniture made it feel unloved and sterile. Its emptiness was constantly highlighted by the sound of thumping feet and chatting, giggling women coming and going on the stairs outside. Only two other people had seen its interior: the nurse whom he had unwisely brought home in his first weeks (and who had ignored him whenever they passed each other since) and, more recently, a Spanish girl from the local language school whom he had met on a train, and who had informed him, at the critical moment when he might normally have forgotten where he was, that she had a boy-friend and subsequently wept for three-quarters of an hour. The money he had paid for her taxi home, he mused, would have fed an Argentinian family of four for a month.

He poured himself a glass of iced tea and lay down on the sofa, propping a cushion under his neck, conscious of the smell of stale perspiration on his clothes. His bones ached with tiredness. He pulled the letter from his pocket and studied the address. He received few, and the sight of his own name against these unfamiliar English words still had the power to jar.

Son, I was going to write that all is fine here, but I realize, with sincerity, that this is only true for a select few. Your father, God willing, is still among them. There is talk of a new government, but I cannot see how things will be any different. There are now two "neighborhood councils" near us, and many of our neighbors have been on the new protests—waving keys at the government buildings. I fail to see what good this will do, but Vicente Trezza, who used to have the offices next to mine, is out there day in and day out with keys, pots, anything that will make a noise. I fear for his hearing. Your mother has refused to leave the house since our local supermarket was robbed by a mob from the shanty towns. Don't misunderstand my report, son. I am pleased to be able to say you are doing well in England. I look forward to our salmon fishing trip.

Your father

PS: I am booked in to do a lady who asks to be remembered to you: Sofia Guichane. She is married to that rogue Eduardo Guichane, the one on television. She wanted liposuction and a breast augmentation. I agreed only to the liposuction for now, as she thinks she may get pregnant soon. Plus she had a fantastic pair. Don't tell your mother I said this.

Baby Boy, My own dear mother (God rest her soul) used to say: "In Argentina, you spit on the ground, and a flower grows and blooms." Now, I tell Milagros, it packs its cases and disappears. I cry for you every day. Santiago Lozano has managed to get a job with a Swiss bank and sends his father money every month in dollars. Ana Laura, the Duhalde's girl, is going to the U.S. to live with her father's sister. I don't suppose you remember her. Soon I think there will be no young people left.

Milagros's daughter-in-law is expecting twins. I pray that when you return to Argentina you will make me a grandmother. There is little love left in my life, all I ask is something to make my existence worthwhile.

I will send on some packets of Mate,

as you asked (I sent Milagros to the supermarket but she said the shelves were empty). In the meantime, across the oceans that separate us, I send you a precious gift. So that you can remember your family. Be safe. And be wary of English women.

With love

Your mama

Alejandro wondered whether his mother was becoming forgetful. He tried to remember whether there had been any packages in his pigeonhole but, sleep-deprived as he was, he was sure that there had been only this lightweight letter. He half hoped she had forgotten: it made him feel guilty when she sent him gifts, even the cheap packets of his favorite drink. He turned the letter in his hands, and rubbed at gritty eyes. Then he reached for the envelope and opened it again.

There, nestling in the corner, light as a feather, so insubstantial he had missed it. Wrapped around with a tiny thread of pink ribbon. A lock of Estela's hair.

Alejandro closed the envelope and put it back on the table, his heart racing. His fatigue forgotten, he stood up, sat down, then stood again and walked over to the television, swearing under his breath.

He stared at the screen for several minutes, then glanced around the room, as if for signs he might have missed. Then, grabbing his keys, he pushed his way out of the flat.

Vivi shielded her eyes against the sun as the familiar figure loped toward her, becoming larger and more distinct as he came closer, his gait only marginally stiffer than that of the man she had married some thirty years ago.

He paused, as if considering whether to ask permission, then sat down beside her, brushing stray seeds from his trousers.

"Your lunch is in the oven," she said.

"I know. Thank you. I got the note."

She was wearing sunglasses. She turned back to the view, pulling her skirt down over her knees as if embarrassed to be caught with her skin exposed.

"Nice day for it. Sitting out, I mean."

She was squinting at something on the far horizon, then waved away a fly several inches in front of her nose.

Douglas's voice was upbeat, casual. "Not often we see you out here."

"No, I suppose not."

"Did you have a picnic or something?"

"No. I just thought I'd sit for a while."

Douglas digested this for several minutes, gazing up as a bird wheeled overhead. "Look at that sky."

He spoke into silence. "Gets you by surprise every summer, doesn't it? A sky as blue as that."

"Douglas, have you walked this far to talk to me about the weather?"

"Er . . . no."

She sat, waiting.

"I've just come from the house . . . Mother wants to know if you'll be able to take her cat to the vet at some point."

"Has she made an appointment with them?"

"I think she was rather hoping you would."

"And is there any reason why she, or indeed you, couldn't have performed this task?"

He looked at her, wrong-footed by her hard tone, then out at the dun-colored fields below. "I've got quite a lot on at the moment . . . darling."

"So have I, Douglas."

In the bottom field a huge red agricultural machine traveled steadily up and down, great arms sending up dust clouds from the neat, planted rows. As it turned, its driver caught sight of the seated figures and lifted an arm in salute.

Absentmindedly, Douglas lifted his own in return. As he dropped it again, he sighed. "You know, Vivi, you can't just dictate how we should all behave." He lowered his head to check that she had heard. "Vee?"

She lifted the sunglasses onto the top of her head, revealing reddened, tired eyes. "I don't dictate anything here, Douglas. I don't dictate to you or Rosemary or Suzanna or even the darned dog."

"I didn't mean—"

"I just try to keep everything running smoothly. And that's been fine."

"But?"

"But it's not fine now."

He waited for a few moments. "What do you want me to do?"

She took a deep breath, like someone preparing to recite a long-rehearsed speech. "I want you to accept that your mother is your responsibility too, and make her understand that I cannot cope with her—her **issues** by myself. I want to be consulted on matters that affect this family, whether you and your mother feel I have an automatic right to be or not. I want to feel—occasionally—as if I'm not just a piece of furniture." She studied his expression, her eyes searching and fierce, as if daring him to suggest that this was something hormonal.

"I—I've never thought of you—"

She pushed her hair off her face. "I want you to hand over more of the running of the estate."

"What?"

"I'd like us to have some time together. Alone. Before I get too old to enjoy it." And if you don't want that, she told herself in the ensuing silence, you'll be telling me what I have feared deep down, all along.

He sat, staring into space. Vivi closed her eyes, trying not to read anything into her husband's silence, trying to muster the strength to continue. "Most importantly, Douglas, you need to bring Suzanna back in," she said slowly. "You need to make her feel she's just as important as the others."

"I'll make sure Suzanna has an equal financial—"

"No, you're misunderstanding me. It's not about the money. You need to allow Suzanna the same sense of family, the same sense of belonging."

"I've never discriminated against—"

"You're not hearing me, Douglas—"

"I've always loved Suzanna just the same—you know I have." His voice was angry, self-justifying.

"It's Athene."

"What?"

"You need to stop behaving as if Athene is a dirty word." At least in one area I can swallow my own feelings and do the right thing, Vivi said silently. She remembered, suddenly, how she had been introduced to Athene formally at Douglas's first wedding. How the girl, exquisite and oddly spectral in her wedding finery, had smiled vaguely and looked straight through her. As if she were invisible.

Below them, the roar died down, leaving just the sound of the breeze.

His hand had crept into hers. She opened her eyes, feeling the familiar roughness, the stiff fingers surrounding her own. Beside her, Douglas coughed awkwardly into his free hand. "I don't know if this is going to be easy to explain, Vee . . . but you've misunderstood me. I don't hate her. Even with what she did." He looked at his wife, his jaw set against remembered pain. "You're right—I never wanted to talk about Athene . . . not because she made me uncomfortable, not because I was frightened of making Suzanna feel different from the others . . . Well, maybe in part that was it, but mainly it was because I didn't want to hurt you. Whether she intended it or not, she damaged so many people. You protected us for all these years, and you pulled it all back together . . . I . . ." He faltered and raised his hand to his thinning hair. "I love you, you know." His fingers closed tightly now around hers. "Really I do. And I just didn't want her to have the opportunity . . . to damage you too."

Suzanna had been sitting alone outside, her long, pale legs stretched out in the sun, her face tipped to the endless blue sky, perversely enjoying the absence of customers. Mrs. Creek had sat over her milky coffee for almost an hour, muttering darkly about the lack of biscuits, while Jessie chattered on about some outfit for a school play she was meant to have made until Suzanna sent the two of them off together to get on with it. It was not the right sort of afternoon for working. Too hot. Too humid. I have lost my London habits in some things, she mused, noting how other traders had also set up chairs outside, loitered on doorsteps, seemingly unworried by the shortage of customers, content to enjoy the moment. She was still having trouble explaining this to Neil: in the capital, shops rose and fell on profit and loss, were judged by their columns of figures, dealt in notions of footfall, turnover, and exposure. Here, she thought, remembering her conversation with Jessie, they were like a public service. A focal point for people who lived often isolated lives.

When she saw him, his long stride too swift, too determined for the sleepy afternoon, she had scooted her legs under her, adjusted her shirt, as if caught doing something she shouldn't. From the end of the lane, he motioned at her as if to indicate that she need not rise on his account, but by the time he reached the shop she had disappeared inside, was already filling the coffee machine in the cool gloom.

She found it difficult to look up when she heard him come in. When she did, keeping her expression neutral, she saw that he looked awful. He was unshaven, his eyes shadowed with fatigue. "Espresso?"

"Yes. No. Do you still have iced tea?" (She had introduced it when coffee sales began to fall in the heat.)

"Sure."

For someone whose movements were normally so measured, whose demeanor was so quiet, he seemed distracted, and unable to settle. "You mind if I smoke?" he had asked, when she handed him the tall glass.

"Not if you take it outside."

He had glanced at the unopened pack of cigarettes in his hand, then out at the bright lane, and decided against it.

"No Jessie?"

"Gone home to make a daisy outfit."

He raised his eyebrows. He drank his iced tea in thirsty drafts, then asked for more.

Perhaps it was because of the brightness outside, but in the gloom, the shop seemed to have shrunk. Suzanna found herself acutely aware of her own movements, of the way she moved around the counter, of the shapes her fingers made as she poured the second glass of iced tea. She gazed at him surreptitiously, taking in the crumpled T-shirt, the faint hint of male perspiration. Set against the delicately fragrant soaps, and the vase of freesias by the till, it was almost aggressively masculine and disturbing. She wished, suddenly, that there were other customers after all. "Smoke in here if you like," she said brightly. "I'll prop the door open."

He stroked his chin.

"You look like you need one."

"No. No, really. I don't smoke anymore. I don't know why I bought them."

"You okay?" she said, pushing the glass toward him.

He breathed out, a deep sigh.

"Bad shift?"

"Something like that."

"I'll be outside," she said and, unsure why she needed to leave him there, walked slowly back into the sun.

To a passer-by, had there been any, Suzanna would have looked relaxed, leaning on her table, sipping a glass of iced water, watching the town's inhabitants meander slowly back and forth on their way to the market square. But she was painfully aware of every minute, felt, or imagined she felt, every glance on her warm back from the shadowy figure inside the shop. So that when he finally came outside and sat beside her, she had to fight the urge to exhale, as if she had been through some demanding test.

"Who is she?"

He looked more at ease, she noted. The almost manic glint in his eyes had dissipated.

"The girl in the painting? It's not you. Your sister?"

Suzanna shook her head. "No, she's my mother. My real mother." The words, for once, came easily.

"You don't keep the picture at your home?"

"It's complicated." He was looking at her. "She was at my family home. My father's home. He's remarried. But when I moved here they gave her to me."

"They didn't want her in their home?"

"I'm not sure it's that, exactly . . ."

"You don't want her in your home."

"It's not that either . . . It's just that she doesn't really belong anywhere anymore."

The conversation already felt less agreeable. She wished she had left the painting facing the wall. She shifted in her seat, reached for the broad-brimmed hat, and put it on so that her face was in shadow.

"I'm sorry. I didn't mean to offend—"

"Oh, it's okay. Jessie's probably told you. I know Jessie tells everyone everything. But it's just that me and my dad have this tricky relationship. And things are a bit difficult with us at the moment."

He had moved his chair to face her. She struggled with the conflicting sensations of wanting to leave him, and a simultaneous, almost fundamental need to explain herself.

"It's to do with inheritance," she said eventually. "Who gets what."

He looked at her steadily.

"My family owns a big estate here. My dad doesn't want me to inherit it. It's going to my younger brother. Perhaps you have the same thing in Argentina?"

"In Argentina it's not an issue." He smiled wryly. "The sons get everything."

"I was obviously born in the wrong country. Or my dad was."

"It bothers you?"

She was a little embarrassed. "You think it's greedy, right? To be so upset about something you didn't earn?"

"No . . ."

"I'm not a greedy person."

He waited.

"I mean, I like nice things, sure, but it's not about the money. It—it's about how he sees me."

She found the intensity of his attention almost too much. She looked down and realized she had finished her water. "Sometimes I think it's because I look like her. I've seen other pictures, you know, photographs, and I'm exactly like her." She stared at her white limbs, which never tanned, the ends of her straight dark hair, just visible, lying sleekly against her shoulders.

"So?"

"I feel like he's making me pay."

He touched her hand, so lightly that afterward she found herself staring at the spot where their skin had met, as if unsure whether it had happened. "For not being your mother?"

Suzanna's eyes had filled inexplicably with tears.

She chewed at her lip, trying to hold the tears back. "You wouldn't understand." She half laughed, made awkward by this show of emotion.

"Suzanna."

"For . . . for being responsible. For her death. I was the reason she died, after all." Her voice had become hard, brittle, her face strained under the smile. "She died in childbirth, you see. No one talks about it, but there it is. She'd still be here if it wasn't for me." She rubbed dismissively at her nose.

"I'm sorry," she said briskly. "I don't know why I'm telling you this. Because you're a midwife, I suppose. You'll have seen it happen . . . Anyway. It doesn't usually get to me like this."

The lane was empty, the sun bouncing off the cobbles. She turned back to him, her smile brave and bright. "Some inheritance, huh?"

For reasons she didn't understand, he took her hand gently between his, bent his head low on their clasped fingers, and rested it there, as if in supplication. She felt the skin of his forehead, the hardness of the bone beneath, and her tears evaporated at the strangeness of what he was doing.

When he eventually looked up, she thought he might apologize. But instead he nodded, almost imperceptibly, as if this had been something he had already known, had been waiting all this time for her to say it.

Suzanna, politeness forgotten, pulled away her

hand like she had been burned. "I—I'll just get some more tea," she said, and ran for the safety of her shop.

Alejandro walked back to the hospital slowly. It was almost a mile and a half, and he was now so tired that he felt nauseated. He took the shortcut, through the Dere estate, his feet moving automatically on the hot pavement. She had shouted his name three times before he heard her.

"God, you look knackered." Jessie and her daughter held hands, their faces bright and open as the sun. He felt relieved to see them, they were so uncomplicated and good.

"We've been making outfits for the end-of-term play. Mrs. Creek has been helping us."

Emma held up a plastic bag.

"Now we're going to the park. You can come if you want and help push Emma on the swings. I'm not good at pushing at the moment," Jessie said. "Bashed my arm."

He might have been tempted to say something—he had thought about it often—but his brain was not clear and he did not trust himself to say what he meant. "I'm sorry," he said. "I didn't hear you very well."

He was thinking about how her hair had glinted blue-black in the afternoon sun. Her aquamarine eyes, when she had looked up at him, had been angry, as if she was scolding him for some previous transgression. He could still feel her skin against his, the cool translucency of it like dew.

I have never met her before, he thought. I know I can never have met her before. So, then, why . . . ?

"What babies came out today?"

Jessie stroked her daughter's hair. "Leave him, Ems. He's too tired to talk babies today. Go on, Ale. Go home. Get some sleep."

"I don't know . . . ," he muttered under his breath, so quiet that, as she later told her mother, she wasn't sure what it was he had said till afterward. And even then she was not sure of his meaning. "I don't think I know where home is."

Suzanna got home long after Neil, just as the shadows started to lengthen, the light summer evening having stretched almost indecently late. She let herself in, found him, feet resting on the coffee table, eyes fixed on the television.

"I was about to ring you," he said, lifting the remote control. "Are you (a) stuck in traffic, (b) having an early Christmas sale that you haven't told me about, or (c) stuck under a heavy piece of furniture and unable to reach your phone?" He tore his eyes from the television and grinned at her, blowing a kiss. "There's some dinner in the oven. I thought you might be hungry. Sorry, I ate mine earlier."

"What is it?"

"Nothing exciting. Spaghetti Bolognese from a jar. I wasn't feeling very inspired."

"Actually, I'm not terribly hungry." She began to pull off her shoes, wondering what it said about her that the sight of him sitting there so contentedly could irritate her, even when he had prepared her a meal. "Isn't he good?" she could hear her parents exclaiming to each other. "He cooks for her as well. I don't think she realizes how lucky she is." She stood in the kitchen for a moment or two, leaning on the sideboard, willing herself to be nice, scolding herself for noticing, as she always did, the crumbs from breakfast and the smeared and splattered pans and surfaces that told of Neil's culinary adventures. Am I always going to be this awful? she asked herself. Am I always going to be so dissatisfied?

"If you want to get yourself a glass," he called, from the other room, "there's a bottle of wine open."

She opened a cupboard, pulled one out by the stem, and walked into the sitting room. She sat next to him on the sofa, and he patted her thigh. "Good day?" he asked, his eyes still on the television.

"All right."

"What was the weather like here? It was gorgeous in London. In the hour I was able to go out, anyway."

"Fine. Pretty hot."

"Look at this guy. He's hysterical." Neil laughed at the television. He had caught the sun, she realized. His freckles had emerged.

She sat, impervious to the comedian on the screen, sipping the wine he had poured for her. "Neil," she said, eventually, "do you ever worry about us?"

He turned his face from the screen after the faintest of delay, as if understanding reluctantly that they were about to have One of Those Conversations, and secretly wishing that he didn't have to be part of it. "Not anymore. Why? Should I?"

"No."

"Not about to run off with the farmer down the road?"

"I meant this. Don't you ever wonder . . . if this is it? If this is as much as we get?"

"As much what?"

"I don't know. Happiness? Adventure? Passion?" As she said the last word, she was conscious that he might read it as some kind of invitation.

She could see him fighting to suppress a sigh. Or perhaps it was a yawn. His eyes kept sneaking back to the television. "I'm not sure I follow you."

"Look at us, Neil, it's like we're middle-aged, and I don't feel like we got to do the exciting bit first." She waited, monitoring his reaction, daring him to look at the television again.

"Are you saying you're unhappy?"

"I'm not saying anything. I just wondered what you thought about us. Whether you were happy."

He turned off the television. "Am I happy? I dunno. I'm happier than I was."

"Is that good enough?"

He shook his head slightly in exasperation. "I don't think I know what kind of answer you're after."

She grimaced, unsure herself.

"Do you not think, ever, Suze, that you can make yourself happy? Or unhappy?"

"What?"

"All this questioning. All this analyzing yourself. 'Am I happy?' 'Am I sad?' 'Is this enough?' Don't you think you can worry it all to death? It's like . . . you're always looking for things to worry about, always judging yourself by everyone else's standards."

"I am not."

"Is this about Nadine and Alistair?"

"No."

"They've been an accident waiting to happen for years. You can't say you didn't notice whenever we went over. At one point they were only communicating through the au pair."

"It's not about them."

"Can't we just enjoy the moment? The fact that, for the first time in ages, we're solvent, we're both employed, we have somewhere nice to live? I mean, no one's ill, Suzanna. There's nothing bad on the horizon, just good stuff, your shop, the baby, our future. I think we should be counting our blessings."

"I do."

"Then can't we focus on that and stop looking for problems? Just for once?"

Suzanna gazed steadily at her husband, until, reassured, he turned back toward the television and flicked it into life with the remote.

"Sure," she said as she stood up, and walked softly into the kitchen.

# 17

Summer had descended fully on the little town, easing Dere Hampton gently into its sweltering embrace. Its narrow streets baked, and cars drove lazily around the market square, their tires sticky on the molten Tarmac. American tourists in sore-footed clusters stopped and stared at intricate masonry, exclaiming into their guidebooks. On the square, market traders sat under canopies, gulping canned drinks, while elderly dogs lay in the middle of the pavement, their tongues lolling.

The shop was quiet: the better-heeled had taken off for summer holidays in other quiet towns, others spent their time shepherding children half crazed with liberation for six weeks from intensive schooling. Suzanna and Jessie, moving at a leisurely pace, cleaned shelves and windows, rearranged displays, chatted to tourists, and made jugs of iced tea, which became increasingly diluted by the melting ice cubes as the afternoons wore on.

Suzanna had felt dissatisfied with the layout of the shop, and furious with herself that she could not work out what was wrong. One morning they stuck up the "closed" sign, moved all the tables and chairs to the other end, and employed a handyman known to Father Lenny to move the shelving units to the opposite side. It had not looked as Suzanna had envisaged, and she paid the man the same amount—to Neil's despair, as he went through the books—to move it all back again. She had decided not to do jewelry anymore (too many pieces had "gone missing") and put the display downstairs in the cellar. As soon as she had done this, no fewer than three women came in separately asking for vintage necklaces. She papered over the wills, and replaced them with colored maps of north Africa. Then she painted the back wall a pale turquoise and immediately regretted the color. Through all this, Athene had sat in her frame on the cellar steps, her smile as enigmatic as the Mona Lisa's, suitable neither for the shop nor home, a constant reminder of Suzanna's inability to shape her world in a way that could be considered satisfactory.

Eventually, infected by a kind of madness, she took one Saturday off to go to London. She had originally meant to meet Nadine but, on a whim, pleaded a family emergency and went to Bond Street where, diving in and out of shops at a speed unusual in those temperatures, she bought two pairs of summer sandals, only one of which could truly be said to fit, a short-sleeved gray shirt, some earrings, a new pair of designer sunglasses, and a pale blue linen suit that might come in handy should she have to go to a wedding. She also bought a bottle of her favorite scent, some painfully expensive moisturizer, and a new lipstick in a color she had seen in some celebrity magazine. She put all but the shirt on the credit card that Neil thought she had cut up. She would pay for it gradually, she rationalized, and had to stop herself crying on the train home.

Alejandro stayed away for three days, then came every day afterward. Sometimes she would emerge from the cellar and find him seated, his aquiline face expectant as if he had been waiting, and she would blush and cover her confusion under some too-loud remark about the weather or the level of coffee in the machines or the **mess** of everything in here!

If Jessie was around, Suzanna said little, content to listen to their exchanges, and store the snippets of information Jessie was able to pry out of him: that his father had written, that he had cooked an English meal, that in the maternity ward a "mother" had been admitted the previous evening with nothing more gestational than a pillow under her nightdress. Sometimes Suzanna felt that, through Jessie, he was telling her things about himself, laying himself out in front of her in little pieces. Sometimes she found herself doing the same, being unusually forthcoming, simply because there were parts of her that she wanted him to see: the better parts, someone more attractive, more together, than the person she felt he usually saw.

Several times now he had arrived when Jessie was out at lunch and Suzanna had found herself almost incapacitated by awkwardness. Occasionally, perhaps when he appeared engrossed in a newspaper or book, she was able to compose herself and then, gradually, they would begin to talk. Sometimes even for the whole hour until Jessie came back.

Once he had told her he wanted to visit the town's museum, a series of overcrowded rooms dedicated to Dere's rather grisly medieval history, and she had closed the shop for a whole hour and gone with him. While they dawdled around the dusty exhibits, he had told her about his own history, and that of Buenos Aires. It was probably not the best business practice, but it was good to hear a fresh perspective from someone. To remind yourself that there were other ways of being, other places to be.

And when he smiled, she noted how his whole face changed.

It was good to have a new friend, she rationalized. She just never seemed to mention him to Neil.

Jessie was in the window, pinning Chinese lanterns around a display, occasionally waving at passers-by when she called out: "Your old man's coming up the road."

"My dad?"

"No. Your husband. Sorry." She backed out, grinning, her mouth full of drawing pins. "I forget you're from the moneyed classes."

"What does he want?" Suzanna stepped forward to the door, saw Neil wave as he drew closer.

"Canceled meeting. I don't need to be in the office till lunchtime," he said, kissing her cheek. He had taken off his suit jacket, slung it over his shoulder. He glanced over at the tables of chatting customers, then at the wall space by the counter. "Shop looks nice. Where's the portrait gone?"

"You wouldn't believe it if I told you." She herself wasn't sure what to think. Her mother and father had come in two days previously. The portrait, they had decided, needed attention. "Thirty years" moldering away in the attic, and now all of a sudden it needs "urgent" restoration. They had been odd with her. Her father had kissed her and told her the shop looked grand. Her mother, unusually, had said almost nothing, but stood back, beaming, as if this were something she had somehow engineered. "I don't understand why it's taken you so long," Suzanna had said. They hadn't mentioned it, but she had had to fight the suspicion that they were using the painting as a way of trying to fob her off about the will.

"So, what are you doing here, anyway?" she asked Neil now.

"Do I need an excuse? Thought I might come and have a coffee with my wife before I head off."

"How romantic," said Jessie straightening some ribbon. "It'll be flowers next."

"Suzanna doesn't like flowers," said Neil, sitting down at the counter. "It means she has to wash up a vase."

"Whereas jewelry . . ."

"Oh, no. She has to earn jewelry. There's a whole points system involved."

"I won't ask what she had to do for that diamond ring, then."

"Hah! If that was on a points system, she would be wearing pull tabs."

"You're both hilarious," said Suzanna, filling the coffee machine. "You'd think feminism had never been invented."

They had met only three times, but Suzanna thought Neil was probably a little in love with Jessie. She didn't mind: nearly all the men she knew were, in varying degrees. Jessie had that cheerful, uncomplicated thing going on. She was pretty in a girlie way, all peachy skin and sweet smiles. She brought out a testosterone quality in them: her size and fragility made the most unlikely men become all caveman and protective. Most men, anyway. Plus she got Neil's sense of humor, an attribute he probably thought went sorely unappreciated at home.

"I never thought of you as a bra-burner, Suzanna."

"I wouldn't describe my wife as militant . . . not unless you count the time they forgot to open Harvey Nichols at the correct hour."

"Some of us," said Suzanna, handing him a coffee, "are working for a living as opposed to sitting around drinking coffee."

"Working?" Neil raised his eyebrows. "Gossiping in your shop? It's hardly working down a mine."

Suzanna's jaw clenched involuntarily. "Whereas selling financial products requires a stunt double, obviously. I don't believe there was any gossiping, darling, until you came in." The "darling" could have cut glass.

"Ooh. Talking of gossip, guess what? Ale isn't gay. He had a girlfriend in Argentina. Married, apparently." Jessie had climbed back into the window, and was rearranging it, her legs folded as neatly into themselves as a cat's.

"What? He was?"

"No, the girlfriend. To some Argentine television star. You'd never guess, would you?"

"Your gaucho?"

"He's a male midwife who comes in here. From Argentina. I know, fab, isn't it?"

Neil grimaced. "Bloke sounds like a weirdo. What kind of man is going to want to spend his working day doing that?"

"I thought you were the one who was so interested in childbirth."

"My own **wife** in childbirth, yes, but I still think I'd rather be up the head end, if you know what I mean."

"How noble of you."

"A plain old gynecologist, now, that's different. I can understand the attraction of that. Although I can't see how you'd ever get any work done."

Jessie giggled. Suzanna squirmed with embarrassment.

"Bit of a dark horse, isn't he? Alejandro, I mean. Jason always says it's the quiet ones who are the worst."

"How do you know all this?"

"He was in the park when I took Emma over there on Sunday. I sat on the bench and we got chatting."

"What was he doing there?"

"Nothing, as far as I could see. Just enjoying the sun. Actually, I won't say enjoying. He looked pretty miserable until I came along." She looked up at Suzanna. "He was doing that **Latino** brooding thing, you know."

"I thought midwives were meant to be female." Neil sipped at his coffee. "I don't think I'd want a male midwife if I was having a baby."

"If you were having a baby, that would be the least of your worries," Suzanna snapped, and began to tack Polaroids of customers above the north African maps.

"I don't think I'd like you to have a male midwife, come to think of it."

"If I was about to go through the hell of pushing a whole human being out of my body, I don't think the decision would be yours, actually."

"I'm going to look this woman up online, just to see what she looks like." Jessie rested the stepladder against the wall.

"Is he still in love with her, then?" Suzanna asked.

"Didn't say. But you know what, Suze, I've got a sneaking suspicion he's the type who likes them married."

"I thought you said there was no gossiping in here," Neil scoffed.

"So he doesn't have to get emotionally involved."

"What do you mean?" Suzanna watched Jessie as she maneuvered the stepladder toward the stairs.

"Well, he's pretty laid back, isn't he? You can't imagine him chasing after someone, or lost in the throes of passion. Some men like to sleep with women who are already involved with someone else. It's safe for them then. The woman isn't going to make any emotional demands. Am I right, Neil?"

"Not a bad strategy," said Neil. "Not one I've ever managed myself."

Suzanna sniffed, trying to disguise the flush to her cheeks. "You read too many magazines."

"You put them here." Jessie threw her bag onto the hook on the cellar door, and held out a starched white apron. "Mrs. Creek made this. Nice, isn't it? Do you want me to get her to do another one for you?"

"No. Yes. Whatever."

Jessie tied the strings around her waist, then smoothed the apron over her legs. "Oh, look, the lady with the children wants serving. I'll go . . . No, he doesn't do it for me. Too . . . I don't know. I just like men with a bit more life in them."

Arturro had sacked all the young men in his shop. Just like that, with no warning. Mrs. Creek was the first to discover it, when she walked past on her way to the market. She told them shortly after Neil had left. "I heard a load of shouting and goodness knows what, and he was blowing off steam like a bull in a field. I was going to go in for some of that nice cheese, the one with bits of apricot in it, but to be honest I thought I'd better give him a chance to cool down."

Jessie and Suzanna stood very still, as they had since Mrs. Creek had begun her story—she had stretched it out over some considerable time, making the most of her unexpectedly rapt audience. When she finished, they exchanged a look.

"I'll go," said Jessie.

"I'll keep an eye open for Arturro," said Suzanna. He hadn't come in yet.

Jessie went to Liliane's, not to pry, of course, just to suss out the atmosphere, as she put it. Initially, she thought, Mrs. Creek must have been exaggerating. Liliane, although reserved as always, was as poised and polite as she normally was. But when Jessie mentioned the delicatessen, she had become distinctly annoyed. She was no longer using it, she said. Some people in town thought their way of treating customers pretty shabby.

"Anything in particular?" Jessie pressed.

"Let's just say," said Liliane, her mouth set in a grim line, her hair as rigid as her jaw, "that there are those who might have been expected to behave like gentlemen but who think nothing of playing practical jokes more suited to the playground."

"Oh, bugger," said Jessie, when she got back. "I've got a bad feeling about this."

"Do we confess?" said Suzanna, feeling faintly sick.

"If the boys have lost their jobs, I guess we have to. It's our fault."

Suzanna thought of them, how they had once occupied an unhealthy portion of her imagination.

"You go."

"No, you."

They were giggling nervously now.

"It was your idea."

"You bought the sugared almonds. It was going fine until the sugared almonds."

"I can't believe I'm thirty-four years old and I'm feeling like I've got to go and see the headmistress at school . . . I can't do this. I really can't." Suzanna leaned back against the counter, deep in thought. "How about if I pay you?" She giggled again.

Jessie put her hands on her hips. "Ten grand. That's my best price."

Suzanna gasped theatrically.

"I know—one does Arturro, one Liliane."

"But you know them better than me."

"So I've got more to lose."

"She scares me. I don't think she likes me as it is. Not since I started stocking those T-shirts. She thinks I'm stealing her market."

"Why? What has she said?"

"It's not what she's said, it's how she looks at them when she comes in."

"Suzanna Peacock, you're pathetic. You're nearly ten years older than me and—"

"Eight, actually. I'm thirty-four. Only thirty-four."

"Neil says you've been thirty-five for about ten years."

Fear had made them hysterical. They clutched at each other, eyes wide, laughter giddy.

"Oh, I'll go—I'll go tomorrow, if you let me off

early this afternoon. I need to take Emma to get some shoes. And I can't do it later because I've got night school."

"That's blackmail."

"You want me to talk to Arturro? Then you owe me, big-time." Jessie began to write out price labels with a fuchsia-colored pen. "And only if he hasn't cooled down and let them all back in anyway."

But the next day Jessie didn't come in. Suzanna was at home drying her hair when the telephone rang. "Sorry," said Jessie, sounding unusually subdued. "You know I wouldn't normally let you down, but I can't make it today."

"Is it Emma?" Suzanna's mind was racing. She had meant to drive to Ipswich to meet a supplier. She would have to change her plans.

There was a pause.

"No, no. Emma's fine."

"What is it? A cold? There's a weird summer one going round. Father Lenny said he felt odd yesterday. And that woman with the dogs." If she rang the supplier now, she thought, she might be able to cancel without too many problems.

"You know what? I'm probably going to need a couple of days . . ."

Suddenly Suzanna switched her attention to the voice on the line. "Jess? Are you okay?"

There was a silence.

"Do you—do you need me to run you to the doctor?"

"I just need a couple of days. I promise I won't let you down again."

"Don't be ridiculous. What's the matter? Are you ill?"

Another silence, then, "Don't make a big deal, Suze, please."

Suzanna sat, staring at her bedside table. She put the hair dryer down, and switched the receiver to the other ear. "Has he hurt you?" It came out as a whisper.

"It looks worse than it is. But it doesn't look pretty. Not the right kind of look for the stylish shop assistant." Jessie mustered a wry laugh.

"What did he do?"

"Oh, Suze, please leave it. Things just got a bit out of hand. He's going to do anger management. He's promised me this time."

The little bedroom had grown chilly.

"You can't keep doing this, Jess," she murmured.

Jessie's voice was hard. "I'm dealing with it, okay? Now, do me a favor, Suzanna, just leave it. If my mum drops by, tell her I'm out with a customer or something. I don't want her going off."

"Jess, I—"

The line went dead.

Suzanna sat on the side of her bed, gazing at the

wall. Then she scraped her wet hair into a ponytail, ran downstairs for her keys, and headed the short distance into the center of Dere Hampton.

There were, as far as Suzanna could see, limited advantages to living in such a small town, but an undeniable one was that there were only so many places for people to be. She found Father Lenny in the tearooms, about to bite into a bacon sandwich. When he saw her he cowered jokingly, as if he'd been caught doing something treasonous. "I'll be in for my normal coffee later," he said, as she sat down opposite. "I promise. I just have to test out the opposition every now and then."

Suzanna forced herself to smile, tried to look more relaxed than she felt. "Father Lenny, do you happen to know where Jessie lives?"

"She's up on the Meadville estate. Near her mother. Why?"

Suzanna remembered Jessie's warning. "Nothing important. She's off with a cold. Thought I'd pop up there and take her some." She smiled reassuringly.

Father Lenny's eyes searched hers and, having presumably found the answers he required, looked down at his plate where his bacon sandwich lay. "Is it a bad cold?" he asked slowly.

"Hard to say. I think she'll be needing a few days off, though."

He nodded, as if digesting the information. "Would you be wanting any company?" he said carefully. "I've not a lot on this morning."

"Oh, no," said Suzanna. "I'm fine."

"I'm happy to come. I'll only stay five minutes if you've got . . . things to discuss."

"That's very kind, but you know what it's like when someone's sick. They don't want to be disturbed."

"No," Father Lenny said. "They don't." He pushed away his plate. "She's at forty-six The Crescent. As you go in off the hospital road, take the first right and it's there on your left."

"Thanks." Suzanna had already risen from her seat.

"Tell her I send my love, will you? And I'll look forward to seeing her back in the shop."

"I will."

"And, Suzanna . . ."

"What?" She hadn't meant to be rude. "Sorry. Yes?"

"I'm glad she's got a friend." Father Lenny hesitated. "Someone to talk to."

But while it was one thing to have the address, it was quite another, Suzanna realized, to push her way in, presumably unwanted, into a potential snake pit. What if he was there? She wouldn't know what to say to him. What was the etiquette in such situations? Did you ignore the woman's appearance?

Make polite conversation? What if he was there and wouldn't let her in? She might make things worse by just turning up.

Suzanna had only ever come up against something similar once: at school, her geography teacher, an apologetic, bespectacled woman, would regularly come in trying to shield purplish marks on her face and arms. "Her husband beats her up," the girls would say knowledgeably to each other afterward, then give it no further thought. It was as if, Suzanna observed now, they had been parroting parental wisdom: these things happened, that was life.

But this was different.

Suzanna felt weak and inadequate. She could just not go, she thought. Jessie didn't seem to want her there. It would be the easier path, and she would be back in a day or two. Yet, the degree of complicity in that course of inaction made her ashamed for even considering it.

It felt almost inevitable that he should go with her. She looked up, still passing her keys from hand to hand, to see him standing in front of her, his long legs for once in pale trousers, a T-shirt in place of the familiar scrubs and jacket. "Locked yourself out?" He looked relaxed, as if wherever he had been in the intervening days had been restorative.

"Not exactly." She thought he might ask for coffee, but he just waited for her to speak. "It's Jessie," she said.

He glanced up and past her into the empty shop.

"I don't know whether to go to her house." She kicked at a stray stone. "I don't know how much it's right to interfere." He didn't need an explanation.

He squatted in front of her, his expression set and grim. "You are afraid?"

"I don't know what she wants. I want to help, but she doesn't seem to want it."

He looked down the lane.

"She talks a lot, Jess," she continued, "but she's actually quite private. I don't know whether she's kind of comfortable with . . . the way things are. Or whether she's secretly desperate for someone to jump in and help her. And—" She scratched her nose. "I'm not very good at confidences and intimacies and all that stuff. To be honest, Ale, I'm out of my depth. And I'm terrified of getting it wrong." She didn't tell him her darker thoughts—that she was afraid of getting too close to the mess of it, to the dark unhappiness—that having salvaged some kind of fragile peace in her own life, she didn't want it corrupted by someone else's misery.

He touched her hand with his fingertips, a reassuring, gentle gesture.

And then he lifted himself to his feet. He held out a hand. "Lock up your shop. I think we should go."

Jessie's house was recognizable outside for its window boxes and its bright purple front door. It was prettier than Suzanna had expected—prettier inside than it deserved to be, considering the uniformly depressed air of its neighbors. Inside, Suzanna had expected a war zone. Instead she found an immaculate sitting room with plumped gingham cushions and carefully dusted shelves. The ungenerously sized rooms were colorfully painted, decorated with cheap furniture that had been customized, loved into something more attractive. The walls were decorated with family pictures and paintings evidently completed by Emma in the various stages of her school career. Jokey birthday cards still lined the mantelpiece, and a pair of slippers in the shape of stuffed animals that announced they were "bear feet" lay on the floor. The only sign of any disturbance was a parcel of newspaper next to a dustpan and brush, presumably concealing broken glass. But what the apparently cheerful interior could not disguise was the air of stunned stillness, an atmosphere quite different from peaceful silence, as if it were still digesting actions that had previously taken place there.

"Tea?" said Jessie.

Suzanna had heard Alejandro's intake of breath as the younger girl opened the front door. Her fine features were swollen, her mouth smeared at a grotesque angle, for both lips had been split by some historic blow. There was a large purplish bruise to her upper right cheek and some kind of homemade splint supported her left index finger.

"It's not broken," she said, wiggling it, as she followed Alejandro's eyes. "I would have gone to the hospital if I thought anything was broken."

She tried and failed to disguise a slight limp when she walked. "Go through to the front room," she said, a parody of a hostess. "Sit down and make yourselves comfortable."

Against the sound of children riding bicycles on the pavement outside, they had sat silently beside each other on the long sofa, which was covered by a pale throw. Suzanna tried not to think what marks on the sofa had led to it needing to be covered.

Jessie brought through a tray of mugs, refused offers of help, and sat down, facing them. "Anyone for sugar?" she said, her voice thick with the effort of speaking through a fat lip.

Suzanna, with an unexpected hiccup, began to cry, brushing at her face in an attempt to disguise her tears. It all seemed so wrong somehow, seeing Jessie like this. She was so far removed from the kind of women she imagined this usually happened to.

Alejandro pulled out a handkerchief. Suzanna took it wordlessly, ashamed that, in the face of such pain, it was she who was crying.

"Please don't, Suze." Jessie's voice was determinedly upbeat. "It looks worse than it feels, honest."

"Where is your daughter?"

"She was staying at my mum's, thank God. Now

I just have to find a way to keep her there another night without Mum kicking off."

"You want me to take a look at your hand?" Alejandro offered.

"It's just bruised."

"You might need stitches in that lip. You should probably get an X-ray too, just to check that your head's okay."

Suzanna watched as Alejandro moved over to Jessie and examined her face, turning it gently toward the light. "You want me to get some butterfly stitches from work? It would help this heal quicker. Or maybe some painkillers."

"I tell you what you could do, Ale. Tell me how I can get the swelling down. I need to have Emma home ASAP and I don't want to scare the living daylights out of her. I've done ice packs and arnica cream, but if there's anything else . . ."

Alejandro was still looking closely at her head. "Nothing that's going to make any real difference," he said.

There was a silence. Suzanna took her tea and stared into it, unsure what to say. Jessie, in her pain and apparently well-rehearsed composure, seemed like a stranger.

"You want me to talk to him?"

Suzanna glanced up. Alejandro's expression was hard; his voice had been tight with restraint.

Jessie shook her head. "I have told him," she said, eventually. "That he's gone too far, I mean."

Outside, the children were squabbling. Their voices were raised against each other at the other end of the street.

"I know what you're both thinking but I won't let this carry on. For Emma's sake, as much as anything. I've told him, the next time he lays a finger on me he's out."

Alejandro looked down into his mug.

"I mean it," said Jessie. "I don't expect you to believe me, but I will. I want to see what happens with this anger-management course before I actually pack up and go."

"Jessie, please go now. Please. I'll help. We'll all help."

"You don't understand, Suze. This isn't some stranger, this is the man I've loved since I was . . . since I was practically a kid myself. And I know the real him and this is not it. I can't throw away ten years just because of a rough few months. He's Emma's dad, for God's sake. And, believe it or not, when he's not . . . like this, we have a good time together. We've been happy for years."

"You're making excuses for him."

"I probably am. And I can see how it looks to you. But I just wish you'd known him before this started. I wish you could have seen us together."

Suzanna glanced at Alejandro. She had thought, given his evident affection for Jessie, that he might get angry, intervene on her behalf despite her protests, but he was just sitting there, holding his mug. It made her feel frustrated.

"I'm not frightened of him, you know. I mean, yes, it's a bit frightening when he loses it, but it's not like I'm walking around the house terrified of setting him off." Jess looked from Suzanna to Alejandro. "I'm not an idiot. This is his last chance. Don't people deserve a chance to change?"

"It's not that—"

"Look, you know what started this off, don't you?" Jessie lifted a mug with her injured hand, then transferred it to the good one and took a sip. "Father Lenny. He had a go at him about losing his temper. He felt like everyone was judging him. He thought I'd been telling tales and that the town had turned against him. You know what it's like around here. I know, because a lot of people wouldn't talk to me when I was a cleaner. Like it somehow made me different."

She put her mug down. "You've got to let me handle this myself. Don't make things worse. If I decide he really has turned into someone I don't feel safe with, I'll pack my bags and go." She tried to smile. "I'll move into the shop, Suzanna. Then you'll never be rid of me."

**Come now**, Suzanna wanted to say, but there was something in Jessie's determined expression that stopped her.

"Here's my number." Alejandro was scribbling on a piece of paper. "You change your mind about your hand, want me to get you some butterfly stitches, anything, you call me. Okay?"

"I'll be back at work the day after tomorrow."

"Whenever you're ready. It's not important." Suzanna stood up and made to hug Jessie, conscious as she did so that she might be pressing on injuries they couldn't see. She stood back, and tried to impart some kind of urgency in the look that passed between them. "You can call me too. Any time."

"I'm fine. Really. Now, get lost, the pair of you. Go and open that shop or I won't have a job to go back to." She shepherded them out of the door.

Suzanna would have protested, but she was also aware that Jason might be on his way, that Jess might have her own reasons for wanting an empty house.

"See you soon." Jessie's voice, cheerful through the net curtains, followed them down the road.

They had walked in silence as far as the Swan hotel on the high street, each alone with their thoughts.

Suzanna stopped at the corner of the road that led

toward the center of town. "I don't feel like opening the shop today," she said. He shoved his hands into his pockets.

"Where shall we go?" he asked.

Neither felt like eating, so they went toward the market. Neither seemed to know where they were going: they simply shared a desire not to be alone, not to resume their normal routine. At least, that was what Suzanna told herself.

They walked companionably around the stalls in the square, drinking bottles of water, until he confessed, apologetically, that he was bored with the market. "I have walked here on almost every one of my days off," he said. He had seen almost nothing, he added, since he got to England. He had thought he would travel to other cities and explore in his spare time, but rail travel had proven pro-hibitively expensive, and he was usually too tired to make any effort. He had been to Cambridge once, and there had been an outing for all the midwives to London, organized by the hospital management, when they had visited Madame Tussauds, the Tower of London, and the London Eye in quick succession, taking in almost nothing. The fact that he was the only man prevented the exclusively female grouping from engaging him in conversation. "I was so glad to find your shop," he said, his hands deep in his pockets. "It is the only place . . . it was just different from everything else."

"So what do you want to see?" she had said.

"Show me where you come from," he said. "Show me this famous estate. The one that causes you so much trouble." He had said it teasingly, and she had smiled despite herself.

"It's hardly an **estancia**," she said. "It's about four hundred and fifty acres. Probably not very big by Argentinian standards." It was, however, big enough to provide a decent afternoon walk. "I'll take you to the river," she said. "If you like fishing, you'd like our river."

It was as if they had made an unspoken decision to step out from the shadow of the morning. Or perhaps, Suzanna thought, as they walked along the bridleway up to the woods, they had both needed to divest themselves of the darkness of that little living room, the violent secrets that suffused its air, and remind themselves of something clean and good and glorious.

Twice he had taken her hand to help her across the path.

The second time, she had had to make a conscious effort to let his go.

They had seated themselves at the top of the forty-acre field and were looking down across the valley. It was one of the few points from which the estate was visible almost in its entirety, its undulating hills and dark patches of forest patchworking their way to the horizon. She pointed to a distant house, set about by outbuildings. "That's Philmore House. It's let at the moment, but my mother and father lived there when they were first married." She stood up, and motioned toward some woods, about five miles west of the house. "That mustard-colored house—you can just see it, right? That's my parents' house now. My brother, Ben—he's younger than me—and my grandmother live there too."

They were standing a third of the way across the field, where it dropped away sharply below them, rolling down to the valley and the river, unseen behind woodland, when she said, "Me and my brother used to come up here when we were little and we'd roll down it. We'd stand here, pretending we didn't know what was coming, and then the other would push us both down and we'd race each other rolling all the way to the bottom. You'd end up with grass in your mouth, your hair . . ." She held up her hands, her elbows in, demonstrating the position, lost in a distant memory. "Dad turned this field over to the sheep one year. We didn't think about it. Ben got up at the bottom looking like a currant bun." She realized she had brought in her family, and didn't want to continue. Sometimes, it seemed, there was no escaping them.

He stood next to her, shielding his eyes as he scanned the horizon. "It's beautiful."

"I don't really see it anymore. I guess when you grow up with something, you don't. It's probably good to see it through somebody else's eyes."

Below them, a sparrow hawk hovered in the air, its eyes trained on some unseen prey. Alejandro followed it as it swooped toward the earth.

"Even on days like this, I think I still prefer the City."

He turned toward her. "Then why do you let it make you so sad?"

"I'm not sad. And I don't let it bother me that much. I just don't agree with the system, is all."

She sat down, pulled up a piece of long grass, and placed its stalk meditatively between her back teeth. "It doesn't rule my life or anything. It's not like I'm sitting in a dark room somewhere sticking pins in a voodoo doll of my brother."

She heard him chuckle, as he sat down beside her and folded his legs beneath him. She heard the quiet rustle of grass as he adjusted himself, watched, surreptitiously, as his legs stretched out beside hers.

"The estate was never yours, right? It belongs to your father?"

"And his father. And his father before him."

"So it was never yours, and it will never be yours. So?"

"So what?"

"Exactly. So what?"

She raised her eyes to the heavens. "I think you're being a bit naïve."

"For telling you not to let your family's land eat up your happiness?"

"It's not that straightforward."

"Why?"

She kicked out at an insect that had landed on her foot. "Oh, everyone's such an expert, aren't they? Everyone knows how I feel—how I **should** feel. Everyone thinks I should just accept things the way they are and stop railing against them. Well, Alejandro, it's not as simple as that. It's not as simple as making yourself not want something. It's about families and relationships and history and injustice and—" She broke off, stole a glance at him. "It's never just about land, okay? If it was just about land it would have been sorted out long ago."

"Then what is it about?"

"I don't know. **Everything**."

She thought suddenly of the greater troubles he had probably seen, of Jessie's situation, and her voice sounded childish, petulant, even to herself. "Look, can we just leave this?"

He pulled his knees up, glanced sideways at her over his shoulder. "Don't get mad, Suzanna Peacock."

"I'm not mad," she said crossly.

"Okay . . . I think maybe you have to make a decision. I think it is very easy to let yourself be swallowed by your family, and by its history."

"Now you sound like my husband." She had not meant to mention Neil, and felt his unwelcome presence in the air between them.

Alejandro pushed back his hair. "Then he and I are in agreement. Neither of us wants to see you unhappy."

She did look at him then, studied his profile, and as he turned toward her, let herself ask silent questions of those brown eyes, the knowing mouth. There was the faintest hint of puzzlement in his face, as if he was trying to work something out.

You are just another crush, she said to herself, then flinched in case she had said it out loud. "I'm not unhappy," she whispered. It seemed important to persuade him of this.

"Okay," he said.

"I don't want you to think I am."

He nodded.

From the way he looked at her, it was as if he understood, as if he knew her history, her guilt, her unhappiness.

He must be a crush, she thought, dropping her head abruptly to hide her sudden blush. I'm getting fanciful, imposing feelings on him that I don't even know he has.

She sat, her forehead resting on her knees—
until she felt his touch, electric on her shoulder.
"Suzanna," he said.

She glanced up at him. Against the sun, she could
see only a blurred, unnaturally slimmed silhouette.
"Suzanna."

She took his proffered hand, made as if to stand,
accepting somehow, in this strange, dreamy afternoon, that she would follow this man anywhere, that
she would let herself be sucked into his slipstream.
He did not stand, but pulled her slightly toward
him, and she watched as he lay back on the grass.
As her breath caught in her chest, he fixed his eyes
on hers, something mischievous in the invitation
they carried. Then, with a childish whoop, he
pushed himself off on a trajectory, and began rolling down the hillside, his legs bumping against each
other as he built up speed.

For several seconds, she stared in disbelief at the
figure flying away from her, and then, the tension of
the past moments released, she threw herself down
after him, letting the sky and the earth dissolve into
a blur, letting her senses be consumed by the rushing grass, the smell of the earth, the gentle bump
of her bones as they met the ground. And she was
laughing, lost in the ridiculousness of it, spitting
out bits of grass and daisies and God knew what
else. She was laughing, her hands stretched above

her head, letting herself fly down a hillside, a child again, knowing she would be caught at the bottom.

He stood over her, as she lay giggling and panting in the grass, her head still spinning from the descent. He swayed above her, one hand reaching forward to help her stand up. She was gradually able to make out his beaming face, the livid grass stains all over his trousers. "Happy now, Suzanna Peacock?"

She could think of no sensible response. And so, giddily, she lay back, laughing, her eyes closed against the painfully blue sky.

They had reached the center of town shortly before seven. They might have made it back sooner, but their pace, by mutual consent, had been measured, perhaps to allow them more time for conversation. It came easily now—their infantile physical release had freed something between them. She knew a little more about him: about his housebound mother, the maid, the political situation in Argentina. He knew about her family history: her childhood, her siblings, her anger at having to leave the city. Sometime later, she would remember that in several hours of conversation they had not mentioned Neil, and would feel not quite guilty enough about the omission.

They were crossing the square when Suzanna noted the three young men leaving the delicatessen, chatting, their bags slung easily over their shoulders.

They glanced at Alejandro's trousers, and said something possibly rude to each other in Italian, then saluted.

Alejandro and Suzanna lifted their hands in return.

"He's taken them back," she breathed.

"Who?"

"It would take too long to explain but it's good news. Jessie will be so pleased." She found she could not stop smiling, a broad, uninhibited smile. The pleasure of the day had been intensified by the uniquely miserable way in which it had begun.

"I'd better go," he said, glancing at his watch. "I'm on a late shift."

"I guess I should head down to the shop," she said, trying not to look as crestfallen as she felt. "See whether any deliveries have been left outside." She didn't want to leave.

She looked down, then back at him. "Thank you," she said, hoping he would understand all that that meant. "Thanks, Ale." He stood there for a minute, then smoothed a stray hair from her forehead. He still smelled of grass, his skin drenched in sun.

"You look like your mother," he said.

She frowned slightly. "I don't think I know what that means," she said carefully.

His eyes hadn't left hers. "I think you do."

———

He wasn't at home when she got there. A message on the answering machine said he wouldn't be in till much later: playing squash with work buddies, he said, he had told her that morning, but he was pretty sure she hadn't remembered. He added, jokingly, that she should try not to miss him too much.

She didn't eat any supper. For some reason she still had no appetite. She tried and failed to find something that would interest her on television, then moved restlessly around the little house, staring out of the window at the fields she had walked earlier that day, until the skies grew dark.

Finally, in her tiny bedroom, Suzanna sat in front of her mirror, which only just fitted under the low part of the sloping roof. She stared at her reflection for some time and then, almost unconsciously, she pulled up her hair, and pinned it at the crown of her head. She outlined her eyes with kohl, painted the lids in the closest approximation she could find to that singular icy blue.

Her skin, pale as her mother's, was untouched by the sun. Her hair, free of dyes and disguises, a deep, almost unnatural black. She stared into her own eyes, lifted the corners of her mouth in an approximation of that smile.

Then she sat, motionless, as Athene stared back at her. "I'm sorry," she said to the reflection. "I'm so, so sorry."

# 18

Isadora Cameron had the sort of springy red hair you didn't often see anymore: once common on impossibly teased schoolchildren, a new generation of relaxants and leave-in conditioners had generally obliterated the kind of mad carrotty frizz that framed her face. Not that she seemed to mind it; since the first day she had come to Dere House, she had let it bounce loosely around her, a kind of russet explosion, dwarfing a face that would otherwise have been almost circular. "Woman looks like a rusting Brillo pad," Rosemary had said with a sniff on the first day that she came. But, then, Rosemary would have been inclined to dislike her whatever the condition of her hair.

To Rosemary, Mrs. Cameron was described as a cleaner, someone to help Vivi now that she was spending more time with Douglas. It was a big house, after all. It was only surprising she'd managed so long without help. To everyone else, Mrs. Cameron was Rosemary's chauffeur, cleaner, underwear launderer, and general home help. "Someone to take the weight off your shoulders," Douglas had said, when he announced her employment. Mrs. Cameron didn't bat an eyelid at unhygienic food cupboards or hazardous refrigerators. She didn't let moth-eaten cats or dishonest terriers trouble her cheerful demeanor. She considered soiled sheets and undergarments simply part of the job. And for four hours every morning, for the first time since Rosemary had arrived, since the children had grown up, perhaps in her entire married life, Vivi now found herself able for several hours a day, to do anything she wanted.

At first she had found the freedom almost intimidating. She had sorted cupboards, gardened, baked extra cakes for the Women's Institute. ("But you don't even like baking," Ben had said. "I know," said Vivi. "But I feel it's a waste of your father's money otherwise.") Then, gradually, she had begun to enjoy the empty hours. She had started a patchwork quilt with fabrics she had saved over the years from the children's favorite clothes. She had driven into town, by herself, to have a cup of tea that she hadn't made and enjoy the luxury of reading a magazine without interruption. She took her dog for proper walks, rediscovering the estate from ground level, taking pleasure in the land she had never really got to see. And she had spent time alone with Douglas, sharing sandwiches with him in the tractor, blushing pleasurably when she overheard one of the men remark that she and the "old man" were like a pair of honeymooners, these days.

"I don't like her," Rosemary would complain, querulously, when Vivi and Douglas returned to the house. "She's very impertinent."

"She's very nice, Mother," Douglas said. "In fact, I would go so far as to say she is a treasure."

"She's overly familiar with me. And I don't like the way she cleans."

Vivi and Douglas exchanged looks. Mrs. Cameron was resolutely deaf to Rosemary's rudenesses, met her bad-tempered complaints with the same soothing cheerfulness with which she had no doubt treated the old men of the nursing home from where Douglas had tempted her. She had been glad to come, she confided to Vivi. Those geriatric men might have been frail, but they weren't above giving you the odd goosing when they had the opportunity. And it wasn't as if you could give them a good whack in return, not with them prone to falling over.

"I'll have a word with her, then, Mother. Make sure she's not missing anything out."

"She should do something with her hair," Rosemary muttered, making her way slowly back into her annex. "I really find it very vexing that she doesn't tidy herself up a bit." She turned and stared suspiciously at her son and daughter-in-law. "Things are going on around here," she said. "Hair and all sorts. And I don't like it."

Rosemary was going to have a field day this morning, Vivi thought, as Mrs. Cameron entered. The muggy heat of previous weeks had broken with a thunderstorm and Mrs. Cameron had been apparently caught without an umbrella, and in the short walk from her car to the door, her hair had sprung up in wild corkscrews around her head. The children used to draw lions with manes like that, Vivi thought, trying not to stare.

"Will you look at it?" Mrs. Cameron said, shaking her headscarf, wiping the rivers from her face with a handkerchief and examining the sleeves of her scarlet cardigan.

"Thank God for it," said Douglas, as he came up behind them. "Thought we were going to have to start irrigating if we didn't get some soon."

"Do you—do you want to borrow a hairdryer?" said Vivi, motioning toward her hair.

"God no. If you think it looks wild now, you should see it after a few volts. No, I'll let it dry naturally. I'll just stick my cardie on the stove, though, if it's okay by you." Mrs. Cameron walked briskly down to the kitchen, a plump red inverted exclamation mark.

Douglas stood by the window, then turned to his wife. "You remember we're off to Birmingham today, to look at trailers? Are you sure you're going to be all right with us taking your car?"

The Range Rover had gone in for its annual

service and, rather than Douglas and Ben canceling their plans, she had offered them hers. "I'll be fine. With the weather like this, I'll just potter around at home. Besides, if I need anything I can always get Mrs. Cameron to run into Dere for me."

He had lifted a hand to her cheek, a wordless gesture, but an acknowledgment all the same. He left it there long enough to make Vivi blush. He indicated upstairs to the gallery. "Have you rung Suzanna?" He was smiling at her high color.

"No, not yet."

"Are you going to get her over here? Today might be a good day, with the rain and all. I don't suppose she'll be doing much business."

"Oh, you never know. Tomorrow, perhaps." Her eyes had not left her husband's. "But I think you should call her. It will mean more coming from you."

He placed his hat on his head, moved in to hold her. She felt his hands enclosing her waist, the comforting security of his chest against hers, and wondered how she could be so embarrassingly happy this late in life.

"You are a remarkable woman, Vivi Fairley-Hulme," he said into her ear. He had placed his emphasis on the "are," as if it were only she who had ever held this in doubt.

"Go on," she said, stepping back and opening the door so that the rain darkened the slate of the hall floor. "Before Ben disappears somewhere and it takes you an hour to find him. He's been itching to go since before breakfast."

By lunchtime the rain had worn out its welcome. Even those who had expressed relief at its arrival, exclaiming at the desperate thirst of their gardens, or the heaviness of the recent heat, were finding the relentless force of the downpour oppressive. It was, said the few visitors to the Peacock Emporium that morning.

"I went to Hong Kong in the rainy season once," said Mrs. Creek, who came in after her lemon sole and boiled potatoes at the Pensioners' Friday Lunch Club, "and it rained so hard the water was actually flowing over the tops of my feet. Ruined my shoes, it did. I thought it was probably a way of getting us to spend more money."

"What?" said Suzanna, who had given up trying to do anything and was watching the downpour through the window.

"Well, it's a good way of forcing you to buy more shoes, isn't it?"

"What—making it rain?" Suzanna had rolled her eyes at Jessie.

"Don't be ridiculous. Not providing proper drainage so the water has somewhere to go."

Suzanna tore herself from the window and tried to take in what Mrs. Creek was saying. A watched pot never boils, that was what her mother had told her. But it didn't stop her looking out for the lithe, dark figure that had become familiar to her. A figure that, today, had so far resolutely refused to show itself. I mustn't think like this, she told herself, for possibly the thirtieth time that day.

Suzanna pulled herself back into the snug interior of the shop, only dimly aware of the soft jazz in the background and the muted chatter of the women in the corner, who had been glad to use the rain as an excuse to indulge in a couple of hours' conversation. Mrs. Creek was poring over a box of antique fabrics, unfolding each piece and muttering under her breath as she examined it closely for loose threads and holes, and a young couple was riffling through a box of Victorian and art-deco beads that Suzanna had not yet got around to pricing individually. It was the kind of rain that usually made the Peacock Emporium feel like an exotic bolthole, had made it glow, snug and bright, against the wet gray cobbles outside, and allowed her to imagine herself somewhere else entirely. Today, however, she felt disquieted, as if the gray clouds, swept in from the North Sea, had brought with them some distant unease and blown it into the shop.

She looked over at Jessie, who had been writing price labels for a box of multicolored Perspex letters for the past half hour, although Suzanna had told her it really wasn't necessary.

Now that Suzanna thought about it, Jessie had

hardly spoken all morning. In the days since she had returned to work she had not quite been herself: not subdued exactly, but distracted, slow to pick up on jokes that previously she herself might have instigated. She had apparently forgotten all about Arturro and Liliane, her former obsession, and Suzanna, preoccupied, had taken longer to notice. External bruises might fade, she thought now, regretting her own distraction, but perhaps internal ones were harder to shift.

"Jess?" she said carefully, when Mrs. Creek had gone. "Don't take this the wrong way, but do you want to take some more time off?"

Jessie looked up sharply, and Suzanna immediately wanted to backtrack. "It's not that I don't want you here. I just thought . . . well, we're not busy at the moment, and you might want to spend more time with Emma."

"No, no. It's fine."

"Really. It's not a problem."

Jessie stared at the table for a moment, then moved her head slowly, taking in the whereabouts of the customers, and turned reluctantly to Suzanna. "Actually, I need to talk to you," she said, not meeting her eyes.

Suzanna hesitated, then moved silently around the counter and sat down opposite her.

The younger girl looked up. "I'm going to have to quit," she said.

"What?"

Jessie sighed. "I've decided it's not worth the aggravation. He's getting worse. We're on the list for his anger management and couples counseling, or whatever it's called, but that might take weeks, months, even, and I've got to do something to get him to see sense."

Her face framed into an apology. "I've dreaded telling you," she said. "Really. But I've got to put my family first. And with a bit of luck it might only be temporary. Just till he calms down a bit, you know."

Suzanna sat in silence. The thought of Jessie disappearing from the shop made her feel ill. Even without her current distractions, it no longer seemed the same on the days when Jessie wasn't there: she didn't feel the same enthusiasm for opening up; the hours stretched, instead of skittering by in ridiculous jokes and shared confidences. And if Jessie disappeared, how many customers would vanish with her? They were barely breaking even as it was, and Suzanna knew well enough by now that the girl's smiling face and her interest in everyone's lives were a draw in a way that she alone could never be.

"Don't be cross with me, Suze."

"I'm not cross. Don't be silly." Suzanna reached out her hand, placed it on Jessie's.

"I'll stay on a week or two if it leaves you in the lurch. And I'll understand if you want to get someone else. I mean, I'm not expecting you to keep the job open for me."

"Don't be ridiculous."

Suzanna saw a tear plop onto the tabletop. "You know the job is always yours," she said quietly.

They stayed like that for some minutes, listening as a delivery van reversed wetly down the road, sending waves of water onto the curb.

"Who'd have thought it, eh?" Jessie's smile was restored.

Suzanna kept hold of her hand, wondering if she could bear to hear it. "What?"

"Suzanna Peacock. Needing people."

The rain beat fiercely on the lane, the view from the windows a gunmetal blur.

"Not people," said Suzanna, trying and failing to sound grumpy, in order to mask the constriction of her heart. "You might have a split personality, Jess, but I don't think even you qualify as people just yet."

Jessie grinned, a hint of her old self shining through, and gently removed her hand. "But it's not just about me, is it?"

The annoying girl left at a quarter past three, taking all that hair, still sticking out as if she had been dragged through a hedge backward, with her. She had taken to shouting at Rosemary, as if she were deaf, and Rosemary, irked by this patronizing treatment, had taken to shouting back, to show her it wasn't necessary. Young people could be so irritating.

She had told the girl, as she left, that if she wanted to hang on to her husband she was going to have to get herself a girdle. "Tidy yourself up a little," she said. "No man likes to see someone who's hanging out all over the place." She had thought, secretly hoped, perhaps, that the girl would take offense and leave. But instead she had placed her podgy little hand on Rosemary's own (another overfamiliar gesture) and hooted with laughter. "Bless you, Rosemary," she had said. "I'll be volunteering my husband for the corset treatment before I do it myself. Hasn't he got several gallons of bitter slooshing around in his?"

She really was impossible. And she was meant to leave at two—**two**, not a quarter past three. Rosemary, checking her watch every few minutes, had become quite anxious for her to leave. Vivi always walked the dog after lunch, and Rosemary was counting on having the house to herself.

She called out, making sure Vivi hadn't come back in through one of the back doors, and then, a little stiffly, began to make her way slowly upstairs, hauling herself along with both bony hands on the banister. They had thought she wouldn't know, she mused bitterly. Just because she no longer went upstairs, they had thought they could ignore her wishes. As if her advanced years meant that she no longer counted. But she wasn't stupid. Hadn't she had her suspicions from the day her son had brought up all that business about dividing the estate again? Even in his sixties he had barely the sense he had been born with, was still swaying with the whims and fancies of women.

She had reached the last but one step and paused, hanging on to the banister, cursing the ache in her joints, the dizziness that prompted the siren call of the easy chair. Old age, she had discovered long ago, didn't confer wisdom and status, but simply a series of indignities and physical collapses, so that not only was one ignored but tasks that one had once completed without thought now required planning and careful assessment. Could she reach the tin of tomatoes in that cupboard? Would her now feeble wrists support it long enough for her to place it on the sideboard without dropping it on her foot?

She took a deep breath, and eyed the wide, even floor of the gallery. Two more steps. She hadn't lived through two world wars to let a couple of stairs deter her. She lifted her chin, took a firmer hold on the banister, and, with a grunt, made it to the gallery.

She straightened slowly, taking in the space she hadn't seen for almost seven years. Nothing much had changed, she decided, with a vague satisfaction. Nothing except the portrait, newly installed, which now glowed, reframed and radioactive with malice.

Athene.

Athene Forster.

She had never deserved the surname Fairley-Hulme.

Rosemary looked up at the pale, smirking figure who seemed, even now, more than thirty years on, to be laughing at her. She had laughed at everyone, that one. At her parents, who had raised her to be a little tramp; at Douglas, who had given her everything, and whom she had repaid by parading her immoral behavior halfway across three counties; at Rosemary and Cyril, who had done everything to keep the Fairley-Hulme line going and the estate intact. And no doubt, again, at Douglas, for not having the backbone to keep her portrait out of the family gallery.

The rain thrummed on the windows, and the air felt damp, loaded with intent.

Rosemary turned stiffly toward the Gothic carver chair by the rail, assessing, calculating. Grasping its arms between two gnarled hands, she hauled it backward, dragging it across the carpet toward the wall, one painful step at a time.

It took several minutes to travel the few feet and, when she finally reached her destination, Rosemary was forced to sit down and fight off dizziness. Fairly confident that she was ready, she stood. Then, with one hand steadying herself on the back of the chair, she gazed again at the girl who had done so much damage, and who was still insulting her family. "You don't deserve to be up here," she said aloud.

Despite having done little in the previous ten years that was more acrobatic than stooping to fill her cat's bowl, Rosemary, with a jut to her jaw, lifted a thin, arthritic foot, and began, precariously, to hoist herself onto the chair.

It was almost a quarter to four when Ale came into the store. Suzanna had long ago given up staring through the rivulets on the window, so she decided to do what she had put off for weeks—sort out the cellar. The shop itself might be immaculate, but she and Jessie had got into the habit of throwing empty boxes down the stairs, shoving goods, and boxes of coffee, into whatever space they could find. Now, however, a major delivery of autumn stock was due the following day, and Suzanna realized that they could not work around the boxes—and the rubbish—unless they were better organized.

She had been down there almost half an hour when she heard Jessie's exclamation of surprise and delight, and stood still for a moment. Then, even against the noise of the rain, she heard his halting, tonal voice, his laughing apology for something. She stopped and smoothed her hair, trying to quell the flutter in her chest. She thought, briefly, of the doctor's appointment she had made earlier that morning, and closed her eyes, feeling a stab of guilt that she could associate with his presence. She took a deep breath and made her way upstairs, deliberately slowly.

"Oh," she said, at the cellar door. "It's you." She had tried, and failed, to sound surprised.

He was seated at his usual table. But instead of facing out to the window, he was looking toward the counter. Toward Jessie. Toward Suzanna. His hair glittered black with rain, his eyelashes separated into starry points. He smiled, a slow, enchanting smile, wiping water from his face with a shining wet hand. "Hello, Suzanna Peacock."

Vivi shepherded the dog through the back door, shaking her umbrella on the kitchen floor, and calling him back before he made a break for it. "Oh, do come here, you ridiculous animal," she exclaimed. She had thought that in lace-ups and with an umbrella she was prepared for the weather, but this rain was in a different league. She was wet through.

The rain-loaded skies had made the kitchen unnaturally dark, and she flicked on several sets of lights, waiting as they stuttered into life. She propped her umbrella against the door, filled the kettle, and removed her shoes. Rosemary's cat was sleeping, stretched out motionless, and Vivi placed her hand against its neck, just to check it was still alive. These days, you could never be sure. She was afraid that when it did die it might be there for several days before anyone noticed.

She pulled the teapot out of the cupboard and got out two cups and saucers. Left to herself, she would have used a mug, but Rosemary liked to do things formally even when it was just the two of them, and she was feeling generous enough to indulge her these days.

She began to prepare the tea. "Rosemary," she called, toward the annex, "would you like a cup of tea?"

Rosemary, through deafness or obstinacy, often required several summonses before she would deign to answer, and Vivi knew she had not yet been forgiven for her outburst. But after the third attempt Vivi placed the tea-tray on top of a stove lid, and knocked on the door of the annex. "Rosemary?" she said, her ear pressed to the door. Then she pushed down the handle and entered.

She wasn't there. Having checked each room twice, Vivi stood in the hallway and tried to think where else her mother-in-law might have gone. Mrs. Cameron had left, so she couldn't be out with her. She wouldn't be in the gardens in weather as filthy as this. "Rosemary?" she called again.

It was then, above the dull rumble of the rain, that she heard the noise: a distant grunting, a shuffling, heralding some unseen effort. She waited, then looked, disbelievingly, at the ceiling and called again. "Rosemary?"

There was a silence that Vivi would remember for weeks afterward. Then, as she made for the door, a muffled exclamation, the briefest pause, and then a terrible, sickening crash from upstairs, overlaid by a furious, strangulated cry.

"I brought you something," Alejandro said, but he was looking down and Suzanna wasn't sure who he was speaking to.

"A present?" said Jessie excitedly. She had perked up when he arrived; he always had that effect on her.

"Not exactly," he said apologetically. "It's the Argentinian national drink. **Mate.** Our version of your cup of tea, if you like." He pulled a brightly colored packet from inside his wet jacket and handed it to Suzanna, who was standing behind the counter. "It's bitter, but I think you might like it."

"**Mate,**" said Jessie, turning the word over in her mouth. "**La Hoja Yerba Mate,**" she read from the packet. "Fancy a cup of **Mate,** Suze? Milk and two sugars, is that?"

"Not milk," said Alejandro, grimacing, "but you can add sugar. Or orange pieces. Maybe lemon, grapefruit."

"Shall I make a pot?" said Suzanna.

"No, no. Not a pot. Here." He walked behind

the counter so that Suzanna was suddenly acutely aware of his proximity. "You make it in a **Mate**. Like this." From the other side of his jacket he produced a voluptuous silver pot, like a miniature pitcher. "Here, let me prepare it. You can both try it and tell me what you think. I will serve you, for a change."

"It looks like Chinese tea," said Jessie, staring at the contents of the packet. "I don't like Chinese tea."

"It looks like a pile of old leaves and twigs," said Suzanna.

"I'll make it sweet," said Alejandro, shaking the **yerba** mixture into the pot.

Suzanna stood back against the blackboard, unaware that today's coffee listings were smudgily transferring themselves to her dark T-shirt. He was so close she could smell him: a mixture of soap and rainwater, and something, underneath it, that made her tense involuntarily. She felt oddly vulnerable.

"I—I've got to get on with moving these boxes downstairs," she said, desperate to regroup. "Call me when it's ready." She looked at Alejandro and added unnecessarily, "We—we've got loads more stock coming tomorrow. And no room. There's just no room." She ran down the rickety staircase, and sat on the bottom step, cursing herself for her weakness as her heart thumped erratically against her chest.

"You're not usually here at this time," she heard Alejandro say to Jessie, his voice betraying none of the turmoil she felt. She had no idea what he felt.

What am I willing to happen here? she thought, clutching her head. I'm married, for God's sake, and here I am, throwing myself headfirst into another crush. Anything to avoid what's really going on in my life.

"Emma's got drama club," said Jessie.

Suzanna could hear her feet moving on the wooden floor, and see the slight give in the timbers above as she traveled from one end of the shop to the other. "I thought I'd stay a bit later, seeing as how I haven't been around much lately."

"Your head? It looks better."

"Oh, it's fine. I've literally plastered myself in arnica cream. And you can't really notice my lip if I have lipstick on . . . Look." There was a brief silence as, presumably, Alejandro examined Jessie's face. Suzanna tried not to wish that it was her face on which his fingertips rested gently. She heard Jessie mutter something, and then Alejandro saying it was nothing, nothing at all.

There was a silence, during which Suzanna's mind was blank.

"That smells," said Jessie, laughing. "Disgusting."

Alejandro was laughing too. "No, wait, wait," he was saying. "I'll add sugar. Then you can try it."

I've got to get a grip, Suzanna thought, and picked up a weighty box of Victorian photograph albums she had bought at auction. She had planned to remove the pictures and place them in individual frames, but failed to get around to it. She jumped as Jessie's face appeared at the top of the stairs. "Are you coming up? We're about to be poisoned."

"Shouldn't we call a few of our favorite customers," she said lightly, "so that they can join us?"

"No, no," said Alejandro, laughing. "Just you two. Please. I want you to try it."

Suzanna ran up the stairs. The shop felt suddenly warm and cozy, brightly lit against the dull, damp outside, infused with unfamiliar smells. She moved toward the shelf, began to pull down cups, but Alejandro, with a touch to her arm, stayed her. "No," he said. "That's not how you drink this."

Suzanna looked at him, then down at the **Mate** pot, from which now emerged a silver straw, twisted like a barley sugar. "You sip it through this," he said.

"What? All of us?" said Jessie, staring.

"One at a time. But, yes, through the straw."

"That's a bit unhygienic."

Alejandro nodded. "It's okay. I'm a trained medic.

"You know, it is a great offense to refuse to share with someone," Alejandro added.

Suzanna stared at the straw. "I don't mind," she said. She held back her hair then sucked up a mouthful of the liquid. She winced—it **was** bitter. "It—it's different," she said.

He offered her the straw again. "Think how coffee tasted the first time you tried it. You have to see **Mate** the same way. It's not bad, just different."

Suzanna, her eyes on his, put her lips around it. Her hand was on the side of the pot, and she stared at her fingers, so pale and smooth next to his, which were tanned and foreign and unmistakably male, shielded from the light by the dark curtain of her hair. Those hands delivered children, wiped tears from female eyes, had met birth and death and lived and worked in places a million miles from here. She took another sip of **Mate**, as Jessie muttered something about needing to buy more sugar. Then she watched as his broad hand moved, just a fraction, to rest on her own.

The lightness of the previous minutes was replaced by something electrifying. Suzanna tried to swallow the pungent liquid, her eyes on their hands, all her senses tuned to his warm, dry palm against her skin, fighting an impulse to lay her mouth against it, press her lips to his skin.

She let out a long, tremulous breath, and lifted her eyes to his. They were already on her. His expression not one of amused complicity, sexual invitation, or even ignorance, as she had half expected, but as if he was bewildered, searching for answers.

His gaze, locked on hers, sent a jolt through her that was almost painful. It made a mockery of reason, sliced through her own beliefs and excuses. I don't know either, she wanted to protest. I don't understand. Then, almost as if they belonged to someone else, her own fingers shifted on the pot until they were entwined with his.

She heard him swallow, and looked away to where Jessie was pulling cups from the shelf, both thrilled and appalled by what she had done, unsure if she could cope with the emotion she appeared to have provoked.

He didn't move his hand.

She was almost relieved when the quiet of the room was interrupted by the shrill ring of the telephone. Suzanna, taking back her hand, could not look at Alejandro. She wiped her mouth, and turned toward the phone, but Jessie had got there first. She felt dizzy, disoriented, and so conscious of Alejandro's eyes on her that at first she could not make out what the other girl was saying. And then, slowly, as her senses came back into focus, she took the receiver. "It's your mum," said Jessie, looking anxious. "She says your gran's had an accident."

"Mum?" Suzanna held the receiver to her ear.

"Suzanna? Oh, darling, I'm so sorry to bother you at work but Rosemary's had a fall, and I desperately need some help."

"What happened?"

"I've got no car. The boys have gone off with mine, your father refuses to carry a mobile phone, and I need to get Rosemary to the hospital. I think she may have cracked a rib."

"I'll come," said Suzanna.

"Oh, darling, would you? I wouldn't ask, but it's that or an ambulance, and Rosemary is absolutely refusing to have one near the house. The thing is, I can't get her down the stairs by myself."

"Upstairs? What's she doing there?"

"It's a long story."

"I'll be as quick as I can."

Suzanna hung up. "I've got to go," she said. "Jess, I'd better shut the shop. Oh, God, where did I put my keys?"

"What about the boxes?" said Jessie. "You've got those deliveries tomorrow. Where are we going to put everything?"

"I can't think about it now. I've got to run my grandmother to the hospital. I'll just have to deal with tomorrow when it comes. Maybe I'll come back tonight if we don't have to wait too long in A and E."

"You want me to come?" said Alejandro.

"No, thank you." Suzanna smiled despite herself at the thought of explaining him to Rosemary.

"Let me ring Mum," said Jessie. "She can pick up Emma and I'll stay here and do it for you. I'll pop the keys in through your door later."

"Are you sure? Will you be okay? Some of the boxes are quite heavy."

"I'll help her," said Alejandro. "You go. Don't worry. We'll sort it out."

It was after six, and the bright evening skies had been prematurely darkened by the thunderous weather. Jessie had piled all the rubbish into black bin bags, which had been relatively easy to carry up the stairs. Now, however, she was having to move the boxes, some of which were weighty, loaded with crockery or books. "God only knows what she's been buying," she said, hauling another up the stairs. "I don't think she knows half the time." She let out a gasp of pain.

Alejandro dived over to take the box from her. "Are you okay?"

"Just put a bit too much weight on my hand. I'm fine," said Jessie, examining her finger, which was still in the homemade splint.

Alejandro put the box on the floor and lifted her hand. "You know, you should get this X-rayed."

"It's not broken. It would have swollen up if it was broken."

"Not necessarily."

"I can't face the hospital again, Ale. I feel those nurses all look at me like I must be some kind of idiot." She sighed. "He's so stupid! I've never even looked at another man. Well, of course I've looked, but I've never—you know—considered doing anything." She wrinkled her nose. "I know every-one thinks I'm a bit of a flirt but I'm actually one of those boring people who thinks there's one man for one woman."

"I know." Alejandro turned her hand over, gently separating the fingers. The bruising was turning a sickly green. "If it is broken, and you don't get it seen to, you could lose some of the use of the finger."

"I'll take the chance." She glanced down at it, raised a smile. "Hey, I never had much use for that one anyway."

He turned back to the box and lifted it. "Okay, from now on I do the lifting. You direct me. Then we both get home faster. Where do you want this?"

She sat on the stool by the counter. "Blue table. I think that's summer stock."

He put it effortlessly at the other end of the shop, the invigorating ease of his movements suggesting a man glad to have a purpose. Outside, in the unlit lane, the rain still came down in sheets, now heavy enough almost to obliterate even the view of the wall on the other side of the road. Jessie shivered, noting that the water had started to creep in under the door.

"It's okay," said Alejandro. "It shouldn't come in any further. It's just because the drains are full." He tapped her lightly on the elbow. "Hey, come on, Jessie. You don't get to sit around, you know. You have to show me which ones to move."

About thirty feet down the lane, Jason Burden sat in the van, unseen by the occupants of the shop. He'd had a few drinks, shouldn't really be driving, but when he'd walked over to Cath's to pick them both up earlier, she'd said Emma was still at drama club, and Jessie was supposedly getting her nails done at some beauty salon. They'd be back soon, her mum said. He was welcome to wait, have a cup of tea with her, and they could walk there and pick Emma up together. He'd gone to the pub instead.

He hadn't really known what had made him come here. Perhaps it was because nothing felt right at the moment. Nothing felt secure, like it had done. Not Jessie, with her fancy friends, her books, shutting herself away from him night after night as she studied, no doubt preparing to build a new life away from him. Not Jessie, too tired to have a laugh down the pub with him now that she was working, always chattering on about people he didn't know, about some girl from the Fairley-Hulme estate, giving herself all sorts of airs and graces. Always trying to get him to come to the shop, meet her new "friends," trying to make him into something he wasn't. Not Jessie, looking at him with a new reproach in her eyes, baring her bruises at him like it didn't hurt him enough already.

Perhaps it was that he'd seen Father Lenny walking toward Cath's house, swaggering like he owned the whole bloody estate, and he'd given him that look, like Jason was no better than dirt, even if he'd covered it up with some phony wave.

Perhaps it was the phone number he'd found in her pocket. The number that had been answered by some foreign-sounding bloke before he hung up.

He wasn't sure why he had come.

Jason sat in the van, listening to the ticking of the engine cooling, the periodic swish of the windscreen wipers as they revealed, every few seconds, in the brightly lit shop, the sight he hadn't wanted to see.

The man holding her hand.

Talking to her with his face inches from hers.

Motioning to her, smiling, to go downstairs to the cellar, to the place where Jason and Jessie had shared their first kiss. The place where he had first made her his own.

They didn't come back up.

Jason rested his buzzing head on the steering wheel.

Then, an eternity later, he placed his hand on the keys in the ignition.

The last box was neatly stacked into the makeshift shelving, and Alejandro dusted off his hands on his trousers. Jessie, sitting on the stairs above him, surveyed the cellar and smiled with satisfaction. "She'll be pleased."

"I hope so." He grinned at her, picked up a piece

of screwed-up paper from the stairs, and tossed it neatly into the bin.

Jessie was watching him, her head tilted to one side. "You're as bad as he is, you know."

"Your boyfriend?" he asked, evidently perplexed.

"Neither of you able to say what you feel. The difference is, he resorts to punches and you just bottle it all up."

"I don't understand." He stepped up toward her so that his head was level with hers.

"Like hell you don't. You should talk to her, Ale. If one of you doesn't do something soon, I'm going to faint under the weight of all the unspoken longing in the air."

He looked at her steadily for some time. "She is married, Jess. And I thought you were the great believer—in fate, I mean. One man for one woman, right?"

"I am," she said. "But it's not anyone's fault if the first time around you get the wrong one."

The jazz compilation playing in the background ended, leaving a silence within the shop, allowing for the dull rumble of an approaching storm outside.

"I think you are a romantic," he said.

"I just think sometimes people need a bit of a shove." She shifted on her step. "Including me. Come on, let's get out of here. My Emma will be wondering where I am. She's coming to watch me get my nails done this evening. First time ever. I can't decide whether to go for some tasteful pink or a lovely tarty scarlet."

He held out his arm, and she took it, helping to raise herself from her seated position. "God," she said, as they emerged into the glowing shop. "I'm absolutely filthy."

He shrugged his agreement, patted himself down, glanced out at the rain. "You have an umbrella?"

"Raincoat," she said, gesturing toward her fuchsia plastic mackintosh. "Essential English summer garment. You'll learn." She moved toward the door.

"You think we should ring Suzanna?" Alejandro said casually. "See if she's okay?"

"She'll be stuck in A and E for hours." Jess checked the keys in her hand. "But I've got to drop these at hers later so I'll tell her you were asking after her, if you like . . ." She grinned, with a hint of mischief.

He refused to answer her, shook his head in mock exasperation. "I think, Jessie, you should keep your schemes to Arturro and Liliane." He stooped to peel off a piece of tape that had attached itself to his trouser leg. Later, he would say he had heard Jessie begin to laugh—a laugh that was interrupted by a rushing noise, a screech of such escalating volume and velocity that it sounded like a vast, angry bird. He had looked up in time to see the blur of white, the ear-splitting crack of what might have been thunder, and then the front of the shop exploding inward in a crash of noise and timber. He had lifted his arm to protect himself against the shower of splintering glass, the flying shelves, plates, pictures, and he had fallen backward against the counter. All he had seen was a flash of bright pink plastic as it disappeared, like a wet carrier-bag, under the van.

It was her fourth cup of machine coffee, and Suzanna realized that if she drank any more her hands would begin to shake. It was hard, though, given the tedium of waiting in the cubicle, and disappearing for coffee seemed to be the only way of legitimately escaping Rosemary's relentlessly bad humor. "If she says, 'The NHS isn't what it used to be,' one more time," she whispered to Vivi, seated beside her, "I'm going to take a swing at her with a bedpan."

"What are you saying?" said Rosemary querulously, from the bed. "Do speak up, Suzanna."

"I shouldn't bother, dear," muttered Vivi. "These days they're made of the same stuff as egg cartons."

They had been there almost three hours. Rosemary had initially been seen by a triage nurse, sent for various X-rays, and diagnosed with a fractured rib, bruising, and a sprained wrist. Then she had been removed from the urgent board, and placed at the end of a long queue of mundane injuries, which she had taken as a personal affront. The young nurse had informed them that it was likely to be another hour at least. Always more accidents in the rain.

Suzanna glanced every few minutes at her left hand, as if it bore the visible sign of her duplicity. Her heart leaped every time she thought of the man who possibly still stood in her shop. This is wrong, she would tell herself. Overstepping the line. And then felt the quicksilver racing of her pulse as she allowed herself, yet again, to replay the events of the previous hours.

Vivi leaned toward her. "You go, dear. I'll get a taxi home."

"I'm not leaving, Mum. Honestly, I can't leave you alone like this." With **her**, went the unspoken addition.

Vivi squeezed her arm gratefully. "I should tell you how Rosemary did it," she whispered.

Suzanna turned, and Vivi glanced behind her, about to impart some piece of information, when the cubicle curtain was pulled back with a loud swishing sound.

A policeman was standing in front of them, his walkie-talkie hissing and stopping abruptly. A female officer was behind him, talking into her own.

"I think you want the end cubicle," said Vivi, leaning forward conspiratorially. "They're the ones who've been fighting."

"Suzanna Peacock?" said the policeman, looking from one to the other.

"Are you going to arrest me?" said Rosemary loudly. "Is it an offense to wait for several hours in a hospital now?"

"That's me," said Suzanna, thinking, **This is like a film.** "Is it—is it Neil?"

"There's been an accident, madam. We think you'd better come with us."

Vivi lifted her hand to her mouth. "Is it Neil? Has he had a crash?"

Suzanna was rooted to the spot. "What?" she said. "What is it?"

The policeman looked reluctantly at the older women.

"They're my family," said Suzanna. "Just tell me, what is it?"

"It's not your husband, madam. It's your shop. There's been a serious incident and we'd like you to come with us."

# 19

Suzanna had spent the last hour and forty minutes, on and off, in the room with the detective sergeant. She learned that he took his coffee black, that he was almost always hungry for the wrong sort of food, and that he thought women should always be addressed as "madam," said with a kind of exaggerated deference that suggested he didn't genuinely believe it. He wouldn't tell her, initially, what had happened, as if, despite her repeated insistence that it was her shop, that her friends had been inside it, all information had to be on a need-to-know basis. She was only allowed odd snippets, offered grudgingly after the detective was called out by whispering underlings, then returned to his desk. She learned about these trivialities because the only one of her senses that seemed to be working efficiently was her ability to register unimportant detail. In fact, she thought she could probably recall any single facet of this room, of the orange plastic chairs, of the stackable public-facility tables, of the cheap foil ashtrays provided in stacks by the door.

What she couldn't do was take in anything that they said and why.

They had wanted to know about Jessie. How long had she worked at the shop? Did she have any—here they hesitated, looked at her meaningfully—**problems** at home? They wouldn't tell her what had happened, but from the unsubtle direction of the questions she had realized it must be to do with Jason. Suzanna, her mind racing headlong into a thousand possibilities, had been reluctant to say too much before she could speak to Jessie, conscious that her friend's hatred of Jason's actions was only matched by her horror of people knowing about them.

"Is she badly hurt?" she would say periodically. "You've got to tell me if she's all right."

"Soon, Mrs. Peacock," he said, scribbling in an illegible hand on the pad in front of him. He had an unopened Mars bar in his top pocket. "Now, did Miss Carter have any"—hesitation, meaningful look—"male friends that you knew about?"

She made the detective promise that if she told him what she knew he would have to tell her the truth about what had happened to her friend. She owed Jason no loyalty, after all. She had told them about Jessie's injuries, about her devotion to and reservations about her partner, about her determination to go through with counseling. She told them, fearful of making Jessie sound like a victim, how determined she was, and unafraid, and how loved she was by almost everyone in the small town. She had become breathless as she finished, as if the words had forced themselves out without sufficient thought, and she had sat in silence for several minutes trying to work out whether there was anything incriminating in what she had just told them.

The detective had noted her words carefully, eyed the woman police officer next to him, and then, in tones that had long learned to disguise shock and horror under an exterior of calm concern, told her that Jessie Carter had been killed instantly that evening when someone drove a van into the front of the shop.

Suzanna's stomach had dropped away. She had looked blindly at the two faces in front of her; two faces, she realized, in a distant, still functioning part of her mind, that were studying her own reaction. "I'm sorry?" she said, when she could make her mouth form words. "Could you repeat what you just said?"

The second time he said it, she experienced a sudden sensation of falling, the same feeling she had had when she was rolling down the hill with Alejandro, the spinning discombobulation of a world off its axis. Except now it was devoid of any joy, there was no exhilaration, just the sickening echo of the policeman's words as they came back to her.

"I think you must have made a mistake," she said. Then the detective had stood, offered her his arm, and said they needed her to come to the shop and determine whether anything was obviously missing. They would call anyone she needed. If she liked, they could wait while she had a cup of tea. They understood it would be something of a shock. He smelled, she noted, of cheese-and-onion crisps.

"Oh, do you know an Alejandro de Marenas?" He had read the name off a piece of paper, pronounced it with a J, and she had nodded dumbly, wondering briefly whether they thought Ale had done it. Done what? she corrected herself. They make mistakes all the time, she told herself, feeling her legs raise her as if they were not connected to her. Who said the police always knew what they were talking about? There was no way that Jessie could be dead. Not **dead** dead.

And then they had stepped out into the corridor, with its stale echoes of antiseptic and old cigarette smoke, and she had seen him, sitting on the plastic chair, his dark head in his hands, the policewoman next to him resting an awkwardly comforting hand on his shoulder.

"Ale?" she had said.

As he lifted his head, the hollow shock, the new landscape of raw, wrenching bleakness on his face as his eyes met hers, confirmed everything the policeman had said. Her hands lifted involuntarily to her mouth as she had let out a great guttural sob; the sound echoed down the empty corridor.

After that the night had become a blur. She remembered being taken to the shop, standing shivering behind the yellow tape with the policewoman murmuring behind her, and staring at the collapsed frontage, the splintered windows, whose top rows still held their Georgian glass as if denying the reality of what had happened below. The electricity had apparently survived the impact, and the shop was glowing incongruously, like the interior of an oversize doll's house, its shelves along the back wall still intact and carefully stacked, alongside the north African maps, all still neatly pasted, as if refusing to bow to the fact of the carnage below them.

At some point, it had stopped raining, but the pavement still gleamed with neon reflections from the floodlights positioned by the firemen. Two were standing under what had been the door frame, gesturing at the wood, and muttering in lowered voices to the policeman in charge. They stopped talking when the policewoman shepherded Suzanna through. "Stand here," the policewoman said in her ear. "This is about as close as we can get for now."

Around her, police and firemen stood in huddles, murmuring into walkie-talkies, taking pictures with flashing cameras, cautioning the few onlookers to move away from the scene, telling them there was nothing to look at here, nothing at all. Suzanna heard the clock in the market square strike ten, and pulled her coat around her, treading carefully on the wet pavement, where her suede-covered notebooks, the hand-embroidered napkins lay sodden, surrounded by shards of glass, price labels smudged with rain. Above her, the sign swung half off, the end of the word "Emporium" apparently carried away with the impact. She moved forward unconsciously, as if to restore it to its place, then halted as she saw several faces glance warily toward her, their expressions telling her it was no longer her shop.

It was evidence.

"We've moved as much stock away from the front as we can," the policewoman was saying, "but obviously until the scaffolders get here we can't vouch for the safety of the building. I'm afraid I can't let you go in."

She was standing, she realized absently, on a photo of herself that Father Lenny had taken when she wasn't looking. She was staring off in the distance, crossly, with Jessie laughing in the background. Jessie had thought it so funny, she had begged to put it up by the register. She bent down and picked it up, wiping her own wet footprint from it with her hand.

"If the rain still holds off, though, you shouldn't lose too much. I take it you're insured."

"She shouldn't have been here tonight," Suzanna

said. "She only offered to stay because I had to take my grandmother to the hospital."

The policewoman looked at her sympathetically, laid a hand on her upper arm. Her tone was oddly confidential. "This wasn't your fault. Good people always think they must be responsible in some way."

Good? thought Suzanna. Then she caught sight of the breakdown truck, which, some thirty feet away, bore the crumpled white van like a precious cargo, its windscreen punched through by some terrible force. Suzanna stepped toward it, tried to read the lettering on the side. "Is that Jason's van? Her boyfriend's van?"

The policewoman looked awkward. "I'm really sorry. I don't know. Even if I did I probably wouldn't be able to tell you. It's officially a crime scene."

Suzanna stared at the photo in her hand, measuring the woman's words in her head, trying to imbue them with some kind of meaning. What would Jessie say about this? she thought. She pictured her face, alive with the excitement of it all, wide-eyed with the sheer pleasure of something actually **happening** in her home town.

"Is he alive?" she said suddenly.

"Who?"

"Jason."

"I'm really sorry, Mrs. Peacock. I can't tell you anything at the moment. If you ring the station tomorrow, I'm sure you'll be able to get some more information."

"I don't understand what has happened."

"I don't think anyone can be entirely sure of what happened yet. But we'll find out, don't you worry about that."

"She's got a little girl," Suzanna said. "She's got a little girl," she repeated. She stood still as the truck, accompanied by several unidentified shouts and a policeman making wheeling motions with his arm, began to tow its unhappy load slowly up the unnaturally lit lane.

"Is there anything personal in there? Anything vital you'd like us to get out for you?"

Suzanna felt the bite of her words, hearing for the first time the request that now could never be satisfactorily answered. Her eyes were too dry for tears. She turned slowly back to the policewoman, placed the photo carefully on the wall beside the shop. "I'd like to go now, please," she said.

The police had rung her mother some time earlier to say that she would probably be at the station for a while. Vivi, having checked anxiously that Suzanna didn't want her there, that her father couldn't come and pick her up, had then promised to ring Neil and let him know. They could give her a ride home if she liked, even send someone to sit with her if she was feeling a bit shaky. It was nearly midnight.

"I'll wait," she said. And three-quarters of an hour later, when Alejandro emerged, his normally tanned face was gray and aged by grief, and Jessie's blood was still grotesquely visible on his clothes. She took his bandaged arm gently and said she would accompany him home. There was no one to whom she could face explaining it; no one else she could bear to be with. Not tonight, at least.

They walked the ten-minute journey through the sodium-lit town in silence, their footsteps echoing in the empty streets, the lights of the windows nearly uniformly extinguished, as above them its inhabitants slept, blissfully unaware of the night's events. The rain had brought forth the sweet, organic smell of grass and rejuvenated blooms, and Suzanna breathed in, her pleasure in it unconscious, until she realized with a jolt that Jessie would not breathe in the verdant smell of that morning. That was how it would feel from now on, the mundane mixed with the surreal: a strange sense of normality, perversely interrupted by great hiccups of horror. Perhaps we are incapable of taking this in, thought Suzanna, wondering how she felt so calm. Perhaps there is only so much to be borne at any one time. She didn't know, she had nothing to judge it against; no one she knew had ever died.

She wondered, briefly, at how her family might have reacted to her mother's death. It was impossible to picture. Vivi had been the maternal core of the family for so long that Suzanna could create no imaginary sense of loss in a family that existed without her. They reached the nurses' quarters, and a security guard, patrolling the perimeter with his straining, whining dog, waved a salute as Alejandro walked her along the path to the block. Probably not such an unusual sight, Suzanna thought absently, picturing them as the security guard must, a nurse and her boyfriend returning from some boozy night out. Alejandro fumbled with the lock, apparently unable to locate the right key. She took them from him, let them both into the silent flat. She took in its emptiness, its impersonality, as if he were determined to only be a temporary visitor. Or perhaps he felt like he had no right to make an impact on the space.

"I'll make us some coffee," she said.

He had washed and changed, on her instructions, then sat down on the sofa, obedient as a child. Suzanna had watched him for a moment, wondering what horrors he had seen, at events she was not yet brave enough to ask about.

It was his paralysis that gave her a kind of strength. She left him there, and set about organizing the coffee, wiping the surfaces of his already orderly kitchen, tidying with a mild madness, as if by doing so she could impose order on the night. And then, emerging from the kitchen, she sat down beside him, handed him a sweetened coffee, and waited for him to speak.

He said nothing.

"You know what?" she said quietly, as if she were speaking to herself. "Jess was the one person who seemed to like me for who I was. Nothing to do with my family, with what I had or didn't have. She didn't even know what my maiden name was for months." She shrugged. "I don't think I even worked it out till tonight, but she didn't seem to think I was a problem. Everyone else does, you know. My family, my husband. Myself, half the time. Living in the shadow of my mother. That shop was the one place I could just be me."

She smoothed an imaginary crease in her trousers. "I've been standing in your kitchen telling myself Jess is gone and the shop is gone. Everything. Even saying the words out loud. But the weird thing is, I can't make myself believe it."

Alejandro said nothing.

Outside a car door slammed and the paving stones echoed with the sound of footsteps, of murmuring voices, which slowly receded.

"I'll tell you something funny. For a while I was envious of her. Because of the way you and she got on," she said, almost shyly. "Jess had that way about her—you know? She got on with everyone. I thought I was jealous, but that's the wrong word. You couldn't be jealous of Jessie, could you?"

"Suzanna—" He lifted a hand, as if to stop her.

"At one point tonight," she continued, persistent, determined, "I thought it was my fault. What happened. Because I made her stay late. But even I know that's crazy—"

"Suzanna."

"Because if you look at it simply, I made her stay. I put her in the path of that van. Because I left early. I can choose to see that, or I can choose to tell myself that I couldn't have done anything to change what happened. That if it was Jason, it would have happened another way."

She blinked back a tear. "I'm going to have to believe that, aren't I? To keep any kind of sanity. To be honest, I'm not sure how well it's going to work."

"Suzanna . . ."

Finally she looked up.

"It is my fault," he said.

"Ale, no . . ."

"It's my fault." It was said with certainty, as if he had knowledge of something she didn't understand.

She shook her head wearily. "This wasn't about either of us in the end. You know as well as I do that this was about Jason. Whatever he did was his decision. His fault, not mine, and definitely not yours."

He didn't seem to hear her. He had turned away from her, his shoulders bowed. Watching him, she felt an encroaching unease, as if he were on the edge of some great abyss that she couldn't see. She started to speak again, compulsively, not sure what she was going to say even as she said it. "Jess loved Jason, Ale. We know that, and we did everything we could to try to persuade her away from him. She was determined to make things work. Look, we were at her house not a week ago, weren't we? There was nothing you could have done. Nothing."

She didn't know whether she believed her own words, but she was determined to lift the weight that had descended on him, desperate to force something out of him, even anger or incomprehension, anything other than this black certainty. "You think Jessie would want you to think like this? She was pretty clear about what she thought was going on. And we trusted her judgment. She wouldn't have thought for one minute that this was anything to do with you. She loved you, Ale. She was always so pleased to see you. Look, even the policewoman said good people always try to blame themselves . . ."

His mouth was set in a grim line. "Suzanna, you don't understand—"

"I do understand. Nobody gets it more than me."

"You—don't—understand." His voice had become sharp.

"What? That you have a monopoly on misery? Believe me, the thought of what you saw will haunt me forever. But this is not helping. It's not going to help either of us. **Ale, please**—" Her voice wavered. "You've got to stop saying that."

"You are not listening to me!"

"Because you're wrong! You're wrong!" she said with a forceful desperation. "You can't just—"

"¡**Carajo!** You've got to listen to me!" His voice exploded into the little room.

Suzanna flinched. "Are you saying you drove the van? You beat her up? What?"

"Suzanna, I bring bad luck to everyone."

She stopped, as if to make sure she had heard him correctly. "What?"

"You heard me." His face was turned away from her, his shoulders rigid with contained fury.

She moved toward him. "Are you serious? Oh, for God's sake, Ale. It's not about luck. You mustn't—"

But he interrupted her, one hand raised. "You remember Jess asked me why I became a midwife?"

She nodded dumbly.

"It doesn't take a psychoanalyst, you know. When I was born, I had a twin. A little girl. When she was born, she was blue. My cord had wrapped itself around her neck."

Suzanna felt the familiar internal lurch. "Did she die?" she whispered.

"My mother never recovered from it. She kept her cot up, bought clothes for her. She even opened a bank account for her. Estela de Marenas. It still exists, for what it's worth." His voice was bitter.

Tears welled in Suzanna's eyes. She tried to blink them away.

"They never said it was me, not to my face. But the fact is that she haunts my house, my family. We are all suffocated by her absence." His voice quietened. "Maybe if my mother had been able to have another child . . . perhaps . . ."

He rubbed at his eyes, and anger crept back into his voice: "I just wanted some peace, you know? I thought, for a while, I had found it. I thought by helping to bring in life, by giving life, I could make it—make her go away. And instead I have this thing, this **fantasma** following me around . . . I must have been a fool." He looked at her. "In Argentina, Suzanna, the dead live among us." His voice was slow now, with the controlled patience of a teacher. "Their ghosts walk among us. Estela lives with me always. I feel her, a presence, always reminding me, always blaming me . . ."

"But it wasn't your fault. You, of all people, should know that." She took his arm now, wanting to make him see.

But he kept shaking his head, as if she couldn't understand what he was saying, lifted his hand to push her away. "I don't even want to get close to you, don't you understand?"

"It's just superstition—"

"Why won't you listen?" he said despairingly.

"You were a **baby**."

There was a long silence.

"**You—were—just—a—baby**," she insisted, her

voice choking. Then, slowly, she put her coffee on the table. She leaned forward and tentatively placed her arms around him, feeling his body rigid against her, desperate to lessen some of what he felt, as if by sheer proximity she could shoulder part of it herself. She heard his voice from somewhere by her hair.

Then he pulled back and she felt her own resolve stagger under the visible weight of his grief, the pain and guilt in his eyes. "Sometimes, Suzanna," he said, "you can do harm just by existing."

Suzanna thought of her mother. Of beautiful horses and sparkling slippers in the moonlight. Briefly, infected by the night and the madness, she wondered whether she contained her mother's soul, whether it was this that so disturbed her father. She tilted her head, her voice cracked with new grief. "Then . . . I'm as guilty as you."

He took her face between his hands then, as if he were only just seeing her, lifted his bandaged hand and wiped her cheek with his thumb, once, twice, unable to stem the flow of tears. Frowning, he brought his face to hers, his eyes so close that she could see the flecks of gold in them, could hear the uneven tenor of his breath. He paused, and then slowly placed his lips on her skin where the tears had been, closed his eyes and kissed the other side, making their salty path his own, winding his hands into her hair as he tried to kiss them away.

And Suzanna, her eyes tightly shut, lifted her own hands to his head as she wept, feeling his soft dark crop of hair. She felt his mouth upon her, breathed in his old leather jacket, and the slight antiseptic hint left over from the police station. Then her lips were on him, searching for his with a kind of urgency, a desperation to obliterate what had gone before. Listening to her own words, as they echoed in the silence around her, the furious, misplaced spirits circling around them as they embraced.

**I'm as guilty as you.**

# 20

It took the building company two days to make the front of the shop safe, for the surveying team to make their official assessment of damage, and another three for the rebuilding work to begin. Fortunately, the insurance company hadn't quibbled. It was two more days before Suzanna was allowed in to begin the laborious process of cleaning up.

During this time, a halting, irregular procession of people had come bearing flowers, small posies, bouquets wrapped in cellophane, which they placed outside the police tape. Many found it easier to mark Jessie's sudden end with a floral tribute than the trickier business of words. At first there were just two, tied forlornly to the lamppost on the day after the accident, their messages making those who stopped to read them exchange glances and mutter sadly about the unfairness of it all. Then, as the news spread through the town, the flowers came in greater numbers. The local florist struggled to keep up, and they formed a cluster, then a floral carpet outside the shop.

It was as if, Suzanna thought, her own grief had been mirrored in that of the town's. The weather had reverted to blue skies and balmy temperatures, the fair had made its biannual visit to the common, and yet there was no joy in Dere Hampton, no gaiety in the bustle of the market square. A small town felt ripples that might go unnoticed in the City, like a tidal wave. And Jessie, it seemed, had been known by too many people for the shock of her death to pass swiftly. The local newspaper made the story its front-page news, careful to say only that a twenty-eight-year-old local man was being questioned by police. But everyone knew: those who knew her and those who claimed to know her speculated on a relationship that had now become common property. Emma Carter's headmaster had twice appealed for local reporters to leave the premises. Suzanna had scanned the reports, and observed in a detached way that her father would be pleased they had only referred to her as Peacock.

In that first week Suzanna had come to the shop twice, once in the company of the detective sergeant, who wanted to talk to her about security arrangements, and once with Neil, who had remarked repeatedly that it was "unbelievable. Just unbelievable." He had tried at one point to talk to her about the financial implications for the shop and she had screamed obscenities at him until he left the room, his hand like a shield over his head. She knew her reaction had been about guilt. Which particular kind, she could not tell. Now she had been given the keys and permission to clear up, even to start trading again. But standing in the steel-framed doorway, flanked by her boarded-up windows and holding the sign that Neil had made for her, which declared her "open for business," she wasn't sure where to begin. It was as if this were a job for Jessie, as if the only possible way to approach it was with her, giggling over trivialities as they wielded brooms and dustpans together.

Suzanna bent to pick up her damaged sign, which someone had propped neatly against the door. She held it for a moment. The Peacock Emporium was her shop. And now only hers alone. The sheer impossibility of the task ahead overwhelmed her and her face crumpled.

Behind her, someone coughed.

It was Arturro, his body blocking out the light. "I thought you might want some help," he said. He was holding a toolbox in one hand, and tucked under his arm was a basket, containing what looked like sandwiches and several bottles of cold drinks. She felt herself collapse a little, imagined briefly what it would be like to let herself be enveloped by his huge, warm arms, to sob against his apron, still infused with the aroma of cheese and coffee from his shop. She needed, just for a moment, the comfort of that solidity. "I don't think I can do this," she whispered.

"We have to," he said. "People are going to need somewhere to come."

She had stepped in through the door then, not taking in what he had said. Within a couple of hours, she understood. Despite its unwelcoming exterior, despite the obstacles of floral arrangements and police cones outside, the shop had become a focal point for those who had known Jessie, those who wanted to share their feelings at her being gone. They came for coffee, to cry tears at the remnants of the display she had made, to leave gifts for her family and, in a few less altruistic cases, simply to gawp.

Suzanna had no choice but to let them.

Arturro had positioned himself behind the counter, and took charge of making the coffee, apparently trying to avoid direct conversation, as Suzanna cleared the floor and tried to organize places to sit. On the couple of occasions that people had spoken to him she had watched him become progressively more uncomfortable, blinking hard and busying himself with the coffee machine. Suzanna, with glazed eyes and the peculiar sensation of operating from the inside of a bubble, cleaned up, answered queries, commiserated, collected the pastel cards and stuffed animals destined for Emma, and allowed people who were seemingly blind to the chaotic nature of their surroundings to fulfill an unstoppable need to talk, with choked voices, about the general niceness, blamelessness of Jessie, and in fierce, accusatory whispers about Jason. They talked in speculative tones about Alejandro: they had heard how he had tried for twenty minutes to save her, about how he had been found, covered in her blood, wedged half under the van himself as he tried uselessly to revive her. Those who had lived nearby talked of how with fists flailing and shouting in Spanish, he had been pulled away from the half-stunned Jason, as he realized his efforts had been in vain. They sat, and wept, and talked—in the way they once had to Jessie.

By the end of the day Suzanna was exhausted. She was slumped on a stool as Arturro moved around her, tidying chairs, nailing the last of the shelves into place. "You should close now," he said, slipping his hammer into his toolbox. "You've done enough. You know there will be more tomorrow."

Through the open doorway the flowers glinted in the afternoon sunlight, some sweating under the plastic. She wondered whether she should get them out to allow them to breathe. It felt somehow wrong to leave them there.

"You want me to come again?"

There was something in his voice . . . Suzanna's mind cleared briefly and she turned to him, her face agonized. "Oh, God, Arturro, I've got something awful to tell you."

He was wiping his hands on a dishcloth. What could be more awful? his expression said.

"Jess—Jess and I," she corrected herself, "we were going to tell you . . . but . . ." She wished she could be anywhere but there. "The chocolates, the ones that Liliane got so upset about. The ones you sacked the boys over. They were from us. Jessie and I sent them to Liliane so that she would think they were from you. We wanted to get you together, you see. Jess—she thought—she said you were meant for each other . . ."

It seemed almost ridiculous now, as if it had happened in another life, to other people, as if its frivolity were part of another existence. "I'm so sorry," she said. "We meant well, honestly. I know it sort of backfired, but please don't think badly of her. She just thought you would be happy together. She was going to tell you the truth. I know it was stupid, and badly thought out, but I encouraged it. If you want to blame anyone, blame me." She didn't dare look at him, wondered whether she should have told him at all. Yet he had been so good, so generous. She could not have made it through the day without him. The least he deserved was the truth.

She waited, fearful of the legendary explosion toward the boys that Mrs. Creek had described, but Arturro continued to pack the last of his tools into his toolbox, and closed the lid. Then he placed a hand on Suzanna's shoulder. "I will tell Liliane," he said, swallowing. He patted her, then walked heavily toward the door and opened it. "I'll see you tomorrow, Suzanna."

She closed up at half past four, then walked home, lay on her bed fully clothed, and slept until eight the next morning.

Alejandro hadn't come. She realized she had been half-waiting for him all day.

The funeral was to be at St. Bede's, the Catholic church on the west side of the square. Initially, Cath Carter had told Father Lenny that she wanted a private service, didn't want everyone gawping and speculating on her daughter's untimely end, not with the police investigation still ongoing and all. But Father Lenny, gently, over a period of days, had told her of the strength of feeling in the little town, of the numerous people who had asked him whether they could pay their respects. How it would help little Emma, in the circumstances, to see how much her mother was loved.

Suzanna sat in front of her dressing-table, pulling her dark hair back into a severe knot. Father Lenny had said the service would be a celebration of Jessie's life, and that he did not want it to be a somber occasion. But Suzanna did not feel like celebrating. Her mother, who had said she would be coming with her father, as much for Suzanna as Jessie, had lent Suzanna a black hat. "I think it's important that you do what you feel is right," she said, laying a hand against Suzanna's cheek, "but formal is never inappropriate."

"Did you say you'd bought me a black tie?" Neil ducked with well-practiced ease as he entered the low doorway. "I can't seem to find it."

"My handbag," said Suzanna, putting in her earrings, gazing at her reflection. She didn't usually wear earrings, wondered whether they would suggest inappropriate gaiety.

Neil stood in the middle of the room, as if in hope that the handbag might leap out at him.

"On the landing." She heard him leave the room, treading the squeaky floorboards to the top of the stairs.

"Lovely day for it. I mean, not a lovely day as such," he corrected himself, "but there's nothing worse than a funeral when it pelts down with rain. Wouldn't have seemed right for Jessie, somehow."

Suzanna closed her eyes. Every time she thought of heavy rain now, she associated it with the images of skidding vans and screeching brakes, of the crashing and splintering of glass. Alejandro had said he heard no scream, but in Suzanna's imagination, Jessie had stared at her approaching death and—

"Got it. Oh, Christ, look—think it could do with a quick iron before I put it on."

She forced away the image and opened her drawer to pull out her watch. She heard Neil muttering about the ironing board, and then a brief silence.

"What's this?"

She hoped Jessie had known nothing when it happened. Alejandro had said he couldn't see how she would have felt anything, that in his opinion she had been dead even as he had scrambled over the timber and glass to get to her.

Neil was at her shoulder. "What's this?" he said again. His face had contorted; it didn't look like his own.

She turned on her stool, and gazed at the doctor's appointment card he held out in front of him, which bore the words "Family Planning Clinic." She knew that her face looked resigned, guilty, but somehow she couldn't form it into an expression that would prove any more satisfactory. "I was going to tell you."

He said nothing, just kept holding it out.

"I booked an appointment."

"To . . ."

"To have a coil fitted. I'm really sorry."

"A coil?"

She nodded awkwardly. "Look, I haven't even been yet. What with Jess and everything, I missed the appointment."

"But you're going to go." His voice was dead.

"Yes," she said, and glanced up. Her eyes looked away as soon as they met his. "Yes, I am. Look, I'm not ready, Neil. I thought I was, but I'm not. There's too much going on. And I need to resolve things first."

"You need to resolve things?"

"Yes. With my dad. My mum—my real mum, I mean."

"You need to resolve things with your real mum."

"Yes."

"And how long do you think this will take?"

"What?"

He was furious, she realized. He turned to face her with manic intent. "How. Long. Do. You. Think. This. Will. Take?" His tone was sarcastic.

"How should I know? As long as it takes."

"As long as it takes. God, I should have known." He paced the room, a television detective explaining the genesis of some long-standing crime.

"What?"

"The one thing I wanted. The one thing I thought we had agreed on. And, oh, look, suddenly, after getting everything she wants, Suzanna has changed her mind."

"I haven't changed my mind."

"No? No? So what is this, then, because it sure isn't up there with oysters and champagne on the getting-pregnant front."

"I haven't changed my mind."

"Then what the hell is this about?"

"Don't shout at me. Look, I'm sorry, okay? I'm sorry, Neil. I just can't do it right now. I can't do it now."

"Of course you can't—"

"Don't do this, all right?"

"Do what? What the hell am I doing?"

"Bullying me. I'm just about to bury my best friend, okay? I don't know whether I'm coming or going—"

"Your best friend? You hadn't known her six months."

"There's a time limit on friendship now?"

"You weren't even sure about her when she started. You thought she was taking advantage of you."

Suzanna stood up and pushed past him to the door. "I can't believe we're having this conversation."

"No, Suzanna, I can't believe that just when I thought we were finally back on track, you've found a way to sabotage everything again. You know what? I think there's something else going on here. Something you're not being straight with me about."

"Oh, don't be ridiculous."

"Ridiculous? So what am I meant to say, Suzanna? 'Oh, you don't want a baby after all. Don't worry, darling. I'll just put my own feelings on hold for a while . . . like I always do.'"

"Don't do this, Neil." She reached past him for her coat, pulled it briskly around her, knowing that she would be too hot later.

He was standing in front of her, refusing to move out of the way when she stepped forward. "So, when is the right time, Suzanna? When does this stop being about you, huh? When do my feelings finally get a look-in?"

"Please, Neil—"

"I'm not a saint, Suzanna. I've tried to be patient with you, tried to be understanding, but I'm lost. Really. I just can't see how we move on from here . . ."

She stared at the confusion in his face. She moved forward, placed her hand on his cheek, an unconscious echo of her mother's gesture. "Look, we'll talk about it after the funeral, okay? I promise—"

He shook off her hand and went to open the door as the taxi arrived, hooting to signify its arrival. "Whatever," he said. He didn't look back.

It was widely agreed that it was a dreadful funeral. Not that Father Lenny hadn't made an effort with his eulogy—which was beautiful and apt and knowing, and had enough humor to raise the odd brave smile among the mourners—or that the church didn't look beautiful, what with the ladies from the supermarket having made such an effort to decorate it with flowers, so that the casual observer might have thought they were about to host a wedding. It was not that the sun didn't shine, as if to offer hope that the place to which Jessie had gone was indubitably wonderful and filled with birdsong—all the things one might hope of a heaven.

It was just that, however you dressed it up, there

was something so unspeakably awful, so wrong
about burying her. About the fact, they all said
afterward, that someone like her should be gone.
About the small pale figure who stood motionless
in the front pew clutching her grandmother's hand,
and the empty place beside her on the pew, which
meant that she was effectively orphaned even if only
one parent had died.

Suzanna had been asked by Cath to come to the
graveside. She had told her that she would be hon-
ored, and taken her place alongside Jessie's distant
relatives and oldest schoolfriends, trying not to feel
like an impostor, trying not to think of where Jessie
had met her death.

He had not even attempted to come, apparently.
Father Lenny had told her the previous day. He had
been to see the lad in the hospital. Even though
it went against his every instinct, he said, his job
was also to comfort the sinner. (And it wasn't as if
anyone else was going to visit him. It had been all
he could do to stop Jessie's neighbors on the estate
from forming a lynch mob.)

In fact, Father Lenny had been shaken by the
lad's appearance. His face stitched and swollen
from his unsupported journey through the windscreen, his skin bruised and purple, his injuries had
uncomfortably echoed Jessie's in previous weeks. He
had refused to say anything other than that he loved
her and that the van wouldn't stop. The doctor said

he wasn't sure his mental state meant he could take in what he had done.

"Would have been better for everyone if he'd died too," Father Lenny had said, his voice uncharacteristically bitter.

The familiar liturgy of dust to dust, ashes to ashes had ended. Suzanna saw Emma with her grandmother's hands on her shoulders, supporting and holding her close. She wondered who gained the most comfort from their seemingly unending physical contact. She thought of the first day she had reopened the shop, when the child and her grandmother had come and stood in the lane. They had refused her invitation to come inside. They had just stood opposite, holding hands, their faces gray and wide-eyed as they absorbed its shattered exterior.

Emma will grow up without a mother, she thought. Like I did. And then, glancing at Vivi, who was standing by the car, felt the customary stab of guilt that she could think that.

It was when they stepped away from the grave that she saw him. Standing a little way back, behind Father Lenny, moving away from Cath, with whom he had evidently been exchanging a few quiet words. Cath was holding his tanned hands, nodding as she listened, her face dignified and curiously understanding in grief. He glanced up as Suzanna stared, and for a moment their eyes locked, exchanging in those brief seconds all the grief, guilt, shock . . . and secret joy of the previous week. She stepped forward, as if to go to him. Stopped as she felt a hand on her shoulder. "Your mum and dad have invited us back, Suze." It was Neil. She looked up at her husband, blinking, as if she was trying to register who he was. "I think it would be a good idea if we went."

She made herself keep looking at him, struggled to gather her thoughts. "To Mum's?" And then, as she took in his words, "Oh, no, Neil. Not there. I don't think I can face it today."

Neil had already turned away. "I'm going. You can do what you want, Suzanna."

"You're going?"

He kept walking, stiff in his dark suit, leaving her standing on the grass. "It's a day for family," he said, over his shoulder, just loud enough for her to hear. "Your parents have been kind enough to support you today. And, to be honest, I can't see the point in you and me being alone right now. Can you?"

Alejandro had walked the length of the grave-yard with Cath and Emma. She had turned back in time to see him reach the gates. When he got there he had squatted down to say something to Emma, and pressed something into her hand. As she left, he might have nodded at Suzanna. At that distance it was hard to be sure.

"Nearly six hundred people came when your father died. The church was so full they had to seat people out on the grass." Rosemary accepted a second cup of tea. She was addressing her son as he leaned back in his chair. "I always thought we should have used a cathedral."

Vivi squeezed Suzanna's arm as she sat beside her daughter on the sofa. She really looked terribly pale. "Lovely cake, Mrs. Cameron," she said. "Very moist. Do you use lemon rind in it?"

"The archbishop had offered to give the sermon. Do you remember, Douglas? Dreadful man with a lisp."

Douglas nodded.

"And four eggs," said Mrs. Cameron. "Good free-range ones. That's what gives it the yellow color."

"I thought your father would rather have the vicar." She nodded, as if confirming this to herself, then eyed Mrs. Cameron as she took away the tea-pot to refill it.

"I didn't like that ham in the sandwiches. It's not proper cut ham."

"It was, Rosemary," said Vivi, in emollient tones. "I got a whole one specially from the butcher."

"Tasted like that re-formed stuff. Scraped off the factory floor and glued together with goodness-knows-what."

"I cut it off the bone myself, Mrs. Fairley-Hulme." Mrs. Cameron turned back from the doorway, with a wink at Vivi. "Next time I'll carve it in front of you, if you like."

"I wouldn't trust you near me with a carving knife," said Rosemary, sniffing. "I've heard about you so-called care assistants. You'll have me changing my will in my sleep next—"

"Rosemary!" Vivi nearly spat out her tea.

"—and then making sure I have a so-called 'accident,' like Suzanna's friend."

There was a stunned silence in the room as its occupants tried to work out which of Rosemary's statements had been the most offensive. Reassured by Mrs. Cameron's easy guffaw as she disappeared into the kitchen, all eyes had fallen on Suzanna, but she appeared not to be listening. She was staring at the floor, locked into the same misery as her silent husband.

"Mother, I hardly think that's appropriate . . ." Douglas leaned forward.

"I'm eighty-six years old, and I shall say what I like," said Rosemary, settling back into her chair.

"Rosemary," said Vivi, gently, "please . . . Suzanna's friend has just died."

"And I'll be the next to go, so I think that gives me more of a right than most to talk about death." Rosemary placed her hands in her lap, then gazed around at the mute faces in front of her. "Death," she said, finally. "Death. Death. Death. There, you see?"

"Oh, for God's sake," said Douglas, rising from his chair.

"What?" She looked up at her son, her expression challenging beneath the immovable pathways of veins and wrinkles.

"Not today, Mother. Please." He moved toward her. "Do you want Mrs. Cameron to take you into the garden? So you can see the flowers? I think a breath of fresh air would be just the thing," said Douglas. "Mrs. Cameron!"

"I do not want to go into the garden," said Rosemary. "Douglas, do not put me in the garden."

Vivi turned to her daughter, still limply acquiescent to having her arm held. "Darling, are you okay? You've been dreadfully quiet since we got back."

"I'm fine, Mum," she said dully.

Vivi glanced at Neil. "Some more tea, Neil?" she said hopefully.

He attempted a smile. "I'm fine, thanks, Vivi."

Outside, they could hear Rosemary protesting furiously at being wheeled around the courtyard garden, punctuated by Mrs. Cameron's cheerfully oblivious exclamations.

"I'm sorry," said Douglas, coming back into the drawing room, wiping his head. "She can be a bit—difficult at the moment. Not been quite the same since her fall."

"I guess she just tells the truth," said Neil.

Vivi could have sworn he looked meaningfully at Suzanna, but he turned away so fast she couldn't be sure. She looked up at Douglas, trying to silently indicate that she was unsure of what to do next. He walked over to the sofa, took her hand in his. "Actually," he said, clearing his throat, "we called you here for a reason, Suzanna."

"What?"

"I know it's been a pretty bad day for you. Your mother and I—we wanted to show you something."

Vivi felt the swell of something hopeful. She took her daughter's hand and squeezed it.

Suzanna glanced at Neil, then at her parents. She allowed herself to be led from the sofa, like a sleepwalker. Vivi, conscious that Neil's part in this was important, placed her arm around her son-in-law's waist, wishing she occasionally saw Suzanna do the same.

"Upstairs," said Douglas, gesturing to them.

They walked silently up to the gallery. Through the window, Vivi could just make out Rosemary, shaking her head as Mrs. Cameron bent toward a flower bed.

"We're thinking of putting some new lights up here, aren't we, darling?" Douglas's voice came from ahead of her. "Brighten this floor up a bit. Always been a bit gloomy," he said to Neil.

They stopped at the top of the stairs, and stood clustered together, Suzanna looking unreceptive, Neil gazing at Vivi's face for clues.

"What?" said Suzanna, eventually, in a thin voice.

Douglas looked at his daughter and smiled.

"What?" she said again.

He gestured toward the far wall. And it was then that Suzanna saw it.

Vivi's eyes never left her as she stood motionless and stared at the oil painting of her mother, undamaged by its brush with Rosemary, now overlit by a narrow brass light. Suzanna's fine profile, so like Athene's, was as still and white as that of a Grecian statue. Her hair, swept back from her face, made Vivi wince. Even after all these years. She reminded herself of her blessings, especially the most recent ones. This is for Suzanna, she told herself. For Suzanna's happiness.

She felt Douglas beside her, his arm sliding around her shoulders, and reached her fingers up to his, gleaning comfort from the gesture. It was the right thing. Regardless of what Rosemary said, it was the right thing.

But when Suzanna turned to them, her color was high, her eyes furious. "And this—this is meant to make it all okay?"

Vivi took in the granite set of Suzanna's mouth, an echo of the worst, most damaged part of Athene. And realized, too late, that the hurt went way deeper than could be addressed by the hanging of a portrait.

"We just thought . . . ," Douglas began, his habitual confidence deserting him. "We thought it might make you feel better."

Neil's eyes were flicking between the three of them, his earlier expression replaced by something less certain.

"Feel better?" Suzanna asked.

"To see it here, I mean," Douglas continued.

Vivi reached out a hand to her. "We thought it would be a good reminder—"

Suzanna's voice pierced through the silent gallery. "Of another person whose death I inadvertently caused?"

Douglas flinched, and Vivi tightened her hold on him. "You didn't—"

"Or how about, I got over what happened to her so I'll get over what happened to Jess too? Is that it?"

Vivi's hand was pressed to her mouth. "No, no, darling."

Douglas had stepped forward. "Suzanna, you've—"

"I can't stay here," Suzanna said, and, her eyes bright with tears, pushed past them toward the stairs. After a split second's hesitation, Neil went after her.

"Get off me!" she shouted, as he caught her up halfway down the stairs. "Just get off me!" The ferocity in her words made him recoil.

It was not often that Vivi felt truly sympathetic toward her mother-in-law but, conscious of the bewildered hurt on Douglas's face as he stood beside her, listening now to the muffled sound of her daughter and son-in-law screaming at each other out on the drive, staring at the far wall at that smirking mouth, those ice-blue eyes, Vivi thought she might finally have understood how Rosemary felt.

Suzanna walked the entire perimeter of the forty-acre field. She walked through the forest, along the bridleway known as Short Wash, up the hill that backed on to the beet field and knelt at its crest where she had sat with Alejandro less than two weeks earlier.

The evening had brought cool, soft breezes from the coast, easing the high temperatures of the day. The land was settling slowly for the evening, bees bumbling lazily across meadows, seeds blown up from meadow grass floating slowly to earth.

Suzanna sat and thought about Jessie. She thought about Arturro and Liliane, whom she had seen together outside the church, her arm linked in his as he stooped to offer her a handkerchief, and wished that Jessie could have seen it too. She thought about the way her father had closed his eyes as she turned from him, a look of quiet despair, so fleeting that it was likely only she had seen it. She had recognized it all right: it was the same expression she had seen on Neil that morning.

A few feet away, a starling was jabbing at the soil, and across the valley, she heard the distant sound of the market-square bell: it struck five, six, seven o'clock, as it had for all the years she had been absent, creating a life for herself many miles from here. Time to get up. Time to move on.

Suzanna laid her head on her knees, and breathed deeply, wondering at the sheer number of people in her life to whom she needed to say sorry.

Only some of whom would ever hear her.

# 21

The shop stayed shut for just over a week. Suzanna had arrived to open it on the morning after the funeral and then, having stood on the doorstep for almost seven minutes—long enough for the woman who ran the pet shop on the corner to enquire whether she was all right—she put the key back into her bag and walked home. Two suppliers had rung to ask her whether there was a problem. She had told them politely that there wasn't, but that she wouldn't be taking any deliveries in the near future. The builders rang to ask if it would be okay if they put a dumpster right outside the door, and she had surprised them with the readiness with which she had said yes. Arturro had rung her at home to make sure she was okay. She fought the suspicion that he was afraid something would happen to her too.

Suzanna had done little that week. She had completed various domestic tasks, which she had somehow never had time for when the shop was open: she washed windows, hung curtains, painted the unfinished part of the kitchen. She made a few cursory attempts at weeding. She cooked several meals, at least one of which was both attractive and edible, none of which she herself had been able to stomach. She had said nothing to Neil about the shop's temporary closure. When he discovered it several days later, having been asked by a fellow commuter when she was likely to reopen, he said nothing in return. And if she was rather quiet, he didn't say much about that either. It was an odd, unbalanced time for everyone. Grief was a strange thing. They were still a little fragile with each other, since the exchange before Jessie's funeral. And even he knew well enough by now that there were times in a marriage when not talking too much was the right thing to do.

On the following Monday, exactly nine days after the funeral, Suzanna got up at half past seven. She ran a bath (the cottage didn't have a shower), washed her hair, put on makeup and a freshly ironed shirt. Then, on a day windy enough to snatch at her hair and turn her pale cheeks pink, she accepted a lift from her husband to the Peacock Emporium. With no visible hesitation, she put her key in the steel anti-squatter door and opened up. Then, having offered the builders a mug of tea, she sorted the pile of post and noted, with mixed feelings, the disappearance of the vast bank of old flowers—and the arrival of several newer bunches, including a posy from Liliane. She pulled out all the things from her bag she had collected over the course of the week, things she had examined and fretted over, things she had remembered and sometimes chosen just because of the way they looked. She laid them out on the pink-painted table, an expression of intense concentration on her face, then began to gather up Jessie's things.

Mrs. Creek, perhaps predictably, was the first customer to appear. The short gap between her and Suzanna's arrival made Suzanna wonder afterward whether she hadn't spent the last days positioned surreptitiously somewhere, one eye on the shop, waiting for the moment when the door would open again. She looked as windswept as Suzanna felt, her silver hair sticking out from under her crocheted beret as if she had been electrocuted. "You didn't tell anyone you were going to close," she said accusingly, as she arranged her bag on the table beside her.

"I didn't know," said Suzanna, moving all the mugs along the shelf in an attempt to find Jessie's favorite.

"It's not very good for business."

She found it. A blue-and-white one with a line drawing of a bulldog and the words "**chien mechant**" on the other side. Jessie had said it reminded her of Jason when he woke up in the morning. She had thought this was funny.

"I had to go to the Coffee Pot instead," Mrs. Creek continued. "I don't like their sandwiches. But you left me no choice."

"I don't do sandwiches."

"That's not the point, dear. You can't have a coffee in there after eleven thirty if you're not prepared to have something to eat. Their cheapest cheese and tomato is more than two pounds, you know."

"Do you want those taped boxes at the back?" Neil emerged briefly from the cellar, checking his trousers for marks. "They've got 'Christmas' written on them, so I'm assuming you don't want them up yet."

Suzanna turned. "No," she said. "The back will be fine. As long as I can get to the other stuff."

"You're lucky the builders took all of this in for you," he said, gesturing to the cellar, where delivery boxes sat in teetering columns, disguising the fact that the area had only recently been cleaned and reorganized. "Some people might have taken them for themselves."

"It's not like that around here," said Suzanna, who didn't feel like being grateful to anyone. Especially not builders who were costing her an excess of four hundred pounds on her insurance policy and apparently drinking almost half that amount daily in finest Brazilian coffee beans. "Did you want another drink or are you going soon?"

"I'm all right for the moment. I'll get as much

done as I can before I have to head off. Leave you free to sort things out up here," Neil said, and disappeared down the stairs again.

"That your husband?" Mrs. Creek was toying with an old magazine.

The way she glanced toward the stairs, as if Suzanna had done something duplicitous in having him here, made her feel intensely irritable. "Yes," she said, and went back to her display.

"I saw him with you at the funeral."

"Oh."

"Have you seen her?"

"Who?"

"The daughter, Emma. Nice little girl, she is. I made her a daisy outfit. Fitted her beautifully, it did. I made it out of an old piece of crepe-de-Chine." She sipped her coffee.

Suzanna had been trying to keep the vision of Jessie's display intact in her head. She had known exactly what she wanted when she left the house, but already her ideas were getting blurred, corrupted by conversation.

"Ball gowns and wedding dresses. Crepe-de-Chine was lovely for those. Of course, most wedding dresses were silk—those who could afford it, anyway."

What was left of her vision evaporated. Oh, please go away, thought Suzanna, fighting the urge to bang her head repeatedly on the counter's hard surface. Just leave me alone. I can't listen to your ramblings today.

The wind rattled down the lane, sending paper cups and the first stray leaves of autumn scuttling in errant circles in its wake. On the other side of the plywood hoardings, she heard the builders calling and exclaiming to each other, interrupted by the occasional burst of an electric drill. The windows would be going in next week, they said. Handmade by a local carpenter. Even better than the old ones. In a perverse way she had decided she quite liked the bare wood enclosure, the dim light. She wasn't sure if she was ready to be so exposed again.

"You couldn't do us another coffee, could you, love?" The oldest builder, a man with silver hair and a strong sense of his own charm, slid his face around the front door. "It's turned bitter out here."

She mustered a smile. Like she had mustered one for Mrs. Creek. "Sure," she said. "Coming right up."

Several minutes later she heard the door open again. But when she finally looked up from the coffee machine it wasn't the builder who stood in front of her.

"Suzanna," he said and, for a second, she could see nothing except him, his blue hospital tunic, his battered holdall, his intimate, lowered gaze. He glanced around the shop, at Mrs. Creek, apparently engrossed in her magazine, and stretched a hand across the counter toward her. "The shop was closed," he said quietly. "I didn't know how to reach you."

His sudden proximity made her short of breath. She blinked hard at the coffees in front of her. "I have to take these out," she said, her voice cracking.

"I need to talk to you."

She glanced at Mrs. Creek, then up at him. "The shop's quite busy at the moment," she said distinctly, trying to convey something—she wasn't sure what—in her voice.

From the other end of the shop, Mrs. Creek called, "Are you charging those men full price for their coffees?"

Suzanna tore her gaze away from him. "What? No," she said. "I'm not charging them anything."

"That's hardly fair."

Suzanna breathed in. "If you'd like to help replace my windows, Mrs. Creek, or compile my insurance claim, perhaps even my accounts, I'd be delighted to give you a free coffee."

"Suzanna," he murmured at her left ear now, equally insistent.

"Hardly very friendly, is it?" Mrs. Creek muttered. "I don't suppose Jess . . ." She apparently changed her mind. "I suppose things will go back to how they were, now." Her tone left no one in any doubt as to what she thought of that.

"I kept thinking about you . . . ," he said quietly. She was focusing on his mouth now, several inches from hers. "I have hardly slept since . . . I feel guilty that I can feel so much joy, so much . . . at a time that's so . . . so bad." Despite the weight of his words, something had lifted in him: his face was glowing.

Suzanna's gaze flickered from his mouth to Mrs. Creek, reading again in the corner. Outside she could hear people talking in the street, the answering tones of the builders, and wondered whether they were leaving more flowers. She was dimly aware of Neil whistling "You Are My Sunshine" several feet below them.

"You think it's wrong?" Alejandro's hand touched hers, the contact featherlight. "To be so happy?"

"Ale—I—"

"Did you say what you wanted done with that garbage bag? I could ask the guys outside if I could dump it in their can."

She jumped, snatching back her hand, and whipped around as Neil, several feet away, rubbed at his nose then examined his fingers as if expecting to see dirt. "Oh," he said amiably. "Sorry to interrupt."

Suzanna struggled to stop herself blushing. She felt, rather than saw, Alejandro take a step away from the counter, and wished she hadn't been a party to his surprise.

"It's fine," said Alejandro stiffly. "I just wanted a coffee."

Neil stared at him for a minute. "Spanish accent,"

he said. "You must be the gaucho. Sorry, the girls didn't tell me your name."

Suzanna's knuckles had whitened on the handles of the tray. She willed herself to grip it less tightly.

"Alejandro."

"Alejandro. You work at the hospital, right?"

"That's right."

"Great job," Neil said. "Great job," he repeated. "Yes, Jessie told me all about you." He paused. "She was very fond of you, old Jess."

"I was very fond of her." Alejandro was looking intently at him, as if he were measuring him, determining his worth, and the strength of his claim on Suzanna. There was something different about his stance, a hint of combativeness in his heightened vigilance, his squared shoulders. Suzanna, her senses vibrating so hard she thought they must be visible, felt both thrilled and appalled by this, conscious of Neil's blindness. She wanted to be anywhere other than where she was. But her feet were rooted to the spot.

"Terrible," Neil said. "Terrible." Outside, someone began hammering. "I'll just pull those shelves out before I go," he said to Suzanna. "Somehow a load of rubble has ended up behind them. God knows how." He disappeared back down the stairs, whistling as he went.

Alejandro glanced past her to the cellar door, to the sounds of boxes being shifted below, and moved forward. "I have to tell you," he murmured, "how I feel. I have to speak to you. It's like the first time I've really spoken."

She lifted her face, her body remembering reflexively. "Please, don't—"

"She saw it, Suzanna. She saw it before we did."

"I'm **married**, Ale."

He shot a dismissive look at the cellar door. "To the wrong man."

At the other end of the shop, Mrs. Creek was regarding them with interest. Suzanna stepped back toward the shelves and fiddled with the coffee syrups, organizing them into a neat row.

"I'm married," she said quietly. "I might even be carrying his child."

He looked at her stomach, then shook his head.

"I can't just ignore that fact, Ale. I'm sorry."

Alejandro came closer, his voice low in her ear as he said, "So what are you telling me, that you're going to stay with him? After everything?"

"I'm sorry." She turned to him, her back against the wall.

"I don't understand." His voice was rising dangerously. Suzanna looked at Mrs. Creek, who was now examining the magazine with the intense concentration of someone trying—or pretending—not to eavesdrop.

She looked at him pleadingly. "Look, I've never done the right thing, Ale, not really." She thought of the previous night, of how she had lain awake in the spare room and then, at half past three, crept into their bed, and curled up, pulling Neil's arm over her, trying to offer herself up as an apology. They had made love, something sad and resigned in it. She had prayed during it that he would not speak.

Neil's voice floated up the stairs: "Do you want to leave these posters down here, Suze? The ones by the trolley?"

Suzanna tried to steady hers. "Can you leave them there, please?" she called.

"I've realized things have got to change," she murmured to Alejandro. "I've got to change."

"You told me, Suzanna. **You told me**—there is a time to let go of the past, of ghosts. You showed me it was time to live." He took her hands in his, apparently no longer caring if they were seen. "You can't go back. You know that. You can't. I can't."

"I can." She stared at their hands. It was as if they belonged to other people.

"Everything has changed, Suzanna."

"No."

"You have to listen to me."

"Ale—I don't know you. I don't know anything about you. You know nothing about me. All we knew was that we loved the same girl, and we lost her. It's hardly enough to base a relationship on, is it?" She stepped sideways, hearing Neil's footsteps in the cellar, his quiet exclamation as something fell heavily into place.

"You think that's it? You think that's all we are?" He had dropped her hands now, was staring at her in disbelief.

Suzanna forced her voice to stay calm. "I'm sorry. But I've done this all my life. I've done it all through my marriage—you're not the first person I've had a crush on."

"You think this is a **crush**?" He was only a few inches away from her now. She could smell the leather of his coat, the faint tang of **Mate** on his breath. The builders had begun banging something against the boarding, and she felt the impact reverberate through her.

"I **know you**, Suzanna." He had her backed up against the boarded window now, his hands on each side of her shoulders, a barely contained fury on his face.

"No," she said. "You don't."

"Yes, I do. I know you as well as I know myself. I knew you the moment I saw you, so beautiful and—and furious, trapped behind the counter of your shop."

She was shaking her head now, the vibrations of the hammer echoing through her, drowning out everything but him, the smell of his skin, the terrible nearness of him. "I can't—"

"Tell me you don't know me," he whispered.

She was crying silently now, no longer caring if Mrs. Creek was watching.

"Tell me. Tell me you don't know who I am." His voice was hoarse, urgent in her ear.

"No—I—"

He slammed the board by the side of her head, so that the banging stopped temporarily. "Suzanna, please. **Tell me you don't know me.**"

She nodded, finally, her face crumpling, her eyes closed against him, lost in the scent of him, the proximity of him. "I do . . . I do know you, Ale. I do."

Vindicated, he turned from her, wiping at his face with one hand.

Her voice came at him from behind, halting: "But that doesn't make it right."

He had left less than a minute later, his face so hurt and furious that she thought she might shrivel and die. That might have been preferable to him ever looking at her like that again. Seconds later Neil, dusty and satisfied, had emerged at the sound of the steel door slamming. "You'll be glad when you get your good one back," he said, fanning his ears. "Sounds like you're being locked up in prison every time that one shuts. Right. I'm done. Do you want to examine my handiwork?"

"No," said Suzanna, biting back tears. "I trust you."

"More the fool you, eh?" said Neil, winking at Mrs. Creek. Before he left, he gave her a supportive hug. "You look washed out," he said kindly. "Why don't you see if there's someone else who can help you for the next few weeks? It's a big job, running it all by yourself."

He couldn't understand why this made her start crying again.

# Part Three

# 22

It is said, among the rare few who have returned from such a state, that the last few moments before drowning are quite pleasant. As the fight ends, and the water floods into the lungs, the victim enters a passive, accepting state, even sees a kind of perverse beauty in their condition.

Suzanna thought of this often over the next few weeks. Sometimes it felt like drowning. Sometimes it felt like sleepwalking, as if she were going blindly through some predetermined motions, not entirely in control of the things she said or did. Some might have said, she thought wryly, that this was an improvement. At home she kept the house tidy and the fridge well stocked, and had failed for some time now to complain about the low beams. She and Neil were gentle with each other, solicitous, each recognizing that the last weeks had damaged the other in some way and not wanting to be responsible for any further hurt. She told Neil she loved him once a day, a sentiment that, to his credit, he was always quick to return. Funny how in marriage a statement that had in its infancy started out as a question, even a provocation, could ultimately become a kind of benign reassurance.

She thought little of Alejandro. Consciously, anyway. At night she often woke crying and wondered fearfully what she had said in her sleep. Neil had put down these nocturnal episodes to Jessie's death, and she felt guilty, apologizing silently to Jessie that she had let him.

Alejandro didn't come into the shop. But, then, not many people did. Once the high drama of Jessie's death had faded, once the flowers had been removed and the mawkish had melted away, Suzanna had been left with just a few regular customers. There was Mrs. Creek—who came, Suzanna suspected, because she had worn out her welcome in most other places. She had once overheard the woman's name mentioned in the market café, followed by a rolling of eyes, and she had felt briefly sorry for her. Except that Mrs. Creek's relentlessly self-involved stories and demands meant that sympathy never lasted for long.

There was Father Lenny, who told her solemnly that if she ever wanted to talk, really talk (here he raised a meaningful eyebrow), he was always there for her. Oh, and if she wanted some beaded lamps at a good price, nice ones, mind, he knew where there were some going. Liliane came in occasionally, glowing with what was possibly new love, and bought

among other things a pigskin wallet for Arturro and
several handmade greeting cards. She didn't speak
to Suzanna more than was strictly necessary, and
despite the apparently happy outcome, Suzanna
knew that in some way she was not forgiven for the
chocolates in the way Jessie might have been.

Arturro came in, at least once a day, to buy an
espresso that she suspected he no longer needed. She
had heard on the town grapevine that he was thinking of having his own machine installed, and was
holding off only out of loyalty to Suzanna, perhaps
in the belief that the shop had suffered enough. He
was endlessly kind, checking that there were no
jobs needing doing, offering to mind the shop for
her so that she could run out to get some lunch.
She didn't take him up on it very often. It was rare,
these days, that she felt hungry enough to make the
effort to buy something, and she was afraid that if
he hung around too much Liliane would eye her
more malevolently than she already did.

Occasionally she would catch him looking at her
with sad, wary eyes, and she would force a bright
smile that said, "I'm okay, really." A smile she found
herself using so often that she had forgotten what
the real one felt like.

Neil told her the shop was failing. He didn't
say it in so many words. He probably didn't want
to make her sadder than she already was. He just
looked at the books every few days, and the way

he rested his forehead on his hand as he examined the receipts told her everything she needed
to know.

She ought to care more than she did, she realized,
but its brightly repainted exterior, the posters someone had put up to hide the ugly hoardings over the
windows, failed to draw her or anyone as they once
had. The brightly colored tables suddenly looked sad
and makeshift, the drinks leaving colored rings on
their surfaces where she hadn't wiped them enough.
The bare patches on the walls where she couldn't
face replacing the photographs and pictures they
had pasted up there, the white emulsion, which
she had one afternoon, with a strange urgency,
painted over the maps, and the lack of display all
somehow conspired to make the shop feel different.
Less welcoming. Less about its people. Less like the
thing that, almost a year previously, she had first
imagined.

Suzanna knew it. Like everyone else did. Somehow, corny as it sounded, the heart of the shop
had gone.

The weather, so the good ladies of the Women's
Institute market had told Vivi that morning, was
definitely on the turn. The seemingly endless weeks
of balmy blue skies and windless heat had been
replaced with stiff breezes, gray skies, and patchy
smatterings of rain for whole days at a time. The

flowers had long blown over, their heads brown and shriveled, while trees were shedding leaves prematurely, showering faded green and gold across the pavement. Perhaps, for a summer like the one they had had, Vivi thought, there had to be a price. She changed her mind about putting the washing outdoors.

"All set?" Douglas stood behind her, his hands on her hips, and kissed her cheek.

"As set as we can be. I've taken you at your word about not wanting a proper lunch."

"Sandwiches in the study will be fine," he said. "I don't imagine any of them will want to stay long. Well, Lucy might if she's taken the day off."

"No, she told me she'd get the train back this afternoon and go into the office."

"Girl's a workaholic," said Douglas, moving over to check the sandwiches. "Can't **imagine** where she gets it from."

The barns were full of hay and straw. The wheat and barley fields had been topped and plowed. Vivi watched her husband as he gazed absently out of the kitchen window, monitoring the darkening skies for the prospect of rain, as he had done, several times a day, all his adult life. The first drops were spitting on the window, and she felt melancholy that the summer was over.

"Have you said anything to your mother?" she asked, peeling the paper off a shop-bought cake.

She had not troubled to lower her voice: Rosemary's hearing was so bad now that she rarely caught anything said in normal conversation.

"I have," said Douglas. "I told her that, despite what she thought, we were not ignoring her wishes. I've told her that this is a happy compromise, and that if she looked at it carefully, she should be able to see it as such."

"And?"

"And I told her the family's happiness was the most important thing. Including hers."

"And?"

"She shut the door on me," he said.

"Poor darling," said Vivi, moving forward to give her husband a hug, then slapped his hand as he dug a roughened finger into the icing.

Suzanna was the first to arrive and Vivi trod on the cat as she hurried down the hallway to open the door. It uttered a wail so feeble that she realized it probably no longer had enough energy to complain.

"I think I've just squashed Rosemary's cat," she said, as she opened the door.

Suzanna didn't appear to have heard. "I can't stay long," she said, kissing her mother's cheek. "I need to open the shop again this afternoon."

"I know, darling, and it's very good of you to make the effort. Daddy won't take long, I promise.

I've put a few sandwiches out so you can eat them while he talks. Will you look at Rosemary's cat and tell me if you think I've broken anything?"

"It's hard to tell." Suzanna's smile was forced. "It's always been a bit bandy-legged. Look, it's walking. I shouldn't worry."

She looked thin, Vivi noted, as she followed Suzanna into the kitchen, where Mrs. Cameron was laying a tray. But it wasn't just the thinness: she looked gray, beaten, as if her essence had somehow been washed away. Vivi wished that in her unhappiness her daughter could have found more comfort in Neil. But, then, these days, she was never sure how much Neil was part of the problem.

"Did you want us to put something else out for Mrs. Fairley-Hulme? If I remember rightly she's not a great lover of sandwiches," Mrs. Cameron enquired.

"Actually, I was going to ask you if you wouldn't mind doing her some scrambled eggs." She lowered her voice. "She's not coming out of the annex today, apparently."

"Is this a protest?" asked Suzanna, leaning against the range, as if she could absorb its warmth.

"Rosemary's whole life's a protest, I think," said Vivi, and felt disloyal. "I'll just finish off the shirts, and then I'll make her up a tray."

A few minutes later she carried it through to the annex, then made up another with a teapot and four mugs. When she returned to the kitchen, Suzanna was looking out of the window. The sadness on her face made Vivi feel suddenly depressed, and conscious that this was an emotion she had felt too often, for too long. There was no such thing as happiness, she thought, if one of your children was miserable. She wiped her hands on her apron and hung it on the back of the door, fighting the urge to put her arms around her daughter as she just had her husband. "Did you have any more thoughts, darling, about whether you wanted us to keep Athene's picture up in the gallery?"

"No," said Suzanna. "I haven't really had time to think about it."

"No, of course not. Well, if you'd like another look, you know where it is."

"Thanks, Mum, but not today."

Vivi, hearing the frozen, subdued little voice, wondered if she was still grieving for her friend. The death was still relatively recent, after all. She remembered the impact of Athene's dying—the shock of it reverberating through their families, the limited number of people who knew the truth about Athene's "extended holiday abroad." Even though Vivi probably hadn't been as sad as she might have been (who had? she thought guiltily), she still remembered the crushing shock of someone so young and beautiful—**a mother**—having been wrenched so brutally from life.

She wondered, with the familiar sense of inadequacy, what she could do to alleviate some of her daughter's pain. She wanted to ask her what was wrong, to offer some remedy, to support her. But she knew, from bitter experience, that Suzanna would talk only when she was ready. And that was quite likely to be never.

"Lucy should be here in a minute," she said, opening the linen drawer and pulling out napkins. "Ben's just picking her up from the station."

Vivi hadn't been going to sit in on their little meeting: she knew what was going to be said, after all. But Douglas had said he would like her there, so she placed herself at the back of the room, leaning against the bookshelves, enjoying the sight of her three children's heads in front of her with a vague maternal satisfaction. Ben's hair had gone quite blond over the summer, working outside all day, and he looked like a parody of a corn-fed farmer's son. Lucy, to his right, was tanned and fit, having just returned from one of her exotic holidays. Suzanna could not have looked more like the odd one out, with her pale, milky skin, dark hair, and shadowed eyes. She would always be beautiful, Vivi thought, but today she looked like someone trying not to be.

"I was going to ring you, Suze," said Ben, as he stuffed a sandwich into his mouth. "Tell Neil I'm getting a list ready for that first shoot. I'll have a place for him if he wants to come."

"I'm not sure we've got the money," she said quietly.

"I didn't intend him to pay," Ben said. His indignation sounded forced against his natural sunny demeanor. "Tell you what, if he's worried, tell him he can pay me back in cleaning out the old pig sheds."

"Or tidy your room," said Lucy, nudging him. "Can't see there's much difference. When are you going to move out, Mummy's boy?"

"When are you going to get a boyfriend?"

"When are you going to get a girlfriend?"

"When are you going to get a life?"

"Hmm," said Lucy theatrically. "Eighty thou' a year plus bonuses, an office overlooking the Thames, my own flat, membership of two private clubs and holidays in the Maldives. **Or** pocket-money wages from Mum and Dad, the room you've had since you were twelve, a car so useless that you end up borrowing Mum's all the time, and your best night out at the Dere Young Farmers' disco. Hmm, wonder who really needs to get a life?"

It was the way they reintroduced themselves to each other, Vivi knew, and reestablished their bonds. But as Lucy and Ben continued their good-natured squabbling Suzanna said nothing, just glanced at her watch and then at their father, who was scrabbling among the papers on his desk.

"So, what is this, Dad?" said Lucy, eventually. "**King Lear**? Do I get to be Cordelia?"

Douglas found his spectacles, placed them carefully on his nose, and eyed his younger daughter over the thin silver frames. "Very droll, Lucy. Actually, I thought it was time I consulted you all a little more about the running of the estate. I have altered my will so that while the estate will be run by Ben you will each have an eventual financial interest in it, as well as some say in its future. I think it's better if, before anything happens to me, you have some idea of what is going on."

Lucy looked interested. "Can I see the accounts? I've always wondered how much this place earned."

"I doubt it'll take you to the Maldives," her father said dryly. "I've made copies. They're over there in the blue folder. I'd just ask that you don't take them anywhere. I feel more comfortable knowing that all the financial information is in one place."

Lucy made for the table and began to study the spreadsheets that Vivi had always found impenetrable. She knew some farmers' wives acted as their husband's bookkeepers, and had warned Douglas at the beginning that she couldn't tell the difference between a debit and a credit.

"The main thing I wanted to tell you is that we have permission to convert the barns by Philmore House into holiday cottages."

Ben shuffled in his chair, making it obvious that he already knew this. Lucy nodded vaguely. Suzanna's face was blank.

"We think there's a potential market, and that, with reasonable occupancy levels, we could clear the cost of conversion within a few years."

"Weekenders," said Lucy. "Cater for the upper end of the market and you'll be laughing."

"And people who want a full week. Less laundry and cleaning," said Ben.

"My boss says there are hardly any really nice weekend cottages for people with money to spend. He says it's all plastic cutlery and nylon sheets."

"Mum, make a note that we don't want nylon sheets."

Vivi leaned forward. "I don't believe they even sell them anymore. Awful things. Used to make you sweat terribly."

"Ben is going to oversee the building work, and manage them." Douglas scanned his three children. "He'll look after the bookings, the cleaning, and the handing over of keys, as well as the money side of things. If he fails, obviously, we'll have him shot."

"Which will save on raising pheasants."

"I've got this image of Ben now, running naked

through the woods, pursued by tweed-clad bankers," said Lucy, laughing. "It's put me right off my lunch."

"Witch," said Ben. "Pass me a cheese and pickle."

"There are some other issues, but I won't bore you with them today, as I know none of you has much time. But, Suzanna, there was one thing I wanted particularly to mention to you."

Suzanna sat with her mug of tea in her lap. She hadn't, Vivi noticed, taken a single bite of her sandwich.

"When I was discussing what to do with the barns, I had a long talk with Alan Randall—you know, the estate agent. He's told me that the owner of your shop is thinking of selling. We wondered if you'd like us to take a financial interest."

Suzanna placed her mug carefully on the table beside her. "What?"

"In the Peacock Emporium. Neil has told me things aren't great for you at the moment, and I know you've been working very hard at it. I think it's a good little business, or has the potential to be, and I'd like to help it have a future."

Vivi, watching her daughter, saw almost as soon as Douglas started to speak that yet again they had done the wrong thing.

Suzanna swallowed hard, then lifted her head, her features rearranged into something painfully controlled. "You don't have to do this, Dad."

"Do what?"

"Compensate me. For our relationship. For Ben's holiday cottages. Whatever."

"Suzanna . . . ," said Lucy, exasperated.

"It's a legitimate business offer," said Douglas.

"I'm not being rude. Really. But I'd rather you all stayed out of my business. I'll decide what happens to it."

"Jesus, Suzanna," Ben said crossly. "They were just trying to help."

Suzanna's voice was icily polite. "I know. And it's very kind of you to think of me, but I don't want any help. Really. I'd rather you all just left me alone." She looked around the room. "I'm really not being difficult," she said, sounding curiously poised. "I would rather you just left me and Neil to it."

Douglas's face had closed. "Fine, Suzanna," he said, his head lowering over his paperwork. "Whatever you want."

Lucy found Suzanna where she had expected, on the stone steps that overlooked the offices. Suzanna had been smoking, hunched over her knees like someone trying to combat stomachache. When Lucy closed the house door behind her, her sister nodded acknowledgment.

"I like the hair," Lucy said.

Suzanna raised a hand to it.

"Why'd you cut it? I thought you liked it long."

Suzanna wrinkled her nose. "Just needed a change. Actually," she said, stubbing out her cigarette, "that's not strictly true. I got sick of people telling me I looked like that stupid painting."

"Oh." Lucy waited for something more. She reached out and took a cigarette from her sister's packet.

"Neil likes it," Suzanna said, eventually. "He's always liked me with short hair."

The sky was cloudy, threatening more rain, and the two pulled their jackets closely around them, each shifting as the cold of the stone step seeped unforgivingly through their clothes.

Lucy took a long drag. "Two years since I gave up, and the odd one still tastes delicious."

"So do the odd twenty," said Suzanna.

There was something peculiar in her tone. Lucy, changing her mind, stubbed out her cigarette and tossed the evidence behind a flowerpot, as if they were still teenagers.

"Are you going to tell me off?"

"For what?"

"For refusing Dad's help. Like Ben did."

"Why would I?"

"It doesn't seem to stop anyone else."

They sat in silence, each alone with her thoughts, watching the clouds race across the sky, occasionally revealing the odd game patch of blue.

"What's up, Suze?"

"Nothing." Suzanna stared straight ahead at the barns.

There was a lengthy pause.

"I heard about what happened at the shop. I tried to ring a couple of times—to make sure you were okay."

"I know. I'm sorry. I keep forgetting to return calls."

"Are you fully back in business?"

"In theory. Neil tells me I can't last long at this rate. I'm not really making any money. It's hard to know what to do to bring people in." She smiled at her sister apologetically. "I don't suppose I'm the most welcoming person at the moment. Not a great draw at the best of times. That's really why I can't see any point in Dad investing in it."

Lucy leaned forward, drawing her knees up to her chest. "And you and Neil?"

"Fine."

"I'm assuming the cigs mean Peacock minor is not yet imminent . . ."

"I think the accepted phrase is 'if it happens, it happens.' I guess I'll try a bit harder when I'm feel-ing a bit . . . brighter." Her voice trailed away.

"Try a bit harder?" Lucy pulled a face. "What are you trying to turn into? Some kind of Stepford wife?" She studied her sister's profile, her smile fad-ing when she saw that there would be no jocular reply. "You don't sound like yourself, Suze. You sound . . ." She couldn't find the right words. "Married, for a change?" When Suzanna turned back to her, Lucy was shocked to see that her eyes were filled with tears.

"Don't mock me, Luce. I'm doing my best. Really. I'm trying to do my best." Her hair, caught on the wind, stood up on one side, looking shorn and brutal.

Lucy Fairley-Hulme hesitated for just a second, then placed her arms around her beautiful, troubled, complicated sister and held her tighter than she had since they were children.

Suzanna was about to close the shop. She needn't have bothered coming back after her parents' lunch. It had probably cost more in petrol to return than she had made in coffee profits. The skies had grown steadily grayer, heralding a premature dusk.

She knew the shop looked as unwelcoming as it felt. Despite the builders' promises, the new windows had still not arrived, and the boards that stood in their place looked increasingly faded and grubby, an unwelcome reminder of Jessie's fate. The previous day she had had to peel off several stickers from the outside, offering the chance for "homeworkers" to make "tens of thousands" if they only rang the phone number advertised, and a crude poster advertising a flea market outside the White Hart.

She couldn't seem to summon the energy to chase the builders. She stared around at the unwanted stock, at the empty gaps on the shelving that she hadn't yet filled from the new boxes, wondering how much she would miss it when it was gone. She had accepted now that it would be gone. If she had cared enough, her father's offer might have seemed like a lifeline. Instead it felt like the latest in a long line of affronts.

Suzanna checked the cartons of milk in the fridge and, out of habit rather than necessity, refilled the coffee machine, noting that with the school-run mothers gone home, she was unlikely to have anyone else in that day. She didn't care. She felt tired. She thought of her cool bed, of the deadening comfort of going home and crawling between the sheets. She would set the alarm for seven thirty that evening so that she would be up again before Neil returned. It seemed to work quite well that way.

The door opened.

"Have you seen the jam in the market square?" said Mrs. Creek.

"I was going to close."

"The cars have got themselves into a complete gridlock. All over one parking space. They're all out there shouting at each other." She removed her hat and sat down at the blue table. "Silly old fools. All because they can't be bothered to pay the forty pence to park behind the church." She had made herself comfortable and was squinting at the blackboard as if it had changed since the previous day, as if Suzanna had ever offered anything but seven different types of coffee. "I'll have a cappuccino, please, with those brown cube sugars on the side. The ones from the pretty box. They taste quite different from what you get at the supermarket."

There was no point protesting. Suzanna wasn't even sure she could raise her voice enough to do it. She thought of showing Neil the till receipts for the day, the fact that this afternoon she would have sold the grand total of three coffees, one for each hour the shop had been open.

She began to prepare the machine, only half listening to Mrs. Creek's chatter, nodding as required. "Nod and smile," Jessie had once advised her. It gave one the appearance of listening.

"I've been asked to make a wedding dress, did I tell you?"

Suzanna had never asked Jessie if she'd wanted to get married. She could imagine her as a bride; some insane bright-pink confection, with beads and feathers and flowers spilling off it. She thought of what Cath Carter had said at the funeral about Jessie's nails, and wished suddenly that she could have had the chance to wear a bridal dress too. Except that that would have implied she was bound even more tightly to Jason. The thought of him brought the van crashing through the front of the shop again, as it did several times a day, and Suzanna willed the image away.

"You've forgotten the sugars. The ones from that box, please."

"What?"

"The sugars, Suzanna. I asked for two sugars."

She thought she might have entered a state where almost nothing could touch her. The pain of Jessie's death had not lessened, but she knew that she was increasingly being cushioned from it by an encroaching numbness, a feeling that little mattered, that circumstances were genuinely beyond her control. Things seemed to be just gently slipping away, and she no longer cared enough to fight for them. It was easier just to allow herself to be carried with these strange new tides. Ironic, she thought, that just as she entered this passive state Alejandro had burst out of his. She could still feel the ringing in her ears from when he had slammed the board beside her head, the whoosh of air that told her he had become someone else. But, then, she didn't think about Alejandro.

"It's for the girl from the library. The one with the teeth—do you know her?" Suzanna placed the coffee in front of Mrs. Creek, and moved toward the remaining window, watching the passers-by, heads down, coats flying up behind them.

"You know, I haven't done a wedding dress

for . . . goodness, must be nigh on thirty-five years.
You wouldn't believe what they charge for a wedding dress now."

It was raining again. As it had rained on the day
that Alejandro had walked in and made them drink
**Mate**. She glanced behind her at the shelf, and saw
that his silver pot was still there, shoved behind a
pile of things still to be sorted out after what everyone politely called "the accident." She could barely
believe she hadn't noticed it until now.

"Yup, thirty-five years. The last one was for a
wedding in this town too."

"Mmm," said Suzanna. She picked up the pot
carefully, held it in both hands, feeling its weight,
its smooth silver contours. I'm sorry, Ale, she said
silently.

"Beautiful it was. White silk, cut on the bias.
Very simple, a bit like what the girls like today. I
modeled it on a dress Rita Hayworth wore in . . .
Ooh, what's that film where she was a real vamp?
**Gilda**, is it?"

"I don't know," said Suzanna. She lifted the cool
pot and held it against her cheek, feeling it warm
gradually against her. The transformation was
comforting.

"The bride was a bit of a fast piece too. Ran
off—what was it?—two years after the wedding?"

"Oh." Suzanna had closed her eyes.

"What was her name? Unusual name. Atalanta? Ariadne? Athene something. That was it. Married one of the Fairley-Hulmes."

The name took several seconds to register. Suzanna turned her head slowly toward Mrs. Creek, who was blithely stirring her cup, her woolen hat beside her on the table. "What did you just say?"

"Pretty girl. Had an affair with a salesman, of all things, and left her husband with the baby. Except it wasn't his baby. Oh, they kept it quiet, but everyone knew."

Time stopped. Suzanna felt as though the shop was rushing backward, away from her, as Mrs. Creek's words dropped heavily into the space between them. "That was it. Athene Forster. You probably won't remember the Fairley-Hulmes, you being so long in London and all, but they were a big farming family out here when I was a girl." She took a sip of her coffee, oblivious to the frozen figure by the window. "Lovely dress, it was. I was very proud of it. I think I've even got a picture of it somewhere. I felt awful afterward, though, because I was in such a rush to finish it and I forgot to sew a piece of blue ribbon into the hem. We used to do that, you know. Just for good luck. 'Something old, something new . . .'" The older woman gave a shrill cackle. "Years later, when I found out the girl had gone and bolted, I said to my husband, 'There you go. It must have been my fault . . .'"

# 23

Rosemary's cat was dying. The fact that they had all known it was coming, had expected it for several years, did not make it any less sad for Rosemary. The tired, bony animal, now featherlight, its flesh lost to the various tumors, slept almost continually, waking only to stagger across the kitchen to its water bowl, often soiling the floor as it went. Vivi hadn't complained about cleaning up after it, despite her husband's private expressions of disgust. She knew that Rosemary was aware that the cat had to be put down but, seeing the old woman's barely contained sorrow, she had not wanted to add to it.

After breakfast on the morning after the children's visit, the uncommon cold meant that the fires were lit for the first time that autumn, and Rosemary had appeared in the doorway of the annex to ask Vivi if she would mind calling the vet out. When he arrived, she asked Vivi to place the cat in her arms, and held him there, stroking him with arthritic fingers. Then she told her daughter-in-law gruffly that she would be fine on her own now. She could still talk to a vet by herself, thank you very much.

Vivi had backed out, the vet briefly meeting her eyes, and closed the door behind her, feeling unaccountably sad.

An almost indecently short time later, the vet had emerged, said he would send his bill, and announced that, as per Rosemary's instructions, he had left the body in a special bag by the back door. He had offered to dispose of it himself, but the old lady had said she would like her cat to be buried in her garden.

"I'll get Ben to help," Vivi said, and that morning, ignoring the rain and the wind, she and her son had donned windbreakers, dug a hole just deep enough to keep the foxes away, and laid the old animal to rest, as Rosemary's impassive face watched out of the window.

"I suppose you think I was selfish, keeping him alive," she said afterward, as Vivi poured tea in the drawing room, her ears still pink from the wind.

Vivi placed the cup and saucer on the table beside her, making sure it was close enough for Rosemary to reach it without shifting position in her chair. "No, Rosemary. I think only you could know when he was ready to go." She wondered whether she should ask Lucy to ring Suzanna. The girls seemed closer than they once had been—it was possible that Suzanna might confide in her.

"That's the trouble, you see. None of us is."

Vivi was wrenched from her thoughts.

"He knew he was a pain," Rosemary began, her face turned to the French windows, "he knew he just got under everybody's feet, that he made rather a mess. But sometimes it's very hard . . . to let go of things."

The teapot was burning Vivi's hand. She put it carefully on the tray, forgetting to pour herself a cup.

"Rosemary—"

"Just because a thing is old doesn't make it useless. It probably feels more useless than you know."

They could hear the faint grinding of tractor gears outside, overlaid inside by the comforting roar of the fire and the regular ticking of the grandfather clock.

"Nobody thought your cat was useless," Vivi said carefully. "I think . . . we all just liked to remember him when he was fit and happy."

"Yes. Well." Rosemary put her cup on the table. "No one ever imagines they will end up like that."

"No."

Rosemary lifted her chin. "He bit me, you know, when the needle went in."

"The vet told me. He said it was quite unusual."

Rosemary's quavering voice was defiant: "I was glad he still had the strength—to tell everyone to go to hell. Right to the last minute . . . he still had something inside." Her rheumy old eyes fixed intently on Vivi's.

"Do you know what, Rosemary?" Vivi found she was struggling to swallow. "I'm very glad too."

Rosemary had fallen asleep in her chair. It was probably the emotion of it all, Mrs. Cameron had said sagely. Death could do that to people. When her sister's poodle had died, it had been all they could do to stop her throwing herself into the grave. But, then, she had always been silly over the dog, had framed pictures of it, and bought it coats and suchlike. Vivi had nodded, then shaken her head, feeling the old lady's sadness seeping, like the damp weather, into the bones of the house.

She had a dozen things to do, several in town, including an invitation to a meeting of the local charity that administered the town's almshouses, and for which Douglas had put her forward when they were first married. But, somehow, Vivi was reluctant to leave the room, as if Rosemary's frailty since the death of her beloved cat had made her fearful for her. She hadn't said any of this to Mrs. Cameron, but the younger woman had seen something: "Do you want me to do the ironing in here? Keep an eye on things?" she asked tactfully.

It would have seemed silly to explain her anxiety. Vivi had told her, with a determined briskness to her voice, that she thought that was a splendid idea.

And, trying to brush off the sense of foreboding, she had gone to the utility room to sort out the apples she had put by for freezing.

She had been there, seated on the old tea chest, dividing the plastic bags of apples into those for cooking and those too rotten to save, for almost twenty minutes, finding comfort in the mindless yearly ritual, when she had heard the doorbell, and Mrs. Cameron whistling as she bustled down the hall to answer it. There had been a brief, muffled exchange, and Vivi, dropping a particular apple into a cardboard box, had wondered whether the lady who left the charity bags for filling had come a day early.

"In here?" She heard the voice, imperious and demanding, on the other side of the door, and Vivi, suddenly upright, flinched.

"Suzanna?"

The door swung open and Suzanna stood there. Her eyes burned dark in a face that was deathly white. There were blue smudges on each side of her nose and her hair was unbrushed, telling of some tumultuous night of lost sleep.

"Darling, are you—"

"Is it true? She ran away from Dad and had a baby?"

"What?" Seeing the scorching knowledge on that face, Vivi felt history leap upward to swamp her, and understood that her previous sense of dread had nothing to do with the cat. She stood and stumbled forward, sending apples spinning across the floor.

"My mother? Was she talking about my mother?"

The two women stood in the little room, which was suffused with the smells of detergent and rotting apples. Vivi heard Rosemary's voice, unsure whether she was imagining it. "You see?" it said. "She causes trouble even after her death."

Her hands hanging by her sides, she took a deep breath and made her voice sound steadier than she felt. She had always known this day might come, but she had never anticipated that when it did she might have to meet it alone. "Suzanna, your father and I had wanted to tell you for some time." She looked for her previous seat. "In fact, we wanted to tell you on Tuesday. Shall I get him? He's plowing up on Page Hill."

"No. You tell me."

Vivi wanted to say that it wasn't her story to tell, that the weight of it had always been too much for her. And, faced with Suzanna's feverish, accusatory stare, that she wasn't to blame. But this was what parenthood was really all about, wasn't it? The protestations of love, that everybody had meant well, that they thought it was all for the best . . . the knowledge that often love was not enough.

"I want you to tell me."

"Darling, I—"

"Here. Now. Right now. I just want to **know**,"

said Suzanna. There was a kind of desperation in her eyes, and a crack of something sadder and stranger in her voice than Vivi had ever heard before.

Vivi eased herself carefully along the tea chest, motioning to her daughter to occupy the empty half. "All right, Suzanna," she said. "You'd better sit down."

The call had come when he had least expected it, on one of the few occasions that he had returned to the house that he had, for two short years, called home. He had walked into the echoing hall in search of his tweed jacket, trying not to think too hard about his surroundings, when the telephone on the hall table had sprung shrilly into life. He had stared at it for several seconds, then moved tentatively forward. No one else would ring him there. Everyone knew he no longer lived there.

"Douglas?" the voice had said, and at that low, heartbreaking enquiry, he found he had lost the ability to stand.

"Where are you?" he had asked, dropping onto the hall chair.

It was as if he hadn't spoken. "I've been trying to get you for weeks," she said. "You are an impossible gadabout." As if they had been two people flirting at a party. As if she hadn't broken him, pierced his heart, and turned his future, his life, to dust.

He swallowed hard. "It's haymaking. Long days. You know."

"I thought you must have gone to Italy after all," she said lightly. "To escape this rotten English weather." Her voice sounded odd, offset by traffic, as if she was in a telephone box. "Isn't it awful? Don't you just hate it?"

He had imagined this moment for so long, had rehearsed so many arguments, apologies, reconciliations in his head, and now she was at the other end of the line. It was as much as he could do to breathe.

"Douglas?"

He noted that his hand was trembling against his leg. "I've missed you," he croaked.

There was the briefest pause.

"Douglas, darling, I can't talk long, but I need to meet you."

"Come home," he said. "Come here." She had replied sweetly that, if he didn't mind, she would really rather not. In London, perhaps? Somewhere they could talk privately?

"Huntley's fish restaurant," he had suggested, his mind stuttering into life. It had booths, where they could talk virtually unobserved.

"Aren't you clever, darling?" she had said, apparently unconscious of the way a phrase, so easily discarded, could fan the flames of hope. Huntley's it was. Thursday.

Now, four interminable days later, he sat in the booth at the back of the restaurant. It was the most discreet in the place, he had been assured by a waiter who had winked at him impertinently, as if he were on some assignation. "It's for my wife," Douglas had said coldly, and the waiter had said, "Of course, sir, of course it is."

He had got there almost half an hour early, had walked past the restaurant several times, willing himself to resist the temptation to go in, knowing that the builders on the scaffolding above probably thought him unhinged. But there was a part of him that feared he might miss her, that fate would intervene and uncross their paths, so he bought a newspaper and sat there by himself, trying to stop his palms sweating, and wishing he could make the slightest sense of the newsprint in front of him.

Outside, girls flashed past in brief skirts, their brightly colored coats incongruous against the grays of London skies and pavement, incurring muffled catcalls. He felt briefly reassured that she had agreed to meet him here, a place where his suit didn't feel provincial, "straight," in modern lingo, a place where he didn't have to feel like an amalgam of all the things she had chafed against.

"Anything to drink, sir, while you're waiting?"

"No. Actually, yes. Just some water, please." He glanced toward the door, as it opened to allow in yet another slim dark woman. The bloody restaurant seemed to cater to no other kind of customer.

"Ice and lemon, sir?"

Douglas shook his paper with irritation. "Oh, for

goodness' sake," he snapped, "however it comes . . . will be fine," he said, collecting himself. He smoothed his hair back from his face, adjusted his tie, and tried to regulate his breathing.

He hadn't told his parents he was coming—he had known what his mother's response would be. She had refused to allow Athene's name to be spoken in the house since the day he had told of her departure. He had moved back home several months previously, leaving the Philmore House like the **Mary Celeste**, exactly as she had left it, down to the ashtray she had filled with her lipsticked cigarette butts. The staff were on strict instructions not to change a thing.

Not till he knew.

Not till he knew for sure.

"Actually," he said to the waiter, as he arrived bearing a glass of water on a silver tray, "get me a brandy, would you? A large one."

The waiter had looked at him for a second longer than suggested completely deferential service. "Whatever you say, sir," he had said, and was gone.

She had been late, as he had known she would be. He had finished that brandy and another in the half hour that crept by after their allotted meeting time. When he looked up from the newspaper to see her before him, the alcohol had already started to blur the edges of his anxiety.

"Douglas," she had said, as he rose slightly and

stared at her for several minutes, not quite able to cope with the reality of her, the fleshed-out version of the specter that had, for almost a year, haunted his dreams. "Don't you look smart?"

He had glanced down at his suit, fearful that he might have spilled something on it. And then he stared at her, aware that he was overstepping some boundary but unable to stop himself.

"Do let's sit down," she said, with a nervous, teasing smile. "People are beginning to stare."

"Of course," he had muttered, and shuffled back into the booth.

She looked altered too, although it was impossible to say whether this was because the Athene of his memory, his imagination, was a perfect creature. This woman opposite, although beautiful, although irrefutably his Athene, was not quite the goddess he had become used to picturing. She looked tired, her skin a little less polished, a little more strained than it had once been; her hair was swept into a haphazard chignon. She was wearing, he noted with a jolt, a suit she had bought on their honeymoon, which she had decided after one wearing was "an abomination," and sworn to throw away. Next to the brightly colored creations of the girls out on the street, it looked old-fashioned. She had lit a cigarette. He noticed, with some relief, that her hands were trembling.

"Can I have a drink, darling?" she said. "You know, I'm absolutely gasping." He waved over the waiter, who looked at her with mild interest. It was when he caught the man staring ostentatiously at her left hand that Douglas realized, with a lurch, that she no longer sported her wedding ring. He took a sip of his own drink, trying not to think about what that might mean.

The important thing was that she was there.

"Are you . . . are you well?" he asked.

"Fabulous. Apart from this awful weather."

He tried to glean some clue from her appearance, to muster the courage to ask the questions that revolved remorselessly around his head. "Do you come up to London much?"

"Oh, you know me, Douglas. Theater, the odd nightclub. Can't keep me away from the old Smoke." Behind her voice was a brittle gaiety.

"I went to Tommy Gardner's wedding. Thought I might see you there."

"Tommy Gardner?" She blew smoke dismissively through painted lips. "Ugh. Couldn't stand either of them."

"I suppose you must have been busy."

"Yes," she said. "Yes, I was."

The waiter brought Athene's drink, and two leatherbound menus. She had ordered a gin and tonic but, when it arrived, appeared to lose interest in it.

"Would you like to eat?" he said, praying she

wouldn't want to leave immediately, that he hadn't already disappointed her.

"You order for me, darling. I can't be bothered to read my way through all those choices."

"I'll have the sole," he told the waiter, reluctantly tearing his glance from his wife long enough to hand back the menus. "Two soles. Thank you."

There was a strange disquiet about her, he noted. Even though she was perfectly still, as languid as she ever had been, there was a visible tension in her, as if she were strung between two taut wires. Perhaps she is as nervous as me, he thought, and attempted to quell the leap of hope prompted by this thought.

There was a painful silence as they sat opposite each other, occasionally catching each other's eyes and raising tight, awkward smiles. In the booth beside them a group of businessmen burst into raucous laughter, and he caught the faint raising of Athene's eyebrows, the look that said they were simply too ridiculous for words.

"You didn't even talk to me," he said, trying to say it lightly, as if it were a mild reproach. "You just left a note."

There was a faint clenching of her jaw. "I know, darling. I've always been useless at those sorts of conversations."

"'Those sorts of conversations'?"

"Let's not, Douglas. Not today."

"Why didn't we meet at Dere? I would have gone to your parents' house, if you'd wanted."

"I don't want to see them. I don't want to see anyone." She lit a second cigarette from the first, and crumpled the now empty packet in her hand. "Douglas, you wouldn't be a darling and order me some more ciggies, would you? I seem to be out of change."

He had done so without hesitation.

"You are a dear," she murmured, and he was not sure if she was even aware what she was saying.

The food arrived, but neither of them had the appetite to eat. The two fish sat balefully in congealing butter until Athene pushed away her plate and lit another cigarette.

Douglas feared that this suggested her imminent departure. He couldn't wait any longer. He had nothing left to lose. "Why did you call?" he said, his voice cracking.

Her eyes met his and widened slightly. "Aren't I allowed to speak to you anymore?" she said. Her attempt at coquettishness was hampered by the strain round her eyes, the fleeting glances she kept casting toward the front of the restaurant.

"Are you waiting for someone?" he said, suddenly filled with fear that He might be there too. That this might all be some elaborate ploy to make a further fool of him.

"Don't be silly, darling."

"Don't 'darling' me, Athene. I can't do this. I really can't. I need to know why you're here."

"You know, it's lovely to see you looking so well. You always did look marvelous in that suit."

"Athene!" he protested.

A woman had arrived at their table, the cloakroom attendant. He wondered, briefly, whether she was about to tell them that there was a call for Athene, and what he would do if she did. It would be Him, of course.

"I'm sorry, madam, but your baby's crying. You'll have to come and get her."

It was several seconds before he had taken in what the woman had said.

Athene stared at him, something raw and unguarded in her face. Then, composed, she turned back to the woman, her smile perfectly poised. "I'm so sorry," she said. "Could you be a dear and bring her to me? I won't stay long."

The girl disappeared.

Athene took a long drag of her cigarette. Her eyes were glittering and unreadable. "Douglas, I need you to do something for me," she said coolly.

"A baby?" he said, one hand clamped to the top of his head.

"I need you to look after Suzanna for me."

"What? A baby? You never—"

"I really can't discuss it. But she's a good baby. I know she'll adore you."

The girl arrived with the child, almost concealed by blankets, whimpering as if in the aftermath of some terrible storm. Athene stubbed out her cigarette and reached for her, not looking at her baby's face. She jiggled her absently, watching Douglas. "Her pram is at the front of the restaurant. It's got everything she needs for a little while. She's no trouble, Douglas, really."

He was incredulous. "Is this—is this some kind of a joke? I don't know what to do with a baby." The child had started to fret again, and Athene patted her back, still not looking at her.

"Athene, I can't believe you—"

She stood up, thrust the baby over the table so that he had little choice but to take the bundle. Her voice was urgent, insistent. "Please, please, Douglas, dear. I can't explain. Really." Her pleading eyes were an echo of a time before. "She'll be much better off with you."

"You can't just leave me with a baby—"

"You'll love her."

"Athene, I can't just—"

Her cool hand was on his arm. "Douglas, darling, have I ever asked you for anything? Really?"

He could hardly speak. He was dimly aware of the occupants of the next booth staring at them. "But what about you?" He was babbling, unsure even of what he was saying. "What about you and I? I can't just go home with a baby."

But she had already turned from him, was packing her bag, fiddling with something inside it, a compact perhaps. "I've really got to go. I'll be in touch, Douglas. Thank you so much."

"Athene, you can't just leave me with—"

"I know you'll be wonderful with her. A wonderful daddy. Much better than me at that sort of thing."

He was staring into the folds of the blankets at the innocent face in front of him. She had managed to find her thumb, and was sucking furiously, an expression of rapt concentration on her face. She had Athene's jet-black eyelashes, her Cupid's-bow lips. "Don't you even want to say goodbye?" he asked.

But she was halfway out of the restaurant, her high-heeled shoes clacking like pins over the tiled floor, her shoulders straight in the abominable suit.

"Her pram's with the hatcheck girl," she called. And without a backward glance she was gone.

He never saw her again.

He had told this story to Vivi some months after it had happened. Until then, she said, Douglas's family had simply told everyone that Athene was "staying abroad" for a little while, but that she thought the English climate better for the baby. They said "the baby" offhandedly, as if everyone should have known there was one. Some believed they must have been told and somehow forgotten. If anyone had not accepted this version of events, they had said nothing. The poor man had been humiliated enough.

He had told Vivi steadily, not looking at her, a short while after they had heard about Athene's death. And she had held him while he cried tears of anger, humiliation, and loss. Afterward she realized he'd never asked if the baby was his.

Suzanna, sitting frozen on the tea chest, was paler, if possible, than she had been when she arrived. She sat there for some time, and Vivi said nothing, allowing her time to digest the story. "So she didn't die giving birth to me?" she said eventually.

Vivi reached out a hand. "No, darling, she—"

"She ran away from me? She just handed me over? In a bloody fish restaurant?"

Vivi swallowed, wanting Douglas to be there. "I just think maybe she knew she wasn't going to be the mother you needed. I knew her a little in her youth, and she was a pretty wild character. She'd had a hard time with her parents. And it's possible the man she ran off with might have pushed her . . . Some men are rather resentful of children, especially if—if they aren't theirs. Douglas always thought he might have been rather cruel to her. So, you see, you shouldn't judge her too harshly." She wished the words sounded more convincing than they had. "Things were different then."

As soon as Athene had left, Vivi had returned

to Dere. Not in the hope of snaring him: she had always known that he wanted Athene back, that he would never countenance anyone else while the possibility remained. But she had adored him since they were children, and felt that at least she could be something of a support.

"I had to listen to a lot of stories of how much he loved your mother," she said matter-of-factly, "but he needed help. He couldn't look after a baby. Not with everything he had to do. And, to begin with, his parents weren't terribly . . ."—she was trying to find an appropriate word—". . . helpful." Two months after Athene's death, he had asked Vivi to marry him.

She pushed her hair off her face.

"I'm sorry we didn't tell you the truth earlier. For a long time we all believed we were protecting your father. He had suffered so much humiliation, and so much pain. And then—I don't know—perhaps we thought we were protecting you. There wasn't the same emphasis then on everyone knowing everything as there is now." She shrugged. "We just did what we thought was best."

Suzanna was crying, had been for several minutes.

Tentatively Vivi lifted a hand toward her. "I'm so sorry."

"But you must have hated me," Suzanna said, sobbing.

"What?"

"All that time I was in the way, always a reminder of her."

Vivi, finally filled with a kind of courage, put her arms around her and held her tight. "Don't be silly, darling," she said. "I loved you. Almost more than my own children."

Suzanna's eyes were bleary with tears. "I don't understand."

Vivi held her daughter's too-thin shoulders, and tried to impart something of what she felt. Her voice, when it came, was determined, and uncharacteristically certain: "I loved you because you were the most beautiful baby I'd ever seen," she said, and hugged her fiercely. "I loved you because none of this was ever your fault. I loved you because from the moment I set eyes on you I couldn't not love you." She paused, her own eyes now filled with tears. "And in some small way, Suzanna, I loved you because without **you**, dearest, dearest child, I would never have had **him**."

Later, when she had extricated herself from Suzanna's arms, Vivi told her how her mother had really died, and Suzanna cried again, for Emma, for Alejandro, and, most of all, for Athene, for whose death she hadn't been responsible after all.

# 24

The first night that Suzanna Fairley-Hulme spent with her family was the scene of huge upheaval on the Dere estate, of high emotion and sleeplessness, of anxiety, and barely hidden fear. Moved from the surroundings in which she had spent her first months, from everything and everyone she had known, one might have expected her to have been rather unsettled, but she slept peacefully from dusk until almost seven thirty the following morning. It was the new adults in her life who achieved only a few moments' sleep.

Rosemary Fairley-Hulme, who had become accustomed to her son's restored presence in the family house, had panicked when he didn't arrive home by late evening, and even more so when she realized that neither she nor her husband had any idea where he had spent the day. She had paced the creaking floorboards until midnight, glancing out of the windows in the vain hope of seeing twin headlights coming slowly up the drive. The housekeeper, roused from her bed, told Rosemary that she had seen Mr. Douglas take a taxi to the station at ten o'clock that morning. The stationmaster, when she got Cyril to ring him, said he had been wearing his good suit.

That was the point at which they had rung Vivi, hoping against hope that although their son appeared to pay her no more heed than the furniture when she came to Dere House several times a week, perhaps just this once, he had taken her into town.

"Gone?" said Vivi, and felt a lurch of fear when she understood that her Douglas, the one who had spent the past months weeping privately on her shoulder, confiding his darkest feelings about his wife's departure, had been keeping something from her.

Vivi had rushed over to the estate, unsure whether she was more afraid that he was lying injured in a ditch or that his disappearance was linked to the reappearance of someone else. He still loved Athene, she knew it. She had been forced to hear him say it often enough over the past months. But that had been bearable when she could believe that his feelings had been dying, like the embers of a fire—one that, now that she had heard all the details, she had not thought would be restoked.

Between the hours of midnight and dawn, split into small groups, armed with flashlights, they had combed the estate, in case he had walked home drunk and fallen into a ditch. A lad had done this several years previously and drowned; the memory of finding that body facedown in several inches of stagnant water haunted Cyril still.

"He's not drunk much since the first weeks," he said, as they strode along, bumping gently against each other in the moonlight. "The boy's past the worst. Much more himself."

"He'll be at a friend's, Mr. Fairley-Hulme. I'll wager he's had a few and stayed in London for the night." The gamekeeper took a sanguine view of the affair and he had remarked four times now that boys would be boys.

"Might have headed over to Larkside," muttered one of the lads. "Most end up at Larkside one time or another."

Vivi winced at the thought of Douglas lowering himself to that level, that he might turn to women like that when she was just waiting for him to say the word . . .

"He's got more sense than to end up there."

"Not if he's had a skinful. He's been on his own a good year."

"This is hopeless," said Cyril. "Bloody, bloody Douglas. Bloody inconsiderate boy."

Vivi glanced up at his set jaw as she trudged along, her cardigan wrapped around her in a vain attempt to stave off the cold. She knew his condemnation of Douglas was to disguise his anxiety. He, like Vivi, knew the depths of Douglas's despair.

"He'll turn up," she said quietly. "He's so sensible. Really."

No one thought to go to Philmore House. Why would they, when he had hardly set foot there since she had left? So it was only an hour after dawn broke, when the two search parties converged in the cold light, chilled and increasingly silent, outside the Philmore barns, that anyone thought of it.

"There's a light, Mr. Fairley-Hulme," said one of the lads, gesturing. "In the upstairs window. Look."

And as they stood on the overgrown, dew-soaked lawn, their eyes raised to the upper floors of the old house, the sound of birdsong building to a swell around them, the front door had opened. And there he had stood, his shadowed eyes betraying his own night of lost sleep, his good suit trousers wrinkled, and a child sleeping peacefully in his arms.

"Douglas!" Rosemary's exclamation had held a mixture of shock and relief.

There had been a brief silence then, as the little group of people properly took in the sight in front of them.

Douglas looked down, and adjusted the shawl around the baby.

"What's going on, son?"

"This . . . is Suzanna," he said quietly. "Athene has given her to me. That is all I want to say on the matter." He looked both bruised and defiant.

Vivi's mouth had dropped open, and she closed

it. She heard the gamekeeper curse vigorously under his breath.

"But we thought—oh, Douglas, what on earth has been—"

Cyril, his eyes fixed on his son, stayed his wife with a hand on her shoulder. "Not now, Rosemary." He nodded at his son, and turned back toward the drive. "Let's all get some rest. The boy's safe."

Vivi felt that she too was expected to leave.

"Thank you, everyone," she heard him say, as she glanced back toward Douglas, who was still gazing at the gently illuminated face of the child. "If you'd like to head back to Dere House I think we could all do with some coffee. Plenty of time for talking when we've had some sleep."

He had gone to Philmore House, Douglas told Vivi long afterward, because he had needed to be alone, unsure whether he could admit even to himself the truth of what had happened that day. Perhaps he went because, carrying Athene's child, he felt some primeval urge to be closer to her mother. Either way, he stayed at the house only two days before he found that coping alone with a baby was beyond him.

Rosemary had, at first, been incandescent with fury. She would not have that woman's child in the house, she exclaimed, when Douglas arrived at the family home. She could not believe he'd been so stupid, so gullible. She could not believe he would expose himself to such ridicule. What next? Would they be expected to put up Athene's lovers too?

That had been the point at which Cyril had told her to go off for a bit, get some air. In a quieter, more measured voice, he had tried to reason with his son. He had to see sense, didn't he? He was a young man, he couldn't be saddled with bringing up a baby. Not with his whole life ahead of him. Especially one who . . . Something in Douglas's implacable stare had halted him midsentence.

"She's staying here," Douglas had said. "That's all there is to it." He already held her with the relaxed dexterity of a young father.

"And how will you support her?" Cyril said. "You can't expect us to carry you. Not with all the work that needs doing on the estate. And your mother won't do it. You know she won't."

"I'll sort something out," said Douglas.

Later he confided to Vivi that his quiet determination had not just been about his desire to keep the child, although he had loved her already. He didn't like to admit to his father that even if he had wanted to give Suzanna back, he hadn't thought to ask Athene how he should get in touch with her.

The first few days had been farcical. Rosemary had ignored the child's presence, and busied herself in her garden. The estate wives had been less condemnatory, or at least to his face, bringing their old high chairs, bibs, and muslins, a whole arsenal of baby necessities that he had not considered might be necessary for the care of one small human being. He had begged Bessie to advise him on the basics, and she had spent a morning explaining how best to heat bottles of milk, how to make solid food digestible by mashing it with a fork. She had watched from afar, disapproval mingling with anxiety for the child as he tried hamfistedly to feed her, swearing and wiping food off his clothes as the little one batted the loaded spoon away from her face.

Within days he was exhausted. His father's patience had been stretched by Douglas's inability to work, the papers piled up in the study, and the men were complaining about lack of direction on the land.

"What are you going to do?" said Vivi, having watched as he jiggled the baby under his arm while trying to negotiate with a feed merchant on the telephone. "Why don't you get a wet nurse, or whatever it is that babies have?"

"She's too old for a wet nurse," he replied, lack of sleep making him snappy. He didn't say what they both thought: that the child needed her mother.

"But you can't possibly manage everything by yourself."

"Don't you start, Vee. Not you with everyone else."

She bridled, hurt at his assumption that she belonged with "everyone else." She watched silently as he walked up and down the room, dangling his keys in front of the baby's grasping hands.

"I'll help you," she said.

"What?"

"I've got no work at the moment. I'll look after her for you." She didn't know what had made her say it.

His eyes widened, hope flickering across his face. "You?"

"I've done toddlers. Babysat them, I mean. When I was in London. She can't be that much harder."

"You'd really look after her?"

"For you, yes." She blushed at her choice of words, but he didn't seem to notice.

"Oh, Vee. You'd really look after her? Every day? Until I can get something else sorted out, of course." He had walked toward her, as if he was already keen to hand Suzanna over.

She hesitated then, suddenly seeing in that dark, satiny hair, the wide blue eyes, the memory of a painful time. Then she looked back at him, at the relief and gratitude on his face.

"Yes," she said. "Yes, I would."

Her parents had been appalled. "You can't do this," her mother had said. "It's not even your child."

"We mustn't visit the sins of the fathers, Mummy," she had replied, sounding more confident than she felt. "She's a perfectly adorable baby." She had just rung Mr. Holstein to tell him she wouldn't be returning to London.

Mrs. Newton, agitated, had gone so far as to call on Rosemary Fairley-Hulme, and had been surprised to find her just as fierce in her opposition to the whole sorry scheme. The young people appeared to have made up their minds, said Rosemary, despairingly. There was certainly no telling Douglas.

"But, darling, think about it. I mean, she could come back at any time. And you have your job, your career. This could go on for years." Her mother had been close to tears. "Think, Vivi. Think of how he hurt you before."

I don't care. Douglas needs me, she said silently, enjoying the sensation of the two of them being united against the world.

They had all softened in the end. They had to: who could hold out against a beaming, beautiful, innocent baby? Vivi found that—as the months went on, as Suzanna's presence in the house became less remarkable, as the explanations for her appearance were less discussed in the village—occasionally, on hearing the child cry, Rosemary would emerge from her kitchen "just to check she was all right," that Cyril, finding her in his son's arms before her bath, would chuck her cheek and blow raspberries at her. Vivi, meanwhile, was besotted, her exhaustion blown away by the uninhibited smiles, the clutching hands and blind trust. Suzanna brought her and Douglas together too: every evening, over a gin and tonic, when he came in from the fields, they would sit and laugh over her little foibles, commiserate over her teeth or sudden, mercurial tempers. When she had taken her first steps, Vivi had run all the way to the forty-acre field to find him, and they had run back together, breathless and expectant, to where she sat with the housekeeper, gazing around her with the benignly merry countenance of the much-adored. And there had been one perfect day when they had taken her out together, wheeling the big old pram across the estate to have a picnic, as if, Vivi thought secretly, furtively, they were a real family.

Douglas had been cheerful that day, had held the child close, pointing out the barns, a tractor, birds slicing through the sky. And something about the perfection of it all, about her own happiness, had forced the question to Vivi's lips. "Will she want her back?" she had asked.

His eyes, which had been bright and cheerful, looked suddenly haunted. "I'm going to tell you something, Vee. Something I haven't told anyone."

With the baby seated between them, he had told her exactly how this child had ended up in his care.

Vivi knew now that the reason he loved this child so much was because she was an abiding link with his former wife: he believed that while he cared for her, there was a strong possibility that Athene might return. And that no matter how much he confided in Vivi, how much he depended on her, how much time they spent talking babies or acting out life as a family, she would never be able to traverse that barrier.

I mustn't begrudge a child its mother, she thought, pretending there was something in her eye and ducking away. It must be enough that he needs me at all, that I am still part of his life.

But she couldn't help it. It wasn't just about Douglas anymore, she thought, as she tucked baby Suzanna into her cot that evening, blessing her face with kisses as she settled her down to sleep. She didn't want to give either of them back.

Six months to the day after Suzanna had arrived, Rosemary had telephoned shortly before breakfast. She knew Vivi had been planning to go to town, but could she possibly take Suzanna for the day? she said, her voice brusque.

"Of course, Rosemary," said Vivi, mentally rewriting her plans. "Is there a problem?"

"There's been . . . it's . . ."

Afterward Vivi realized that, even then, Rosemary had been reluctant to say her name.

"We've had a call. It's all a bit difficult." She paused. "Athene has . . . has passed away." There was a stunned silence. Vivi's breath stuck in her throat. She was sorry, she said, but wasn't sure what Rosemary had just told her.

"She's dead, Vivi. We've had a call from the Forsters." It was as if each time she said it, Rosemary gained a little more confidence, until eventually she could be matter-of-fact about it.

Vivi sat down heavily on the hall chair, heedless of her mother, who, in her dressing-gown, was trying to gauge what was going on. **Are you all right, darling?** she kept mouthing, stooping in an attempt to meet her daughter's eyes.

Athene would not be coming back. She would not be returning to take Douglas and Suzanna away from her. Stunned as she was, Vivi saw that her shock was tinged with something uncomfortably close to elation.

Douglas had mourned for two months, revealing a level of grief that many around him felt excessive, considering his wife had bolted more than a year previously and everyone knew she had taken up with another man.

Vivi didn't. She didn't dwell on Athene's death, finding it impossible to settle on the right balance of sympathy and disapproval, so instead focused on Suzanna, as if she could atone for her mean-spirited thoughts by flooding the child with love. She had taken sole charge of the child for weeks now, finding that without the threat of Athene's return, an almost shocking amount of it poured from herself into the now motherless child.

Suzanna seemed to respond to Vivi's uninhibited affection and became even sunnier than she had been before, placing her soft, cushioned cheek against hers, wrapping fat starfish fingers around her own. Vivi would arrive shortly after seven thirty, and take the child for long walks around the estate, removing her from Douglas's grief, which hung over the house like a dark cloud, and from the whispered conversations of his parents and the servants, all of whom seemed to consider Suzanna's presence a problem of some pressing urgency.

"We can't get rid of her now," she had heard Rosemary saying to Cyril, as she passed the study. "We've told everyone the child is Douglas's."

"The child **is** Douglas's," Cyril had said. "He'll have to decide what he wants to do with her. Tell the boy to pull himself together. He's got decisions to make."

They were clearing Philmore House. The home that had remained a shrine to Athene—whose wardrobes still bulged with her dresses—had fallen into Rosemary's list of responsibilities. Douglas and Suzanna were now firmly ensconced in Dere House. And Rosemary, who had long itched to remove the physical evidence of "that girl" from the estate, had taken advantage of her son's newly passive state to deal with it.

Vivi stood on the brow of the hill, holding her hat on her head as she watched the men come out, bearing armfuls of brightly colored dresses and laying them on the front lawn, while the women, kneeling on rugs and braced against the chill, sorted through bags and boxes of jewelry and cosmetics, exclaiming among themselves at their quality.

For someone who had professed herself so unconcerned with belongings, Athene had had a prodigious amount of things—not just dresses, coats, and shoes but records, pictures, lamps, beautiful things bought in haste and discarded, or received as gifts that had been soon forgotten.

"Anything you want to take, help yourselves. All the rest into a pile to be burned." She heard Rosemary's voice, clear and commanding, perhaps lifting with the restoration of her own domain, and watched as she marched back inside to bring out yet another box. She wondered if she felt the same small thrill of excitement at Athene's final, enforced removal. A small, mean thrill that she was hardly able to admit to herself.

"You don't want any of this, do you?" Rosemary called, catching sight of Vivi as she walked over slowly, pushing Suzanna's pram.

Vivi glanced at Athene's going-away suit, the beaded slippers she had worn at that first hunt ball, now lying in a heap by the geranium border, occasionally stirring in the stiff breeze. "No," she said. "No, thank you."

Athene's own parents had wanted nothing. Vivi had heard her parents discussing it when they thought she wasn't listening. The Forsters had been so embarrassed by their daughter's behavior, so keen to distance themselves from her even in death. They had had her cremated in a closed ceremony, had not even put an announcement in **The Times**, Mrs. Newton had said, in a shocked whisper. And they had not wanted to meet their own grandchild.

Vivi wheeled Suzanna slowly through the piles of belongings, stooping forward to make sure the sleeping baby was shielded from the wind. She winced as she caught sight of a drawerful of Athene's undergarments, diaphanous pieces of lace and silk, items that spoke of nights of whispered secrets, of unknown pleasures, now exposed and discarded. As if there was no part of her that deserved to remain sacrosanct.

She had thought this might bring her some secret satisfaction. Now that she was here, this hurried disposal of Athene's things seemed almost indecent. Douglas no longer talked of her. Rosemary and Cyril had forbidden mention of her name. Suzanna was too young to remember her—her age allowed her to accept the love of the strangers around her as a happy substitute. But, then, one didn't know how much Suzanna had been loved before.

Vivi picked her way past a heap of expensive wool coats and stood on the edge of the lawn, as a man dumped a box of photographs beside her. Afterward she wasn't sure what had made her do it. Perhaps the thought of Suzanna's rootlessness, perhaps her own discomfort at what seemed an almost fervid desire among those who had known Athene to obliterate her from history.

Vivi bent down, pulled a handful of photographs and newspaper cuttings from the box and stuffed them into the bottom of the pram, under her bag. She wasn't sure what she would do with them, or if she even wanted them. It just seemed important that, no matter how unpalatable, or how many awkward questions it might raise, when she was older Suzanna might have some idea where she had come from.

As Vivi made her way back up to the brow of the hill Suzanna had begun to cry. She lifted her from the pram and whirled her around, letting the baby's cheeks pink in the brisk air. "Who's my beautiful, beautiful girl?"

"She certainly is."

She spun around to find Douglas standing behind her, and flushed. "I'm sorry," she said haltingly. "I didn't know you were there."

"Don't be sorry." His tweed collar was lifted

against the cold, his eyes weary and red-rimmed. He stepped closer, adjusted Suzanna's woolen bonnet. "Is she okay?"

"She's fine." Vivi beamed. "Very bonny. Eating everything in sight, aren't you, precious?" The baby thrust out a fat hand and pulled at one of the blond curls that emerged from under Vivi's hat. "She's doing very well indeed."

"I'm sorry," said Douglas. "I've neglected her. Both of you."

Vivi flushed again. "You don't have to . . . nothing to apologize for."

"Thank you," he said quietly. He glanced down toward the lawn, where they were already tidying up now. "For everything. Thank you."

"Oh, Douglas . . ." She was unsure of what else to say.

Douglas had placed his coat on the ground and they had sat on it in silence for a while, facing the house, he staring at the lawn, at the child whose fingers grabbed the blades of grass, from the safety of Vivi's lap.

"Can I take her?"

She handed over the baby. "I keep thinking it's all my fault," he said. "That if I'd been a better husband . . . that if she'd stayed here, none of this—"

"No, Douglas." Her voice was unusually sharp. "There was nothing you could have done. Nothing."

He looked down.

"Douglas, she was gone from you a long time ago. Long before this. You must know that."

"I know."

"The worst thing you could do is make her tragedy your own." She wondered at the strength of her own words. This certainty came somehow easier to her these days. There was pleasure in supporting him. "Suzanna needs you," she said, pulling the child's rattle from a pocket. "She needs you to be cheerful. And to show her what a wonderful daddy you are."

He made a mild scoffing noise.

"You are, Douglas. You're probably the only father she's known, and she loves you to bits."

He looked at her sideways. "She loves **you** to bits."

Vivi reddened with pleasure. "I love her. It's impossible not to."

They watched as Rosemary's erect figure marched backward and forward between the remaining piles, gesturing and pointing with military efficiency. And then at the bonfire, which had started to burn, just out of sight, its plume of smoke hinting at the irrefutable end of Athene's tenure of the house. As the gray column gained in strength, lost its translucency, she felt Douglas's hand creep across the grass to hers, and squeezed it reassuringly in return.

"What's going to happen to her?" she said.

He stared at the child between them, and let

out a long sigh. "I don't know. I can't look after her alone."

"No."

At that Vivi felt something shift inside her, the stirrings of a confidence she had never felt before. The sense of being—for the first time in her life—indispensable. "I'll be here," she said, "for as long as you need me."

He had looked up at her then, his eyes—too old and sad for his youthful face—seeing her as if for the first time. He had observed their linked hands, and then he had shaken his head slightly, as if he had been missing something all these years and was chastising himself for doing so. At least, that was how she liked to remember it afterward.

Then, as her breath stalled in her chest, he had lifted his free hand to her cheek, in almost the same way as he had to the child's. Vivi's sweet, generous smile broke through, willing strength, joy, love into him as if she could do it by willpower alone. So when his lips met hers, it was no great surprise.

"**Darling**," she had said, marveling at the determination, the certainty that requited love could bestow. And her blood sang when he answered her in the same way, his arms enclosing her in an embrace that said as much about his need as it did hers. Not quite a fairy tale, but no less momentous, no less real, for that.

**I'll be here.**

# 25

The passengers emerging through the arrivals gate from flight BA7902 from Buenos Aires were a conspicuously handsome lot. Not that the Argentinians weren't a good-looking nation generally, Jorge de Marenas observed afterward (especially when compared to those Spanish **Gallegos**), but it was perhaps inevitable that a hundred and fifty attendees of a plastic surgeons' convention—and their wives—would be a little more aesthetically pleasing than most: tanned Amazonian women with hourglass figures and hair the color of expensive handbags, men with uniformly thick dark hair and unnaturally firm jawlines. Jorge de Marenas was one of the few whose appearance related to his biological age.

"Martin Sergio and I played a little game," he told Alejandro, as they sat in the back of the taxi, speeding toward London. "You look around and work out who's had what. The women, it's easy." He held an imaginary pair of footballs to his chest, and pouted. "It's too much of everything. They start off with a little nip and tuck here, then they want to look like Barbie. But the men . . . We were trying to start a rumor that the plane had run out of fuel to see who could still form frown lines. Most of them were like . . ." He mimed a frozen expression of benign acquiescence: "'Are you sure? But that's terrible. We're going to die!'" He laughed heartily and slapped a hand on his son's thigh.

The plane journey, and the prospect of seeing his beloved Alejandro, had made him garrulous, and he had talked so much since their embrace in the echoing arrivals hall that it wasn't until they reached the outskirts of Chiswick, and the taxi slowed on the motorway, that he realized his son had said barely anything. "So, how long do you have off work?" he said. "Are we still on for our fishing trip?"

"All booked, Papa."

"Where are we going?"

"A place about an hour's drive from the hospital. I've booked it for Thursday. You said you'd be finishing your conference Wednesday, right?"

"Perfect. **Buenisimo**. And what will we be catching?"

"Salmon trout," Alejandro said. "I bought some flies in Dere Hampton, the place where I'm living. And I've borrowed a couple of rods from one of the doctors. You need nothing apart from your hat and your waders."

"All packed," said Jorge, motioning toward the trunk. "Salmon trout, eh? Let's see if they'll give us a bit of a fight." He sat, heedless of the flat west London sprawl that was building in density through the window, his mind already thinking of clear English rivers, the whir of the line as it flew through the air and landed a length of water in front of him.

"How's Mama?"

Jorge regretfully left the bubbling waters behind. He had wondered for much of the plane journey how much to tell him. "You know your mama," he said carefully.

"Has she been anywhere lately? Will she go out of the house with you?"

"She . . . she's still a little worried about all the crime. I cannot persuade her that things are improving. She watches too much **Crónica**, reads **El Guardian**, **Noticias**, that kind of thing. It's not good for her nerves. Milagros has been living with us full time—did I tell you?"

"No."

"I think your mother likes to have someone else in the house when I'm not around. It makes her . . . more easy in herself."

"She didn't want to come here with you?" His son was staring out of the taxi window, and it was hard to tell from his voice whether he was regretful or glad.

"She's not so keen on airplanes these days. Don't

worry, son. She and Milagros rub along quite well together."

The truth was, he was glad to have a little break from her. She had become obsessed with the idea of the supposed affair he was having with Agostina, his secretary, while simultaneously berating him for his lack of interest in her. If he would only agree to tighten her waist, lift her cheeks, he might find her more attractive. He tended to avoid denial— years of experience had shown him that this often made her worse. Nor could he articulate the truth: with age, he no longer felt the intense need for physical reassurance he once had, but the years of slicing these young girls open, of reshaping them, of padding them out and hauling them in, of carefully sculpting their most intimate parts, meant that he no longer had much more than a detached, artist's appetite for female flesh.

"She misses you," he said. "I'm not telling you this because I want you to feel guilty. God knows, you should have some fun as a young man, see the world a little. But she misses you. She's packed you some **Mate** in my bag, and some new shirts, and a couple of things she thought you might want to read." He paused. "I think she would like it if you wrote a little more often."

"I know," said Alejandro. "Sorry. It's been . . . a strange time."

Jorge looked sharply at his son. He was going

to probe further, but changed his mind. They had four days together, and if Alejandro had something on his mind, he would find out soon enough. "So, London, eh? You'll like the Lansdowne Hotel. Your mother and I came here in the 1960s when we were first married, and we had a ball. This time I have booked us a twin room. No point in being separated, not after all these months. Me and my boy, eh?"

Alejandro grinned at him, and Jorge felt the familiar pleasure at being in the company of his handsome son. He thought of how Alejandro had held him tightly, pulling him close at the airport gates, kissing his cheeks, a drastic progression from the reserved handshakes he had habitually bestowed, even as a small boy returning from board-ing school. They said travel changed you, Jorge thought. Maybe, in this cold climate, his son was finally thawing out a little. "We'll be boys together, eh? We'll hit the best restaurants, a few nightclubs. Live a little. There's a lot to catch up on, Turco."

Jorge's conference finished every day at four thirty, and while the other delegates met in bars, admired glossy photographs of each other's handiwork, and muttered about their colleagues' supposed butchery behind their backs, he and his son set out on a fran-tic bout of evening activities. They visited a friend of Jorge's, who lived in a stucco-fronted house in St John's Wood, went to see a West End show, although neither liked theater, took drinks at the bar of the Savoy, and had tea at the Ritz, where Jorge insisted the waiter take their picture ("It's all your mama asked for," he said, as Alejandro tried to disappear beneath the table). Drunk, they clapped each other on the back, and said what a great time they were having, how good it was to be together, how the best times were to be had by men alone. Then, more drunk, they became tearful and sentimental, expressing their sorrow that Alejandro's mother couldn't be there too. Jorge, while gratified to see these unusual displays of emotion from his son, was aware that something was yet to be told. Alejandro had said a friend had died, and this explained something of his change in character, something of the sorrow that hung about him, but it didn't explain the tension, a fine yet increasing anxiety that even Jorge, a man with the emotions of a carthorse, as his wife often told him, could sense in the atmosphere.

He asked him nothing directly.

He was not sure that he wanted to know the answer.

Cath Carter's house was two doors along from her late daughter's, a throwback to the days when council policy tried to put family members near each other. Jessie had told Suzanna stories of families whose members occupied whole cul-de-sacs, grandmothers next to mothers, sisters, and brothers, whose children had melded into an amorphous family group, running in and out of each other's homes with the confident possession of the extended family.

Cath's house, however, couldn't have been more different from her daughter's. Where Jessie's front door and gingham curtains spoke of an esoteric taste, a love of the bright and gaudy, an irreverence reflected in her character, Cath's spoke of a woman certain of her own standing; its neat floral borders and immaculate paintwork betrayed a determination to keep things orderly. Suzanna averted her eyes from Jessie's front door. She did not want to think of her last visit to that house. She wasn't convinced she wanted to be there at all. The morning school run had just finished, and the estate was dotted with mothers pushing prams, others carrying cartons of milk purchased from the mini-mart down the road. Suzanna walked on, her hands thrust deep into her coat pockets, feeling the envelope she had prepared half an hour earlier. If Cath wasn't there, she wondered, should she push it through the door? Or was this the kind of conversation that needed to be had face to face?

There was a photograph of Jessie in the front window, her hair in bunches, the familiar grin on her face. It was bordered in black and there were around forty cards of remembrance around it. Suzanna glanced away from them, and rang the doorbell, conscious of the curious stares of passers-by.

Cath Carter's hair had gone white. Suzanna stared at it, trying to remember what shade it had been before, then caught herself.

"Hello, Suzanna," Cath said.

"I'm sorry I haven't been over," she said. "I wanted to. I just—"

"Didn't know what to say?"

Suzanna blushed.

"It's okay. You wouldn't be the only one. At least you came, which is more than most. Come on in." Cath stepped back, holding open the door, and Suzanna walked in, her step leaden on the immaculate hall carpet.

She was shown into the front room and directed toward a sofa, from where she could see the back of the framed picture and the cards, a few of which were turned inward toward the little room. It was the same layout that Jess's house had been, the interior just as pristine, but the atmosphere heavy with grief.

Cath moved heavily across the room, and sat down on the easy chair opposite, folding her skirt under her with careworn hands.

"Emma at school?" Suzanna asked.

"Started back this week. Half-term."

"I came . . . to see . . . if she was okay," Suzanna said awkwardly.

Cath nodded, glanced unconsciously at her daughter's picture. "She's coping," she said.

"And to say—if there's anything I can do to help . . ."

Cath tilted her head enquiringly.

There was a photograph behind her on the mantelpiece, Suzanna noted, of the family all together, with a man who must have been Jessie's father holding Emma as a baby. "I—I feel responsible," she said.

Cath shook her head briskly. "You're not responsible." There was a huge weight in the words she left unspoken.

"I really just wondered . . . perhaps if I could"— she reached into her pocket and held the envelope in front of her—"contribute anything?"

Cath stared at her outstretched hand.

"Financially. It's not much. But I thought if there was a trust fund or something . . . for Emma, I mean . . ."

Cath's hand reached for the little gold cross around her neck. Her expression seemed to harden. "We don't need anyone's money, thank you," she said crisply. "Emma and I will do just fine."

"I'm so sorry, I didn't mean to offend." Suzanna stuffed the envelope into her pocket, scolding herself for her tactlessness.

"You haven't offended me." Cath stood up, and Suzanna wondered if she was about to be told to leave, but the older woman moved over to the serving hatch at the end of the room, reached through, and flicked the switch on the kettle. "There is one thing you could do," she said, her back to the room. "We're making Emma a memory box. Her teacher suggested it. You get people to write their memories of Jessie. Nice things that happened. Good days. So that when she gets older Emma can still have . . . a full picture of what her mum was like. What everyone thought of her."

"That's a lovely idea." Suzanna thought of the shelf in the shop that bore a small shrine of Jessie's things.

"I thought so."

"A bit like our displays, I suppose."

"Yes. Jess was good at those, wasn't she?"

"Better than I was. I don't suppose you'll be short of those sorts of memories. Good ones, I mean."

Cath Carter said nothing.

"I'll try to do something that matches up, that does her justice."

The older woman turned. "Jess did everything to the full, you know," she said. "It wasn't much of a life, a pretty small life to some. I know she didn't really do anything, or go anywhere. But she loved people, and she loved her family, and she was true to herself. She didn't hold back." Cath was staring at the picture above the mantelpiece.

Suzanna sat, motionless.

"No . . . She used to divide people into drains and radiators. Did you know that? Drains are the type that are always miserable, that want to tell you their problems, suck the life out of you . . . Radiators are what Jess was. She warmed us all up."

Suzanna realized with some discomfort where she had probably sat in the equation. Cath no longer seemed to be speaking to her: she was addressing the picture, her face softened. "I'm going to teach Emma to do the same. I won't have her growing up frightened, cautious of everything, just because of what happened. I want her to be strong, and brave, and . . . like her mother." She adjusted the frame, moving it a fraction along the shelf. "That's what I want. Like her mother."

She brushed nonexistent fluff from her skirt. "Now," she said, "about that tea."

Alejandro stood up suddenly in the little boat, making it rock dangerously, and threw down his rod in disgust. At the other end, his father looked up at him in incomprehension. "What's the matter? You'll frighten the fish!"

"Nothing is biting. Nothing."

"Have you tried one of these damsel nymphs?" Jorge held up one of the brightly colored flies. "They seem to be biting better on the smaller lures."

"I tried them."

"Then a sinking line. I don't think your floating one is any good."

"It's not the line. Or the lure. I just can't do it today."

Jorge pushed back his hat. "I hate to remind you, but it's the only day I have."

"I can't fish anymore."

"That's because you are fidgeting like a dog with fleas." Jorge leaned over and made Alejandro's rod secure within the boat, then laid his own next to his landing net of stunned, glistening fish. He was nearly up to his ticket allowance of six. He was going to have to eat into his son's soon.

He shifted on his seat and reached into the hamper for a beer, holding it up like a peace offering. "What's going on? You were always a better fisherman than me. You're like a five-year-old today. Where's your patience?"

Alejandro sat down, shoulders hunched. His formerly languid air had vanished over the past days.

"Come," said Jorge, with a hand on his shoulder. "Have something to eat. Another beer . . . Or something stronger?" He tapped the whiskey flask in the pocket of his fishing vest. "You've hardly touched this food."

"I'm not hungry."

"Well, I am. And if you keep thrashing about like you have been, there will be nothing left in the water for miles."

They ate the sandwiches Alejandro had made in

silence, letting the boat drift in the middle of the lake. It was not a bad flat, Jorge told him. Spacious. Light. Secure. Lots of pretty young nurses going past. (He hadn't actually said the last bit.) Yes, he had been pretty taken with the area, the rolling countryside, the quaint cottages, the low-ceilinged English pubs. He liked the tranquility of this lake, the fact that the English were considerate enough to restock it with fish every year. England seemed to stay the same, he said. It was reassuring, when you could see a once-proud country like Argentina going to the dogs, to know that there were some places where civilized standards, a little dignity, still mattered. Alejandro had told him then of the landlords who had rejected him for being "dark," and Jorge, spluttering, had said the place was obviously full of half-wits and ignorants. "Calls itself a civilized country," he muttered. "And half the women wearing men's shoes . . ."

Alejandro stared into the water for some time, then turned to him. "You can tell Mama," he said, and let out a deep sigh, "that I'm coming home."

"What is wrong with a nice woman's shoe?" Jorge stopped, and swallowed the last of his sandwich. "What?"

"I've handed in my notice. I'm coming back in three weeks."

Jorge wondered if he had heard him correctly.

"Your mother will be pleased," he said carefully. Then he wiped his mustache and put his handkerchief back into his pocket. "What happened? The pay is no good?"

"The pay is okay."

"You don't like the work?"

"The work is fine. It's pretty universal, you know." Alejandro did not smile.

"You can't settle? Is it your mother? Is she plaguing you? She told me about the lock of hair—I'm so sorry, son. She doesn't understand, you know. She doesn't see it like other people. It's because she doesn't get out enough, you know? She thinks too much about things . . ." Jorge was suddenly swamped by guilt. This was why he was more comfortable with reticence. Conversation inevitably led to awkwardness. "You shouldn't let her trouble you."

"It's a woman, Pa. She's killing me."

The fact that they were in the middle of a thirty-acre lake meant that no one saw Jorge's eyes widen slightly, then raise to heaven as he uttered a near-silent "Thank God!"

"A woman!" he said, trying to keep his voice free of blatant joy. "A woman!"

Alejandro's head dropped onto his knees.

Jorge straightened his face. "And this is a problem?"

Alejandro spoke into his knees: "She's married."

"So?"

Alejandro looked up, bewildered.

The words bubbled out of Jorge. "You're getting older, son. You're not likely to find anyone that doesn't have a little . . . history." He was still fighting the urge to dance a little jig round his son.

"History? That's only part of it."

A **woman**. He could have sung it, let the sound burst forth from his lungs. Carry across the lake and bounce back at him off the shore. A woman!

Alejandro's face was hidden, his back bent as if he were in acute pain. Jorge composed himself, tried to focus on his son's misery and introduce a more somber tone to his voice.

"So. This woman."

"Suzanna."

"Suzanna." Jorge said the name reverentially. "You—you care for her?"

It was a stupid question. Alejandro lifted his head and Jorge remembered what it was like to be a young man, the agony, the volatility of love.

His son's voice was stilted: "She—she's everything. I can't see anything but her, you know? Even when I'm with her. I don't even want to blink when I'm near her in case I miss a single moment . . ."

Perhaps if he had been someone else, Jorge might have uttered a few platitudes about first love, about how these things became easier, about how there were plenty more fish in the sea. But this was his son, and Jorge knew better.

"Pa? What do I do?" He looked like he was about to explode with frustration and misery, as if talking about the cause of his unhappiness had made his suffering more acute.

Jorge de Marenas straightened himself up, his shoulders a little squarer, his expression dignified and paternal. "You have told her how you feel?"

Alejandro nodded miserably.

"And do you know how she feels?"

The young man looked out across the water. Eventually he turned back to his father, and shrugged.

"She wants to stay?"

Alejandro made as if to speak, but his mouth closed before it had the chance to form words.

If they had been seated side by side, Jorge would have put his arm around his son. Instead he leaned forward, and laid his hand on his son's knee. "Then you're right," he said. "It's time to go home."

The water lapped against the side of the boat. Jorge adjusted the oars, opened another beer, and handed it to his son. "I meant to tell you. This Sofia Guichane . . . the one who asked to be remembered to you." He leaned back in the boat, blessing God silently for the joy of fishing. "**Gente** says she and Eduardo Guichane are to split."

———

As Suzanna left Cath's house, she bumped into Father Lenny. He was walking along the pavement, holding a bag under his arm, his robe swinging. "How is she?" he said, nodding at Cath's house.

Suzanna grimaced, unable to convey what she felt.

"I'm glad you came," he said. "Not enough do. Shame, really."

"I don't know if I was any help," she said.

"What's happening with the shop? Are you headed off there now? I notice you've been shut a lot lately."

"It's been . . . difficult."

"Hang on in there," he said. "You might find things easier after the inquest."

She felt the familiar clench of discomfort. She was not looking forward to giving evidence.

"I've done a few," he said, closing the gate behind him. "They're not so bad. Really."

She forced a smile, braver than she felt.

"I don't think your man was too keen either, from what he told me."

"What?"

"Alejandro. Told me he was off to Argentina."

"He's going back?"

"Shame, isn't it? Nice guy. Still, can't say I blame him. It's not the easiest town to settle in. And he's had a bumpier ride than most."

———

Suzanna lay awake for most of the night. She thought of Cath Carter, and of Jessie, and of her broken, empty shop. She watched as the dawn broke, the blue light filtering through the gap in the curtains that she had never liked.

Then, as Neil sat in the kitchen cramming toast into his mouth while he searched the work surfaces for his cuff links, she told him she was leaving him.

He seemed not to hear her. Then, after several seconds, "What?" he said.

"I'm leaving. I'm sorry, Neil."

He stood very still, a piece of toast protruding from his mouth. She felt rather embarrassed for him.

Eventually he removed it. "Is this a joke?"

She shook her head.

They stared at each other for some minutes. Then he turned, and began to pack things into his briefcase. "I'm not going to discuss it now, Suzanna. I've got a train to catch, and an important meeting this morning. We'll talk this evening."

"I won't be here," she said quietly.

"What's this about?" he said, incredulity on his face. "Is this because of your mother? Look, I know it's all been a shock to you, but you've got to look on the bright side. You don't have to live with all that guilt anymore. I thought you all understood each other better now. You told me you thought things might improve."

"I do."

"Then what? Is this about having children? Because I've backed off, you know I have. Don't start making me feel bad about that."

"It's not—"

"It's just stupid to make life-changing decisions when you're not thinking straight."

"I'm not."

"Look, I know you're still upset about Jessie. I feel sad about her too. She was a nice girl. But you will feel better after a while, I promise." He nodded to himself, as if in confirmation. "We've had a tough few months. The shop is a drain on you, I know that. It must be depressing having to go in to work with it looking . . . well, with all that still in the air. But the windows are going in—when?"

"Tuesday."

"Tuesday. I know you're unhappy, Suzanna, but just don't overreact, okay? Let's just get it all in proportion. It's not just Jessie you're grieving for, it's what you thought was your family history, probably your mother, even. It's your shop. It's your way of life."

"Neil . . . it's not the shop I wanted."

"You did want the shop. You went on and on about it. You can't tell me now you didn't want it."

She had heard an edge of panic in his voice. Her own was almost unnaturally calm as she said, "It was always about something else. I know that now. It was about . . . filling a hole."

"Filling a **hole**?"

"Neil, I'm really sorry. But we're kidding our-selves. We've been kidding ourselves for years."

Finally he was taking her seriously. He sat down heavily on the kitchen chair. "Is there someone else?"

Her hesitation was just brief enough for her answer to be convincing. "No."

"Then what? What are you saying?" He stood up, began pacing the room. "You can't just throw everything up in the air, keep shopping around, just because you're not waking up singing every morn-ing. You've got to work at something, to stick at something in your life. That's what life is like, Suze, it's about persistence. About sticking with each other. And waiting for the happy times to come back. We've had a lot of them, Suzanna, and we will again. You've just got to have a little faith. Be realistic in your expectations."

When she didn't speak, he sat down again, and they were silent for some time. Outside, one of the neighbors slammed a car door and shouted an instruction at a child, then drove off.

"You'll have your family, Neil," she said quietly. "You've got loads of time, even if you think you don't."

Neil got up and walked over to her. He squatted down and took her hands in his. "Don't do this, Suze. Please." His blue eyes were pained and anxious. "Suze."

She kept staring at her shoes.

"I love you. Doesn't that mean anything? Ten years together?" He dipped his head, trying to see her face. "Suzanna?"

She lifted her face to his, her eyes steady. She shook her head. "It's not enough, Neil."

He looked back at her, evidently hearing the certainty in her voice and seeing something final in her expression, and let go of her hands. "Then nothing's going to be enough for you, Suzanna." His words were bitter, spat out in the realization that this was really it. "You're after a fairy story. And it's going to make you very unhappy."

He got up and wrenched open the door. "And you know what? When you realize it, don't come running to me because I've had enough. Okay? I've really had enough."

She had hurt him so much already. She didn't say that she would rather take that risk than live with what she already knew would be a lifetime of disappointment.

# 26

Suzanna lay on the bed she had slept in as a child, as the sounds of her childhood resonated through the wall. She could hear her mother's dog whining, its claws scrabbling on the flagstone floor downstairs, its flurry of staccato yelps proclaiming some unseen outrage. She absorbed the muffled sound of Rosemary's television: the forecast was gray with scattered showers, she noted, smiling wryly at the plaster wall's inability to offer any resistance to the evidence of Rosemary's faded hearing. Outside, on the front drive, she could hear her father talking to one of the men, discussing some problem with a grain chute. Sounds that, until now, had only ever made her feel alien in this environment. For the first time, Suzanna was comforted by them.

She had arrived late at night two evenings ago, having packed her belongings while Neil was at work. Despite what he'd said, she knew he was hoping that she would change her mind while he was gone. That what she said had been perhaps an unhappy side effect of grief. And she thought, in his heart of hearts, that he probably knew that the grief had delayed the decision, clouded her certainty that it had to be done.

Vivi had met her at the door and listened without saying a word when Suzanna announced tearfully why she was there. Suzanna had thought she would leave the cottage without a second glance, but had been taken aback by how emotional she felt at packing her clothes. Surprisingly Vivi hadn't pleaded with her to give it another go, or told her what a wonderful man Neil was—even when Neil turned up, as she'd known he probably would, drunk and incoherent later that night. Vivi had made him coffee and let him rant, ramble, and sob. She had told him, Vivi said afterward, that she was so sorry, that not only was he welcome to stay in the cottage, but that he would be part of their family for as long as he wanted. Then she had driven him home.

"I'm sorry to have put you through that," Suzanna had said.

"Nothing to be sorry for," replied Vivi, and made her a cup of tea.

She had been static for years, Suzanna thought, gazing at the rosebuds on the wallpaper, noting the corner by her wardrobe where she had, as an adolescent, scribbled in pen her hatred of her parents. Now, as if unleashed by her actions, things were moving rapidly, as if time itself had decided she had too much to make up.

There was a knock at the door. "Yup?" Suzanna pushed herself upright, and saw, with shock, that it was nearly a quarter to ten.

"Come on, lazybones. Time to shake a leg." Lucy's blond head peered in, a tentative smile on her face.

"Hey, you." Suzanna rubbed her eyes. "Sorry. Didn't know you were coming so early."

"Early? It doesn't take long for you to revert to your old habits." She moved forward and hugged her sister. "You okay?"

"I feel like apologizing to everyone for not being a wreck."

That was the worst thing, how easy it had been to leave. She felt guilty, of course, for having been the cause of his unhappiness, and sadness at having to break a habit and routine; but there was none of the crushing sense of loss that she had anticipated would come with her marriage ending. She had briefly wondered whether it meant some kind of emotional disability on her part. "Twelve years, and so little wailing and gnashing of teeth. Do you think I'm odd?"

"Nope, just honest. It means it's the right thing," Lucy said, pragmatically.

"I keep waiting to feel something—something else, I mean."

"Perhaps you will. But there's no point in looking for it, trying to make yourself feel something you don't." She sat down on Suzanna's bed, and riffled through her bag. "It was time to move on." She held an envelope aloft. "Talking of which, I've got your tickets here."

"Already?"

"No time like the present. I think you should just go, Suze. We can sort out the shop. I don't think it's fair on Neil if he has to see you around everywhere. It's a small town, after all, and it's never been short on gossip."

Suzanna took the tickets and stared at the date. "But that's not even ten days away. When we talked, I thought you meant next month. Maybe even a couple of months."

"But what's there to stay for?"

Suzanna bit her lip. "How am I going to pay you back? I won't even have time to sell off the stock."

"Ben will help. He thinks you should go too."

"Probably glad to have me out of the house. I think he's been rather put out at having me home again."

"Don't be ridiculous." Lucy grinned at her sister. "Love the thought of you backpacking," she said. "Hilarious. I'm almost tempted to come too. Just to witness it."

"I wish you would. I feel quite nervous, to be honest."

"Australia's not the end of the world." They

giggled. "Okay, it is the end of the world. But it's not exactly roughing it."

"Have you spoken to your friend? Is she still happy to put me up for a few days?"

"Sure. She'll show you around Melbourne. Get you started. She's looking forward to meeting you."

Suzanna tried to picture herself in foreign vistas, her life, for the first time, a blank, waiting to be populated by new people, new experiences. The kind of thing Lucy had urged her to do in her early twenties. It felt terrifying. "I haven't done anything on my own. Not for years. Neil organized everything."

"Neil infantilized you."

"That's a bit strong."

"Yeah. It probably is. But he did let you behave a bit like a spoiled child. Please don't get arsy with me for saying it," she added quickly, "not while we're having our sisterly bonding session."

"Is that what this is?"

"Yup. About fifteen years later than it should have been. Come on, show me where your bags are and I'll start sorting your things for you." Lucy unzipped the big black holdall with determined speed. "Bloody hell!" she said. "How many pairs of stilettos do you own, Imelda?" She zipped the bag shut again and hauled it to the other side of the room. "You won't need any of those. Get Dad to put them in the attic. Where are your clothes?"

Suzanna pulled up her knees under the duvet and hugged them, thinking of the infinite possibilities before her. And all the ones she had missed. She was trying to fight the sensation of being rushed, that she should sit still for a while and take stock. But her sister was right. She had caused Neil enough harm already. It was the least she could do.

"Are you getting up today, you fat lodger?"

Suzanna rested her face on her knees, watching Lucy's blond head bob up and down as her sister sorted through her clothes—clothes that looked, suddenly, as if they didn't belong to her. "I told Mum there wasn't anyone else," she said, eventually.

Lucy stopped, a pair of socks balled in her hand. She slowly put them into a pile on her left. When she looked up, her face was a careful blank. "I can't say I'm surprised."

"He was the first."

"I didn't mean that. I just thought it was going to take something pretty radical to shake you out of your safety net."

"You think that's what it was?" Suzanna realized she felt vaguely defensive about her marriage. It had lasted a lot longer, and survived a few more slings and arrows, than many.

"Not just that."

Suzanna stared at her sister. "It wasn't just a casual fling."

"Is it over?"

Suzanna hesitated. "Yes," she said, eventually.

"You don't sound very sure."

"There was a time when . . . when I thought it might be right . . . but things have changed. And, anyway, I should be by myself for a while. Sort myself out. Something Neil said made me think a bit."

"You told Neil about him?"

"God, no. I've done enough damage. You're the only one who knows. Do you think I'm awful? I know you liked Neil."

"Doesn't mean I ever thought you two were right for each other."

"Ever?"

Lucy shook her head.

Suzanna felt relieved though a little part of her felt betrayed by her sister's apparent certainty. Then again, she reasoned that even if Lucy had said anything she would have taken no notice—she had taken little heed of her family's opinions for years.

"Neil's a simple soul," Lucy said. "Just a nice, straightforward chap."

"And I'm a complicated old cow."

"He needs some nice Home Counties **gel** to lead a nice simple life with."

"Like you."

Do you really believe that? Lucy's eyes asked, and Suzanna discovered that she didn't know because she had never looked hard enough.

Lucy paused, as if judging her words carefully. "If it makes you feel any better, Suze, one day I'll probably drop my own little bombshell on Mum and Dad. Just because my life looks simple to you, it doesn't mean I am."

It had been said lightheartedly, but Suzanna, gazing at the young woman opposite, thought of her sister's furious ambition, her determined privacy, her lack of boyfriends. And, as the germ of a notion grew, she started to see how blind, how self-obsessed she had been.

She slid out of bed, crouched beside her, and ruffled her sister's short blond hair. "Well," she said, "when you do, my prodigal sister, just make sure I'm around to enjoy it."

She found her father by the Philmore barns. She had walked the long route, up the bridleway and past the Rowney wood, carrying the basket Vivi had made up, which she had offered to run to them in her car. It was okay, Suzanna had said, she fancied the walk. And she had walked meditatively, ignoring the fine rain, conscious of the glowing swell of autumnal colors on the land around her.

She heard it before she saw it: the grind and bump of the bulldozer, and the creaking and crashing of timbers. She had to shut her eyes for a second and remind herself that such sounds didn't always mean disaster. Once her breath had come back to her, she had walked on, closer to the house. And then, coming upon the flurry of activity, she stood at the edge of what had once been a yard and watched as the bulldozer crashed against the rotten wood, bringing down the semi-derelict buildings that had been there for centuries, which even the most fervently antiquarian listings officer at the council admitted were not worth saving.

Her father and brother were at the other side, motioning to the men in the bulldozers, her father breaking off occasionally to talk to two others, one of whom appeared to be in charge of the bins.

By the time she had arrived, two buildings were already down, their metamorphosis from shelter to sculpture almost dismayingly swift.

Ben had seen her. He pointed to his father and she nodded, watching as he walked over to interrupt the older man's conversation. He and Ben walked with the same stiff-legged gait, shoulders hunched forward as if permanently ready to do battle. Her father, tilting his ear toward his son, ended his conversation and, following his son's hand, gestured toward her. She stood still, not wanting to have to make polite conversation. Finally, perhaps sensing her reticence, he came across to her, dressed in a thin cotton shirt that she remembered from her youth, oblivious, as he seemingly always had been, to the elements.

"Lunch," she said, handing over the basket. And then, as he was about to thank her, she added, "Got a minute?" He indicated to the one remaining barn, and passed Ben's sandwiches to him on the way.

They had not seen each other in the twenty-four hours she had been in the house. He had been out with the demolition team, and she had spent much of her time in her room, a good portion of it asleep. She rested carefully against an old fertilizer sack as he hauled one over for himself.

There was an expectant pause.

"Looks strange, without the middle barns."

He glanced up to the holes in the roof. "I suppose it does."

"When do you start work on the new houses?"

"It'll be a while. We'll have to level the ground first, put in new drainage, that sort of thing." He offered her a sandwich, and she shook her head. "It's a shame," he said. "We'd originally thought we could convert the lot. But there are times when you have to accept that you're just going to have to start from scratch."

They sat side by side, her father breaking off from his sandwich to drink from a flask of tea. She found herself staring at his hands. She remembered Neil telling her that when his own father had died, he had realized, with shock, that he would never see his hands again. Something so familiar and mundane, suddenly to disappear.

She glanced down at her own. She didn't need to see a picture to know that they were her mother's.

She placed them between her knees, and looked out to where the men had stopped for lunch. Then, finally, she turned to her father. "I wanted to ask you something." Her palms pressed against each other, her skin surprisingly cool. "I wanted to ask if you'd mind if I took a little of my share of the estate money now."

She saw from the way he looked at her that he hadn't known what was coming. That what he had perhaps expected was somehow worse. His eyes were both questioning and relieved, checking that this was what she wanted.

"You need it now?"

She nodded. "Ben will do good things with the estate. It . . . it's in his blood."

There was a brief silence as the words descended between them. Silently, he took a checkbook from his back pocket, scribbled a figure, then handed it to her.

Suzanna stared at the check. "That's too much."

"It's your right." He paused. "It's what we spent putting Lucy and Ben through university."

He had finished his sandwich. He screwed up the grease-proof paper it had been wrapped in, and put it back into the basket.

"You might as well know," she said, "that I'm going to go abroad with it. Spread my wings."

She was conscious of his silence, of the silences with which he had spoken to her all her life. "Lucy's got me a ticket. I'm going to Australia. I'll be staying with a friend of hers for a while, just till I find my feet."

Her father shifted position.

"I haven't done much with my life, Dad."

"You're just like her," he said.

She felt herself boil up. "I'm not a bolter, Dad. I'm just trying to do what's right for everyone."

He shook his head, and she realized that the look on his face had not been one of condemnation or judgment. "I didn't mean that," he said slowly. "You . . . need to strike out. Find your own way of doing things." He nodded, as if reassuring himself. "You sure that money will be enough?"

"God, yes. Backpacking's pretty cheap, from what Lucy says. Actually, I'm hoping not to spend too much. I'm going to leave most of it here in the bank."

"Good."

"And Father Lenny's going to sell off my remaining stock for me. So that will be a bit more coming in, hopefully."

They watched as Ben moved between the two bulldozers, apparently issuing instructions, breaking off once to answer his mobile phone and laugh uproariously.

Her father stared at him for a while, then turned

to her. "I know things haven't been easy between us, Suzanna, but I do want you to know something." His knuckles were white around the flask. "I never did a test, you know—we didn't have DNA and suchlike in those days—but I knew from the start you were mine."

Even in the darkened barn Suzanna could see the intensity of his gaze, heard the love in what he was saying. She realized that even he was bound by the past, by deeply ingrained beliefs about blood and heritage. There were ways to be certain about these things. But suddenly she understood they were irrelevant. "It's all right, Dad," she said.

They were quiet for a moment, conscious of a gap widened by years of silence, hard words, and misunderstanding, of the ghost that would always come between them. "Maybe we'll visit. When you're in Australia," he said. He was now close enough so their arms rested against each other. "Your mother has always fancied a bit of foreign travel. And I wouldn't want to go too long—without seeing you, I mean."

"No," said Suzanna, allowing the warmth of him to seep into her. "Me neither."

She found Vivi in the picture gallery, staring at the portrait.

"Are you going to your shop?"

My shop, thought Suzanna. It no longer felt like

the right phrase to describe it. "I'm going to pick up the last of my clothes from Neil's first. I think it's fairer on him to do it while he's out."

"Just clothes?"

"A few books. My jewelry. I'm going to leave the rest." She frowned. "Will you keep an eye on him while I'm gone?"

Vivi nodded.

She had probably already decided as much, Suzanna thought. "I'm not completely heartless. I do care about him, you know," she said. She would have liked to add, I want him to be happy. But she was glad that she wouldn't be around to witness that. Her selflessness didn't stretch that far.

"Will you be happy?"

Suzanna thought of Australia, an unknown continent on the other side of the world. She thought of her own tiny world, of what had once been her shop. Of Alejandro. "Happier than I have been," she said, unable to explain quite what she felt. "Definitely happier."

"That's a start."

"I suppose it is."

Suzanna stepped forward, and they stood side by side, gazing up at the gilt-edged painting. "She should be here," said Vivi. "If it's all right by you, Suzanna dear, I shall probably be on that wall opposite. Your father, silly old fool, thinks I should be up there too."

Suzanna wrapped her arm around Vivi's waist. "You know what? I'm not sure it shouldn't just be you. It might look a bit odd otherwise. And that frame of hers doesn't really go with the surroundings."

"Oh, no, darling. Athene has a right. She has to have her place too."

Suzanna was transfixed briefly by the glittering eyes of the woman in the portrait. "You've always been so good," she said, "looking after all of us."

"Goodness has nothing to do with it," said Vivi. "It's just the way we were made—I was made."

Then Suzanna turned from the portrait to the woman who loved her, who had always loved her. "Thanks, Mum," she said.

"Oh, by the way," Vivi said, as they made their way toward the stairs, "something came for you while you were out. It was delivered by the most extraordinary old man. He kept smiling at me as if he knew me."

"An **old** man?"

Vivi was examining the wood of a table, rubbing at its surface with a fingertip. "Oh, yes. Well into his sixties. Foreign-looking chap with a mustache. No one I've seen in town."

"What was it?"

"He wouldn't explain who it was from. But it's a plant. **Roscoea purpurea**, I think it is."

Suzanna stared at her mother. "A plant? Are you sure it's for me?"

"Perhaps it's from one of your customers. Anyway, it's in the utility room." She walked down the stairs, then called over her shoulder, "We used to know it as the peacock eye. Not one of my favorites, I must admit. I'll give it to Rosemary if you don't want it." With a noise that sounded like a gasp, Suzanna almost pushed past her mother and ran down the stairs.

# 27

She had thought she knew almost all there was to know about Jessie. Now, an hour and a half into the inquest, she learned that the late Jessica Mary Carter had been exactly five feet two and a half inches tall, that she had had her appendix and her tonsils removed more than ten years previously, that she had a birthmark on her lower back, and that the index finger on her left hand had been broken at least three times, the last time relatively recently. Among her other injuries, many of which Suzanna had chosen not to listen to, there were bruises that could not be explained by the events of the night of her death. She didn't sound like Jessie: she sounded like an amalgam of physical elements, of skin and bone and catalogued damage. That was what was so disturbing: not that there were so many injuries she hadn't known about, but that nothing of her essence was there at all.

Inside the court, Jessie's friends and relatives who had braved the inquest, some because they still could not accept that she was gone, others because they were secretly enjoying being part of the biggest thing that had happened to Dere Hampton since the 1996 pet-shop fire, murmured among themselves, or wept silently into handkerchiefs, cowed by the occasion. Suzanna shifted in her seat, trying to look from the edge of the public gallery to the other door. She had to fight the suspicion that he was, at this moment, sitting outside on the bench with Cath Carter's chain-smoking sisters. It would be disrespectful to keep leaving the courtroom to check.

He hadn't been there when she arrived, and he had not been there when she had left the court twenty minutes previously to visit the ladies' room. But as the sole witness to the event, he would have to give evidence.

He would have to come.

Suzanna smoothed back her hair, feeling the familiar clench of her stomach, the winding coil of excitement and fear that had possessed her for the last twenty-four hours. Twice, to comfort herself, she had stared into her bag at her trove of peculiar treasures. There was the label from the plant that had arrived that first day; then, addressed to her at her parents' house, a paper butterfly sent in an unmarked envelope, which Ben, an amateur enthusiast in his teens, had identified only as **Inachis io**. She had written the name on the back. Yesterday, when she had gone to the shop to complete her final task before handing over the keys, she had found an oversize feather pinned to the door frame. It now stuck incongruously from the lip of her shoulder-bag. There had been no messages. But she had known they had to be something to do with him. That there must be some meaning.

She tried not to think too hard of the possibility that they might have come from Neil.

The coroner had finished with the postmortem report. He leaned solicitously over his bench and asked Cath Carter if there was anything she would like clarified. Cath, sandwiched tightly between Father Lenny and an unidentified middle-aged woman, shook her head. The coroner returned to the witness list in front of him.

It would be her turn next. Suzanna gazed down at the bespectacled reporter in the corner, faithfully scribbling shorthand in his notebook. Suzanna had spoken to Father Lenny earlier of her fears that if she told the coroner **everything** she knew, Jessie would be painted as a domestic-abuse victim in the newspapers. She hadn't wanted to be seen as a victim, Suzanna had told him. Didn't they owe her that small dignity at least? He had told her that Cath had similar concerns. "But there is a bottom line here, Suzanna," he had said, "and that is where you'd rather see Emma growing up. Because although there won't be a criminal verdict in this court, you can bet that what gets said here will go on to be used in any criminal case. I think even

Jessie wouldn't mind sacrificing her privacy a little for the sake of her daughter's . . . stability." He had chosen the word carefully.

That had then made it a pretty straightforward decision. Suzanna heard her name called and stood up. Under the surprisingly gentle prompting of the coroner, she told him in measured tones of Jessie's injuries during the time she had worked for the Peacock Emporium, of the sequence of events that had led to the evening on which she died, and of the gregarious, generous personality that had inadvertently led to her death. She had been unable to look at Cath as she spoke, feeling still as if she were betraying the family's trust, but as she stepped down she had caught the older woman's eyes, and Cath had nodded. An acknowledgment of sorts.

He had not come in.

She sat down in her seat, feeling herself deflate.

**You okay?** Father Lenny mouthed, turning in his seat. She nodded, trying not to let her eyes drift again to the wood-paneled door, which threatened to open any minute now. She smoothed her too-short hair for the fortieth time.

Three other people gave evidence: Jessie's doctor, who confirmed that in his opinion Jess had not suffered from depression but had intended to leave her partner; Father Lenny, who, as a close friend of the family, told of his own attempt to remedy what he called her "situation," and of her fierce determination to sort it out herself; and a cousin whom Suzanna had not met. The latter had burst into tears and pointed an accusatory finger at Jason Burden's mother: she had known what was going on and should have stopped it, stopped the bastard. The coroner suggested that she might like to take a break to compose herself. Suzanna listened with half an ear wondering at what point she could legitimately leave the court again.

"We now turn to our sole witness," said the coroner, "a Mr. Alejandro de Marenas, an Argentinian national, formerly resident at Dere Hampton hospital, where he was working in the maternity ward . . ."

Suzanna's heart stopped.

". . . who has provided a written statement. I will pass this to the court clerk to read aloud."

The court clerk, a plump woman with enthusiastically dyed hair, stood and, in a flat, estuary accent, began to read.

A written statement. Suzanna slumped forward as if winded. She heard almost nothing of Alejandro's words, the words she had heard whispered into her ear on the night of Jessie's death, words uttered through tears and kisses, words she had stopped with her own lips.

Then she stared at this woman, who should have been Alejandro, and tried to stop the wail of exasperation that was building inside her.

She couldn't sit still. She fidgeted in her seat, fever-ish and despairing, and when the woman stopped reading, she slid rapidly along the bench and, with a nod of apology, fled to the hallway where two of Jessie's aunts, her cousin, and a friend from school were already seated on the bench.

"That murdering bastard," said one, lighting a cigarette. "How can his mother show her face in here?"

"Lynn says the boys are going to have him if they let him out."

"It's not Sylvia's fault," said the other. "You know she's devastated."

"She still visits him, doesn't she? She still goes to see him every week."

The older woman patted the girl's arm. "Any mother would," she said. "He's blood, isn't he? Whatever he's done." She called to Suzanna, "You all right, love? Found it too hard to listen to, did you?"

Suzanna, leaning against the wall, could not reply. Of course Alejandro hadn't come. Why would he, after everything she had said? She stood for a second, her face crumpling, her hands lifting to her head as if she could physically hold it together. She felt an unfamiliar female arm around her, smelled the acrid aroma of just-smoked cigarettes. "Don't fret, love. She's with the angels now, isn't she?"

Suzanna muttered something and left. She didn't need to know whether the death would be recorded as misadventure, manslaughter, or even as an open verdict. Jessie was gone. That had been the only relevant fact.

She could only pray that Alejandro hadn't gone too.

There had been several delays, ascribed variously to engine trouble, security matters, and bad weather, and Heathrow airport was packed with people milling around, dragging suitcases on wheels, or stacked high in trolleys that swerved mutinously on the shining linoleum floor. Exhausted travelers stretched out proprietorially across multiple seats while babies wailed and small children did their best to get lost in brightly lit cafés, fraying their parents' already shredded tempers.

Jorge de Marenas, a little too full of airport coffee, looked up at the flight board, stood, and picked up his suitcase. He gestured toward the departure gate, where a snaking line of fellow Argentinians were queuing patiently, boarding passes in hand. "You sure you want to do this?" he said to his son. "I don't want you to think about me. Or your mother. This should be about you and what you want."

Alejandro followed his father's gaze to the departure board. "It's okay, Pa," he said.

The nurses' accommodation block at Dere Hampton hospital was bigger than Suzanna had remembered.

It had two entrances, and a wide grassy area surrounding it, punctuated by straggly looking shrubs that she didn't remember at all. It looked so different in the light, dotted with people, frosted with autumnal leaves, that it was hardly recognizable as the place that had been the backdrop of her dreams.

She stood for several minutes, trying frantically to work out which entrance to use. Alejandro had lived on the ground floor, she knew, so she walked over the grass and stared in at several windows, trying to see through the net curtains that appeared to be standard issue in the block.

The third flat she had peered into looked like it might be his. She could just make out the sectional sofa, the white walls, the beech table. But the net curtains made it impossible for her to tell if anyone was living there now.

"Why the hell are there so many bloody net curtains?" she muttered.

"To stop people looking through the windows," said a voice behind her.

Suzanna blushed. Two nurses, one red-headed, one West Indian, were beside her.

"You'd be surprised how excited some people get at the idea of a building full of nurses," said one.

"I'm not a peeping—"

"Are you lost?" she asked.

"I'm looking for someone. A man."

She caught their amused response, realizing she

was a nanosecond away from a bad joke. "A specific man. He works here."

"This is a female block."

"But you had one man here. A midwife. Alejandro de Marenas. Argentinian?"

The nurses exchanged glances. "Oh . . . him."

Suzanna could feel herself being assessed, as if her association with Alejandro had put her in a new light.

"That's his flat, all right, but I don't think he's there. He's not been around for a while, has he?"

"Are you sure?"

"The foreign ones don't last long," said the West Indian woman. "They get all the crappy shifts."

"And they get lonely," said the Irish girl. "Yeah." She looked at Suzanna, her expression unreadable. "I'm not sure if **he** was lonely."

Suzanna blinked furiously, daring herself to collapse in front of these women. "Is there anyone who would know whether he's gone?"

"Try Admin," said the Irish girl.

"Or Personnel. Fourth floor of the main block."

"Thank you," said Suzanna, hating the girls for their knowing looks. "Thank you very much." She fled.

The woman in Personnel had been courteous but wary. "We've had a few cases where foreign nurses have run up considerable debts while they were here," she said, in explanation. "Sometimes the ones that come from third-world countries get a bit carried away with the lifestyle."

"He doesn't owe me any money," said Suzanna. "He doesn't owe anyone money. I just really need to know where he is."

"I'm afraid we're not able to give out personal staff details."

"I have his details. I just need to know if he's still around."

"And that would be a hospital employment matter."

Suzanna tried to regulate her breathing.

"He's a friend."

"They always are."

"Look," Suzanna said, "please. If you want me to humiliate myself, I will—"

"No one's asking you to humiliate yourself—"

The woman was staring at her now.

"I don't even know if it's near Patagonia, or Puerto Rico, or what. I just know it's got lots of cows, and drinks that taste like twigs and water, and horrible mean fish, and that it's really, really big, and if he leaves here I haven't got a hope of finding him. I don't know if I'd be brave enough to try. Please. **Please** just let me know if he's still here."

The woman gazed at Suzanna for a minute, then

moved to the back of her office and pulled a file from a bulging drawer. She stood over it, reading carefully, too far away for Suzanna to see its pages. "We're not allowed by law to reveal the personal details of staff files. What I can tell you is that he's no longer an employee of the hospital," she said.

"So he no longer works for you?"

"That's what I said."

"So you can tell me where he is. If he no longer works for you, he's no longer staff."

"Nice try," said the woman. "Look, you could try his agency—the people who brought him over and placed him with us in the first place." She scribbled a number on a piece of paper and handed it to Suzanna.

"Thanks," said Suzanna.

"And it's next to Uruguay."

"What?"

"Argentina. It's next to Brazil and Uruguay."

The woman, smiling to herself, turned away from the counter and headed back toward her filing.

Arturro hadn't seen him. He asked the three young assistants, who shook their heads theatrically, then continued their graceful lobbing of large pieces of Stilton, and jars of quince paste. Arturro hadn't seen him for more than a week. Neither had Mrs. Creek, nor Liliane, nor Father Lenny, nor the woman who ran the antiques stall, nor the thin man who ran the Coffee Pot, nor the assistants at the café by the garage where he had once been known to get a newspaper.

"About six foot? Quite tanned? Dark-haired?" she said to a nurse outside the newsstand, just on the off chance.

"Shove him my way if you find him." She smirked.

When it started to get dark, Suzanna went home.

"Are you all packed?" said Vivi, handing her a cup of tea. "Lucy rang to say she'll be here at midday tomorrow. I was wondering whether you'd mind having a little sit with Rosemary before you left. It would mean a lot to her, you know."

Suzanna was on the sofa, wondering whether it was madness to head to Heathrow now. The local airport didn't do flights to Argentina, and Heathrow wouldn't give out names on their passenger list, as a matter of security, obviously. "Sure," she said.

"Oh, and you know you said you couldn't get any reply from that number earlier?" said Vivi. "Well, they called back. A nursing agency, they said. Is that who you wanted? I didn't think it could be right."

Suzanna leaped up and snatched the piece of paper from her mother's hand. "It is right," she said.

"A nursing agency?"

"Thank you," she said. "Thank you, thank you." She threw herself along the sofa toward the telephone table, heedless of her mother's bemused look.

The man at the agency was very nice. Almost too nice. But Alejandro de Marenas had signed off their books two weeks previously. Having paid their "introduction fee," he was under no obligation to keep in touch. He was probably back in Argentina. The average stay in England was under a year for midwifery. "I'll take your number, if you like," he said. "If he contacts us again I can keep it on file for him. Are you NHS?"

"No," she said, staring at the feather in her hand. She'd just remembered you weren't meant to keep them in your house because they were bad luck. "Thanks, but no," she whispered. And then, finally, her head dropping gently onto the telephone, she wept.

It was almost nine thirty, and the slight increase in pedestrians that constituted Dere Hampton's rush hour was easing, as the last of the shops opened and the trailing mothers returned home from the school run.

Suzanna stood in the Peacock Emporium for the last time. The windows were in place, their frames freshly painted, a sign advertising next week's one-day closing-down sale. "All stock half price or less," it read in bold black letters. That was the left-hand side, though. The right-hand window would fulfill a different purpose.

She checked her watch, noting that Lucy would be there in two and a half hours. She had only invited a few people, Arturro and Liliane, Father Lenny, Mrs. Creek, those who could be considered to have had daily contact with Jessie, those to whom the objects might mean something, might add to their memory of her.

She looked out through the gauze curtain she had placed in the window that morning, an uncomfortable reminder of the net curtains of the days before, watching as they stood in a little huddle. She had wondered whether this was the right time to do it, but Father Lenny, the only one who had known her plan, had said it was exactly the right time. He had been at previous inquests. He had known that after a death there were images and words that should be blocked out, painted over with something sweeter.

**Are you ready?** she mouthed at him, from behind the door, and then as he nodded she stepped to the window, lifted the gauze curtain, and stepped outside, to where the others stood, a few feet back from the shop, watching with a little anxiety as they took in the display in front of them.

The window was filled with pink gerberas draped from above with the stenciled Mexican fiesta decorations that Jessie had planned to take home at an arranged staff discount, and twisted around with the white fairy-lights that had previously decorated the shelves.

It contained the following items: a pair of net wings that Jessie had once worn all day for a bet, a sequined purse she had loved but regretted she could not afford, and a circular box of pink-wrapped chocolates. To the side there were several magazines, including **Vogue** and **Hello!**, and a piece of handwritten work she had brought back from night school, with "very promising" scrawled in red on the margin. There was a salsa CD, which Jessie had played until Suzanna had begged for mercy, and a drawing of Emma's that she had pinned above the till. In the center there were two photographs, one of which had been taken by Father Lenny and showed Suzanna and Jessie laughing with Arturro beaming in the background, and the other was of Jessie with Emma, seated outside, both wearing pink sunglasses. It was all arranged around a piece of cream parchment, on which Suzanna had penned, in cursive handwriting and fuchsia ink:

**Jessie Carter had a smile as bright as August, and the dirtiest laugh this side of Sid James. She loved Mars bar ice creams, bright pink, this shop, and her family, not in that order. She loved her daughter, Emma, more than anything in the whole world, and for someone so full of love, that meant a lot.**

**She wasn't allowed the time to achieve everything she had wanted, but she changed**

**my shop, and then she changed me. I know that nobody in this town who met her could not have been changed by her too.**

The display glowed, bright and gaudy, at odds with the bare brick and wood around it. At the very front there were two coffee cups. One was empty.

Nobody spoke. After several minutes, Suzanna began to get anxious and glanced at Father Lenny for reassurance. "Having the townspeople displays were Jessie's idea," she said, into the silence, "so I thought she'd like it."

Still no one spoke. Suzanna felt sick suddenly, as if she had reverted to her former self, always saying and doing the wrong thing. She had got it wrong here too. She felt a hiccup of panic rising, and fought to keep it down.

"It's not meant to be everything she was—say everything about her. I just wanted to do a little celebration of her. Something happier than what's been . . ." She trailed off, feeling useless and inadequate.

Then she felt a hand on her arm, and looked down at the slim, manicured fingers, then up at Liliane's now softened, carefully made-up face. "It's beautiful, Suzanna," she said. "You've done a lovely job."

Suzanna blinked hard.

"It's almost as good as one of hers," said Mrs. Creek, who had leaned forward to peer at it. "You should have put in a packet of those heart sweets. She was always eating those heart sweets."

"She'd love it," said Father Lenny, placing his arm round Cath Carter's shoulders. He squeezed her, and murmured something in her ear.

"It's very nice," she said quietly. "Very nice."

"I've taken a few pictures of it for Emma's memory box," Suzanna said. "For when . . . it has to come down. When the shop closes. But it'll be in here till then."

"You should get someone from the paper," said Mrs. Creek. "Get them to put a picture in the paper."

"No," said Cath. "I don't want it in the papers."

"I like that picture of Jessie and Emma," said Father Lenny. "I always liked those sunglasses. They looked like you should be able to eat them."

"I should think they'd taste awful," said Mrs. Creek.

Behind them, Suzanna realized, Arturro was in tears, his heavy shoulders turned away from them in an attempt to disguise his grief. Liliane stepped toward him, and put an arm around him.

"Hey . . . big man," said Father Lenny, leaning forward. "Come on, now . . ."

"It's not just Jessie," Liliane said, turning. She was smiling, her expression indulgent. "It's . . . everything. He's really going to miss your shop."

Suzanna noticed that Liliane's slim arm stretched barely halfway across his back.

"We'll all miss the shop," said Father Lenny. "It had . . . a certain something."

"I just liked the feeling. Coming in." Arturro blew his nose. "I even liked the word. **Emporium.**" He enunciated it slowly, savoring each syllable.

"You could rename your delicatessen Arturro's Emporium," said Mrs. Creek, and bridled as everyone looked blankly at her.

"We have a lot of reasons to feel fond of your shop," said Liliane, carefully.

"Feels almost like it was more Jessie's shop," said Suzanna.

"If it doesn't sound too mawkish," Father Lenny put in, "I like to think there's another one up there somewhere, with Jessie serving."

"You **are** being mawkish," said Cath.

"Serving and talking," said Suzanna.

"Oh, yes," said Father Lenny. "Definitely talking."

Cath Carter, with a faint smile of pride, nudged him. "She talked at nine months," she said. "Opened her mouth one morning and never closed it again."

Suzanna was about to speak, then jumped as she heard a familiar voice.

"Can I add something?" it said.

Her breath was knocked out of her. The last time she had seen him he had radiated such urgency and anger that the air around him had seemed to crackle. Now his movements were easy and fluid, his eyes, which she had last seen accusatory and disbelieving, were soft.

He was looking at her intently, waiting for an answer.

She tried to speak, then nodded dumbly instead.

He stepped past them into the shop, reached up to a shelf, and placed his silver **Mate** pot in the corner of the window. "I think we should be happy," he said quietly, as he emerged. "She was my first friend in this country. She was good at bringing joy. And I think she would want everyone to remember her that way."

She couldn't take her eyes off him, still hardly able to believe that he was there, in front of her.

"Hear hear," said Father Lenny, with a hint of determination in his voice.

There was a long silence, which became slowly awkward. Liliane shifted uncomfortably in her high heels, and Mrs. Creek muttered something to herself. Suzanna heard Father Lenny murmur to Alejandro, and watched as he responded with something that made Father Lenny look directly at her. She blushed again.

"We ought to go." It was Cath's voice.

Shaken from her reverie, Suzanna realized that she hadn't heard from the one person whose opinion mattered most. She turned and searched for the blond head. She hesitated for a moment, then: "Is it all right?" she said, crouching down.

The child did not move or speak.

"It'll be there for at least two weeks. But I'll change it if you want, if you think there's something missing. Move it, if you don't like it. I've got time to do that before I go." She kept her voice low.

Emma stared at the window, then looked at Suzanna. Her eyes were dry. "Can I write something to put in it?" Her voice had the glacial composure of childhood. It made something deep within Suzanna ache.

She nodded.

"I want to do it now," said Emma. She glanced up at her grandmother, then back at Suzanna.

"I'll get you a pen and paper."

Suzanna held out her hand. The little girl let go of her grandmother's and took it. The silent group standing in the lane watched as they walked inside the shop holding hands.

"It was you, wasn't it?"

The shop was empty. Suzanna had just finished pinning Emma's words into the display, fighting the urge to edit the last painful sentences from what she had written. It was important to tell the truth. Especially about death. She straightened her knees and backed out of the window.

"Yes," Ale said.

Just that. A simple affirmative.

"It's bad luck. You should know that."

"It was just a feather. It doesn't have to mean anything." He glanced at the iridescent plume protruding from her handbag. "And, besides, it's beautiful." He let the words hang between them as he walked slowly around the shop.

"And the other things? The butterfly? The plant?" She had to fight the urge to keep sneaking looks at him, to stop her face lighting up at the sheer pleasure of having him nearby.

"A peacock butterfly. The plant too."

"I didn't understand," she said. "About the butterfly, I mean. We only looked up its Latin name."

"Then it's lucky I didn't catch you a cichlid."

They sat for a moment in silence, Suzanna wondering at how, having spent years existing in a kind of low-grade nothingness, her emotions could swing so dramatically from despair to elation and then to something less clear-cut and infinitely more confusing. A group of young girls was peering in at the window, making exaggerated expressions of sentimentality when they read Emma's words.

"It's beautiful, what you did," he said, nodding at the display.

"She would have done it better."

Suzanna struggled with the things she had wanted to say, things that now felt awkward and overblown. "I thought you were in Argentina," she said, trying to sound noncommittal. Now that he was here, she felt suddenly complicated, as if the urgency of the previous day had been an overreaction, had given too much away. "You didn't come to give evidence so I thought you'd already gone."

"I was going to go. But . . . I decided to wait." He leaned against the door. When she looked up, he was gazing at her intently, and that, combined with the slowly settling meaning of his words, made her blush again.

She stood up and began to sweep the floor, conscious of the need to do something, to stay focused. "Right," she said, unsure of why she had. "Right." Her hands tightened on the broom. She pushed it along in short strokes, the heat of his gaze still on her. "Look, you probably know I've left Neil, but I need you to know that I didn't leave him for you. I mean, not that you didn't mean anything to me—don't mean anything to me . . ." She was conscious that she was rambling already. "I just left him to be on my own."

He nodded, still leaning against the door.

"It's not that I'm not flattered by what you said. Because I am. But so much has happened over the past days—stuff that even you don't know about. To do with my family. And I've only just started to work things out. Things about me, about how I'm going to live."

He was looking over at the display.

"So I just want you to know that you are—will always be—really important to me. In ways you probably don't realize. But I think it's time for me to grow up a little. Stand on my own two feet."

She stopped sweeping. "Do you understand?"

"You can't run away from this, Suzanna," he said.

She was shocked by his certainty, by the absence of his previous reticence. Reticence she had always felt fueled by her own.

"Why are you smiling?"

"Because I'm happy?"

She made a sound of exasperation. "Look, I'm trying to explain something here. I'm trying, for once in my life, to be an adult."

He tilted his head to one side. "Did you cut your hair like that to punish yourself?"

At first she didn't trust what she had heard. "What?"

Suzanna's heart was thumping uncomfortably, and now, given his bizarre reaction, all the rage of the previous weeks, all the emotion she had been forced to contain, came spilling out. "Have you lost your mind?"

"It's not so bad." He moved forward, lifted his hand as if to touch it. "I still think you look beautiful."

"This is ridiculous!" She ducked away from him. "You're ridiculous! I don't know what's happened to you, Alejandro, but you don't understand. You don't understand even half of what I've been working through. I've tried to tell you nicely. I've tried to make you understand, but I'm not going to save your feelings if you're going to be too obstinate to listen to them."

"I'm not listening to my feelings?" He was smiling now, and for some reason this enraged her more than ever. Almost unaware of what she was doing, she began to shove him, to physically force him out of the shop, knowing only that she had to be away from him, that she needed him far from her to restore her peace of mind.

"What are you doing, Suzanna Peacock?" he asked, as she forced him through the door.

"Go away," she said. "Go back to bloody Argentina. And just leave me alone. I don't need this, okay? I don't need this on top of everything else."

"You do—"

"Just **go**."

"You do need me."

She closed the door on him, her gasping breaths veering dangerously toward sobs. Now that he was actually there, a reality, she wasn't ready for it. She needed him to be like he was before. She needed things to move slowly, so that she could be sure of what she felt, that she wasn't getting it all wrong. Nothing felt secure anymore: all the elements of her life had swooped and fallen under her like the decks of a storm-ridden ship, threatening to overwhelm her.

"I can't just—I can't just be like you. I can't let go of it all." She wasn't sure he had heard her through the door. She leaned against it, feeling his voice vibrate through it. "I'm not going anywhere."

He was shouting, apparently unafraid of being heard. "I'm not going anywhere, Suzanna Peacock."

The shop seemed to have shrunk. She sat down as it diminished around her, the sound of his muffled voice echoing through her, filling up the remaining space.

"I will haunt you, Suzanna," he yelled. "I will haunt you worse than they ever did. Because they are not your ghosts. They are your mother's and father's and Jason's and poor Emma's. But they are not your ghosts. I am. I'm here to tell you to be happy."

He paused.

"You hear me? I'm not going anywhere."

Eventually she stood, and moved to the window. Through the small frames of curved glass, she could see him, a foot away from the door, addressing it with a kind of evangelical determination, his face relaxed as if he was already sure of the outcome. Behind him, she made out the distant figures of Arturro and Liliane, watching, bewildered, from the door of the Unique Boutique.

"I'm not going anywhere."

His voice echoed down the cobbled lane, bounced off the flint walls, the water fountain. She leaned against the window frame, feeling the fight seep out of her and something give inside her.

"You are a ridiculous man," she said. She wiped her eyes, and he caught sight of her. "A ridiculous man," she said, louder, so that he could hear. "You sound like a lunatic."

He looked right at her and raised his eyebrows.

"You cut your hair like this and I'm the lunatic?"

"A **lunatic**," she yelled.

"So let me in," he said, and gave a distinctly Latin shrug. He was still smiling.

She moved to the door and opened it.

He looked back at her, this foreign man from thousands of miles away, more strange yet more familiar than anything she could have imagined, a broad, uninhibited smile across his face, that spoke of freedom and uncomplicated pleasure, a smile that held promises it didn't have to explain. A smile that was finally matched by her own. "You get it now?" he said quietly.

She began to nod, and then laugh, not even sure why she was doing so—feeling a great bubble of emotion forcing its way out of her in short, breathless bursts. And for some time, they stood in the door of the shop that used to be the Peacock Emporium, talked about in dismissive and curious whispers for weeks after by those who knew them in the small town and those who didn't. Barely touching each other, and watched by the few people who had once been its customers, the Argentinian man, and the woman with the short black hair, a woman who, considering all that had happened, should have been a little less elated, perhaps a little more discreet. The girl, after all, was the image of her mother.

Much, much later, Suzanna stood on the painted step of the shop, locked the door for the final time, and looked around. He was seated, fiddling with the paper butterfly, waiting as, for the seventeenth time, she checked that everything she needed was there. "You know I'm meant to be going to Australia. In about an hour. I've got the ticket and everything."

He reached over and put his arm around her legs as she came to him, a gently proprietorial gesture. "Argentina is closer."

"I don't want to rush into anything, Ale."

He smiled at the paper butterfly.

"I mean it. Even if I do come to Argentina, I'm not sure whether we're going to be together, not yet anyway. I've just come out of a marriage. I want to go somewhere for a while where my history doesn't count."

"History always counts."

"Not to you. Not for us."

She sat beside him and told him about her mother, and how she had run away. "I should hate her, I suppose," she said, feeling the warmth of his hand around hers, savoring the fact that it could now linger there. "But I don't. I just feel relief that I didn't cause her death."

"Well. You have a mother who loves you."

"Oh, I know. And Athene Forster." She looked at the photograph Vivi had given her, which was sitting on top of a cardboard box. "I look like her, I know, but I feel like she has nothing to do with me. I can't mourn someone who left me without a backward glance."

Alejandro's smile faded as he thought of a baby in a Buenos Aires maternity ward, spirited away by a blond woman determinedly oblivious to someone else's pain. "Perhaps she never wanted to leave you," he murmured.

"Oh, I think she knew what she was doing." She was surprised at her lack of animosity. "I had her down as this glamorous, doomed figure. I think perhaps I was half in love with the idea of being the same. Now I just think Athene Forster was probably rather a stupid, spoiled little girl. Someone who just wasn't meant to be a mother."

He stood up and held out his hand to her. "It's time to be happy, Suzanna Peacock," he announced. He tried to make his face solemn. "With me or without me."

She smiled back, accepting the truth in this. "You know what?" she said. "Your gifts were way off the mark. Because there is no Suzanna Peacock. Not anymore."

She paused. "My name is Suzanna Fairley-Hulme."

# 28

The girl in the blue boucle suit descended backward from the train, struggling with the huge pram, whose wheels had stuck on some ledge. It was a cumbersome thing from the 1940s, and as she nodded her thanks to the guard who helped wrestle it onto the platform, she thought of her landlady, who had complained for weeks about its presence in her narrow hall. She had twice demanded its removal, but the girl knew the old woman was intimidated by her accent, and had used it to devastating effect. Just as she did now on the guard, who grinned at her, checking that she had no other bags that also required carrying, and gave her long, slim legs an appreciative glance as she walked away.

It was a blustery day, and outside the station she leaned forward and tucked the blankets more securely into the sides of the pram. Then she smoothed her hair and pulled up her collar, watching wistfully as the latest of several taxicabs roared past. It was at least a mile and a half to the restaurant and she had only enough money for her return ticket. And a packet of cigarettes.

She was going to need those cigarettes.

As she reached Piccadilly, perhaps predictably it began to rain. She flipped the hood up on the pram, and walked faster, her head down against the wind. Because she had not worn stockings, her ridiculous shoes were rubbing her heels. But some vestige of vanity had meant she didn't want to be seen in a pair of cheap shoes. Not today.

The restaurant was in a side street behind a theater, its dark-green exterior and stained-glass windows advertising its discreet quality. She slowed as she approached, as if she were reluctant to reach her destination, and stood outside, staring at the menu, as if trying to decide whether to go in. A row of builders were leaning against the scaffolding above her, temporarily taking shelter from the light rain, one whistling to Dionne Warwick's "Walk On By," which issued furrily from a transistor radio. They watched with unconcealed interest as she attempted to repin her hair, sabotaged by the wind and the lack of a mirror, then peered into a nearby window in an attempt to see whether her makeup had smudged.

She lit a cigarette and smoked it in short, urgent gasps, shifting on her feet and peering distractedly down the street. Finally she turned to the pram beside her, and glanced inside at the sleeping baby.

Suddenly she stood immobile, the intent look on her face still and strange, oblivious to the builders, to the foul weather. She reached in, as if to touch the child's face, her other hand gripping the pram handle tightly, as if to steady herself. Then she leaned under the hood, stooping so that her face couldn't be seen.

Sometime later, she straightened up, let out a slow, shaky sigh, and muttered something under her breath. Then, she wheeled her pram slowly toward the door of the restaurant.

"Cheer up, love," called a voice from above her, as she entered. "It might never happen."

"Oh," she murmured, not loud enough for anyone to hear, "that's where you're quite, quite wrong."

The fat girl with the permanent wave had been rather difficult about taking temporary charge of the pram, huffing and puffing about restaurant policy, so Athene, using her most determinedly cut-glass accent, had been forced to tip her the cigarette money, and promise that she would be no longer than half an hour.

Athene had sat in the ladies' room for almost ten minutes before she had control over her breath.

It had been fun at first. She had never lived like that, hand to mouth, unsure where she was going to sleep, even what town she was going to be in: it had been an adventure. And she, cocooned from the less pleasant bits—the crummy rooms, the appalling food—by the first flush of passion, had reveled in the sheer naughtiness of it all. She had laughed at the thought of her mother, trying desperately to explain her absence at her Wednesday bridge session; of her father, harrumphing over his newspaper as he considered her latest outrage; of sour-faced, disapproving Rosemary, who had always been so blatant in her judgment, who had told Athene with her first look that she knew quite what kind of a girl she was, even when Athene was trying hard not to be.

She had tried not to think about Douglas. She and Tony were like peas in a pod. She had known, from the moment he had stood at her door and smirked as she opened it, as if she should have known very well she was in the wrong place.

She finished her cigarette, and made her way slowly out of the ladies' room and into the clamorous noise of the restaurant to where he sat, staring into his newspaper.

He had always looked handsome in a good suit, this one's cut and color an uncomfortable echo of their wedding day. Now as he turned, she saw that new lines of experience had given his face a handsome maturity.

"Douglas?" she had said, and he had flinched, as if the very word wounded him.

They had stuttered into a dreadful dinner-party conversation. She winced at the pain in his voice.

She was amazed that she could summon any words at all.

"Do you come up to London much?"

She wondered, distantly, whether he was mocking her. But, then, Douglas had never been smart like that. Not like Tony.

"Oh, you know me, Douglas. Theater, the odd nightclub. Can't keep me away from the old Smoke." Her head hurt. Her ears strained, as they had since she had sat down, for Suzanna's cry, the signal that she had woken up.

He was trying to talk to her, but she was having trouble hearing what he said. She thought, briefly, watching his mouth move, that she didn't have to go through with this. That she could simply sit down, eat a meal with Douglas, and travel home again. No one was forcing her to do anything. It would all work out in the end, wouldn't it? Then she thought of the telephone conversation she had had with her parents earlier that week, the day before she had phoned him. "You've made your bed, Athene," her mother had said. "You can jolly well lie in it." She'd not get a penny out of them. Her father had been even less forgiving: she had disgraced the family, he had said, and she needn't bother thinking she could return. As if he hadn't, by his actions, done twice as much damage. She hadn't bothered to tell them about the baby.

She thought about the bottom drawer of the

rather horrid pine chest that Suzanna had as her cot, the drying nappies draped around their room, the landlady's repeated threats of eviction. Of Tony's despair at his inability to find another job.

It was better this way.

"Douglas, you wouldn't be a darling and order me some more ciggies, would you?" she said, mustering a smile. "I seem to be out of change."

When the waiter had returned with them, he had left Douglas's change on the table, and she had stared at it, conscious that she could keep them fed with that money for several days. Or pay for a bath. A really hot bath, with a few bubbles thrown in. She stared at the money, thinking of a time, not so long ago, when she would not have noticed it, when that small amount would have been irrelevant. Just like her coat, her shoes, a new hat would have been irrelevant: easy come, easily replaceable. She stared at it, and then at Douglas, realizing that there was another answer to her problems, which she had not yet considered. He was a handsome man, after all. And it was obvious he still cared for her—even their short telephone conversation had told her that. Tony would survive without her. He would survive without anyone.

"Why did you call?"

"Aren't I allowed to speak to you anymore?" she said gaily.

She had looked—really looked—at him then, at

the hurt and desperation on his face. At the love. Even after everything she had done. And she knew why she could never do the thing that would solve everything at a stroke.

"Don't 'darling' me, Athene. I can't do this. I really can't. I need to know why you're here."

He was angry now, his face coloring. She tried to focus on what he was saying, but she had become aware of a jangling vibration within her, tuned to some invisible maternal frequency. And she lost the thread of the conversation.

"You know, it's lovely to see you looking so well," she said bravely, wondering whether she should just get up and go. She could run now, snatch Suzanna from the horrid old pram and disappear. Nobody would have to know. They could go to Brighton, perhaps. Borrow the money and go abroad. To Italy. They loved babies in Italy. Her voice emerged from her mouth, as if it belonged to someone else, as her thoughts scrambled in her head: "You always did look marvelous in that suit."

She could hear Suzanna now, in the distance, making everything else irrelevant.

"Athene!" he protested.

And then the fat girl was there, standing in front of her with her insolent face, taking in the lack of a wedding ring, the untouched meal in front of her. "I'm sorry, madam," she said, "but your baby's crying. You'll have to come and get her."

Afterward, she found she could remember little of the next minutes. She vaguely remembered Douglas's shocked face, the color draining from it almost as she watched; she remembered being handed Suzanna's pram and realizing as she held her, for what she knew to be the last time, that she could no longer look at her face. Suzanna, perhaps with some terrible foreboding of her own, had been fretting, and Athene had been glad of the need to jiggle her—it disguised the trembling of her own hands.

Then the bit that she wished she could forget, the bit that would haunt her waking moments, her dreams, that would leave her arms empty, a child-size hole next to her heart.

Almost unable to believe she was doing it, Athene Fairley-Hulme took the child she loved with a pure uncomplicated passion of which she had not believed herself capable, and thrust her small, soft weight, her blanket-wrapped limbs, at the man opposite.

He held her carefully, she noted, with a faint, piercing gratitude. She had known he would. Oh, God, forgive me for this, she said silently, and wondered, briefly, if she might faint.

"Athene, I can't just—"

She felt the dim panic then, that he might refuse. There was no alternative. Tony had told her so, many times.

She had made her bed.

She placed her hand on his arm, trying to convey everything in one pleading look. "Douglas, darling, have I ever asked you for anything? Really?"

He had gazed back at her then, his faltering confusion, the brief nakedness of his expression telling her she had him. That he would care for her. Love her, as he, in his own childhood, had been loved. It's better this way, she told herself silently, repeatedly. It's better this way. As if by saying it enough times she could make herself believe it. She forced herself to stand then, and began to walk, trying to stop herself from falling over, trying to keep her head up. Trying to keep her mind blank so that she didn't have to think about what was behind her, just focusing on making one foot move in front of the other, as the sounds of the restaurant receded into nothingness. She had wanted to leave Suzanna something—a small sign that she had been loved. But they had nothing. Everything had been sold for the simple necessity of eating.

Bye-bye, darling, she said silently, as the restaurant door loomed closer, her heels echoing on the tiled floor. I will come back for you, when things are better. Promise.

"Don't you even want to say goodbye?" His voice came from behind her. And Athene, feeling the last of her resolve begin to crumble, fled.

It was the strangest thing, the hatcheck girl said

to the wine waiter afterward. That snobby girl, the one with dark hair, had walked around the corner, sat down on the pavement, and cried as if her heart would break. She had seen her when she went out for a breather. All crumpled up against the wall, howling like a dog, not even caring who saw her.

When she returned Tony was lying on the bed. It was not surprising, although it was only late afternoon: there was nowhere to sit in the little room.

Athene opened the door. He startled, as if he had been asleep, and pushed himself into an upright position, blinking as he scanned her face. The room smelled musty: they hadn't had the money to take the sheets to the launderette for several weeks, and the window didn't open enough to air it properly. She watched as he rubbed at his hair with his broad, even hands.

"Well?" he said.

She couldn't speak. She walked toward the bed, not bothering to move the newspaper from the crumpled candlewick bedspread, and lay down, her back to him, her shoes slipping from her bloodied heels.

He placed his hand on her shoulder, squeezed it hesitantly. "You okay?"

She said nothing. She stared at the wall opposite, at the green flocked wallpaper that had started to peel from the skirting, at the bar heater they didn't have the coins to feed, at the chest of drawers, the bottom one padded with Athene's old jumpers, lined with her one silk blouse, the softest thing she could think of to lay next to Suzanna's skin.

"You did the right thing, you know," Tony murmured. "I know it's hard, but you did the right thing."

She didn't think she would ever be able to lift her head from the pillow again. She felt so tired, as if she had never previously understood what tiredness was.

She was dimly aware of Tony kissing her ear. Her reticence had made him needy. "Sweetheart?" She could not respond. "Sweetheart?" he said again.

"Yes," she whispered. She could think of nothing else to say.

"Things will get better, 'Thene. Really. I'll make sure of it."

She would be almost back at Dere Hampton by now, if he had taken the train. Douglas would have struggled with that pram in the same way she had. She could picture him now, demanding that the guard help him lift it in, wrestling with the hood, the oversize handle. Then, inside the carriage, leaning in to check that the baby was okay. Please don't let her cry too much without me, she thought, and a large, solitary tear trickled down her cheek toward the pillow.

"She'll be better off with him. You know that."

Tony was stroking her cold, white arm, as if that might comfort her. She heard his voice in her ear, urgent, persuasive, yet distant. "We could never cope with two, not in here. We can barely afford to feed ourselves . . . Athene?" he said, when the silence became too much for him.

She lay on the crumpled classified ads, her face cool against the stale cotton pillow, still staring at the door. "No," she said.

Athene lay on the bed for four days and nights, not leaving the little bedsit, weeping helplessly, refusing to eat or speak, her eyes unnervingly open, until on the fifth day, fearful for her health, if not her state of mind, Tony took matters into his own hands and called the doctor. The landlady, who enjoyed a bit of drama, stood on the upper landing as the doctor arrived, and proclaimed noisily that she had a respectable house, clean and proper. "There's no disease in this place," she said. "Nothing unclean." She was peering around the door, hoping to get some indication of what was wrong with the girl.

"I'm sure," said the doctor, eyeing the sticky hall carpet with distaste.

"I've never had an unmarried before," she said, "and this'll be the last. I can't be doing with the inconvenience of it."

"She's in here," Tony said.

"I don't want anything infectious in my establishment," the woman called excitedly.

"Not unless a big gob is infectious," the young man muttered, and shut the door.

The doctor eyed the little room with its damp walls and grimy windows, wrinkling his nose at the stale, tidemarked bucket of soaking laundry in the corner, wondering how many people in this district routinely lived in habitation more suited to animals. He listened to the young man's hurried explanation, then addressed the woman on the bed.

"Any pain anywhere?" he said, peeling back the covers to knead the belly that was just beginning to swell. When she replied, he was a little surprised to hear her cut-glass accent after this bluff northerner's. But that was the way things were going these days. The so-called classless society.

"Any problems with your waterworks? Sore throat? Stomachache?"

The examination didn't take long: there was plainly no physical problem. He diagnosed depression, unsurprising when you considered the circumstances in which she was living. "A lot of women get a bit hysterical during pregnancy," he said to the young man, as he closed his case. "Just try to keep her calm. Maybe take her for a walk in the park. Be good for her to get some fresh air. I'll write you a prescription for some iron tablets. See if you can get some color in her cheeks."

The young man saw him out, then stood at the door of the little room, his hands thrust uncomfortably into his pockets, patently out of his depth. "But what do I do?" he kept saying. "She doesn't seem to be listening to me."

The doctor followed the young man's anxious gaze to the bed, where the girl had fallen asleep. Sympathetic as he was, he couldn't waste any more time here. "Some women find motherhood a bit harder than others," he said, placed his hat firmly on his head, and left.

"But I was told my mother died in childbirth," Suzanna had said, when Vivi had told her what she knew of her mother's last days.

"She did, dear." Vivi had taken her hand, a gentle, maternal gesture. "Just not yours."

# 29

My daughter was born on the night of the power cuts, the day that the whole hospital, and half the city, was plunged into darkness. I like to think it was portentous now: that her arrival in this world was so important it had to be marked by something. Outside, the lights had disappeared, room by room, building by building, dissolving their way across town like bubbles in champagne, as we sped by in our car until the night sky met us at the hospital gates.

I had laughed hysterically between the contractions, so that the thick-jawed midwife, who couldn't understand what I was saying, thought there might be something wrong with me. I couldn't explain. I was laughing because I had wanted to have her at home and he had said I couldn't, that he couldn't stand the risk of something happening. It was one of the few things we have ever disagreed about. So there we were, him apologizing and me laughing and gasping in the entrance, as nurses shrieked and swore, and the walking wounded collided in the dark.

I don't know why I laughed so much. They said afterward that they had never known someone laugh like that in labor, not without the benefit of Entonox. Perhaps I was hysterical. Perhaps the whole thing was just so unbelievable that I couldn't accept it was happening. Perhaps I was even a little afraid, but I find that hard to believe. I am not afraid of much, these days.

I didn't laugh so much once it got really painful. Then I chewed on the mouthpiece for the gas and air, and shouted, betrayed that no one had warned me it could feel like this. I don't remember the last part; it became a blur, of pain and sweat and hands and encouraging voices urging me in the dim light to bear down, to go on, telling me that I could do it.

But I knew I could do it. In spite of the pain, and the strange, shocking sensation that heralded the birth, I didn't need their encouragement. I knew I could push that baby out. Even if there had been no one there but me. And as I stared down my naked torso in our final minutes as one, my hands white-knuckled as they gripped the sheets, she slid out with something of the same determination, the same confidence in her own abilities, her arms already raised as if in victory.

He was there to meet her. I don't know how, I don't think I had seen him move. I had made him promise beforehand that he wouldn't stand there, that he would not spoil his romantic view of me. He had laughed, and told me I was ridiculous. So he was there when she breathed her first in this world, and even in the dim light I could see tears glistening on his cheeks, as he cut the cord and lifted her, holding her up to the candlelight so that I could see her, believe in her too.

And the midwife stood back while he held her, kissing her face tenderly, wiped the blood from her limbs, her dark hair, all the while crooning a love song I didn't understand. He said her name, the name we had agreed: Veronica de Marenas. And, as if by magic, the lights began to go on again, illuminating the city, district by district, thrusting the quiet streets back into light.

As that woman cleaned me up, both brusque and tender, I watched my husband and my daughter move around the little room, their faces lit by candles, and finally began to cry. I don't know why: exhaustion, perhaps, or the emotion of it all. Disbelief that I could produce this perfect, beautiful little girl from my own body, that I could be the unwitting creator of such joy.

"Don't cry, **amor**," Alejandro said, beside me, his own voice still choked with tears. He had moved to the side of the bed. Hesitating, he gazed at her, then leaned over and handed her gently to me. Even as his eyes filled with love, his hands moved slowly, as if he was reluctant to let go. And as she looked up at us, blinking in that wise, unknowing way, he hugged me close to him, so that we were all enclosed in a single embrace. "There is nothing to cry for. She will be loved."

His words cut through everything then, leaving no dark corners, as they do still.

She will be loved.

# Acknowledgments

I would like to thank Sophie Green and Jacquie Bounsall, who, while being nothing like my lead characters, did, together with Sophie's shop, Blooming Mad Sophie Green, provide me with the inspiration for **The Peacock Emporium**. And to all the customers whose individual stories, snippets of gossip, scandals, and jokes helped shape this book. I am still amazed by what people will tell you if you stand behind a till long enough . . .

A huge thanks to everyone at Hodder & Stoughton for their continuing support and enthusiasm, with special thanks to Carolyn Mays, Jamie Hodder-Williams, Emma Longhurst, and Alex Bonham, as well as Hazel Orme. Thanks also to everyone at Pamela Dorman Books / Viking and Penguin in the US.

Thanks to Sheila Crowley and Jo Frank, whose agenting skills bookended this book, as well as Vicky Longley and Linda Shaughnessy at AP Watt. Thanks to Brian Sanders for his fishing wisdom, Cathy Runciman for her knowledge of Argentina. To Jill and John Armstrong, for space to work away from overflowing laundry baskets, and

James and Di Potter for their knowledge of animal husbandry and agriculture. Thanks also to Julia Carmichael and the staff of Harts in Saffron Walden for their support, and to Hannah Collins for Ben, the best work avoidance ever.

A belated thank-you to Grant McKee and Jill Turton, who first got me into print: I'm sorry I sold your car.

Apologies and thanks also to Saskia, Harry, and Lockie, who now understand that when Mummy talks to herself and occasionally forgets to make supper she is not displaying early signs of madness but actually paying the mortgage.

And most of all to Charles, who puts up with me periodically falling in love with my male leads and now knows so much about the process of writing novels that he might as well publish his own. For everything else. XX

A PENGUIN
READERS GUIDE TO

THE PEACOCK
EMPORIUM

Jojo Moyes

# An Introduction to The Peacock Emporium

Jojo Moyes became a household name with her
**New York Times** bestselling **Me Before You**
trilogy (**Me Before You**, **After You**, and **Still
Me**), and especially for her trademark memorable
characters and complex, true-to-life relationships.
Moyes brings all of that to **The Peacock
Emporium**, a rich story of a young woman with
a mysterious past who finds both safety and
salvation in the quirky shop she opens in her
small town.

Athene Forster was untouchable. Dubbed the
"Last Deb," she was gorgeous, rich, and could have
anything—or anyone—she wanted, including
young heir Douglas Fairley-Hulme. Two years
into their marriage, however, scandal engulfs the
couple after a young salesman catches Athene's
eye, ultimately causing her fall from grace.

Thirty-five years later, Suzanna Peacock is
drowning in the shadow of her late mother,
Athene. Unhappy in her marriage and desperate
for a fresh start, Suzanna opens The Peacock
Emporium, an eclectic shop that attracts an
eccentric cast of characters. In her new role,
Suzanna begins opening up, and even finds a

true friend in Alejandro, a male midwife. But despite her efforts, Suzanna is unable to escape the specter of her mother. It will take tragedy, heartbreak, and ultimately healing for Suzanna to learn that only by confronting the ghosts of her past can she finally begin to live in the present.

Like all Moyes's books, **The Peacock Emporium** will steal your heart—and is an absolutely unputdownable, unforgettable read.

# A Conversation with Jojo Moyes

The characters in the novel—Suzanna, Alejandro, Vivi, Athene to name just a few—are incredibly complex, though some sober and reflective, while others have a much louder joie de vivre. What led you to these characters, and how did this story come about?

I never really know what leads me to characters. Most fall, to some extent, into my lap—or at least their skeletons do. And then I build bits of them on top of that framework. Sometimes I look back and realize they reflect something in my own life—in the case of **Peacock**, I wrote it when I was adjusting to life in a small town after spending thirty years in London so I'm sure there's a bit of me in Suzanna.

Family and class are both significant themes in this book—and in some of your other books as well—and we see Suzanna, Douglas, and others chaffing at their tethers. What is it about issues of class that makes it important to you?

I think if you live in England it's very hard to escape issues of class, especially in market towns where the house you live in or the family you come from often give away your background. I suppose I just find it a useful source of tension as a writer—there is always someone in the wrong place.

**Without giving anything away, the ending is truly a remarkable and unexpected twist. Did you know in advance that this is how you would end it, or did the conclusion come about as you worked, slowly revealing itself to you?**

If I have a twist (and I usually do) I always plot it beforehand. I don't think it's possible to write free-form toward one. I wanted the reader to think of Athene a certain way—to see her largely through the eyes of everyone else—and then realize that the story they've been told might have been something else entirely. So yes, I always knew what I was working toward.

**Suzanna flounders beneath her eccentric mother's legacy, but eventually finds her way with the success of the Peacock Emporium. It is only when she takes the initiative in seeking her own happiness that she finds contentment. Why was it important to you to show this transformation, especially in a female character?**

I think it's become an undercurrent in my books—female contentment and emancipation through work! Or at least working out what you love to do. I didn't think Suzanna was the kind of character who would ever be properly satisfied without that—she reminded me of some mothers I was around when writing this who poured their energy into soft furnishings or playgroups but were somehow always restless and dissatisfied. I think it's such a gift to know what really makes you happy.

**How did you decide to structure the novel as you did? The first few chapters highlight Athene's wild beginnings, and then you soon turn to Suzanna's much more conventional story. Did you ever consider alternating their perspectives chapter by chapter?**

It's probably the most challenging structure I've ever attempted—at least for the reader. I didn't consider alternating the chapters because sometimes that can make the narrative flow a little choppy, and I thought the reader needed to spend a little time with the background. But I do love playing with structure so who knows? Perhaps I should have done.

**You have written both contemporary and historical novels, and some, like this one, have dual timeframes within them.** (The Last Letter From your Lover **is another one, as is** The Girl You Left Behind.) **What attracts you to these kinds of dual stories?**

I think the key difference with the older work and the work from **Me Before You** onward is the humor. Most of the books I've written since 2010 have a lot of humor in them. And I don't know what attracts me to dual timeframes—really it just depends on the story that won't leave my head and how I think it can best be told. The book I've just completed is almost completely linear, bar the prologue.

**What are you working on now?**
I'm just editing my new book, which is completely different—and a bit of a departure. I'm probably more excited about it than anything I've ever worked on. I don't want to say too much but it's set in Kentucky and based on something that happened in real life, and while researching it I totally fell in love with that state in a way I'd completely not expected. So I hope readers enjoy it!

# Questions for Discussion

1. **The Peacock Emporium** is about Suzanna coming to terms with her family and her past, but it is also a love story, as well as an ensemble piece about the ways a small town reacts around issues of domestic violence. Do you think the elements came together to create a realistic and cohesive narrative? Why or why not? Which storyline compelled you the most?

2. In this novel, Suzanna must reckon with her mother's scandalous past and the way in which this history affects her own identity. How important a role do you think parents' lives should play in the foundation of one's own identity?

3. Suzanna, the protagonist, is an enigma to the end. She continually denies her true feelings, and is stalled in life out of passivity, confusion, and fear, yet these are very understandable human reactions. Did you understand why Suzanna decided to keep everything to herself, and why she had trouble letting others get close to her? What do you think motivates her? Is it her unhappiness and feelings

of not belonging or being good enough—or something else entirely? Or why do you think she's so unhappy in her marriage?

4. Some of the great joys of this novel are the wonderful secondary characters, such as Arturro, Father Lenny, Mrs. Creek, etc. Which of these characters stood out most for you? Did you relate personally to any of them? In what ways?

5. Suzanna makes a point of not inviting her husband, Neil, to the opening of the Peacock Emporium, because she "wanted something that was hers, pure and pleasurable, untainted by her and Neil's history. Uncomplicated by **people**" (p. 122). What do you think she meant by this?

6. Suzanna is so different from the rest of the Fairley-Hulmes—both emotionally and in terms of her outlook on life. How do you think these differences helped or hindered her relationships within her family? How do they shape her choices regarding the shop?

7. How did you come to understand Suzanna and Neil's marriage? Did you understand and believe in the relationship that develops between her and

Arturro, and did you anticipate what happened between them?

8. Did you like the way the ending connected to the beginning of the novel, having come full circle? Did you think it made for a satisfying ending?

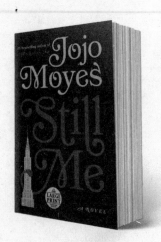
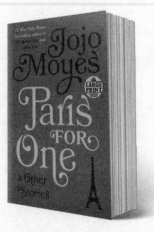